Milayna

BOOK ONE

BY: MICHELLE K. PICKETT

Milayna

clean teen
PUBLISHING

ISBN: 978-1-63422-038-5
Cover Design by: Marya Heiman
Typography by: Courtney Nuckels
Editing by: Cynthia Shepp

For more information about our content disclosure, please utilize the
QR code above with your
smart phone or visit us at
www.cleanteenpublishing.com.

This book is dedicated to the everyday angels we find in life.

Magnolia, Texas, EMTs, thank you for the care you gave my dad.
You are one of my family's angels.

Do not be overcome by evil, but overcome evil with good.

~St. Paul

1
The Pool

THAT NIGHT, I DREAMT OF DEMONS.
They chased me. No matter how fast or where I ran, they chased me.

Brown, curling horns protruded from their heads. They looked like wood with the bark whittled away. Some demons had two horns—one next to each pointed ear—and some had just one in the center of their forehead. Their gray skin was covered with a layer of dark ash that curled behind them as they ran, bringing with it the smell of sulfur and rotting flesh. Their eyes were black orbs. They were dull, dead eyes.

I screamed for my parents.

"Don't fight it, Milayna. This is your destiny," my dad told me.

I ran to Muriel's house. My best friend—surely, she'd help. She waited for me at her door.

"Help me," I screamed and reached for her.

She smiled, and horror filled me. Her jaw protruded and her mouth filled with long, yellow teeth, which were pointed like daggers. She grabbed my arms and held me for the demons.

"Muriel, help me," I gasped, trying to pull free.

"I am helping you. You'll see. You'll be so much happier with us," she hissed through her fangs.

I struggled against the demons. Their black nails bit into my arms, drawing blood. They pulled me to their leader, who stood silently watching, adjusting the sleeves of his black robe as if he were bored.

He looked like the devil. His skin was ruddy, and his eyes glowed amber.

1

Michelle K. Pickett

Jet-black hair, slicked back on his head, hung to his shoulders. But the demons didn't call him Devil, Satan, or even Lucifer. They called him—

Azazel.

The sun beat down on my back. It felt good after swimming in the pool's cool water. I looked at the trees surrounding the park while I squeezed water from my hair. The leaves looked like someone had dripped orange and yellow paint on them. I loved autumn in Michigan, but it meant the end of swimming outdoors, which I preferred to the tiled, sterile pool at school.

The water sparkled a silvery blue. I watched the children play, splashing and giggling as their mothers sat poolside, no doubt gossiping about the latest scandal in the neighborhood.

A young girl, maybe six or seven years old, caught my eye. I watched her strawberry-blonde curls float around her in the water. She was cute, at least as far as kids go. They just weren't my thing. A whiny younger brother was all I needed. I didn't even babysit, except when my mother needed help. But my gaze was drawn to the girl.

What is it about her? I can't stop looking at her.

I felt like I had a knot in the pit of my stomach. It grew like a growth, moving into my throat. It was hard to pull in a breath. The strange feeling wasn't directed toward the girl, although she was part of it. It was more a feeling that something wasn't right. I could feel the cold fingers of evil slide up my spine.

I sucked in a breath, and the hairs on the back of my neck stood on end. I dropped my towel and focused on the girl.

She climbed out of the pool. Her mother was still deep in conversation with another woman. The redheaded girl yelled to her mom, but she waved her off, never looking away from the woman talking animatedly beside her.

It must be juicy gossip.

Happy, the young girl—why was I fixated on her?—scampered off to the playground next to the pool. She plopped down on a swing and pumped her legs back and forth until she swung high. Leaning back, she stretched her legs out, her chubby face to the sky, and smiled.

And then I saw him.

He stood just inside the trees at the edge of the playground. Watching. Waiting.

I don't think he cared which kid it was. She just happened to be there. Either way, his stance changed. His face became animated. An ugly grin slid across his mouth as he waited next to a towering pine tree. He knew his chance was coming soon, and his gaze followed the girl. His prey had just entered his line of sight.

The knot lodged in my stomach twisted, as if someone were tying my insides together like they would their shoelaces. I sucked in a breath through my teeth and tensed against the pain.

Without thought, seemingly without my conscious control, I rose from my seat and circled the pool. I continued into the parking lot, where the sharp, small stones embedded themselves in the bottom of my feet, but I hardly noticed. I was on a mission. Why, or what I was going to do, I wasn't sure.

It's her mother's responsibility to watch over her. Well, that's not exactly true. We should—no, we're required to watch over each other. At least, that's what Mom and Dad pound into my brain every chance they get, usually right before they ask me to babysit Ben.

I continued through the gravel parking lot to the hill on the edge of the tree line. Glad to feel the cool grass under my burning feet, I picked up speed. He wasn't hard to spot when I entered the trees. The sorry son-of-a-bitch stood watching her with his hand down his pants.

Eww and ick.

He was so engrossed that he didn't hear me behind him. I picked up a fallen tree branch about the size of a baseball bat. It felt heavy in my hands, and the bark scraped against my fingers. With visions of his hands on the little girl running through my mind, I swung the limb as hard as I could. It cracked against the back of the man's balding head.

I had no emotion as I watched him crumple to the ground. I stood over him, images of him with the girl mingled with images of him with other children. As I watched his blood trickle through the grass, I realized what I'd done. My hands started to tremble, and the branch slipped from my fingers and landed on top of him. My heartbeat was frenzied in my chest, and I turned and ran from his scrawny body.

Thoughts scrolled through my mind at triple speed. What caused the unstoppable desire to save the kid? I would've never let him touch her. But normally, I'd tell her mother that she'd wandered too far or call the police and alert them to the possibility of a child predator roaming the park. I never would have stepped in myself, but I wasn't able to stop. Drawn to the girl, to her safety, I couldn't walk away.

I went back to gather my things at the edge of the pool, looking over my shoulder to check on the girl. Her red curls bounced as she swung in the sunlight. Her mother was still unaware of where she was or how close she'd come to losing her childhood innocence.

Before climbing into my beat-up Chevy, I stopped at a pay phone near the restrooms, shaking my head with a smile.

I can't believe I found one. Everyone uses cell phones. I thought these things were only in museums. It's gotta be older than me.

Using my wet towel, I picked up the receiver, dialed 911, and reported the man—and I used the term *man* very, very loosely.

"You'll find a man unconscious just inside the trees. Hurry before he hurts another child."

3   *Michelle K. Pickett*

"What's your name?" the nasally dispatcher asked.

I dropped the receiver, letting the cord hang limp, and walked away.

Let them trace the call. There's nothing pointing to me. I don't want anyone finding out I was here. What do I say? I had a funny feeling and... what? I had a vision of him doing stuff with kids so I bashed his head in? Yeah, right. No, they just need a valid trace so they can get here and catch the pervert before he wakes up.

As I drove away, I was struck by two things. First, what drew me to the girl? My eyes weren't drawn to any other. In fact, I couldn't remember the face of any other kid at the pool. My eyes wanted only her... searched her out. I knew I needed to watch her, knew that something was wrong.

And second, how did I know?

2

More

EIGHT WEEKS, ONE DAY UNTIL MY EIGHTEENTH BIRTHDAY.

"What'd you do yesterday? I called you." Muriel twirled her pen in circles on the dirty Formica table.

"Nothing exciting. Just laps at the pool," I lied. I hadn't stopped thinking about what happened at the park. I couldn't get my mind wrapped around how I knew the man was going to hurt that girl.

She slapped her hand on the pen to stop it and looked at me. A perfect, jet-black eyebrow arched over her almond-shaped eye. "Gee, ever think of asking your best friend and swim teammate to go along?"

I cringed. "Sorry, it was a last-minute decision."

She pointed at me. "Don't let it happen again," she said through clenched teeth. Her black, stick-straight hair fell over her shoulder. I burst out laughing. She dropped her finger and shoved my shoulder, laughing with me.

Our calculus teacher marched into class like one of the British Royal Army's soldiers in a parade with those red uniforms and the knee-high marching steps—arms full of books and files.

I wonder what Muriel would've thought about the guy in the trees—what she would've done.

Halfway through class, Muriel texted me. I reached for my cell phone and looked to make sure the teacher wasn't watching before I read the message. That was when I saw him.

His body angled in his seat, and his head turned slightly toward me. The

5

Michelle K. Pickett

corner of his mouth twitched slightly, like he'd started to smile but decided against it just before it materialized.

I'd noticed him before—it was hard not to. Talk about easy on the eyes. We had English together. I knew him, but we didn't travel in the same circles. In fact, as far as I could tell, he didn't travel in any particular circle. He kept to himself and seemed to prefer it that way.

I looked away quickly, feeling my cheeks warm.

Great, I'm blushing. Nice look. Red cheeks and red, curly hair—just like Bozo the Clown. Homecoming queen material. No need to vote; I'll just take my crown. Yeah, sure.

When my eyes darted back in his direction, he'd turned and faced forward. I felt a small pang of disappointment. Looking down, I read Muriel's text.

> Muriel: Go to the mall after school?
> Me: Sure.
> Muriel: I'll drive.
> Me: K
> Muriel: What was that look?
> Me: What look?
> Muriel: Between you and the hottie.

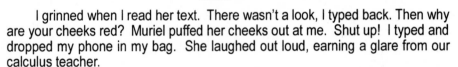

I grinned when I read her text. There wasn't a look, I typed back. Then why are your cheeks red? Muriel puffed her cheeks out at me. Shut up! I typed and dropped my phone in my bag. She laughed out loud, earning a glare from our calculus teacher.

I sighed when I turned the corner to my English class. He was waiting for me outside the door. *Joe.* I guess he had a crush on me. He always walked with me when our classes were near each other, and he parked his car conveniently next to mine, or Muriel's if I rode with her, so he could walk into school with me. And he taped little drawings on my locker door. He was a great artist, but still.

Then there was the thing. The thing I dreaded, but happened every week. My hands started sweating and my stomach roiled when I looked at him—I knew it was coming. I hated it because I hated what I had to do. I didn't want to hurt Joe's feelings. He was a really nice guy, but I didn't find him the least bit attractive or interesting with his mousy-brown hair, too-big glasses, and his constant prattle about the AV club.

"Hey, Milayna." Joe smiled when he saw me, pushing his glasses up with his middle finger. I smiled back and stifled a groan.

"Hi, Joe." I tried to blend in with a group of students walking into class and brush past him before he asked me the inevitable question.

"Hey, wait up," he called.

I stopped just inside the doorway, sighed, and then walked back to where he stood, with his shoulder leaned against the lockers lining the wall. "What's up?" I twisted my pencil in my fingers.

"You look pretty today. I like it when you wear your hair down and all... all... red and curly."

"Um, thanks." I shifted and adjusted the strap of my bag on my shoulder. *That's good since my hair is red and curly.*

"I was wondering..."

Oh no, here comes the thing. Please don't ask me again. I squeezed the strap of my messenger bag so tightly my fingers ached. *There's only so many ways I can say no without being mean.*

"...if you wanted to go out to a movie this weekend?" Joe reached out and put his warm, sweaty hand on my arm.

And there it is.

I sighed and moved my arm to push my hair behind my ear, so he had to pull his hand away. "Joe—" I started when movement caught my attention.

The hottie from calculus walked up beside me. "Hey, there you are." He stood beside me, at least a head taller, his muscles flexing under his white T-shirt, which clung to him in just the right way as to hint at what lay beneath. His arm brushed against mine, and the unintentional touch was enough to send my nerves crackling. "I saved you a seat." He winked.

What is he talking about?

"Thanks." I turned back to Joe. "Uh, Joe, I can't this weekend. Sorry," I told him, my voice soft.

"Maybe another time?" He gave me a tight smile before looking the hottie up and down with narrowed eyes.

The so-hot-he-could-be-an-underwear-model guy from calculus gave Joe a friendly slap on the back. "I don't think so, buddy."

"Oh. Okay." Joe looked between me and the tall, dark-haired guy, blowing out a breath. "See ya around, Milayna." Joe turned and was swallowed up by the current of people rushing from one class to the next.

"'Bye." I turned, looking at the guy who saved me from Joe, and was sucked in by his marbled, blue-green eyes. "Thank you."

"No problem. I'm tired of watching you try to turn him down without hurting his feelings. Better just to be done with it." He turned away, and I fumbled for something to say to keep him from leaving.

"I'm Milayna. You're Chay, right?"

He nodded once. "Be careful. They're here for you," he murmured over his shoulder before he slipped into the classroom.

"Wait! What are you talking about?"

What the hell kind of freaky thing to say and then just walk away.

I watched the clock tick the seconds off one by one. As soon as the bell rang, I was going to tackle him. My body wanted to tackle him for a totally differ-

Michelle K. Pickett

ent reason than my mind, but my mind won out—I wanted information.

When the bell rang, Chay swiped his books off his desk and slipped out of the door. I ran out of the classroom to catch him, but he'd already disappeared into the hoard of students.

"Where do you want to go first?" Muriel asked as we drove to the mall after school, looking over at me from the driver's seat of her car.

"I dunno." I typed out a quick text to my mom, letting her know I was going to the mall.

"Food court?"

"Yeah, I could go for a soft pretzel." As if on cue, my stomach growled.

"Food court it is," Muriel said and pushed up her sunglasses. "Guess what I heard about..."

Muriel's words were shoved away and pain, swift and sharp, took their place. My stomach scraped together like someone punched through my gut and scrubbed my insides with sandpaper. My breathing became ragged and shallow, my head pounding in rhythm with my heart.

The sights and sounds around me moved in slow motion. Muriel spoke, but I couldn't understand her, her voice too deep and slow. It sounded like she was underwater. *What's going on? What's happening to me?*

I gripped the armrest on the car with one hand and wrapped my other arm around my stomach. It felt as though someone were drilling holes inside me. I ground my teeth together against the pain.

Muriel continued her story, maneuvering her car down the street toward an intersection. The light was green, and we inched toward it.

I knew something was going to happen—the same feeling I'd had at the park rolled in the pit of my stomach. Licking my lips, I tipped my head forward so my hair created a curtain between Muriel and me. I didn't want her to see my eyes darting back and forth and the sweat beading on my upper lip.

A yellow car was on our right. The driver talked on her cell phone, and a baby slept in a car seat behind her, its thumb dangling from its lips. A blue minivan merged into the left turn lane on our left. We all sped closer and closer to the intersection.

A red car. The stoplight.

I saw it. Not with my eyes, but in my mind. I saw what was going to happen. My breath rushed out of my lungs, and time sped up around me.

"Muriel, watch out for the red car!"

"What red car?" Muriel looked to the side.

"It's gonna run the stoplight." I pointed to the left.

Just as I said it, the red car came into view. Muriel slammed on the brakes.

Milayna   8

We lurched forward before the seatbelts snapped us back against our seats. The car whizzed in front of us, narrowly missing the yellow car.

I covered my mouth with a shaky hand and watched the car as it sped out of sight. A shiver ran down my spine.

We could have died! What the hell...?

"Whoa! That was way too close." Muriel let out a shaky breath and looked at me. "How did you see that car?"

I'd like an answer to that question too. What the freaky hell is going on?

"Where are the police when you need them, huh?" I puffed out my cheeks and blew out a breath.

It was the second time in as many days that I had a vision, or premonition. Whatever they were, they scared the crap outta me.

My fingers squeezed together so tightly that they turned white and began to throb in time to my heartbeat. Sucking in a deep breath through my nose like my mom's meditation DVD instructed, I forced each finger to relax and straighten. I counted to ten as I let the breath out through slightly parted lips so I didn't draw Muriel's attention. I repeated the breathing exercise—deep breath in and deep breath out. My insides that felt as though they'd slid out of place slowly righted themselves, and I stopped shaking.

"Milayna?" Muriel grabbed my arm. "How'd you know that car was going to run the red light?"

Should I tell her how? I don't even know what's happening to me! Oh, by the way, Muriel, I can see the future. That's how I knew about the car. Yeah, she'd think I was crazy for sure. I already feel like I need a padded cell. I don't need her to confirm it.

"Um—he was coming too fast to stop."

Muriel narrowed her eyes at me. "I'm just glad you saw him because I sure didn't."

"You were just focused on the road, that's all." I bit the inside of my cheek and hoped she'd just drop the subject.

Muriel nodded and turned to look out of the windshield.

"What do you know about Chay?" I looked at Muriel across the table in the mall's food court. Pieces of pretzel dropped to the paper wrapper below as I ripped it apart.

Muriel shoved a bite of pretzel in her mouth, mustard dribbling down her fingers. "Not much. Why?" she asked around the blob.

"He saved me from Joe this afternoon before English class." I scooted my chair over to make room for a lady pushing a stroller to pass by.

"Poor Joe." She frowned. I immediately tuned her out, focusing on the oldies

Michelle K. Pickett

music piped through the speakers that were spread through the court and hidden behind plants. "He's such a nice guy, Milayna. You really should—"

With a sigh, I finally interrupted Muriel's list of reasons I should date Joe. "He is nice, Muriel, but there's nothing there. About Chay?"

"You like him?"

I shrugged. "I don't know him. Just curious."

"Why'd he care about Joe?" Muriel took a sip of her Coke.

"Said he was tired of watching me try to turn him down without hurting his feelings. Then he said something really weird."

She leaned closer to me. "Yeah? What?"

"He told me to be careful. That they were here for me, or something like that." I dropped what was left of my pretzel, brushing off my hands.

A strange look crossed Muriel's face. "Huh. That is weird. Kinda creepy." She looked away.

Raising my arms over my head, I arched my back and stretched the muscles that were tired from sitting all day. I looked around the food court, and my eyes landed on his blue-and-gold jersey—oh, and his body. Couldn't leave that out. "Hey, look who's here!" I flicked my eyes toward Jake, who was standing in line at Little Caesars. My heart did a little tap dance inside my chest, just looking at him.

"Yeah, and look at who's with him. Too much PDA." Muriel rolled her eyes.

"Heidi, ugh. She's so close to him that she looks like she's been Krazy Glued to his side. Someone needs to explain to her that Jake and I are meant to be together. I mean, she's dating my future husband." I never took my eyes off him. "Geez, he's like a blond-haired, blue-eyed, muscled package of perfection."

Muriel laughed. "Are you ready? I think we need to leave before you start drooling."

"Yeah, yeah." I crumpled up the pretzel wrapping and threw it in the trash. "Let's go."

The rest of the afternoon, we combed the mall for deals on the hottest trends. Muriel was good at window-shopping. She would try on all the cute outfits and look at all the cool shoes and accessories, but she rarely bought anything. I hadn't mastered the art of window-shopping, though, and spent what little money I had on some wicked new boots, a messenger bag to match, and two kinds of lip stain because I was looking for the perfect shade—not too pink, but not too peach. As it turned out, that color was more elusive than the Loch Ness monster.

As we walked along the hall, passing Old Navy and a group of teenagers drinking slushies, I glanced at Muriel and sighed. "I hate that you can do that."

"What?" Muriel looked over at me, her eyebrows pulled down.

"Look at everything and buy nothing," I said.

"Eh, I didn't really see anything I had to have."

"Me either, but I'm still carrying bags while your hands are empty." I hefted up the bags I was lugging around and rattled them in the air.

Milayna   10

She smiled and arched a brow. "You just need a little more self-control, that's all."

"Yeah, easy for you to say. Oh, ma'am," I called to a lady walking toward us. Her toddler bounced along in front of her in one of those baby harnesses. "Ma'am? The latch on that harness is going to break. You don't want him to get loose and run into the crowd."

The mother knelt to look at the clasp. "It's almost bent in half. Thank you!" She glanced up and smiled at me. "I guess I'll have to buy a new one."

"No problem." I turned to Muriel and pointed down the hall. "Onward to Abercrombie. Where I can't afford to buy anything, but I'm still going to try on the clothes and pretend."

"How'd you see that?" Muriel asked as we continued walking.

Crap. How did I know? I didn't even look at the clasp. The words just blurted out of my mouth. I didn't even have any weird feelings like before.

I let out a breath to stay calm. "I saw the clasp bending. I didn't want the kid to start running around getting in the way—hey! Here's Victoria's Secret. Want to go in?" Muriel kept walking. I took one last look at the store and jogged a few steps to catch up to her. "Okay, we don't want to know Victoria's secrets today," I muttered.

"You couldn't have seen the clasp, Milayna," she said as I caught up to her. "We weren't even close to the woman when you called out to her the first time. There's no way you saw it." Muriel shook her head. Her strides were long and quick, and her glossy black hair shimmered as it swung with each step.

I stopped in the middle of the aisle. People moved around me—some knocked into my sides, others gave me a wide berth, and a few even tried to walk through me by barreling right into me. But I stood there anyway. At five foot nine, Muriel was taller than I was, and her stride was longer than mine, too. She also ran track, so she had the stamina to power walk the mall all night if she wanted.

"I'm not chasing you, Muriel," I yelled over the din of voices. I walked to the benches in the center of the hall, leaned a knee on top of one, and waited. Muriel turned around, walked to me, and stood with her hands on her hips.

"You're losing it. I was standing right next to her when I told her. I happened to look over, saw the bent clasp, and told her to watch it. Otherwise, that kid would be running around, touching people with booger-smeared hands." I shuddered.

Muriel looked at the floor and shook her head. "Something's wrong. What's going on?"

"Nothing's wrong." My voice came out at a higher pitch than normal, and I blew out a frustrated breath. *How do I get her to drop this?* "Come on, I need to get home for dinner. Abercrombie will have to wait for next time. I've done enough damage to my bank account—"

I glanced up, and the same blue-green eyes from calculus pulled me in. He sat a few benches away and watched us. I stared back at him until Muriel

Michelle K. Pickett

grabbed my arm and broke my gaze. I was too far away to say hello, so I gave him a small smile and a finger wave. He barely nodded his head in answer before he looked away.

Muriel drove us to my house. Thankfully, I didn't have any more weird visions or whatever they were. I didn't think I'd be able to explain away another one. Muriel was already suspicious. When we parked in my driveway, I grabbed my bags from the backseat and walked with Muriel to the front door where my mom waited. Her blonde hair, usually pinned up for work, hung loose in the same soft waves I had. Dressed in distressed jeans and an old Rolling Stones T-shirt, she looked like a teenager, not a mom of two.

"Hi, Aunt Rachael," Muriel said to my mom as she stepped inside.

"Hi, Muriel. Have a good time at the mall?"

"Yeah. Milayna bought the place out again."

My mom smiled, shaking her head at the bags I hauled inside. Then she looked at Muriel. "Do you want to stay over for dinner?"

"Yeah, stay and we can work on our calculus together." I jerked the last bag inside and stood up, brushing a stray curl out of my eyes.

Muriel and I did everything together, especially since we were both on our school's swim team and softball team. She was my best friend, too, and my cousin. That was why I had to be extra careful when she was around. I wasn't ready to tell her about my visions, if that was what they were. I didn't know if I'd ever tell anyone, but I knew I wouldn't until I understood what was happening to me.

We were lying across my bed doing homework when she brought it up again. "What happened with you today?"

"What do you mean?" I shook my mechanical pencil, trying to get some lead out.

Just drop it already, Muriel. Geez, you're like Ben and his annoying "but why" questions.

Muriel blew out a frustrated breath. "The car? The kid?"

"I already told you—" I was looking inside the hole of my pencil when Muriel swiped it out of my hand and dropped it on the bed.

"There was no way you saw that car, Milayna. It wasn't there."

"Yes it was! I saw it start to run the red light and yelled to you." I reached for my pencil, but she covered it with a pillow. Tossing her own pencil onto her calculus book, she rolled over and glared at me.

"No, you said you saw it was coming too fast to stop, not that you saw it at the light."

"What difference does it make? We'd have been toast if I hadn't told you that it was coming. Who cares where it was when I saw it?" I flipped the page in my book and looked for another pencil in my bag.

"And what about the kid's leash thingy?"

I sighed and dropped my head against the textbook.

I want to get the Duct Tape craft kit Grams got me and tape her mouth shut.

"What about it? We walked by, I saw the latch, and I turned to tell her it was breaking. It's no big deal."

"You didn't turn."

I raised my head and looked at her. "Huh?"

"You didn't turn around and tell her. You called to her as we walked toward her. Milayna." She paused and looked at me. Her big, hazel eyes were filled with emotion. "If there was something wrong, you'd tell me, right?"

"Yes." I nodded and poked her side to get her to laugh. "But nothing's wrong."

Nothing much. Just that I've turned into a freak of nature.

"Okay," Muriel said between giggles when I poked her again. "Just checking."

"Can we finish our calculus now?" I pointed at my book.

"Yup." She grabbed my pencil from where she held it hostage under the pillow and tossed it to me.

An hour later, Muriel had gone home. After I'd slipped into my favorite PJ bottoms and a soft hoodie, I went outside and sat on the swing on the back deck. With one leg curled under me, the toe on the other gently pushed the swing. I leaned my head back and looked at the expanse of the velvet sky and the twinkling dots spread across it. It made me feel small. Small and confused. The visions scared me. And I was scared to tell anyone about them. I didn't want them to think I was a freak. Maybe I was. That scared me, too.

It was Thursday, two days after my last vision at the mall, and Muriel and I were at swim practice, getting ready for a big meet against a rival school. Everyone was there, even the boys' team. Usually the girls and boys' teams practiced on different days, but that day was different—and so was my vision.

I saw three boys walking behind Miranda. She was stuffing her hair into one of the horrendously ugly swim caps the school made us wear, and the boys were snickering about something, and then their thoughts slammed into me. Two of the boys were daring the third to reach out and undo the clasp on Miranda's swimsuit. It wouldn't have done much good since the swimsuit had another strap holding it in place, but just the thought of what he wanted to do, what he wanted to happen, made me angry and the feeling took over. It was almost like I was in a trance, but I was aware of what was happening. I just couldn't stop it.

Do it, one boy urged, bumping his friend's arm toward Miranda.

Are you a chicken shit? the second boy taunted.

I jumped. I was too far away to hear them whispering, so why could I hear them when Miranda couldn't? It was like the way I'd just seen what was about to

13 *Michelle K. Pickett*

happen. Now I was hearing them, too. *Great.*

Walking faster, I passed the boy just as he reached out. I rammed my body into his before he was able to touch Miranda.

"What the heck!" he yelled. He started to get up, his hand slipped on a puddle of water, and he hit the floor a second time. His face turned tomato red. A thick vein pulsed down the side of his neck.

Miranda swung around, looking at the boy who was still on the floor.

I shrugged. "Sorry, I slipped."

"Dude, she totally body checked you," one of the stupid idiots said.

Darn straight I did. Just be thankful I didn't break out and go all Tae Kwon Do on your ass.

Smiling, I glanced across the room. Muriel was watching me with an odd expression. Knowing she saw everything, I turned away quickly, hoping if I ignored it, she would too.

3

Freak

SEVEN WEEKS, FIVE DAYS UNTIL MY BIRTHDAY.

I'm a freak. There's no other explanation for what's happening to me.

Lying on my back across my bed, looking up at the ceiling, I stared at the posters taped there. I'd gone home right after swim practice, not even waiting for Muriel like usual. Staying wasn't an option, though. She'd ask questions about what happened with Miranda, and I didn't know what to tell her. How could I explain what happened when I didn't understand it myself?

I turned over and looked out of the window with a sigh. Part of me needed—wanted—to talk to someone. Muriel seemed like the logical choice. She was my best friend, after all. She was family. Or I could've talked with my parents. We'd always been open with each other. I got along with them fine, as far as parents go. But I didn't want any of them to know.

I'm a freak. That's all there is to it. And I want to keep my freakishness a secret.

The doorbell chimed, and I rolled off the bed. It was Muriel. I knew she'd come looking for me when I didn't wait for her after swim practice. I walked down the hall toward the stairway but stopped short at the corner of the stairs, skidding on the hardwood floor. It wasn't Muriel's voice I heard but my aunt's. And she was talking about me to my mother. I held my breath and strained to listen to their quiet voices.

"Muriel thinks it's started. She says Milayna's showing signs."

"She hasn't said anything to us," my mom answered.

Michelle K. Pickett

"It's only been a few days, but Muriel is pretty sure. She's almost positive Milayna's had some sightings."

Sightings? What does she mean? Visions?

I adjusted my weight to my other leg, and the floorboard creaked. They heard and changed the subject.

My mom and aunt stopped talking and looked at me when I bounded down the stairs. A frown pulled at my mom's lips, and the skin between her eyes wrinkled.

"What's started?" I looked between them.

My mom wouldn't look at me. "Oh, um, old Mrs. Haggarty is complaining that Muriel's dog is digging up her flower bulbs again. You know how she is."

Yeah, and you're lying to me.

"Oh." I looked at my aunt and smiled. "Hi. Where's Muriel?"

She smiled, but her lips quivered at the sides. She was so faking it. "She's doing homework. She said to tell you she'd call later."

"Okay." I looked between them one more time before I wandered into the kitchen to help my dad make dinner. He was silent, and that put me even more on edge. He usually never shut up when we made dinner together. His silence was like a scream telling me that something was wrong. Whatever my mom and aunt were talking about, he was in on the secret.

And it definitely wasn't about Muriel's dog.

Muriel called just after dinner. "Hey," I mumbled.

"Whatcha doin'?" she chirped, and I cringed. I wasn't in the mood for bubbly.

"I'm finishing my English homework." I drummed my fingers and waited for the inevitable questioning to begin. It didn't take long.

"What was up in swim practice today? You almost pushed that guy right into the pool." She laughed. It was too high and too loud. So fake.

"Yeah, well, he deserved it." The scene replayed in my head. "He was a tool who was going to undo Miranda's swimsuit."

Shit. Why did I just tell her that?

"Really? How'd ya know?" She sounded skeptical, and I knew I'd said too much.

"I heard one of the other guys dare him." I doodled on my notebook and tried to sound bored.

"How? You weren't close enough to hear him. Besides, if you heard them, Miranda would've heard it too."

"Miranda was busy putting her swim cap on. She wasn't paying attention," I said with an exasperated sigh. "And what's with all the questions and watching everything I do?" I pushed too hard on my paper and broke my pencil lead.

"Nothing." The word hung between us like a brick. Something was happening to me. Something very strange. Even more strange was that my family seemed to know what it was, but they didn't want to tell me.

I'm a freak.

"I think we should go see Grandma tomorrow after school," Muriel said.

"Grandma? Okay. Why?"

"We haven't gone to see her in a few weeks. We should go. I'll call and ask her to make some butterscotch brownies."

"Okay." I shrugged. "I'm down for some brownies."

The next day at school, it happened again. I started to worry that it was going to be an everyday thing.

I walked through the crowded cafeteria. Long, rectangular tables lined the aisle. The room roared with the noise of people laughing and joking, and a person had to yell to be heard over the chaos. But I heard giggles and whispers in my ears—no, in my *head*. I sucked in a breath and braced myself.

The same feeling washed over me each time it happened. I could feel it building in the pit of my stomach, filling it. It was as if someone were blowing up a balloon inside of me. It rose from my stomach to my throat, making it hard to breathe. My head started to pound, and I could hear the blood rushing behind my ears. I had only one thought screaming through my head.

Stop them.

The scene fast-forwarded through my mind. They were going to trip a poor freshman as she walked by. She was scrawny, shy, wore braces and glasses, and had a bad acne problem. She had enough on her plate without some idiot tripping her in the lunchroom and embarrassing her in front of half the school.

It's just like the little girl... I don't even know her, but I'm drawn to her. But it isn't my problem. I shouldn't have to step in. I should have a choice!

I did know the other kids, though. They were notorious bullies. I knew if they were joking about tripping her, they were gonna do it.

I don't remember walking toward their table. I didn't choose to—I just did. Like a puppeteer moves a puppet, the feeling moved me. I had no control, even though I fought against it. The more I fought, the stronger the feeling became.

Stop them.

The girl walked toward me. I could see the bullies watching her. I approached from the opposite direction, gripping my lunch tray tightly in my hands. One of us would have to move to let the other pass, and I knew it would be her. In my mind, I could see the scene play out.

With a quick glance up, she stepped to the side so I could pass. I slowed just in front of the bullies' table, putting myself between her and the group of overgrown two-year-olds.

A foot shot out. A wave of viciousness swept over me, and I stepped down

Michelle K. Pickett

on it with all my weight, bending his foot at a painful angle. The boy howled. I tried not to smile. It was really, really hard.

I gave him a small shrug. "Gee, I'm sorry. You really should be more careful," I said before walking away with a smile and an unexplainable feeling of peace. I sat across from Muriel. She looked at me with a slight frown, but thankfully, she didn't say anything.

I took in two deep breaths, letting the air hiss through my teeth. Slowly, my mind righted itself. Their voices faded—but not before I heard him call me a bitch—and the feeling disappeared. The freak show was over.

Muriel and I drove to Grams' after school. I knocked on the black apartment door, which according to Grams was 'hideous,' and listened as Muriel told me the latest gossip from her sixth-period class. She hadn't brought up what had happened at lunch. Maybe she didn't notice. *Yeah, right.*

I jumped when the door flung open and my grams looked up at us. "Hey, Grams." I gave my grandma a hug and kissed her baby-soft skin. It was smooth and smelled faintly of gardenia. She laid her hand, her fingers crooked from arthritis, against the side of my face.

"It's about time you two showed up! I was beginning to think I'd have to drag you here by the nape of your necks."

I laughed. "Sorry, Grams."

Muriel leaned down to give Grams a hug before we went inside. "So." Grams wheeled her wheelchair into the large, bright yellow living area and swung it around. "What brings you by?"

"Just visiting," I said, plopping down on a vintage, purple couch. I loved that couch. It was a place I felt safe and loved. Not to mention it was wicked cool, with its back shaped like the Nike swoosh and its velvety feel. I leaned back into the couch cushions and flipped off my shoes.

"Actually," Muriel started, sitting on the edge of a red, purple, and yellow paisley chair.

Oh, crap.

"We need to have the talk, Grams."

"Ah. It is that time, I suppose." Grams nodded, her snow-white curls bouncing in all directions.

"What talk?" I looked between them.

Grams took a big breath and glanced quickly at Muriel, who looked like she had a mouthful of Warhead candy. "Well, Milayna, since you're almost eighteen, there are some things you should know—"

I shot up like I was on a springboard. "Eww, Grams. Mom already had that talk with me."

"Good gracious, if you'd just let me finish. Cripes, that isn't the talk I want to have with you." She held both hands up and waved them down at me.

"Then what?" I shook my arms out at my sides.

"Get comfortable, child. This is going to turn your life sideways."

Michelle K. Pickett

4

Angels

"YOU'RE SPECIAL, MILAYNA." GRAMS RESTED HER ELBOW ON the arm of her wheelchair and put her chin in her upturned hand.

"Isn't everyone?"

"No, I mean, you're *really* special. You're a demi-angel," she told me as if it should've been obvious.

"Demi what?" I'd decided Grams was more senile than I thought.

"Angel, dear, keep up." She patted my knee. "See, your mother is a mortal…"

This is gonna be priceless.

"…and your dad is an angel. So there you go."

"Huh? What are you talking about?" Shaking my head, I knew if I looked in the mirror just then I'd look like a fish, with my mouth opening and closing and my eyes bulging. I don't think I blinked for a whole minute as I stared at my grandmother, waiting for her to laugh and say *'Gotcha.'* I was always too gullible and fell for her practical jokes too easily.

"You've completely lost me, Grams. I think you need a brownie fix as much as I do. The sugar will clear your head." I wiped my hands down my thighs. "You did make brownies, right? You feel okay?"

She sighed. "Yes, I made you some, but first, we need to discuss this. See, your mother is a mortal, and your father is an—"

"Yeah, I heard it the first time you said it. Funny. You had me going there for a minute. I thought you'd bought two one-way bus tickets, senile-ville for you and gullible-city for me." I laughed and stood up to rummage through her small, galley-style kitchen in search of something to ease my brownie fix. "But you know I hate those jokes you pull on me, so can we just have some brownies like normal people?"

"Milayna! Sit down, child. This is important."

"Come on, Grams." I threw my arms in the air and let out a frustrated sigh. My hands slapped against my thighs when they fell. "You can't really expect me to believe we're a family of angels." I stared at her, eyebrow raised.

"No—"

"Good. Let's have brownies, huh? I've been waiting all day for some." I pulled the plates out of the low cupboard made to accommodate her wheelchair.

"We're a family of angels and half angels."

Blinking at her persistence, I turned slightly and studied her. Her expression didn't hold a trace of humor.

Okay, their joke was cute at first. Now, they're starting to piss me off.

"Okay, whatever." I set the plates down a little too hard on the counter, and they rattled against each other. I rolled my eyes. "The joke isn't funny anymore." I paused. My eyes narrowed, and the muscles in my neck tensed. I didn't like practical jokes, especially ones that made my family sound like they had a padded cell reserved in their name. "Oh, I get it. Ha-freakin'-ha. You're both hilarious."

"Milayna, I know this is hard to believe, so I'm going to start over from the beginning. Now, like I said, you're a demi-angel, a child of an angel parent and a human parent."

"Wait." I gave a half-laugh. "You really believe what you're saying?" Grams nodded. I looked at Muriel, who'd been quiet. "And you?" She nodded once and turned her face away.

I paced the small kitchen, mulling over what Grams was telling me. One hand massaged the tension growing like a tumor in my neck muscles, and the other rubbed at the migraine knocking its way out of my forehead.

We're either a bunch of angels, which makes me a freak like I thought and makes everyone else in my family a freak, too. Or Muriel and Grams have lost it completely—or are really trying to activate my bitch-mode with this joke.

I turned and pointed at Grams. "Angels are immortal."

"Not necessarily. Your father is just as mortal as anyone else, but he is definitely an angel."

"Not always, according to my mother," I grumbled under my breath. Grams cackled at that, and I jumped before squeezing my arms around my stomach.

"No, probably not," she agreed. "Anyway, when an angel leaves Heaven, or in some cases, is asked to leave, they become mortal. Unless they go south of the border."

I was so confused. "Mexico?" I squeezed my eyes shut. Maybe if I kept my eyes closed long enough and pretended they weren't there, they'd go away, and I wouldn't have to deal with this. Whatever *this* was.

"No, Hell. Keep up, would you, child? If they choose to serve in Hell, they

21

Michelle K. Pickett

retain their immortal status, becoming a demon angel instead."

I put my hands on either side of my head and bent over. It felt like it was spinning so fast that it was going to pop off and fly across the room like a balloon.

This is a great fairytale, but there's no frikkin' way it's real. My dad is just Dad. Not a flippin' angel. I've had enough of this crap. I just want a damn brownie without all the stupid practical jokes, is that too much to ask?

Slowly, I opened my eyes in time to see Grams pick a piece of lint off her shirt. When she noticed my gaze, she continued. "In the case of your father, he fell madly in love with the woman he was assigned to protect—"

I sighed. "He was her guardian angel." I made a *blah, blah, blah* motion with my hand. Muriel glared at me, but she stayed quiet.

"Yep, and he left Heaven for her. He gave up his immortality and chose a life with her here on earth, which is about as close to Hell as you can get without burnin' your toes." She laughed at her own joke.

I stared at her and tried to figure out exactly when it was that everyone in my family went nutso. Surely, she didn't believe what she was telling me. "Lemme guess," I said in a sarcastic tone, walking around the kitchen counter and sitting on the couch—in the corner furthest from my grams in case whatever she had that made her go batty was contagious. "That woman was my mother?"

"Yes indeedy, speedy. Your dad lost his wings, gained a wife, and a few years later, you were born. Then they got a big surprise when little Ben made his appearance ten years later. Anyway, the two of you were born from a human and an angel, making you demi-angels. You know, like demi-gods?" Grams waved her hand in the air like she was batting them away. "They don't exist, by the way. That whole Zeus and human thing? Who'd believe that?" She looked at me with a smile.

"Yeah. Who'd believe it?" I whispered, staring back at her. A chill ran up my spine, and I watched my grams' steady gaze.

"But demi-angels do exist, Milayna, and I'm staring one square in the face. Actually, two. Muriel's also a demi-angel. That's how she knows you're having the visions."

I swung around in Muriel's direction, feeling my heart speed up. "What do you know about my visions?" My hands clenched. I had the oddest fight-or-flight sensation come over me.

"I know that you see things before they happen. Bad things. I know that you can't help yourself. If it is in your power to stop whatever is going to happen, you have to," Muriel answered quietly. She wouldn't meet my gaze. Instead, her eyes stayed on her lap, where she twisted her fingers together.

"Why didn't you tell me? You knew what was happening to me, and you didn't tell me? How could you do that to me, Muriel?" I had a heavy feeling in my chest and a lump lodged in my throat. The thought that Muriel, the one person I shared everything with and thought she did the same with me, kept something so big a secret from me? It physically hurt.

She raised her head, her eyes wide. "You would have thought I was insane. *I* thought I was insane."

"You've let me think I'm a freak! You could have *tried*, Muriel. You could have tried to tell me, so I wouldn't have been so scared that something was really wrong with me—that I wasn't going insane." Tears pushed at the back of my eyes, but I fought to keep them from falling. I was too angry to cry in front of Muriel. As far as I was concerned, she'd betrayed our trust.

"I'm so sorry, Milayna, but you wouldn't talk to me when I asked. And until it happens to you, it's pretty hard to explain. Or believe." Muriel held out her hand to me, pleading, but I pushed it away.

Grams tsked behind me. "How long have you known, Muriel?"

"I didn't know for sure until the day in the cafeteria. I started wondering the day at the mall." Muriel dropped her hand.

I turned my back on Muriel and met Grams' gaze. I asked, "So my dad and Muriel's dad are angel brothers?"

"No. They're just angels who happened to find each other on earth. They think of each other as family. And they are, if you think about it. They love each other like brothers. I think that makes them just as much of a family as anyone else." She folded her hands in her lap, the sparkle in her eyes introspective. "See, angels don't have blood family, dear. We're created, not born like humans. Other than your mom, your brother, and you, your father is alone in this world."

"We? You're an angel too?" My voice went up several octaves. "Geez, all I wanted was a brownie, but what did I get? Family members jumping around, telling me they're angels." I rolled my eyes and tossed my hands in the air. "Okay, you have my attention. Prove it. Fly around the room. Show me your angel wings." Throwing my arms out, I spun around. "Prove you're an angel, Grams, because I don't believe a word you're saying."

Grams' mouth pinched down at the corners. "When we leave our home to come to earth, we become mortal. We aren't quite human, but we lose most of our angelic abilities. I can't fly around the room. I don't have wings stuffed in my bra that I can whip out and show you."

I lowered my arms and huffed. "Yeah, okay, joke's over, guys."

All of a sudden, the lamp on the table next to me turned on. I swung around to see who else was in the room and felt a chill trickle down my spine—no one.

"I can turn it off, too."

The light went out, and I stared at it before turning around again. "So you got one of those clapper things that turn your lights on and off automatically—big freakin' deal. That isn't proof of anything," I said slowly. Trying to be inconspicuous, I looked around for the clapper thing.

But she didn't clap. She didn't do anything.

Grams leaned back in her wheelchair and crossed her thin arms over her chest. "Okay, try this, then."

Every light in the apartment came on. The ceiling fans started to whir above

23

Michelle K. Pickett

us, and the blender buzzed in the kitchen. I jumped, a small scream slipping past my lips. My breaths came as fast as my racing heart. "What the hell...?" I looked around the room.

"Can I turn them off now? My electric bill will be outrageous this month if I have to keep turning lights on and off," Grams said with an eye roll. Everything turned off simultaneously, just as they'd turned on.

"How'd you do that?" I stared at the floor where I'd let my shoes fall earlier, but I didn't really see them. I didn't see anything. In truth, I wasn't thinking much of anything either. My mind was a mishmash of information. Angels, demi-angels, visions... My insides quivered like I was sitting on top of the washer during the spin cycle. But this wasn't a fun kind of quivering, this was the change-your-life kind. "Angels. Angels? So, wait, if you really are an angel—"

"I am." She folded her hands in her lap, and her gaze locked on mine.

"And angels are created, then you aren't my real grandma? I mean, if you really were created, then we can't be related." It hurt to say those words out loud. My grams was everything to me. Next to Muriel, she was my best friend. I told her everything. The thought of her not really being my grandmother brought bile up my throat.

"Technically, no."

Oh. Not the answer I wanted. Sometimes, you should keep your big mouth shut, Milayna.

"And Muriel's not my real cousin," I said quietly. I already knew the answer, and it was crippling. My body felt weak. If they gave me one more piece of information, I was going to crumble beneath it.

"I'm still me, Milayna! Nothing's changed." Muriel moved from the chair to the couch. Before I had time to react, she'd pulled me into a hug. "We are still the same people, still the same *family*, we were before you learned we're angels and demi-angels."

Grams nodded and tapped her perfectly manicured nail on the arm of her wheelchair. "It all depends on what you consider to be real, Milayna. Your relationship with us hasn't changed. Does it really matter what title we hold? I'm your grandmother in heart. Doesn't that count for something?"

Everything I knew to be true walking into my grandmother's apartment had shattered in a matter of minutes. My aunt and uncle weren't really related to me. My cousin was just another friend. My grams wasn't really my grandmother. And my father was a friggin' angel. Fury pounded against my veins, and like betrayal, demanded to be satisfied.

I narrowed my eyes at Grams. "Is there anyone else in our family who is an angel or demi-angel?"

"No."

I jumped off the couch and paced the entryway hall. "So Mom is human and Muriel's mom is human. But Muriel, me, and my brother are demi-angels." I ticked each person off on my fingers. "Dad, you, and Uncle Rory are angels.

Right? Do I have it right? Because when I came in here, I thought we were one big, happy family of humans. Now I find out we're one big, happy *sort-of*-family of freaks!"

"Milayna!" Grams snapped, and flicked all the lights on and off again.

I turned and looked at her. "Yeah, I get it. One of your angel powers is becoming your very own clapper."

Grams pointed a tiny finger at me. "I wish I had some of my full angel powers. I'd clap you right on your ass," she snapped.

I heard Muriel suck in a breath at the same time my mouth dropped open. Grams had never spoken to me like that.

I let out a breath, and my shoulders slumped forward. Suddenly, I was just tired, and all I wanted was to go home and crawl into bed. Maybe if I pulled the blankets over my head, everything else would go away. Deflated, I sat down on the couch and put my hand over Grams'. "I'm sorry, Grams."

"Look, you can be angry. You can be confused. What you can't be is disrespectful, so don't get pissy. Learn to live the life you've been dealt," my grandma said, sounding nicer but still firm.

"That's just it," I whispered. "I have no idea what my life is now."

I stood, kissed Grams' cheek, tried to smile in Muriel's direction, and slowly walked out of the apartment. I hoped I had enough money to take a taxi home because I didn't want to ride with Muriel. I didn't even want to look at her.

I heard Muriel yell my name. Then Grams' soft voice floated after me as I shut the door. "It's okay, child. Let her be."

I stood outside my grandmother's senior citizen apartment complex, digging around in my purse for my wallet. A sudden squeezing in my stomach choked the air from my lungs. "Damn it!" I yelled. My head started to pound, and I nearly dropped my purse. Voices screamed through my head.

A woman crying. A man laughing.

Shaking my head to clear it, I held out my arm to hail a cab driving down the street. The yellow taxi pulled to the curb beside me, and I opened the door just as a scream pierced my ears. Jumping, I dropped my purse and slapped my hands over my ears. I looked around; there was no one there. Then another scream came, and my vision began to blur.

A woman in a blue dress. A man in an alley. She screams. He's grabbing at something— What is it?

"C'mon, kid," the taxi driver yelled. "I ain't got all night. Are you gettin' in or what?"

The vision fizzled away. "Yeah. Just a second." I took in a big breath and started to shove the stuff back into my purse when I saw her—the woman in the blue dress. She was trying to hail a cab, but several drove past.

25   *Michelle K. Pickett*

She's gonna leave. Stop her.

The woman turned from the road and started walking toward me.

Stop her.

The vision became clearer. She'd walk down the sidewalk, past an alley. A man would be there, waiting. He'd grab her and... Oh!

Stop her!

"Ma'am?" I called, waving at her.

She looked around. "Me?" she asked when she realized we were the only two in front of the building.

"Yes." I smiled. "I saw you were trying to get a cab. Do you want to share?"

"Yes." She took a deep breath. "Thank you. I didn't want to have to walk to the next street to get one. I hate walking alone at night."

She asked where I was going. When I told her, her shoulders sagged. "I'm heading in the opposite direction. Maybe you could just drop me at the next street?"

The vision played in my head like a video. It didn't change. If I gave her a ride to the next street, she'd still meet the man. He'd cut through the alley and grab her on the other side. She'd still be in danger.

My skin prickled. "No, that's okay. I don't really need a cab. My cousin is here; I can catch a ride with her." I stepped aside to let her get into the taxi.

"Are you sure? I feel bad taking your cab."

"Yeah, I'm sure. You take it."

"Thank you." She smiled and got into the cab. "I appreciate this so much."

"No problem. Have a good night." I waved as the cab pulled away from the curb. The vision fell away, and the stabbing pains in my stomach eased. The physical relief from pain was always the most pronounced after a vision. Stopping the claws from ripping me apart from the inside out was definitely a bonus. There was also a kind of peace mixed with joy that came after the pain eased. For a short time, I think I felt how it would be if evil didn't exist in our world.

Muriel walked out of the apartment building just as the cab disappeared down the street. I was digging through the never-ending crap in my purse for my cell phone. Silently, Muriel handed me hers. I stared at it for a few beats. Finally, deciding it was better to use her phone than stand there for the week it would take me to actually find mine, I took it and punched in 911.

"911. What's your emergency?"

"The rapist that's been on the news? I just saw him."

"Where?"

I rattled off my grandmother's address and told the dispatcher that he was in one of the alleyways lining the main road.

"What's your name, miss?"

I clicked off the line and handed the phone back to Muriel. "Thanks," I said. Climbing into Muriel's car, I turned to look out of the passenger window. We didn't speak on the ride home.

As soon as I got home, I went into the family room where my parents were watching the news.

"You're an angel?" I blurted, staring at my dad. He looked the same as he had that morning, but so much had changed since then.

My dad straightened and reached for the remote, putting the TV on mute. "Grams said you'd talked. I wish she'd given me a little bit of a heads-up." He leaned forward in his chair, his hands falling between his knees like he always did when we had a serious talk, but it seemed wrong somehow. Like he was an imposter of my real dad. "Yes, I'm an angel. But it's not quite that simple."

"Really? You needed a heads-up? I think I'm the one that needed a little warning." I pointed a finger at my chest, my voice rising with each word.

"There was no reason to tell you before; it would've only confused you. But now, you are maturing as a demi-angel and you need to know the truth."

"Well, gee, thanks for including me," I bit out through clenched teeth. My hands balled into fists at my sides. "I think you could've told me a little sooner. I've had reasoning skills for a few years. It's not like I'm seven, like Ben."

My dad nodded and clasped his hands together. He sat for several seconds, staring at the floor before he said, "You're right. But please understand that this is new territory for your mom and me. We weren't—aren't—sure how to handle this either. We've done the best we can." He lifted his gaze to mine, and I saw regret. "We wanted you to have as normal a childhood as you could before all this stuff was thrown at you, so we waited to tell you. We were wrong to wait so long. Sit down, Milayna. Let's talk."

I stepped back and leaned against the wall behind me. "I can hear you from here."

My dad nodded and sighed. "Angels have been studied by scholars for years. There is very little accurate information on us. I was a Watcher—the official name is Qadishin. It's what man has termed a guardian angel. I left my post as a Watcher and came to earth twenty-five years ago to live out my life as a mortal. I'm an angel, but I've given up most of my powers. I'm not immortal. I'll age, get sick, injured, and eventually die just as any mortal human would. I've also relinquished my status as a Qadishin. I can never go back."

"So you're a fallen angel?"

My dad fiddled with his watch clasp. "No."

"But we're taught in church that angels who leave to come to earth are fallen—"

"Like I said, men have tried to understand the angelic world for centuries. They don't have all the facts correct. Not all angels on earth are what man terms 'fallen.'"

"I don't understand." I walked to the couch and sat next to my mom, the only

Michelle K. Pickett

other human—non-freak—in the room. She wrapped her arm around me, and I snuggled against her where I felt safe and the world made sense, or at least, where it used to.

"There are two groups of Watchers. The Iri are the obedient, or faithful, Watchers. The Irin are disobedient, or fallen, angels. I'm an Iri."

"And Uncle Rory?" My mom hugged me closer but stayed silent, letting my dad tell me about his history and his people.

"Iri, and so is Grams."

"I guess if I must have a freaky family of angels, I'm glad they come from the Iri line," I muttered.

My dad chuckled, spinning his wedding ring on his finger. "Yeah, I guess that's the silver lining in all of this."

"But where's the proof? I want to see something other than Grams turning her blender on from the living room." I stood and walked to the window.

Dad laughed, and the suddenness of it in this otherwise quiet room made me jump. "The blender trick, huh? Yeah, she likes that one." He shook his head slowly with a grin. "Ah. Well, let's see. You believe in good and evil, right?" I nodded. "That's your proof."

"What are you talking about?" I made a *what-the-hell* face.

"Faith. That's about the only proof you have right now. You'll get hardcore, tangible proof soon enough, unfortunately. And once you see it, you'll spend the rest of your life wishing you could un-see it."

I leaned against the window and stared at a portrait on the fireplace mantel. The faces of the people I'd called family smiled back at me. "I can't believe you didn't tell me. Nothing about our family is what it seemed." Tears pressed against the back of my eyes, and I blinked to hold them in. They were a watery mixture of anger and sadness. At that point, I hadn't figured out which outweighed the other—or if it even mattered.

"Milayna." My mom spoke for the first time. "Our family is the same now as it was yesterday. You've just learned some things about your heritage. Just because our family is different doesn't mean we don't love each other as much as any blood relations could love one another."

I nodded. "I still wish you would've told me."

My parents looked at me, their faces soft with love and understanding. A shimmer of sympathy stirred in their eyes. "I'm sorry, Milayna, but we just didn't think you were ready," my dad whispered. "Or maybe, we weren't ready."

"What makes me more ready today than yesterday?"

"Your visions. You need to know why you're having them." My dad reached for my hand, but I moved it away from him.

"Why? Because I'm this... this demi-angel? Well, I don't want to be a demi-whatever, and I don't want the visions." The fury and betrayal bubbled up inside me, singeing my stomach lining. The acid burned my throat. "I don't want the visions!" I yelled, jamming my hands through my hair. Fisting my fingers in the red waves, I pulled at them. "They're horrible. They aren't just *visions*, either. I feel things too. They're painful. And sometimes, I hear things. And the stuff I see? I shouldn't be seeing it!" I looked at my parents. "No one should."

My dad's shoulders sagged. "I'm sorry—"

"Whatever." I grabbed my book bag off the floor. "I have homework to do."

I took the stairs two at a time. My sneakers squeaked against the wooden floor as I ran to my room. Slamming the door behind me, I fell across the bed and grabbed a black pillow. It was covered with hundreds of different colored smiley faces. Disgusted, I tossed it across the room and buried my face in a plain black pillow that matched my mood.

Michelle K. Pickett

5
Rebellion

SEVEN WEEKS, FOUR DAYS UNTIL MY BIRTHDAY.

Though I'd heard the expression '*seeing red*' before, I'd never actually believed a person saw the color red when they were mad. It was just an expression—a way to tell someone that a person wasn't just mad but pissed. I was wrong. I'd know. I was that mad. It was the morning after I'd learned I was supposedly a demi-angel, and the more I thought of it, the angrier I became. I was mad at my parents. Mad at Muriel. Mad at my grandma. Mad at the world in general. I wanted to be mad.

I'd gone from shocked and confused to thoroughly pissed off. Demi-angel, my ass. I refused to take part in their little family of angelic freaks.

I spent the entire weekend in my bedroom. I even skipped our traditional Saturday morning family breakfast, opting to sleep late instead. Well, actually, I wasn't sleeping. I was sitting on the window seat overlooking the front lawn when my mother knocked on my door and asked if I was coming down. I didn't answer. I couldn't sit across the table from my dad after he'd lied to me. I didn't even want to be in the same room with him. It was his fault. My life was ruined because of my dad, and I hated him for it.

I only left my room to go to work or grab something to eat when my parents went out. Somehow, I managed to steer clear of both of them.

I didn't wait for breakfast Monday morning, and I didn't wait around to ride with Muriel. Instead, I got up early and drove to school in my beat-up Chevy, which was filled with old burger wrappers and Coke cans.

The day progressed quickly. I wasn't ready to face Muriel, even at school, so I cut second-period calculus class. I felt the sting of betrayal run through my veins when I thought about her. We'd always told each other everything. At least, I thought we did. Now, I wondered what else she'd kept from me.

But beneath the noxious betrayal ran another emotion. One just as strong, or maybe even stronger. Muriel and I had a bond, and I missed her. Longing tore through me like scissors through a ribbon. I felt like I was on the other end of that ribbon—a helium balloon, floating farther and farther away from my family.

No. I gave my head a quick shake and pinched the bridge of my nose with my fingers. *I'm pushing them away. I'm not floating away from them; I'm shoving them away from me. They lied. All these years, all the lies, how can I forget that?*

A vision pulled at me on my drive home from school that afternoon. It jerked and pushed for control of my thoughts and actions. I struggled to lock it out. But it seemed that the more visions I had, the stronger they became. And the more dangerous the situation, the stronger the vision. But when my chest tensed and a knot twisted in my stomach, sending bile up my throat, I was determined to ignore the vision I knew would follow.

I'm not giving up my free will and having something that I didn't ask for shoved on me.

This time, I heard it before I saw it. My ears felt like they were full of cotton, and the normal sounds of my surroundings were muted in the background. Like an explosion, the sounds of the upcoming vision bombarded my mind. They were all I could hear, all I could focus on.

I'm not listening this time. I'm going to ignore, ignore, ignore. Demi-angel or not, I'm not going to let these visions control me!

What kind of life would I have if I could have a vision anytime, anywhere? I could see myself standing in front of a church full of people. Flowers and candles filled the room. I was in a gorgeous white gown about to give my wedding vows to Jake, then BAM! A vision. *Nope, no thanks.*

I turned on the radio to drown out the sounds. It didn't help. My mind focused on them, even as I cursed it.

Kids laughing. Singing.

"No! I'm not listening," I said through clenched teeth, banging my fist against the steering wheel.

Laughing. Playing.

My vision started to crackle, and I shifted in my seat and gripped the steering wheel tighter. I couldn't have a vision while I was driving. I'd cause an acci-

Michelle K. Pickett

dent. Sweat covered my back and my shirt stuck to my skin. But the vision came anyway. It was transparent, playing like a video over my normal sight.

A ball. A toddler. The ball rolling into the road—a teenager racing down the road, not paying attention.

"No! It's a baby!"

A child's life was in danger. There was no question—I gave in.

Once I stopped fighting the vision, it guided me. It was like I was a remote-controlled toy, and someone used the remote to drive me to the kids playing in the yard. I saw the red ball and the blond-headed little boy.

Reaching the house, I steered my truck so it blocked the road. I saw the old Trans-Am barreling toward me on one side of my truck and the little boy, running in that wobbly way little kids do, on the other side. The driver of the Trans-Am slammed on his brakes just in time to keep from hitting my truck. At the same time, the little boy picked up his ball and held it over his head with a loud giggle. He threw it, and it bounced back into the yard. He ran after it. As soon as the toddler was safely in his yard again, the vision cleared and my hearing returned to normal. The clenching pain in my stomach eased, but adrenaline still zinged through my veins like electricity shooting across my nerve endings.

The idiot in the Trans-Am got out of his car and stalked to my window. "What the hell are you doing?"

I rolled down the window, reached through the opening, and poked him in the chest. "Listen, idiot, you should be thanking me. Stop speeding through these streets; there are little kids playing. Now move your dumb-ass car." I rolled my window up and tapped my finger on the steering wheel, waiting for him to move.

He stared at me with a stupid expression before turning and slowly walking to his car.

Once he was gone, I drove to the bakery where I worked part time. I had a closing shift that night, so I didn't get home until after eight. I grabbed a frozen dinner and threw it in the microwave.

"Milayna?" my mom called.

I rolled my eyes. I didn't want to talk, but I knew she'd expect an answer. "Yeah."

She walked around the corner into the kitchen and leaned her hip against the counter. "How are you doing?"

The microwave beeped. "Fine. I'm just really hungry, and I have a ton of homework. I'm going to take this to my room." I grabbed my dinner from the microwave and threw it on a plate. She stood silent and watched me. "See you later." I carried my things to my room and locked myself inside. Maybe if I locked myself in, everything would go away.

Seven weeks until my birthday.

Tuesday, I skipped school and went to my grandmother's. I needed to talk to her. I needed to stretch out on her purple couch and let my problems and worries float away. My grams and I had a lot of talks on the purple couch. Maybe that was why I always felt pulled to it when life turned upside down.

"Hi, Milayna," one of my grandmother's friends called when I walked through the foyer and into the great room. She was short and plump, with her hair dyed jet-black, which she insisted was her natural color. She smiled wide and waved. Her teeth were stained with bright red lipstick.

"Hi, Mrs. Richardson." I waved back.

Telling everyone *hi* as I passed, I made my way to Grams' apartment. She opened the door before I could knock.

"Come in, child." She motioned me inside and rolled her chair into the living room. The overhead lights gleamed down on the white hair that curled against her round face.

"Hi." I bent down and kissed her on the check. The familiar scent of her perfume tickled my nose, and I forgot I was mad. She was just my funny, old grandmother again. Not a freakin' angel.

"No school today?"

"Not for me." I shrugged a shoulder and plopped down on the couch.

"Ah. Well, I knew you'd be back sooner or later." She fiddled with the knitting she had on her lap. "A scarf." She held it up. "Do you like it?"

"Yeah. It's pretty, Grams. Everything you knit is pretty. I like the pink and black."

"Well, that's good. It's for you," she said with a laugh. "So, I guess you're not here to talk about my knitting."

"No." I picked at the hem of my shirt.

"Well, get on with it then." She tossed the yarn in a basket next to the sofa where I sat. I loved that my grandma was a fun, eccentric person—the kind that would have a purple sofa in a bright yellow room.

I frowned. "I don't want it."

"Well, dearie, there's nothing you can do about that."

"I didn't ask to be born this way." My voice grew louder. "I want to give it away."

Grams shook her head while I was talking. When I finished, she shrugged and said, "You can't just give it away, Milayna."

"Why not? I don't want it."

"It'd be like someone trying to give away their brain." She tapped her forehead with her fingers. "It just can't be done. This is a part of you. You can't separate yourself from it." Her hand dropped to her lap.

"Grams, I just want my regular life back."

"You still have your regular life. You're just learning more about yourself. Everyone has growing pains. Consider this one of yours."

Michelle K. Pickett

"Not everyone finds out their father is a flippin' angel. I think that's one helluva growing pain." I stood and walked to the window. It had started to rain, and the drops covered the glass blurring everything outside.

"True."

"There's gotta be a way for me to get rid of this. Help me find it, Grams, please?" I turned from the window and knelt in front of her wheelchair. "Grams, how do people like Muriel and I have normal lives? Will we be able to go to college, have the job we want, or go on school functions with our kids?" I laughed, but it was a short, bitter sound. "Or even have kids? Can you imagine having a vision in the middle of labor?"

Grams chuckled. "A woman in labor hunting down a demon? Yes, that'd be quite a sight." She smiled and patted my cheek. "The way I see it, you have two choices. You can sit around your whole life and pout like a spoiled brat because things aren't going the way you think they should." She ran her hand over my hair. "Or you can get on with life and find a way to be happy. It's your choice, but I know which one I'd make if I were you."

"I don't want it, Grams. I'm gonna find a way to get rid of it." I ground my teeth together and clenched my fists.

"Well, good luck with that. What I'm hearing is a bunch of '*I, I, I, I.*' When you can talk without your thoughts centering only around yourself and what *you* want, then we can have a real discussion about what this demi-angel thing really means and what it can do—if you let it."

I looked at my lap and twisted my fingers together.

I have made it all about me.

"Now," Grams said, clapping her hands together, "let's make some brownies. I'll show you my secret recipe, but if you tell anyone, I'll have to hunt you down and run over your toes with my wheelchair." She tapped her finger against my nose and winked.

I grinned. "Okay. I swear I won't tell anyone." Standing, I went into the kitchen. I grabbed the measuring cups and a bowl, waiting for instructions from Grams.

"All righty. Grab the boxed brownie mix out of the cupboard—"

"Wait! You said your brownies were homemade."

Grams cackled and turned her wheelchair, rolling into the kitchen. "They are homemade, child. I make them at home. I never said they were made from scratch."

"Sneaky old angel, aren't you?" I said with a laugh and opened the cupboard to get the brownie mix.

That night, I had the nightmare again. Demons chased me through nothingness—just a black void that seemed to go on forever. It was hard to move, as if the dark was closing in on me, swallowing me.

Their leader stood watching, waiting. "Milayna," he called. "Stop running and listen to the truth."

Stopping, I turned to him. I could see him clearly, but blackness framed him. His eyes were soulless and cold. Terror ran up my spine, digging into my skin and leaving a warm, sticky trail in its wake.

"They lied to you." He brushed an invisible piece of lint off his shoulder. "You can rid yourself of your awful visions." Pausing, he rocked on his heels. "I can help you."

"How?" I asked, trying to keep the tremor out of my voice.

"Give them to me. It's simple." He spread his hands wide at his sides. "I take them, and you go back to your pathetic little life."

"How do I do that?"

"Come with me, and I'll show you." He held his hand out to me, a smirk on his face.

I backed away. Evil surrounded him, and I knew I wasn't meant to go with him. "No," I said, my voice firm.

A demon grabbed me. Heat radiated from his body, and he smelled of sulfur and burnt flesh. I struggled against his grip, crying and screaming, as he dragged me by the hair to his leader.

"Help me!" But no one came. The blackness surrounding us lifted, and I saw my family and friends watching as other demons grabbed me and pulled me into a glowing, yellow hole.

"You shouldn't have fought your destiny, Milayna," someone said as the demon jerked me down, down, down—

I woke up screaming and sat up in bed. My body trembled, and sweat dripped from my hair. Barely breathing, I tried to force myself to hold still and listen. My eyes darted around the room, looking for shadows that were out of place or movement that signaled I needed to get my skinny ass out of there.

Once I was reasonably sure the monsters didn't follow me out of my dream, I slid out of bed, went into my bathroom, and splashed water on my face. A soft knock sounded on my bedroom door, followed by the handle rattling.

"Milayna? Are you okay?" my mom called.

I shook my head and leaned forward, bracing myself against the sink. "Just a dream."

It'd been days since my last vision. I thought maybe by saying I wasn't going to accept being a demi-angel, I'd somehow cured myself. With spirits lifted, I practically skipped out of school. The visions were gone, the sun was shining, and I didn't have homework. I even had the day off work. Things were looking up.

Humming, I unlocked the door of my truck when a sharp, burning sensation sizzled through my stomach, like someone had impaled me on a white-hot poker.

Michelle K. Pickett

I doubled over. It radiated upward until it swelled and lodged itself in my throat. Gritting my teeth, I leaned against my truck for support as my vision started fading in and out.

A girl. The parking lot.

I shook my head. The vision cleared for a few beats before crashing into me stronger than before.

She drops something. She bends over. A car.

"No!" I said through clenched teeth, earning strange looks from the people around me.

I'm not getting involved. I refuse to get sucked into these demi-angel visions. I didn't ask for it, and I don't want it. They aren't going to control my life.

But the vision didn't go away.

A car, driving through the parking lot. A girl.

I could hear the sounds and see what was going to happen. If someone didn't step in, the car was going to plow right into the girl. She'd bend over to pick up what she'd dropped, the driver wouldn't see her, and—nope, I wasn't getting sucked into it. It. Wasn't. My. Problem.

A teacher driving. My history teacher.

I figured I had three choices. Try to ignore the vision and hope everything worked out on its own, go to my history teacher and stall him the few seconds it would take to change the vision, or talk to the girl to keep her from walking out in the middle of the parking lot.

I decided on the first one—ignore the vision and hope everything worked out okay on its own. After all, if I weren't a demi-angel, I wouldn't have known about it anyway.

As it turned out, I had fewer choices than I thought. My feet took on a life of their own, and I started running toward my history teacher.

Ambulance. A girl lying on the pavement. Blood seeping around her.

I couldn't do it. The vision was too strong, and my own sense of what was right propelled me forward. Dropping my books and purse next to the open door of my truck, I ran. I ran as fast as I could and then even faster. The vision flipped picture after picture in front of my eyes: The girl bending down, the car hitting her, Mr. Rodriguez with tears in his eyes, and blood. So much blood. I pushed myself to run faster, dodging cars and pushing by other people. Another picture scrolled across my vision. The girl's limp body on a stretcher just before it was pushed into an ambulance.

I let all resistance crumble, opening myself to the vision completely. I gave it what I was so afraid of losing. What I'd been fighting to hold on to—total control.

The vision directed me to Mr. Rodriguez. A warm, tingling sensation started in my chest and radiated through my body. It felt like I'd stuck my tongue on a nine-volt battery. I pushed my body harder. I had to get to him.

Wait. Just wait. I'm almost there.

"Mr. Rodriguez!" I screamed.

Milayna

He opened the car door, and I gasped, struggling to breath around the burning in my lungs. *Don't get in the car. Give me just a second longer.*

"Mr. Rodriguez!" I screamed again. "Wait!"

He didn't hear me, and dread filled me as I watched him slide into his car and shut the door. The effects of the visions intensified. I felt a stabbing behind my eyes, like someone was hammering nails into them.

Turning in a circle, I searched the crowd, frantic to find the girl. But there were too many people, and I could sense my time was running out. I pushed my way through the sea of students to the end of the sidewalk. I'd find her there. She'd have to pass me when she crossed into the parking lot. I'd grab her and say something stupid, like, *'Don't we know each other? Are you in Mr. Matelli's English class?'* She'd stop to answer, and it'd delay her long enough to avoid the car. Right? *Right.* Unless she was rude and wouldn't talk to me. Then I'd make something up on the fly. Maybe I'd tackle her. Not very angelic, but better than getting hit by a car. *Yeah. Okay.*

I jammed my way through the massive crowd, making my way toward the sidewalk. Sweat dripped down my back, and the muscles in my arms strained from pushing people out of my way. And my legs burned from running, but I was almost there. Just a little more. I just had to get past a group of guys—but they wouldn't move.

"Excuse me," I yelled, jamming into the guy closest to me. Tears were building behind my eyes, and my chest burned.

I'm running out of time. Move, move, move!

The guy didn't bother to stop texting and look at me. "Go around."

I jabbed my elbow in his side and plowed through. Then I heard it. At first, I thought the boy was screaming at me, but it wasn't him.

I was too late.

I rammed myself through the people standing in front of me and stumbled forward onto the curb. Sights and sounds faded into the background until all I saw was the girl lying on the pavement. Blood pooled around her head like a gruesome halo, and deep red stained her long, blonde braid.

Tears sprang to my eyes. *I'm too late. I didn't save her. I did this to her. My selfishness. My pride. Me. I hurt this girl. What kind of monster am I to let this happen?*

Students screamed. Some grabbed their cell phones and dialed 911, and a couple boys ran into the school and brought back the nurse. But I just stood there, motionless. Useless. Guilty. People ran into me, jostling me, pushing me out of the way.

It's my fault. If I hadn't been so stubborn—if I hadn't fought the vision so hard and done something sooner—she'd be driving home right now instead of lying on the ground in her own blood.

Mr. Rodriguez stood next to his car door with both hands on top of his head, looking at the girl. Tears ran down his face. He was a nice man. If I hadn't been

Michelle K. Pickett

so selfish, so stubborn, I could have spared him the agony of knowing he'd hurt a student.

It's my fault. I'm to blame.

I jumped when I felt a soft touch on my elbow. "Come on, Milayna. I'll drive you home. There's nothing you can do." I turned and saw Muriel. A fresh wave of tears blurred my vision.

"It's my fault, Muriel. I saw it coming. I waited too long. I fought it."

"C'mon. Let's go home." She went to my truck, picked up my purse and bag from where I'd dropped them, and locked the doors. Then she pulled me toward her car.

We drove in silence. I cried, and Muriel would occasionally look over at me with an expression of pity? Disappointment? Blame? Yeah, with an expression of a mixture of all three on her face.

When we got to my house, she walked me upstairs and pulled a pair of yoga pants and a T-shirt from my dresser.

"Here, put these on." She handed the clothes to me.

I peeled off my clothes and slipped into the clean ones before I climbed into bed. The soft, flannel sheets pulled me in with their soothing smell of lavender. I grabbed a pillow, buried my face in it, and screamed before crushing, ugly sobs took over. Muriel sat on the edge of my bed and put her hand on my shoulder.

"She's gonna be okay, Milayna."

"How do you know?" I wiped my tears away with the backs of my hands and sniffed.

"I just know."

"Another angel thing?" My voice was raspy and when I turned to her, she was blurry from the hot tears filling my eyes.

"Yeah, something like that." She gave me a small, sad smile. "We all have visions. Some of us just see different things."

"And Mr. Rodriguez?" A sob slipped out at the thought of him, and I put my fist to my mouth to hold it in.

Muriel's gaze drifted to the floor. "He'll be fine once he knows she's okay. Besides, there was nothing he could've done. He didn't see her. She was kneeling down. It wasn't his fault."

"No, it was my fault."

I'm to blame. What kind of demi-angel will I make? I just let someone almost die.

She didn't deny it. We both knew that if I hadn't fought the vision, the accident wouldn't have happened.

Muriel sat with me until my parents got home. Then she kissed my cheek, said she'd see me at school the next day, and left to go downstairs.

I heard her tell my parents what happened. Telling them it was me who caused it.

When I woke the next morning, the sun streamed through the window blinds and glittered through the stained glass suncatchers I had hanging from the ceiling, creating rainbows on the walls. The birds chirped happily in the treetops. I stretched all the way to my toes under my warm blankets. It was a beautiful morning. And then I remembered—

It was my fault.

Michelle K. Pickett

6

Acceptance

I padded down the stairs and into the kitchen to grab a granola bar for breakfast, finding my parents sitting at the kitchen table. My mom's curly, blonde hair was smoothed into an elegant French twist, and she wore a navy suit that made her blue eyes look like laser beams. My dad wore his normal jeans and a polo, and his auburn hair was cut short, military style.

The sudden realization made me tense up and forget about breakfast. They'd both gotten ready for work earlier than usual so they could wait for me to come downstairs and then pounce.

Damn it. They set a trap, and I walked right into it.

"Sit down, Milayna," my mom said.

I shook my head and crossed my arms over my chest. "I don't want to talk."

"Too bad. Sit down." She pushed a chair out for me with her foot and pointed.

I walked slowly to the table, dragging my messenger bag behind me. Then, dropping into the chair, I crossed my arms around my waist and hunched over.

"We've been patient," my mom said. "We've tried to give you time to work through your feelings. Well, it's time to get over it and get on with life. This hiding in your room is going to stop." My mom picked up her mug and took a sip of coffee. Her gaze never left my face.

"Sorry," I mumbled. And then the tears came. I sobbed, laying my head on the table. I couldn't get the image of the girl lying on the pavement, her blonde hair soaked in her own blood, because of me.

Milayna

40

"You can't fight them," my dad said quietly. He leaned over and rubbed my shoulder.

"It's my fault."

"You have to give into your visions or things like that will keep happening." My mom smoothed my hair over my ear. "Learn to look at the visions as a gift, Milayna, rather than a curse. You have the ability to help people in a way others can't."

It is kind of awesome. If I stop fighting it and learn to use it

My dad cleared his throat. "There's more we need to tell you."

"Oh," I said between hiccupped sobs, "something tells me I don't want to hear it."

My mom slapped her hand flat against the tabletop, and I flinched. "You will listen, Milayna! It's important. There are far worse things you could be than a demi-angel. People don't get to choose their lot in life. This is the life you've been given. So stop whining and bitching and learn to deal. We'll talk after school."

My parents stood and walked out of the room, leaving me slouched in a chair at the kitchen table. I was supposed to leave for school, but instead, I sat at the table most of the morning, thinking.

Emotions tumbled through my brain like a dryer set on high. Some sliced through me, like my family's betrayal and lies, leaving wounds still open and hurting. I opened my heart and pushed those emotions out. They were toxic and not something I had room for. Not something I wanted to keep. Other emotions were raw, but welcomed. Memories of family game nights, traditional Saturday morning breakfasts, trips to the mall with Muriel. That was my life. Was it really going to change as drastically as I pictured?

I was in my room when my parents got home from work that evening. I heard them talking and laughing when they came in. It was rare they came home at the same time, so I figured our impending conversation had something to do with that. I bounded down the stairs to meet them.

"You should change out of your work clothes. I made dinner." Shoving my hands in the back pockets of my jeans, I rose on the balls of my feet and then lowered myself down again. "And I took Ben to Grams'."

"Really? I thought something smelled good in here." My mom smiled at me. We walked into the kitchen, and she went to peek in the oven. "Roasted chicken. It's perfect."

Dad took the lid off a pot on the stove. "Mashed potatoes." He smiled and looked at me. I winked at him, and his smile widened. That was our secret sign that let him know I used extra butter—and not the diet kind that Mom used.

My parents went upstairs to change and wash up for dinner while I set the table. When we all sat down, my mom looked over the table and gave a happy

Michelle K. Pickett

sigh. "This is nice, Milayna. I didn't feel like cooking tonight. Thank you. And thanks for taking Ben to Grams' house. I wasn't looking forward to fighting rush-hour traffic."

I fiddled with my fork and nodded. "I wanted to help."

We ate in a semi-comfortable silence until my dad spoke. "You skipped school today." He took a bite of mashed potatoes.

"I had a lot to think about."

"Yes, I suppose you did."

I picked off a slice of chicken with my fork. "I've come to a conclusion," I said. "I don't like it, but hiding in my room and trying to fight my visions doesn't change what I am. And I don't particularly like the person I've been the last few days. I don't want to be bitter and nasty the rest of my life."

"That's good, Milayna." My mom nodded. "I'm really glad to hear you aren't happy with how you've been acting because, well, you've been almost unbearable to live with." She smiled to take the sting out of her words.

"I know. I really am sorry."

We ate in silence for a bit. The only sound in the room was the scraping of utensils against plates and the ice maker dropping cubes of ice in the bin.

Shifting in my seat, I turned toward my dad. "So, what did you want to tell me? You said this morning there was more I needed to know. I think I'm ready to know the whole truth. I don't want anyone else getting hurt because of something I did or didn't do."

"Well, first," my dad said around a bite of asparagus, "it might help you deal with things knowing there are others like you out there."

"I know. Muriel." I nodded and picked up my water glass.

"Yes, she's a demi-angel too, but there are others." My dad wiped his mouth on a napkin and reached for another biscuit. "Including you and Muriel, there are ten demi-angels at your school. They all know about their powers. You are the youngest, so you're the last to show signs that your powers are maturing."

"Signs? Like the visions?"

"Yes, that's part of your power. You have the ability to change the course of some people's lives. Sometimes, you'll be able to step in and change it for the better, and sometimes you won't. But once you mature, you'll have the power to fight Azazel and his demons. Your visions will help you track him, see his plans, and stop him before he can unleash his evil on earth."

He finished buttering his biscuit, set it and his knife down, and pushed them out of the way. "Milayna, I was the third highest-ranked angel. On earth, I am the highest-ranked angel. That means my children are the highest-ranked demi-angels. Your power is far greater than any other demi-angel. Your job, your power, is to track Azazel and his demons. Keep them from doing harm, making sure humans are as safe as possible from their evil. But above all—keep the underworld from taking over the earth. It would be a massacre if the evil of hell were let loose on unsuspecting humans. It's that power, the power to track, stop, and kill his demons, that Azazel wants from you. And He. Will. Kill. To. Get. It."

I swallowed hard against the lump forming in my throat. Setting my fork down, I wiped at the tears building in my eyes. Thinking of Mr. Rodriguez and the girl burned a piece of me, like a brand or a tattoo. That memory was bound to me. "Um, why was I able to fight the vision so hard yesterday? If I have to step in, if that's my duty, why was I able to wait until it was too late?"

My dad shrugged a shoulder. "I'm not sure. It's probably because your visions are still weak. Your power hasn't reached its full strength yet, but the more you have the visions, the closer to your birthday you get, the stronger they'll become. You'll come to a point where you won't be able to fight them."

"Good. I don't want that to happen again. Ever. I may not be completely thrilled with them, but I know I don't want anything to happen to anyone because of me again." I thought of the girl lying on the pavement. Just two seconds, that was all. If I'd gotten there just two seconds earlier, it could've been avoided. The guilt was like a giant mouth that swallowed me whole.

"I'm glad to hear that."

I forced the memory of the girl out of my head. "Who are the others?"

"They'll come to you. Muriel will help introduce you to the group. Listen, Milayna, this is very important. Right now, your powers are stronger when you're with another demi. They won't be fully mature until your eighteenth birthday, and until then, you are susceptible to outside forces." There was an urgency in his voice that pulled me to him and caused goose bumps to spread on my skin.

"What kind of outside forces?"

"Well, it'll be easier for you to understand if I explain a little about me. Then you'll be able to understand what sets you apart from the other demi-angels." I nodded my head for him to keep going. "I was a high-ranking angel when I left. Third in charge of the Iri Council."

"What's that mean?" Putting my elbow on the table, I rested my chin on my upturned palm. I had the feeling we'd be talking for a long time.

He flipped his chair and straddled it. "The Council is the government of the Iri. I had a high position, and my high ranking made my powers stronger. As my daughter, that power transferred to you. You are a high-ranking demi, so your powers will be stronger than other demis." My dad stopped and took in a big breath. "It also means you'll be the leader of the group and other stuff after you turn eighteen," he said so quickly the words blended together in to one long word. "But until then... Well, until then, you have to be careful. There are *people* who want to harm you."

This just keeps getting better and better. First, I was just a demi-angel, but now, I'm like a demi-angel general. Go me! Ugh!

"For every good force in the world, there is an evil force." Dad ran his hand down his face. I studied him; he looked worried. His eyes were dull and smudged underneath with dark bruises. Tiny lines fanned out from his eyes. His mouth was pinched. For the first time, I thought my dad looked old.

43　　Michelle K. Pickett

"So evil wants to get me? I don't understand what you mean."

"The Irin are our enemy, and one of the main jobs of the Fallen is to convert or kill the Iri. Azazel, a high-ranking Irin, wants your powers. He'll do anything to get them, even if that means killing you so you can't use them." He doodled on the table with his finger. "Until you are eighteen, you are susceptible to his influence. But after your eighteenth birthday, your powers will strengthen and you'll become immune to him. He won't be able to touch you."

My hands began to shake and were slick with sweat. I wiped them up and down my pant legs.

You said kill. That's more than touching! That's ending, like ending a life. Over, done, finished, caput. I don't like this demi-angel thing. At. All.

"Why not?" I asked, hoping my voice wouldn't give out. "What makes me so special when I turn eighteen?"

"Your ranking as a demi-angel will supersede Azazel's ranking as an Irin. Essentially, when my Iri rank and power transfers to you, it will make you the strongest demi-angel on earth. You will hold more power than Hell's Angel. And when Ben reaches eighteen, well, the two of you together? You will have control of the angelic army, which will be so strong that the demons of Hell won't have any footing on earth. The thousands-year-long fight to reign over the earth with evil will be stopped."

"Wait—" Questions were rolling around in my brain so fast it was hard to concentrate enough to ask one. "If I'm so vulnerable, why hasn't he tried to get to me before now? And, I mean, if I'm so vulnerable, how come you're just telling me this now? He could have grabbed me!" I smelled the coffee my mom was making and inhaled deeply, the smell oddly comforting. "And why didn't you prepare me before now? I mean, isn't there some kind of class for this? A special school like Harry Potter had? I mean, come on, really? I find out a few weeks before my birthday, just sitting in my kitchen."

A chill ran through my body as I thought about Azazel and him actually wanting to kill me. If this wild fantasy were true, then I'd been walking around for days with a huge target on my back and didn't know it. Nothing said "*kill me*" like a person who didn't know to protect herself! My lungs hurt when I took a breath. I rubbed my chest with the palm of my hand and gripped the edge of the table with the other.

"You were safe. The other demi-angels were following you. Keeping watch—"

I slapped both hands on the table and stood. "You had me followed!"

"It was for your own protection. Once the visions started, we knew you were vulnerable, but we hadn't prepared you yet. Plus, you weren't in the best mood for us to tell you all this." My dad rubbed the back of his neck. "You were having enough trouble just finding out you were a demi-angel. I was afraid if I dumped this on you too, you'd really lose it."

The tension leaked from my shoulders, and I slipped back in my seat and nodded. "Yeah. Yeah, I guess that's fair. I wasn't listening to you."

My mom set a cup of coffee in front of my dad, and he took a sip before answering. "Before your visions, you were in a safety period. Azazel only has two opportunities to get to a demi-angel: before you reach the age of accountability and then again in the months leading up to your eighteenth birthday."

"Age of accountability?"

"Yes, the age a person is able to understand the difference between right and wrong, good and evil. Once they understand the difference, they choose which to embrace. Azazel can try to influence their choice, but when they reach the age of accountability—regardless of the choice they've made—they enter a safety period. This is the time during their childhood when they are too young to protect themselves from Azazel's evil. But when their demi-angel powers emerge in the months or weeks leading up to their eighteenth birthday, they lose that safety. Azazel has one more opportunity to convert or take the demi-angel's powers before they fully mature."

I stared at my hands and twisted my fingers one after the other, thinking about everything my dad had told me. So far, he'd made the visions seem like fun in comparison to this Azazel. *Azazel.* Even his name sent shivers through me. I couldn't stop shaking, and I couldn't get my mind to stop spinning. I could die. Muriel could die. Geez, this was way too much. My body felt brittle. Put the least bit of pressure on me, and I'd snap.

As I glanced to my right, the pink sticky notes counting down the days to my birthday caught my eye. I tilted my head, stared at them, and had the oddest sensation. *It was funny.* I wasn't sure why. Maybe laughing about it was a way to release the stress building inside me like steam in a teakettle.

I laughed and pointed at the refrigerator. "That's why you made the little countdown calendar on the refrigerator, right? I thought it was because you were excited about my big birthday: turning eighteen, becoming an adult, and all that. But you're really counting down the days I have to either fight off Azazel or die." I laughed harder.

I'm losing it. This is so not funny. Why am I laughing? It's not funny, but it totally is funny, too

My mother sighed. She wrapped her arms around her middle and sat down. Her lips clamped together in a straight line as she glanced at my dad. Her eyes were soft and swimming with emotion. I could almost see her irises swirling like waves in a storm. "Sort of," she answered finally.

I laughed so hard that I snorted. "Wow, when people say turning eighteen is a milestone, they really have no idea!"

My dad chuckled. "Look, Milayna, the bottom line is that you have to be aware at all times. He'll use anything or anyone to get to you. If he is able to convert you and pull you to his side, he'll control your powers, making him even stronger than he already is."

"Wait, he'll use anyone? What keeps Mom safe?" I looked between the two of them.

Michelle K. Pickett

My mom pulled the collar of her shirt down her back and showed me a patch of raised skin. I'd seen it before when she'd worn a tank top or swimsuit, but I'd never examined it before. Now I saw it was an intricate design, the layers of skin weaving above and under each other. "It's a rune for protection. All human family members get them. It doesn't keep us completely untouchable, but it gives some protection."

I ran my fingers over the patch of skin. "Good. That makes me feel better." I smiled at my mom and she pinched my side, tickling me. When I stopped laughing, I looked at my dad and asked, "So, what is he waiting for? I mean, I'm not in the safety period anymore."

"The closer it gets to your birthday, the stronger you'll become. That means there'll be more power for him to absorb. He's greedy. He'll wait until the last possible second so he can absorb the most power from you."

"So what do I do now?"

"Your powers are weakest when you're having a vision. Azazel will exploit that. He'll force visions on you by creating situations that will require your involvement. Knowing that, I want you to make sure you're always with another demi. They can protect you, and you can protect them."

Taking a drink of his coffee, he wrinkled his nose. He dumped some creamer into it and tasted it again. With a nod, he turned his focus back to me. "Because you are the highest-ranking demi and the leader of the group, the others in the group are also vulnerable until you turn eighteen. You must, you *must,* work as a team, Milayna. I can't stress that enough. You're strongest when you are a united front. Alone, you are at your weakest, and Azazel has a better chance of defeating you. It's very important you understand that."

Okay, then, this Azazel guy was really serious. Taking in a deep breath, I glanced at my mom. She'd been silent while my dad talked. She stared into her coffee mug with glassy eyes, and I could see a slight tremor in her hands. My dad was also acting strange, downing coffee like it was water, and he was in the middle of Death Valley in July. They seemed as worried and scared as I was, and my heart rate kicked up another beat. I thought this was all about my demi-angel status and me, but looking at my parents, I could see it was also affecting them.

I forced a smile. "How do we fight him, Dad? This Azazel guy? Do I have laser beams for eyes or spider webs that shoot from my hands?" I asked, only half joking. If Azazel was as evil as they said, what could a group of teenagers do to stop him?

My dad laughed. "No, you don't have spider webs or laser beams. You'll have to rely on good, old-fashioned, hand-to-hand combat against his demis."

"The Tae Kwon Do and every other type of self-defense class you could find—is this why you made me take them?"

"Yes." My mom set down her coffee mug and moved to pull me into a hug. I squeezed her to me, breathing in her comforting scent.

"As your powers increase, you'll have telekinetic energy, but it will be weak.

You won't be able to rely on it until your powers fully mature."

"Wow." My brain was slogged down with information. It was so full that I had trouble focusing on one thing to process. But telekinesis? Really? I was really starting to believe my dad was embellishing the story a little. Everything I'd heard so far seemed mega far-fetched, but the telekinesis tipped it over the mountain into bizarro world.

"It's a lot to take in, I know. Think about things for a while. When you have questions, and I'm sure you will, I'll be here to answer them," my dad said with a sad smile.

Nodding at him, I grabbed my music player from the counter and started to clear the kitchen table, rinsing the plates for the dishwasher. I hummed along to the song playing through my earbuds while my parents still sat at the table, drinking the last of their coffee. I could hear them talk about getting the oil changed in the cars and other boring stuff that parents had to do.

I tried to clear my mind of everything we'd talked about and just let the music distract me for a little while. I needed some downtime away from demons, visions, and evil people named Azazel who wanted to kill me for powers I wasn't sure I had.

Hey! My powers…

I pulled out my earbuds and leaned over the kitchen island. "Dad, I have a question now."

He turned so he was facing me. "Okay."

"You said I'd have telekinetic powers, right? What about mind reading?" I tapped my temple with my finger. "Will I have that, too? Because it would really be killer this Friday when I have my calculus exam."

"You can't read minds, but you will develop the ability to read people's emotions and perhaps even know what they might do just before they do it. This will help you with your visions," he paused and narrowed his eyes, "but when it comes to calculus? You're on your own."

"Bummer." I drummed my fingers on the counter. Putting my fingers to my temples, I glared at my dad's coffee cup.

"What are you doing?" my mom asked. One side of her mouth curled up.

"I'm trying to move that cup."

My parents laughed. I concentrated on the coffee cup, but it didn't budge.

"I guess I'll have to work on this telekinesis thing. It'll come in handy when Ben is hogging the TV remote and forcing me to watch Teenage Mutant Ninja Turtles for the fifty-millionth time."

That night, I sat in my room and tried to move everything. I wasn't sure how the whole telekinesis thing worked, so I just stared at stuff and chanted, "Move, move, move."

Everything ignored me and stayed where it was.

Telekinesis, my ass.

47   *Michelle K. Pickett*

7
The Group

Six weeks, four days until my birthday.

I was doodling across the front of my notebook when Muriel came into class. Interestingly enough, it was a picture of angel wings.

Muriel slid into her seat beside me and brushed a lock of hair from her cheek. "I think you need to come over tonight. Have some pizza?" She bounced her pen off her notebook. "There are some people you need to meet."

"Yeah. My parents told me."

The instructor began speaking, and I snuck a smile at Muriel before turning forward in my seat. But I wasn't interested in looking at the stodgy, old professor. My eyes searched out another. When my gaze fell on him, he was staring back at me, his blue-green eyes thoughtful. Chay. Tall, lean, and gorgeous with his dark hair, odd eyes, and a body that looked sculpted in all the right places under his perfectly fitted clothes. I could definitely see why all the girls were crushing on him. But my heart was saved for another. Jake.

And that was why I was floored when I walked into Muriel's house later that evening and saw Jake sitting on her couch in all his perfect glory. My heart did a little nosedive right to my toes before bouncing back and lodging in my throat. I couldn't believe it. I'd always thought he looked like an angel with his golden blond hair and denim-blue eyes, but I didn't know he actually *was* an angel—well, half angel, anyway.

Oh, holy hotness, Batman! He's amazing.

Tearing my gaze away from Jake, I looked around the room. Nine sets of eyes stared back at me. Most I knew from school: Muriel and Shayla, who were both on the softball team with me; Jen from my history class; Steven and Jake, who played on the school's football team together; and I didn't know Drew, Lily, or Jeff very well, but they seemed nice enough. The ninth person, Chay, was a surprise.

"Hey." I gave a small wave and then rubbed my sweaty palms up and down my thighs. They stared silently back at me, unmoving. I wondered if there was a secret word or handshake I was supposed to know that Muriel forgot to tell me.

Why am I so nervous? We're all on the same side, and we're all going through the same thing. Why do I feel like they're sizing me up? Because they are, genius. I don't particularly like it.

"So, what now? Is there some kind of initiation or rite of passage or something?" I scanned the faces looking at me.

"Nope. Now's pizza!" Jake lunged off the couch, and I flinched. He made it to the kitchen in three large strides.

"Pizz-uh," Steven called out in a deep baritone that made me jump. Getting up, he pushed Jake out of the way and made it to the pizzas first.

"Oh. Okay." Standing at the door, I watched them swarm to the steaming pizzas, confused. I thought we were going to discuss things, not have a party.

"They're not much for small talk," Chay said as he walked by me and into the kitchen.

Neither was he, apparently.

The ten of us gathered around Muriel's small kitchen table, ate pizza, and talked about our secret. It was the only place we could interact freely and be ourselves.

"Ever dress up like an angel on Halloween or play one in a Christmas pageant?" Drew asked, smiling.

"Yeah." Picking a mushroom off my pizza, I flicked it on my plate. I missed, and it plopped on Muriel's arm. She shrugged a shoulder and ate it. I giggled.

Drew laughed and grabbed another piece of pizza. "Betcha didn't think you really were one, huh?" He scarfed down a bite without even chewing it.

I popped a piece of pepperoni in my mouth and shook my head. "Nope."

"My mom collects angel figurines and only decorates our Christmas tree with angel ornaments." Jen shook her head. "I should've figured something was up. Talk about angel overload."

We all laughed.

Shayla looked at me. "What about you, Milayna? What weird things do your parents do?"

I nibbled at the crust of my pizza. "Um, hmm, nothing. They're just boring, angel-human parents."

"I guess that's why you freaked out when you found out about being a demi, huh?" Lily asked, her tone cutting.

"Yeah. I guess." I glanced at my plate and tore apart my pizza crust.

49

Michelle K. Pickett

She leaned back in her chair and crossed her arms over her chest. "And now you've had some great epiphany and everything is A-okay." Sarcasm dripped from her words, and a frown darkened her face.

Looking at her, I tilted my head. "I wouldn't say that. I do have a few demons after me." I smiled at her.

"Don't we all." Lily stared at me, not returning my smile. "But now we have our fearless leader in the group." She threw her hand toward me like I was a vowel on the Wheel of Fortune.

"I don't look at myself that way."

Whoa, down girl. I'm not here to step on anyone's toes. You want to be the leader? You got it. I don't know what the hell I'm doing anyway.

"Yeah, but everyone else does. That's the problem." She pushed away from the table and stood. "I gotta go. See you guys at school." Grabbing her bag from the floor, she tossed it over her shoulder and walked out.

Dumbfounded, I watched Lily leave. Her attitude surprised me. She seemed hostile, which was odd since we didn't really know each other. Scrolling through the times I'd talked to her in the past, which were minimal, I tried to find something I may have said that offended her.

"Milayna, whoo-hooo!" When I focused on him, Jake smirked. "There you are. What planet were you visiting? Anyway, don't bother with Lily." He waved his hand in the air, as if brushing her aside. "She has ego issues."

"Yeah, when she found out she was a demi-angel, she was disappointed. She thought she was a demi-god." Jeff rolled his eyes. "Apparently, being an angel is beneath her, especially when she's not in charge

I spun my empty can of Coke on the tabletop. "Why? Would she have been the leader if I hadn't stepped up?"

"Her? Nah. Like I said, ego issues," Jake said.

"Well, I hate to break up a good thing, but the pizza's gone and it's getting late. I'm outta here." Drew stood and smiled. "Thanks for the pizza, Muriel."

Everyone echoed their thanks. "You know I'd do anything for pizza. Even have you freaks around." She giggled when Drew tickled her side.

I was slipping into my sneakers when Chay walked over to me. I looked up at him through my lashes. "Hi," I said for lack of anything earth shattering to say.

"Dad, right?"

"Huh?"

"It's your dad, right?" Chay asked slowly, like he needed to break out the crayons and draw me a diagram. I could feel my cheeks heat with a blush.

"Oh, my dad. Yeah, he's the angel."

Profound. Really.

He nodded once and flipped his car keys around his finger. They jangled when they hit his palm. "See ya," he said and walked out of the door. His car roared to life a minute or two later.

I looked at Muriel, and she shrugged a shoulder.

I wondered what Chay's story was. He seemed so closed off. Standoffish. Not shy, though. There was nothing about him that made me think he was shy. In fact, it was the opposite. He almost commanded a room, even without speaking. But what did I care? I wanted Jake and, for once, things were on my side. We were both demi-angels. We'd probably see a lot of each other. Heidi could put that in her pom-poms and shake it!

By the time I left Muriel's, I felt better than I had in days. I wasn't the only freak. I smiled. We were a group of demi-freaks.

But the Azazel thing wasn't the greatest—it was downright scary. I felt like I was standing on a precipice. If I made one wrong move, I'd fall down, down, down into the abyss, and meet my tormentor face-to-face. But now I knew I had people watching my back. Things didn't seem quite so off-balance. It felt as though maybe, just maybe, I'd be all right with this whole half-angel thing.

Five weeks, five days until my birthday.

Muriel and I were at swim practice a week later when it happened again. I had almost forgotten about them. *Almost.*

My hands started sweating. That should have been my first clue, since I was cold from the pool water. Then my stomach tied itself in a bow so tight I doubled over gasping from the pain, and I knew. The visions always started out the same—pain. My dad, who also had occasional visions, taught me some breathing exercises to help me relax. It didn't work, but I wouldn't tell him that. He wanted to help.

The blue water of the pool splashing against the tiled sides. The water getting foggy, hard to see through. It's not blue anymore. Red.

I sucked in a breath through my teeth, making a hissing sound.

Muriel put a hand on my arm. "What's up?"

"I don't know yet," I answered, distracted. For once, I was trying to focus on the vision rather than fight it.

Running. Splashing water. Chlorine.

"Someone is going to run through water and slip, I think. I see them running. I see the blood in the water and taste chlorine."

Kids! Kids. I can't fail this time. I can't fail again.

I pressed my fists to my eyes, sucked in a deep breath, and tried to empty my head of anything but the vision. This was my duty as a demi-angel—to protect humans. I was created for this.

Blowing out a breath, I swung toward Muriel and grabbed her arms. "Is the youth organization using the pool today?"

"It's Thursday. I guess so."

I tightened my grasp on her arms and shook her. "You've got to listen to me. One of the kids is going to get hurt." My head started to pound, and then the room

51

Michelle K. Pickett

grayed out around me, replaced by a clearer picture of the vision.

"Okay, okay. Just tell me what you see." Muriel tried to keep her voice calm, but I could sense the tremor and feel how tense she was. "Dark curls bounce in front of me. I can only see her back. She's wearing a red and white polka-dot bathing suit."

Please, please, find her.

"Here they come, Milayna!" She grabbed my hand and squeezed. "It's fine. It'll be fine. Just keep telling me what you see," Muriel said all in one breath. Her fingers gripped mine tighter, and I started to lose feeling in my fingertips.

"They're singing. There are at least two of them. Maybe three. Red and white bathing suit!"

"I don't see her."

"Hurry." I gasped for air. The clenching in my stomach rose up my throat, squeezing the oxygen from my lungs and closing off my throat. I couldn't get a breath. I tasted chlorine; it burned my nose. "She's gonna drown."

"How do you know?" I could hear the panic in Muriel's voice.

I felt dizzy. The pounding in my head was unbearable, and the room started to tilt to the side. My body felt light, like I was floating in the pool. I could hear the water whooshing in my ears.

"I feel it."

"Oh, damn."

"Hurry," I whispered.

Can I die from a vision? It feels like I'm drowning with the girl. Will I die if I can't save her?

"I see her! There she is, Milayna." I felt Muriel leave my side.

Moments later, the feeling started to fade. The chlorine burning my nose and throat disappeared, and my lungs filled with air. The pounding in my head lessened. It subsided gradually, but after what seemed like minutes, the vision faded away completely.

Muriel rejoined me, and I let out a sigh of relief. "Thank you. What'd ya say to them?"

"I told them if I caught them running, I was going to tell their counselor, and they wouldn't be able to swim for the rest of the year."

"What'd they say?"

"*Yes, ma'am.* Which, by the way, I take great offense to. I am not a *ma'am*!"

A giggled bubbled from my lips. With the vision over, I almost felt normal again. I always felt drained after one. My energy was zapped, tapped out. But otherwise, I felt fine.

Muriel and I hurried and dressed to go home. Walking out of the pool room, I stopped short. Chay stood outside the girls' locker room door. One shoulder leaned against the wall, and a thumb hooked through a belt loop on jeans that rode low enough to make every girl pant.

"Uh, hi," I said.

He rubbed the back of his neck with one hand and slowly, and I mean *slowly*, looked me up and down. "You look fine," he said matter-of-factly.

I narrowed my eyes at him. "Thanks, I think."

"I got the feeling something was wrong. I'm just checking on you two."

I fiddled with the strap of my messenger bag and tried not to stare. "Oh, well, thanks, but everything is fine here."

Now go away. You make me feel weird. I don't know why, but I don't like it. Or maybe I do? Either way, shoo.

"You had a vision?"

"Yes." I shifted my weight and put my hand on my hip.

"It's gone?"

I didn't answer right away. I just stared at him. He didn't break eye contact with me, which made me feel uncomfortable, but I wasn't sure why. Finally, I answered, "Yes."

He nodded, pushed off the wall, and walked away.

"Hey! Wait, how'd you know?" I yelled after him.

He didn't turn around. I stood and stared—he looked pretty good from that angle, too. Coming or going, he was definitely easy on the eyes.

When Chay was out of view, I turned to Muriel.

"Wow, Milayna, I think he has a thing for you," she teased.

"Stop," I said with a giggle, nudging her shoulder with mine.

"Seriously, I think that's the most I've heard him talk since I met him."

"He just seems quiet. And wait." I looked at her with an arched brow. "I thought you said you didn't know him?" I asked as we walked out of the school.

"I only know him because he's a demi, and anyway, I couldn't tell you until the group made sure you were okay with everything. I met him when he transferred to our school. He started showing signs, so his parents sent him here so he could be with other DAs."

"DAs?"

"Demi-angels." She flicked the back of my head and smiled. "Goofball."

"Ah, I should have figured that one out." I threw my messenger bag in the backseat of Muriel's car and tilted my head. "When did you show signs?"

Muriel looked at me over the roof of the car. "About a month and a half before my eighteenth birthday, just like you."

"Ah, right about the time you had Mono and couldn't come to school for three weeks." I arched an eyebrow, and she grinned.

We climbed into the car, and I reached for the seatbelt. "Is everyone else eighteen?"

"Everyone but you." Muriel started the car and looked at me. "When your birthday gets here, we'll all be stronger. And it can't happen soon enough."

Michelle K. Pickett

8

Hobgoblins

FIVE WEEKS, FIVE DAYS UNTIL MY BIRTHDAY.

I worked a two-hour shift after swim practice, and then a friend from the bakery drove me home. When I unlocked the door and walked into the house, it was unusually quiet—I was alone. Dad had to work late, and Mom was out with friends. And my brother, Ben, was at Grams'.

Generally, I didn't mind being alone. I kinda liked it. I could read, watch something other than cartoons on television, and get takeout for dinner. It was pure bliss. But that night was different. I was edgy, full of restless energy.

I swayed on the old, wooden swing on the back deck, watching the clouds float across the dying sun. The sky was filled with streaks of reds and oranges—it almost made it look on fire.

The breeze shifted toward me, carrying a smell that made me wrinkle my nose. It smelled like something was burning—tinged with something else.

What is that smell? It's putrid.

Not long after the smell, I noticed a change in temperature. The cool night turned warm, and I started sweating under my sweatshirt. I could feel my hair sticking to the back of my neck.

I was looking at the floor of the deck, fanning the back of my neck with my hand, when I heard a puff of air. Looking up, I saw a puff of smoke in the yard a few feet from the deck. When the smoke cleared, I saw a small figure about the size of a toddler standing in the grass. It was short and fat with stumpy legs under a big, round belly. Its skin was red, and it had a shock of black hair standing atop its oval head. I jumped backward against the swing, a little scream coming out of my mouth.

What in the hell...?

I rubbed my eyes with my fists and looked again. It was still there, staring at me.

I'm dreaming. This is too out there. Wake up. Wake up now!

As if my life wasn't weird enough already, the short, fat thing spoke, its ruby, bulbous lips bouncing. "Hi, Milayna," it said, its voice high pitched like a little girl's.

I stood up so fast that the swing flung out behind me, hitting the house. The pipsqueak kept still, smoke curling around its body. The strong smell of something burning nearly suffocated me, and the temperature had risen another few degrees. I was sweating heavily, my sweatshirt damp.

What? What—oh, damn. Oh, no. That's not real. No. That can't be real.

I inched toward the door, keeping my eye on the thing in my yard. I had to call my dad. Then I had to call the police and tell them... what? A little red man popped into my backyard? No, I needed my dad.

Another pop sounded and I jumped with a scream. I slapped my hand over my mouth and watched the smoke billow and float away, revealing another creature much like the first. Their red skin against the green lawn made them look like peculiar Christmas decorations, and the smell reminded me of scorched meat.

The creatures were alike in almost every way, except the second had a scar running down the left side of his face, from his ear to the corner of his mouth. He also seemed grumpier.

"She doesn't speak," the first weird gnome-like creature said to Scarface.

"We don't need her to speak. We just need to bring her back," Scarface answered. He waved me away with both hands and then put his fists on his hips. "Then we can go home and get away from this horrid place. It's too cold up here."

I stared at them as they talked, my eyes moving between them like I was following the ball in a tennis match. My mouth was open, and my mind whirred as it tried to process the scene.

What. The. Freakin'. Hell. Is. Going. On?

"Milayna."

I thought it was the one of the creatures talking, but realized the voice was lower, smoother—not an ear-piercing squeal.

"What?" I didn't want to take my eyes off my uninvited visitors, but I glanced toward the gate where the voice came from.

"Go inside."

I wasn't sure why I listened to the person—I didn't even know who it was for sure—but I did as he asked.

Once inside, I stood by the patio door and peered out of the window. The red—whatever they were—wandered around and walked through my mother's flowerbeds. Scarface plucked blooms from the plants, inspected them, and crushed the flowers into the ground. He then tried to climb a tree, cursing violent-

Michelle K. Pickett

ly when his stumpy legs were too short.

An ear-piercing sound sliced through the air. I cringed and slapped my hand over my mouth to keep from screaming. My gaze swung to the other creature. It was laughing as it pushed the swings on the swing set. It climbed up the ladder to the cyclone slide my brother loved so much, took a leap, and slid down. Its cackling echoed off the walls of the slide until he came out the other end and plopped on his ass.

"Milayna," Scarface called, "we're getting tired of waiting. Come out and play with us."

I took a step back from the window where I'd been watching them. The first creature pressed his nose against the glass and looked at me. "I can see you," it sang.

Movement caught my eye. I turned and saw Chay round the corner. The weird red men froze. Their faces turned demonic as their eyes grew wide and glassy black, and their lips pulled back against their yellowish-brown teeth. They watched Chay's movements closely.

"Chay," Scarface said.

"What are you doing here?" Chay asked, his voice hard.

"Ah, don't worry, we're just looking around. There are so many fun things to do at Milayna's house." Scarface laughed, an ugly, garish laugh, and I cringed.

Chay hooked his thumb around his belt loop and leaned casually on one leg. "Leave."

"We're not done playing," the friendlier one said.

"Leave or I'll send you back."

"Tsk, tsk, Chay. You really need to work on your temper. Angels are supposed to be passive." Scarface brushed one finger over the other in a shame, shame gesture.

"I'm only half angel." They slowly backed up as Chay advanced on them. He seemed apathetic, bored even. "I'm only going to ask you nicely one more time. Leave."

"Make us," the friendly one said, sticking his tongue out like a child.

My hands were damp with sweat, and I ran them up and down my thighs. I watched as Chay walked toward whatever the hell the red things were. It was hard to breathe. I felt like I'd just run the Boston Marathon in an hour. I couldn't catch my breath.

This isn't possible. I think I'm having a nervous breakdown or something, because this is just way too bizarre. What are those things?

Biting my bottom lip, I watched as Chay grabbed them by the back of their necks and knocked them together. Their heads clunked, making a thud so loud I could hear it in the house. He let go, and their fat little bodies fell to the ground.

A bright flash of light lit the yard, and I had to shield my eyes. When it dimmed, the red mini-trolls were gone, leaving behind nothing but two puffs of smoke and the same putrid smell I'd noticed before they popped in. I covered my nose and mouth with my hand to stifle it.

Chay jogged up the deck stairs two at a time. He didn't wait for an invitation to come inside; he just opened the door and walked into the house, brushing ash off his jacket.

I looked over his shoulder and peered into the backyard. It was still empty. Other than the trampled flowers and the swaying swings, there was no sign that the freaky red things had been there.

"Um, you want to tell me what the hell just happened? What were those things?" I looked up at Chay. I was gonna lose it any second, and it wasn't gonna be pretty.

"Hobgoblins," he said.

"And?" I asked slowly.

"They're harmless for the most part."

"But hobgoblins are the cute and likeable mischief makers of fairy tales. They're not spawn from Hell!"

"The fairy tales got it wrong. They usually do."

"What did they want?" I stood by the kitchen sink and looked out of the window. My bottom lip between my teeth, I bit it harder waiting for his answer. I had a feeling it wasn't going to be one I liked. And for once, just once, since this started, it would be nice to get some good news.

"You."

"Oh. Will they come back?" I had butterflies in my stomach, and not the lovey-dovey kind. The *I'm-officially-freaked-out-and-scared-shitless* kind.

He hooked his thumbs in his back pockets. "Probably not."

Probably not. I was just visited by fat little demons from Hell, and he says they probably *won't come back.*

"What do you mean probably? I'm really not all that comfortable with *'probably'*." I said, using air quotes—which was funny since I hated it when people did that. "I'd like to be ready next time."

"They were just messengers for Azazel."

I stared and waited for him to elaborate. It wasn't hard, actually. Staring at him. He was handsome in an understated way. Not movie-star handsome like Jake, but definitely swoon-worthy. He had a strong jaw, full lips, and a golden complexion that was clear except for a slight scar on the left side of his chin, which only added more character to his wicked handsome face. Add to that the most beautiful blue-green eyes I'd ever seen all framed by dark, almost black, hair. And don't even get me started on his body—yeah, staring at him was easy. Talking to him, or at least getting him to talk, was a bitch.

"And?" I crossed my arms.

"They were just seeing if you were alone."

"I was."

He leaned his back against the wall. "You're not now."

"What would they have done if you hadn't come over?" I rubbed my hands

Michelle K. Pickett

up and down my arms. The temperature had returned to normal, but I was chilled even with my sweatshirt on.

Do you get cold when you're in shock? Consider me sufficiently shocked. Mini demons in my backyard. I so didn't sign up for this.

"They would have summoned some demons or Azazel."

An icy finger ran down my spine and seemed to coil inside me. I shivered and wrapped my sweatshirt tighter around me.

"Why are you here?"

"You should be glad I am," Chay answered. His tone was neutral, never changing.

"I am. I mean, I wouldn't have known what to do with the hobgoblins without help. But, where did you come from and how did you know to come?"

"I live on the next street."

"And?"

Why can't he just finish an answer without me squeezing it out of him?

"I smelled the sulfur and knew something was coming."

"Thanks." I scrunched my nose. "That smell is nasty."

"When will someone be here?" He looked out of the window.

"My dad should be here any minute."

Chay nodded and walked outside. I followed. He sat on the porch swing. "I'll wait." He leaned forward and rested his arms on his thighs, his hands hanging between his knees.

"Okay." I wished he'd just leave. He made me feel uncomfortable. But considering he'd just saved me from two little red men, I was glad he hung around. I was still standing next to the door, my hand on the knob, when my dad pulled into the driveway minutes later. I heard his car door slam shut. "I think my dad's home."

"Later." He stood and walked away, cutting through my backyard and jumping the fence to get to his street without a backward glance.

Weird. Very weird.

Chay definitely had the uncanny ability to set me on edge. He made me feel off-balance. I couldn't decipher what he was thinking, and he wasn't exactly forthcoming in his answers.

I heard my dad come into the house and stood in the kitchen, waiting for him to stow his junk in the mudroom. When he walked into the kitchen, I let loose.

"What are hobgoblins, and how come you didn't warn me about them?" My voice came out quieter than I'd expected. I thought I'd be upset because he didn't tell me about them before they showed up, but I was exhausted. Seeing little demon creatures swinging on my swing set was about enough excitement for one night.

"Hobgoblins?" He froze in place. "They've been here?"

"Yeah."

"And what'd you do?" he asked. He started moving again, going from window to window and looking outside before he pulled the blinds closed.

"*I* didn't do anything. *I* didn't know what to do, because *you* didn't mention anything about the fat, roly-poly demons or what *I* should do about them." I over-enunciated each word to show my irritation, but my dad seemed oblivious. I turned in a circle and watched as he jumped from window to window.

"Are they still here?"

I wrapped the hem of my sweatshirt around my finger. "No, Chay came over. Said he smelled sulfur and knew something was wrong."

"Yeah, I know Chay. Good kid. Quiet. He's acquired a sort of sixth sense through this mess. It's kind of like your ability, but his is a little different. It only works with you, not with other people."

"Me?"

"Well, not just you. The entire group. He can usually tell when a member of the group is in danger." My dad waved his hand in the air when he talked as if it wasn't a big deal. I rubbed my temples, trying to push in all the information I'd gotten the last few days.

Well, that explains why he was standing outside when I left swim practice today.

"And just how often is one of the group members in danger?"

"Until your eighteenth birthday, a lot. Especially since the hobgoblins are already showing up and making mischief. They're usually the first visitors that come around. Kind of like scouts checking things out and reporting back." He looked out of the window and tsked. "Your mother is gonna be pissed when she sees her flower beds."

"Flower beds? Flower beds. That's what you think about?" I held my arms out to my sides and let them fall, slapping against my legs. "I just told you little red demons were running around the backyard while you were at work, and you're worried about Mom's damned flower beds?"

Flowers. Thanks, Dad. I'm okay, really. You don't need to worry about me. Go take care of Mom's flowers.

"Yeah, they tore down all her clematis. She loves that stuff." He looked at me, his stance tense. "Listen, Milayna, the hobgoblins aren't very dangerous, although if they catch you alone, they can be. From now on, you aren't allowed to be alone. You need to be with another demi-angel or angel. Give notice at the bakery—"

My eyes widened. "What? Why? I like working at the bakery!"

My dad rubbed his forehead. "There's no way to protect you there. You'd be alone. That's unacceptable."

I stared at him for a second with my mouth open. Finally, planting one fist on my hip, I glared at him. "I've worked there for a year, Dad. I like it. I'm good at it, and they're really nice to me! It's not fair to make me quit because of this." My voice rose with each word.

"And what if you had a vision while you were working? The bottom line is,

Michelle K. Pickett

you can't be alone until your birth time." He took off his glasses, tossed them on the kitchen counter, and pinched the bridge of his nose between his finger and thumb.

"My birthday."

He puffed out his cheeks and blew out a breath. "No, your birth time. The exact moment you took your first breath. Until then, none of you are safe. Especially you."

9

Information Overload

"I heard you had visitors last night." Muriel glanced at me and tapped her fingernail on the table.

"Yeah, thanks a whole bunch for warning me about the red pipsqueaks."

Muriel cringed. "Um, yeah, sorry about that. I was on my way over when I smelled the slight scent of sulfur, but Chay got there first. I knew he could handle it better than I could. It must have been pretty scary, huh?"

"Yeah." I looked down and picked at my fingernail polish. "It was scary."

"I'm sorry. But it all turned out okay, right?" She pulled me into a quick hug.

"Right as rain, like Grams says. So, Chay actually spoke to you?" I whispered with a teasing grin. We were in calculus class waiting for our teacher to pass out our torture—the weekly exam.

When I said Chay's name, he turned and glanced over his shoulder, one eyebrow raised. His lips pursed into a straight line. He stared at me, and I looked back at him.

"No. Why?" Muriel's chair squeaked across the tile when she shifted it.

"Why what?" I asked, distracted by Chay's stare.

"Why'd you think Chay and I talked?"

"You knew what happened when he came over last night."

"Well, I know about the hobgoblins. But that's all. So start talking about what happened after that." She leaned toward me and smacked her palm in front of me on the table. "Hey!" I jumped and looked at her. "Do you think you can tear

Michelle K. Pickett

your eyes off him long enough to talk to me?"

I turned in my seat so I was facing her. "He said he smelled sulfur and came over to check things out. After the goblins were gone," I whispered, "he sat on the deck until my dad got home, and then he jumped the back fence and went to his house. I bet he didn't say more than a handful of words the entire time he was there."

"Oh."

"Gee," I gave a quick laugh, "I'm sorry my gossip isn't raunchy enough for you."

"I should have known it'd be all business with him. He doesn't talk much, other than when it's necessary, and it's very seldom necessary unless something," she lowered her voice so much that I almost had to read her lips, "otherworldly is happening."

"He's mysterious," I said with a wicked grin and arched brow, twiddling my fingers in front of Muriel's eyes. She knocked my hand away, and I laughed. "Do you have a thing for the new hottie DA?"

"Nope. Dark and brooding isn't for me."

I wasn't sure why I was relieved to hear that. I certainly didn't have a thing for Chay. What did I care who he did or didn't date? Jake was my passionate love affair. Of course, he didn't know it. Neither did the head cheerleader, Heidi, who was *Jake's* passionate love affair. I was in a love triangle with two other people who had no idea I even existed. Well, I guess Jake knew me, but that was only because we were both DAs. Otherwise, I was off his radar.

"Give it up," Muriel said, patting my shoulder. "You're too good for him anyway."

"Who? Chay?"

"Now why would your mind automatically go to him? I was talking about Jake. That's who you were thinking about right? Or... is someone else giving Jake some competition? Maybe, I mean, have you ever thought that dark and brooding might be your thing?" She arched a brow and tapped her pencil against her lips.

"Pssh, no." I waved off her words. He was maddening. He didn't talk, he was a complete loner, and I couldn't deal with that. It wasn't like I wanted to be the center of attention—no thank you—but I liked to hang out with my friends. No, definitely not Chay. He was hella smexy, but the last thing I needed was a boyfriend to deal with. I had demons, that was plenty, thank you very much.

"Hmm, too bad." Muriel inspected her perfectly painted nails and shrugged a shoulder.

"Why?"

"Because he hasn't stopped looking over here since you walked into class this morning," Muriel answered with a grin.

"Oh, please. He probably just has the feeling we're talking about him. Which we are, so let's change the subject," I whispered.

"Let's not just change the subject, ladies. Let's stop talking altogether." Our calculus teacher flung two exams toward us.

I tried to read the instructor's mind just in case I was telepathic, since I couldn't seem to make telekinesis work. No luck..

I didn't get a chance to talk to Muriel again until lunch. I had another vision. The poor freshman girl I'd saved from certain embarrassment last week was back on the bullies' to-embarrass-and-harass list. They just wouldn't leave her alone.

This time, I just stood in front of their table with my hands planted on my hips until she passed by.

As the vision receded, I saw Chay walk toward me. I shot him a glare. I didn't need his help. Nothing the oafs said about me, or to me, mattered. I was focused on the poor target of their amusement. She didn't deserve it. I remembered how hard it was being a freshman. She didn't need any additional heartache.

When the girl—I'd learned her name was Susie—walked safely by and sat with her friends at the other end of the cafeteria, I gripped the edge of the bullies' table and leaned forward, showing them just enough cleavage to grab their attention.

"Listen up. Find someone your own size and low IQ to pick on, but leave that freshman alone," I said quietly.

"Or what?" the biggest idiot asked.

"I'll hurt you."

The hulking teenager stood to his full height. He was a good head taller than I was and twice as wide. My first instinct was to apologize, beg forgiveness, and run away. But I stood my ground.

"Oh, sit down before you embarrass yourself," I snapped, thankful my voice didn't quiver. "I've got a brown belt in Tae Kwon Do, and I've studied Krav Maga. Your dumb ass doesn't scare me." Smirking, I walked away. I had to remind myself to walk, not run, to where Muriel sat.

"What's going on?" she asked.

"Oh, they have this thing for little Susie Freshman over there. I keep having visions of them doing embarrassing things to her, and I'm sick of them. The visions make me feel weird and tire me out, and the boys make my skin crawl. So I just told them to back off." I shrugged a shoulder, unwrapped my chicken salad sandwich, and pulled the sides of the bread apart to inspect it before taking a bite.

"That wasn't very smart." I knew the voice instantly. I didn't have to look up to know I'd see the oddest eyes looking at me. Not quite blue and not quite green. Chay.

"I had to do something—"

"You only have to do what needs to be done to right the wrong and make the vision go away."

63 *Michelle K. Pickett*

"I've had the same vision about them hurting that girl before. I'm tired of spending my lunch finding new ways to step in without being obvious."

"Oh, and threatening them wasn't obvious?" He flung his arm toward their table.

"You threatened them?" Muriel's eyes grew wide. "They're huge!"

"I didn't threaten them. I just warned them away. Maybe now the girl will have some peace."

"And maybe you just angered a demon," Chay said through clenched teeth. "They're hard enough to deal with. We don't need you going around making more trouble for us. We don't know who works for Azazel. Do you understand that? It could be anyone in this school—from the principal to the janitor, even your pet freshman over there. So do me a favor and don't antagonize anyone else. Your job is to step in and protect humans. My job is to protect you until your birthday, and I don't need you making my job any harder than it already is." He pushed away from the table and stalked out of the cafeteria.

Geez, even angry, he's a hella-hottie. Wait. No, that's Jake. "Well." I cleared my throat. "That got him talking."

Muriel laughed, but her eyes looked worried. "He's right, Milayna. We don't know who we can trust."

"Okay. I'll keep a leash on my temper from now on. I promise." I looked down at the fake wooden tabletop. I ran my finger along the words *"Charlie loves Anna"* written in black marker. I didn't really see the words. I saw the faces of people I knew with horns and fangs. I saw Jonathan, my supervisor at the bakery, turning into a demon, and the little old lady who lived two doors down in the cute, yellow house growing fangs. My parents always warned me not to talk to strangers when I was little, but now I couldn't trust anyone. A shiver ran up my spine. "I promise. I'll be more careful." I glanced up at Muriel. She gave me a quick smile. "What do you know about him?"

"Who? Mr. Dark and Brooding?" I nodded, not looking at her. "Uh, nothing you don't already know. He's smart, at least judging by his AP classes. His dad's the *"A"*. He's eighteen, and he has an unusual gift none of us have, but no one knows why."

"Yeah, the ability to see when one of the group is in danger. Why do you say it's unusual? Don't we all have powers?" I whispered, leaning my head close to Muriel's.

"We all have the same visions you do, only you have them a lot more often and they are a lot stronger because your dad was a stronger, higher-ranking Iri. But beyond that ability, most of us don't have other gifts."

"My dad said that we are sometimes telekinetic, and we can feel what humans are feeling or thinking—whatever that means."

"Yeah, everyone in our group is telekinetic, but not every demi is. A DA friend of mine in Indiana isn't. And from what she says, no one in her group is. And none of us have been able to figure out how to use our telekinesis," she whispered. Our heads were so close that they nearly touched. "So far, beyond the visions and the telekinesis, no one in our group has additional powers, so Chay's ability is unusual. But it sure comes in handy, like last night."

"Yeah. Back to this subject, I wish you guys would tell me about these things instead of just letting me come face-to-face with them," I snapped.

"You mean the hobgoblins? I told you, we didn't think they'd be around so soon. We're trying to ease you into things so you don't go all kung-fu on us like you did with the table of gigantic baboons over there." She giggled.

"My dad was surprised they were around, too."

"It's usually closer to their birthday when DAs start seeing them, but I guess Azazel wants you pretty bad." Muriel took a bite of her lunch and made a face. "Good Lord, what *is* this?"

"I think it's time you guys tell me everything there is to know before I come up against something deadlier than a couple of red rugrats in my backyard."

"We should talk to our dads, maybe go see Grandma again. There are definitely some things you should know now that the hobgoblins have made an appearance. Which ones came?" She picked up her Coke and took a drink, swishing it around in her mouth.

"I don't know. They didn't give me names. They both looked pretty much the same. Short, fat, and red, but one had a scar running down the length of its face." I ran my finger down the side of my face where the scar was.

"Oh. I know those two. They aren't too bad. They mostly just deliver messages from Azazel. Usually, the same message over and over and over again." She waved her hand in the air in a *blah, blah, blah* motion. "Change sides. It'll be wonderful. Azazel is a great guy. Blah, blah. You're gonna get really sick of seeing them by the time this is over."

"Great. Sounds like I just made some new friends." I rolled my eyes. "So there are worse things than the hobgoblins?"

"Oh, hell yeah. You've only seen the tip of the iceberg." She pushed her tray away and scrunched her nose up. "It should be illegal for them to serve this."

"Great." I threw down my half-eaten sandwich. My appetite had disappeared.

"Are you going to eat that?" Muriel pointed at my sandwich. I shook my head. "Good." She snatched it up and took a big bite.

I chuckled at her, but it was just a façade. I didn't feel like laughing or smiling, not even crying. I just wanted to sit in a quiet corner somewhere to figure things out. Maybe if I could make sense of it all, I wouldn't be so scared.

After school Friday, the group met at my house for dinner. Muriel and I were going to talk with our dads about what I should expect, but my dad thought it would be better if I heard it from the people going through it with me.

"There's a hierarchy in the demon world," Shayla told me. "First, hobgoblins.

Michelle K. Pickett

They're the lowest and least deadly form of demons. They'll cause a lot of trouble for you, though."

"How?" I leaned toward her.

"They'll create problems, and you'll have to intervene. When you're having a vision, you're the most vulnerable. So the hobgoblins try to force you into visions by creating things for you to deal with."

"So they intentionally put people in dangerous situations?" The concept didn't surprise me, I supposed. What worried me was how much I'd play a part in it. Was I going to be the reason they'd create dangerous situations? And would I be strong enough to do what needed to be done? Would my visions tell me what to do? Where to go? What if I couldn't save the people? Then it'd be my fault.

"That's what evil does every day. It doesn't matter how many demi-angels fight to protect innocent humans, there'll always be evil to fight back. Sometimes, we'll win," Drew shook his head and looked down, "and sometimes, we won't."

Shayla cleared her throat and continued, "Then there are the Evils. They are demi-angels that have flipped sides. They started out demi-angels like us, but Azazel was able to convince them to join forces with him. Their sole purpose is to get you to join Azazel. They aren't able to do much more than help the other demons. Azazel absorbs most of their power." Shayla popped a French fry into her mouth.

"After the Evils are the demi-demons," Jen said, her hands fisting. "They're half human like us, but their other parent is a fallen angel—a demon angel. An Irin. Their angel parent chose to give up immortality and live on earth, but instead of serving good, they serve Azazel. They have the same powers we do. This level starts getting dangerous. They are able to fight us on an even playing field. Whatever we can do, they can match. If you are caught alone with a group of demi-demons, it's very likely they could drag you straight to Azazel." Jen shuddered. "You definitely need to watch your ass around them."

I watched Jen as she explained the demi-demons to me. When she'd finished, I asked, "How will I know who they are, the Evils and demi-demons? Do they wear some kind of mark, a rune or tattoo?"

"You won't," Chay said quietly from the corner of the room where he sat watching the rest of the group. "They look like any other person, just like we do. Now are you finally starting to get it through your thick skull why you have to be more careful?"

I nodded. "Yeah. I think I'm starting to get it," I said quietly.

It isn't simple like in movies or on television. The good guys don't wear white and the bad guys black. We don't know who our enemies are until they decide to show themselves, and that's kinda scaring the hell out of me... or into me, whatever.

"After the demi-demons are your standard-issue demons. They're strong, ugly, and can inflict more damage than any other demon, except Azazel himself," Jake said around a mouth full of burger. "You do not want to meet one of those bad boys alone."

"I'm pretty sure I don't want to meet any of them," I said.

"Yeah, none of us do," Drew murmured, "but unfortunately, we have. Well, all except Azazel. None of us have seen him." Drew was a nice guy, soft-spoken and very polite. With his wavy, brown hair and chocolate-colored eyes, he was good-looking, too, and judging by how often he stared at her, he had a thing for Muriel. I wondered if she knew and made a mental note to tell her after everyone went home.

"You've seen them before?" My eyes swung to Muriel. I couldn't believe she'd been doing something so dangerous, and I had no idea.

Muriel put her hand up, palm facing me. "Just a few times. Another group of demis lost a lot of their group to Azazel. He converted too many, and they needed extra help. They'd sent for help when our group was small and needed it. So we went."

I puffed out my checks and blew out a breath to calm myself. Licking my lips, I looked around at everyone's faces. "Okay, now I know about the demons. What else is there?" I pushed my plate away from me. I'd only taken one bite of my burger and ate few fries. My stomach was churning thinking of all the dangers we faced.

This seems like we're fighting a losing battle. There's so many of them and just ten of us... not the best odds.

"Hello?" Jake waved his hand in front of my face. "Earth calling Milayna. Are you gonna eat your burger?" I shook my head, and he grabbed my plate, digging into the burger like he hadn't just eaten two.

"Are you okay? You kinda zoned out there for a minute." Muriel looked at me. The skin between her eyebrows wrinkled.

"Yeah, I'm good. Just tryin' to let everything soak in, that's all." I tried to smile, but I wasn't sure I pulled it off.

"Basically, it boils down to this," Steven said, spinning his Coke can in circles on the table. "Azazel wants you to become one of his Evils, and he's gonna do anything and use anybody to get to you. You equal power for him. A lot of power. And he wants it."

"And if he doesn't get it?" Every muscle in my body tensed, waiting for the answer. I was like a rubber band that was pulled back and ready to be shot across the room.

"He'll kill you," Chay said, tossing his half-eaten burger on his plate.

Yeah, that's what I thought. I'm really not amenable with that option.

"He wants your power or he wants you dead. What he doesn't want is you completing your transformation on your birthday," Muriel added. "Now that the hobgoblins have been around, the next demon you can expect to see is an Evil. One of us turned bad. You won't know who it is, and you won't know when you'll see them. That's why our parents want us to stay in pairs, or larger, at all times. Azazel wants you bad, Milayna. You're a big target. It wouldn't surprise me if he

Michelle K. Pickett

skipped over the Evils and went straight for the demi-demons."

I stood up and started clearing the table of the empty burger wrappers and fry boxes. Shoving them into the garbage can, I grabbed the sanitizing wipes to scrub the ketchup that had oozed onto the table. My hands shook and my insides felt like Jell-O, wobbling all out of place. I was scared, confused, and overwhelmed. I didn't want to hear anymore, so I played Molly Maid to distract myself. I'd just have to learn on the fly, because the more they talked, the more I panicked. I was polishing the water faucet when Muriel ushered everyone out of the kitchen.

The other group members went into the living room and sprawled out on the floor, playing video games and joking around to blow off steam. I sat at the dining table and watched, drumming my fingers on the table. It felt like my fear was pressing down on me. I couldn't get up, I couldn't talk, all I did was sit and think— something I didn't want to do. Seeing I was upset, my dad shooed the group out of the house about an hour later. I stood at the door, saying goodbye as they left.

"See ya, boss lady." Lily gave me a tight smile and brushed by me. She hadn't said anything to me all night. She sat in the corner with her arms folded over her chest and listened, never saying anything. But her tone told me she was ticked about something.

"'Bye," I answered quietly and watched her walk to her car.

Chay was the last to leave. He stood at the door, his eyes boring into mine. "So now that you know the types of demons you'll be dealing with, do you feel better?"

"No." I shook my head and wondered why standing so close to him seemed to steal the breath from my lungs.

"Good. As soon as you start feeling comfortable, that's when you'll find your-self in a situation that will send you straight to Hell or get you killed." He nodded once, slipped into his U of M hoodie, and walked out of the door without another word.

He sure has a way with words.

10

The Vision

THEY'RE CHASING ME. I'M ALONE. IT'S DARK OUTSIDE. NONE of the houses on the block have their lights on. I run home. The door is locked. I reach for my key, but it isn't in my pocket.

I run across the street to Muriel's. Pounding on the door, I scream for her to let me in. No one answers.

I dart around a group of demons and through my backyard. Chay. I don't know which house is his. I find the only one in the neighborhood with lights on and pound on the door with both fists.

"Help me," I scream.

The demons advance. I can smell the sulfur and see their gray skin as they enter the pool of light created by a street lamp just a few feet away.

The door opens. I fall inside and hit the floor with a grunt. Scrambling away from the door, I kick it closed.

"Thank you." My breath comes out in pants, my chest heaving so hard it hurts. Like someone is squeezing the air out of me.

"I told you not to get too comfortable." I look up and see his blue-green eyes. He stares back at me. It's cold, hard. Chay opens the door and the demons walk inside, grotesque smiles pulled across their yellow, dagger-like teeth.

I bolted upright with a scream, my breathing heavy and heart racing. Pushing my sweaty hair off my face, I took two deep breaths to calm myself, kicked to free my legs of the sheets twisted around them, and crawled out of bed.

Standing at the bathroom sink, I stared at my reflection in the mirror. My hair

69

Michelle K. Pickett

was soaked with sweat; the red waves hung limp around my face. My green eyes were dull and had dark smudges under them. They were swollen and bloodshot from crying in my sleep.

"Milayna," my mother called. "Are you okay?"

I jumped when I heard her voice and then rolled my eyes.

Stop being so jumpy. It's just Mom. Big baby.

Sticking my head out of the bathroom door, I answered, "Just a nightmare, Mom."

"Evils. Demi-demons. Chay said I wouldn't know who they were. Why does my subconscious mind think it's him?" I whispered in the empty room.

Five weeks, one day until my birthday.

I rolled out of bed an hour before my alarm went off. It didn't really matter. After the nightmare, I hadn't gone back to sleep. And when the one thing you didn't want to do was think, lying in bed in a dark room all alone was not the best place to be.

I walked across the street to meet Muriel. We were riding to school together because of the whole buddy system thing. Demis had to be in pairs or larger. So Muriel drove, which she did normally, and it suited me just fine. She had a nice sporty car. I couldn't tell you what it was, other than it was blue, about twenty years newer, and definitely cleaner than my truck.

"You look horrible," Muriel said as soon as she saw me.

I rolled my eyes. "Yeah, and you're a freakin' supermodel."

"What's up? And don't tell me *nothing*. Even if I didn't know you, I could tell something's the matter. So spill."

"Just couldn't sleep last night. All the talk of demons and Azazel got to me." I wrapped the hem of my T-shirt around my finger.

She must've sensed I didn't want to talk about it, because she changed the subject to more exciting news—school gossip. We caught up on everything that happened over the weekend on the short drive to the school.

Muriel and I grabbed our books out of our lockers. I turned to go to my first class when she grabbed my arm. "It'll work out, Milayna."

"Yeah." I forced a smile. "It'll be fine."

I walked into AP chemistry, dropped my books on the table, laid my cheek against them, and closed my eyes. After my nightmare, I couldn't sleep. I was tired with a killer headache, not the greatest combo. I took two painkillers before I left for school, but my headache just laughed at them and pounded harder. It felt like I had one of those toy monkeys that play the cymbals inside my skull. We had a lab to do that day in class or I would have slept through it.

I got three hours of sleep last night. Yeah, today's the day I need to be playing around with dangerous chemicals. I hope the school is up-to-date on their insurance.

I didn't pay attention to who was coming and going. Boyfriends walked girlfriends to the door. Friends gossiped. People filed in and out of the room. I tried to ignore them.

Just a few minutes of sleep. That's all I need.

A large book bag slammed on the table next to me, and I jumped up in my chair, stifling a scream.

"I told you not to get too comfortable."

What the crap? Who let him in here and why is his bag on my table?

"What are you doing here?" I glared at him.

"Getting ready for class. Same as you, I suspect," Chay answered, unperturbed. He opened his bag, pulled out a mechanical pencil, and clicked it a few times.

I turned in my seat to face him, smacking the table in front of him. "You're not in this class. Since when are you in this class?"

"Since now." He pulled out the gigantic chemistry book we were forced to lug around all day. "We're lab partners."

Oh, hell to the freakin' no! Put that book back in your pack and go away. Lab partners? I might just blow the school up just to get away from you.

"What?" I looked wide-eyed at him. "I don't have a lab partner."

"Do I need to use smaller words?" He looked sideways at me.

"Why are you here, and why are you my lab partner?" I bit out through clenched teeth.

"This is the only class you don't share with one of the group. You need someone here. There's at least two people in here you should be watching. I noticed them the first few seconds I was here. You aren't paying attention, Milayna."

Why does it have to be him? Why can't Muriel transfer? Or Jake? Anyone but him.

"Oh, really? Who?" I folded my arms across my chest.

"Girl in the pink sweatshirt. She doesn't want anyone to notice, but she keeps looking over here." He flicked his eyes in her directions.

"She's not looking at me. She has a thing for the guy that sits in front of me." I turned and looked at her. Her eyes followed every movement the guy in front of me made. I bit my lip to keep from giggling. He was being ridiculous.

"Second, Robbie Reynolds. He's been staring at you since I walked in. Now, he's scowling. He either has a thing for you, or he's picturing dragging you to Hell."

"I've known him since kindergarten. He's fine." I looked over my shoulder. Robbie was looking at me. The tips of his prominent ears turned red when he realized he'd been caught staring. I waved my hand once. "Hey, Robbie. What do you think of this class, huh?" I made a face because everyone hated this instructor.

"The class wouldn't be so bad if we had a teacher who actually knew some-

Michelle K. Pickett

thing and did more than assign every damn problem in the book as homework."
He flipped the cover of his book.

I nodded, turned around, and glared at Chay.

"Doesn't matter." Chay shrugged a shoulder. "You need to be aware at all times. How many times do we have to warn you before it gets through?"

"Geez, you're an ass."

He laughed, and I jumped at the sound. I didn't think he'd laughed since I met him. I wasn't sure he was capable.

Why did I like the sound of it? Like fine silk sliding over rough rock. It sent warm waves down my spine and the hairs on the back of my neck stood up and did a little dance. I wondered what I could do to make him do it again.

"I've been called worse."

"Why? You're so charming." I rolled my eyes.

He laughed again. "You look like hell, Milayna."

Evidently, I just have to insult him and he'll laugh. Okay, I can do that. Because I totally want to hear that sound again.

"There's that charm I was referring to." I flipped my book open and pretended to be enthralled with the lab we'd be doing.

"Nightmare?"

I nodded, not looking at him. I was supposed to be the daughter of this big shot Iri council member. Supposed to be a big-deal demi-angel—whatever that was—and I was scared of a nightmare. Worse, he knew it. And if he knew, everyone else probably did too. So they'd see me as a failure—weak and unfit to be a demi-angel.

He cleared his throat and leaned close to me. His mouth near my ear, he said, "We all have them, you know."

I looked at him. His expression was soft, his eyes liquid—the blue and green seemed to swirl together. The instructor started class, but I held Chay's gaze a few seconds longer before I gave him a small smile and turned to face the front.

My heart rate had nearly doubled and I felt light-headed from breathing too quickly, but looking into his eyes... I didn't see the smartass, know-it-all Chay I thought I knew. I saw someone else. Someone who understood. Who knew what I was going through. Someone who maybe even cared. I saw, for just a second, behind his mask. And what I saw there was magical.

After the instructor explained the lab exercise we'd complete in mind-numbing detail, going over the safety procedures and warnings at least five times, Chay and I started to work on the assignment. Heads close together, we consulted the lab form, measured, mixed, and recorded our results. I could smell his cologne, fresh and clean, like the outdoors. His warm breath skimmed the side of my face and sent chills down my spine.

What is wrong with me? I don't even like him.

But when we both reached out to turn the page in the book we were sharing, our hands grazed and electrical currents zinged up my arms. I jerked my hand

Milayna

back, glad I wore long sleeves so he couldn't see the goose bumps that dotted my skin.

I'm losing it. This is messed up. I can't fall for him. I'm in love with Jake. Besides, there are probably rules about DAs dating each other.

When the torture of chemistry was over, I grabbed my book, shoved it in my messenger bag, and slung the strap over my shoulder. I hurried to the door, embarrassing myself by stumbling over the leg of my chair.

"Milayna."

I sighed. I just spent an hour with him. What did he want now? "What?" I looked at him over my shoulder.

"Wait for me. I'll walk you to class."

"It's okay. Muriel's meeting me." *And I need a breather from you.*

"Safety in numbers and all that shit." He didn't look up from putting his book in his bag.

"Fine." I let my bag fall from my shoulder, and it hit the floor with a thud. "Hurry up."

The corner of his lips tipped up.

Muriel arched a brow when Chay and I walked into the hall together.

"Yeah." I nodded my head toward Chay. "We have chemistry together now. Isn't that fantastic?" I rolled my eyes.

Muriel looked between me, who no doubt looked irritated, and Chay, who looked amused. She shrugged and walked between us to calculus.

The rest of the day went smoothly. Thankfully, Chay didn't make any more surprise appearances in my classes.

I sat at the kitchen table, eating a sandwich and talking with Muriel on the phone, when the vision hit. My stomach clenched; I gagged on my sandwich, ran to the sink, and spat it out.

"Milayna?"

"I have to go. I'll call you when it's over."

Who is it? No one is here for me to protect. Oh, geez, maybe it's a neighbor. Or the red rugrats are coming. Then what do I do?

"I'll be right there." She slammed the phone in my ear.

My stomach roiled, and my mouth was filled with the rancid taste of stomach acid. My breathing came in gasps, like I was running. My head and heart pounded in time with each other like a pair of drums. The sound bounced through my head.

I heard Muriel come in the back door just as the first of the vision appeared.

Mom's building. She's leaving work, walking to her car in the parking garage.

"Call my mom," I said.

"What's the number?"

73 *Michelle K. Pickett*

I jumped when I heard Chay's voice. "Speed dial two on my cell. On the table." I pressed the heels of my hands to my eyes and focused on the vision.

The parking garage is dark. I see our car. I smell damp cement and exhaust fumes.

"I'm here, Milayna," I heard Muriel tell me.

My breathing grew faster. My heart beat so hard it hurt, and I rubbed my chest with my hand.

"Your mom is on the phone, Milayna," Chay said quietly. I could barely hear him over the blood rushing behind my ears. "She wants to know what's going on."

"Has she left work?"

"No."

"Tell her to call a cab. Don't go into the parking garage. It's dangerous."

Sulfur. Coughing. Hobgoblins.

"Wait! It's not her. The vision hasn't changed."

The smell of sulfur is stronger. Red high heels.

"Red high heels. Tell her to look for someone wearing red high heels... and... and... red nail polish. I see her fingers. She's holding a black notebook. "

A force jerked me forward, and I screamed. Tears pushed behind my eyes. I tried to pull away, but it squeezed my wrist so hard it was painful. I tried to jerk away. But I couldn't. I tried, I really tried, but it was too strong. Much stronger than me. So big, too. How could we do it? How could we win against something like that? I jerked again and again, but it held me easily.

A manhole cover moved to the side. The hole is open. A gray face... horns.

"Oh, shit, it's disgusting," I choked.

The wood-like horns curled back from its face and were so long they almost made a perfect circle on each side of the gray demon's head. The smell of burning flesh wafted off its skin. Smoke and ash billowed around it. Its large, jutting bottom jaw didn't align with the top and it couldn't get its mouth to close all the way, so saliva and remnants of its last meal dripped from its mouth. Its large, gray forehead was bare but for three circles in the center. The circles were in a line. Their sides touched but did not overlap. A line with a slight curve extended from the center of the middle circle. It almost looked like the picture of a cherry on a Vegas slot machine.

Its unblinking, black eyes stared at me. A reflection bounced back to me. But it wasn't me I saw reflected in its eyes. It was the woman in the parking garage. Her face was twisted in pain and horror. Her mouth was open as if she were trying to scream, but no sound came out.

A gray hand grabbed my other wrist and jerked me forward. I fell out of the chair, hitting the kitchen floor on all fours.

Dragging her toward the hole. The smell is unbearable—sulfur and burning flesh. Screaming. The hem of a black dress scraped across the asphalt, her knees bleeding.

"A black dress. Red high heels and red fingernails. Tell her to find that woman now!" I panted. I couldn't catch my breath.

"She says it's the secretary. She's talking with her now. Has it changed?"

I couldn't answer. A gray hand wrapped around the woman's throat. I felt everything. Its hands burned into her skin, squeezing so hard that she couldn't take a breath. It pulled her toward the hole.

I shook my head no.

"Take the secretary somewhere. Out for coffee or something, but take a cab," Chay told my mother.

I couldn't breathe. I clawed at the invisible hands clutching my throat.

"Chay, they're here." It was Muriel's voice.

"Damn it!" He dropped the phone and ran out of the house.

I struggled to stay conscious. Stars floated in front of my eyes. The thing in my vision still held the woman by the neck. Her head and shoulders were in the hole.

It's hot. The hole glows at the bottom. It squeezes harder and pulls her by the neck... down... down... down. The heat is unbearable.

And then my arms buckled, and I fell face-first on the tiled floor, gulping in air. My lungs burned. My throat felt like sandpaper, and the smell of sulfur still stung my nose.

"It's over," I whispered.

"Aunt Rachael, Milayna says it's over. Okay, okay... Bye." Muriel ended the call. She knelt down and looked at me. "Are you okay?"

I pulled myself up to a sitting position and nodded, but tears stung my eyes. "I could feel it, Muriel. It was choking her, and I could feel it. The smell of sulfur burned my nose, and I could see the, oh good Lord, I could see its face."

"Hobgoblins?" Chay asked.

I shook my head. I hadn't heard him come back into the house. He knelt next to me.

"Muriel, get her something to drink." He looked at me. "Then who?"

"How the hell am I supposed to know?" I whispered. The tears filling my eyes fell to my cheeks. I didn't know what the monster was I'd seen. I just knew I didn't want to see it again. Ever. Because as sure as I knew my own name, I knew that the creature was evil. It brought death.

Chay helped me up from the floor. He glided the pads of his thumbs over my cheeks and wiped away my tears. His touch was soft, and my heart stuttered. "They're getting bad fast."

It wasn't a question, so I didn't answer. I didn't trust my voice. Chay's hands still cupped my cheeks. I shivered.

"Let's get you into the living room," he murmured. He guided me to a big, overstuffed chair. I fell onto it and gripped the fluffy throw pillows. I pulled them over me like a shield. Chay knelt on the floor in front of me. With his hands resting on my knees, he studied my face. "You okay?"

"Yeah."

Michelle K. Pickett

I looked over Chay's shoulder and realized we weren't alone. In fact, there were five others in the room. Muriel was there, handing me a cold Coke. Jake and Drew were walking through the back door. Jen and Shayla stood behind Chay, their faces worried.

"How'd you guys get here so fast?"

"Muriel started the call chain," Jen answered. "We all live in the same subdivision. Demis tend to gravitate to one another, so it doesn't take long to get to each other's houses."

"What happened?" someone asked. I couldn't tell who.

"Oh. Uh, I had a vision." I hated that my voice quivered, though I wasn't sure if it had to do with the vision or the fact that Chay was still touching me.

"A bad one," Muriel added.

"Well, at least they're gone. It wasn't too difficult tonight." Drew stood next to Muriel.

"Who?" No one answered me. "Who?"

"Demi-demons," Jake answered, sitting on the beige-tiled floor next to the patio door.

"Demi-demons. In my backyard?" He nodded. "Oh." I wasn't sure how to respond. I wasn't even sure why I was surprised. They'd told me what to expect.

"What'd you see in your vision?" Chay's gaze held mine.

I shrugged a shoulder. "Probably some kind of hobgoblin like you said. I don't know."

Yeah, keep dreaming. There's no way that thing was related to one of those crazy, red gnomes.

"What'd it look like?"

"Gray face, wrinkled skin. Two curling horns on its head. They looked like ram's horns. Um, long, black fingernails." I rubbed my neck. I could still feel it clutching me, its fingernails poking my flesh. "Black eyes."

"It wasn't a type of hobgoblin, Milayna. It was a demon."

11

FOUR WEEKS, SIX DAYS UNTIL MY BIRTHDAY.

The nightmares were getting worse. They kept me up most nights. I'd pace my room, waiting for something to happen. The closer my birthday drew, the more anxious everyone became. It scared me.

At six o'clock, I heard my mother moving around in the kitchen. I wandered downstairs and sat at the table, watching her make coffee.

"You look like you didn't sleep at all last night," she said.

"I don't think I did." I rubbed my hands up and down my face, inhaling the smell of the freshly brewed coffee. I'd always loved the smell. It reminded me of Saturday mornings, eating breakfast with my parents and little brother Ben. It was one of my favorite family traditions.

"You should let Doctor Preston give you something to help you sleep, Milayna." My mom cupped my face and ran a finger over the dark purple smudge under my eye.

Doctor Preston was Jen's father. He knew of our situation, since Jen's mother was an angel. He'd offered to give me something to help with the nightmares. I didn't want it.

"I can't, Mom. What if something happened?"

"We'd be here. Muriel and Chay are close. The others don't live that far away. You'd be protected." My mom kissed my cheek and squeezed my face to hers before turning to the coffee maker to pour herself a cup.

"I'm not worried about me. Well, I am, but I'm worried about everyone else.

Michelle K. Pickett

Dad said that until I turn eighteen, everyone is in danger."

"They've been dealing with this a lot longer than you. They'll be fine. Besides, you can't help if you're so tired that you can't think straight. You can't keep this up. The visions drain your strength. You need sleep to recharge."

"Maybe." I shrugged a shoulder and grabbed the apple-cinnamon oatmeal out of the cupboard.

"I'll have Doctor Preston drop something by just in case you change your mind." She looked at me over her coffee mug.

"Okay, but no slipping it in my food." I narrowed my eyes at her and smiled.

"Me? I'd never do such a thing." She winked at me.

"Yeah, right." I smiled at her and stood next to the microwave waiting for it to nuke my instant bowl of oatmeal goodness.

A good night's sleep would feel so good. Maybe I'll try the pill. Just for one night.

"You look like dog shit baked in the sun," Muriel said on the drive to school.

I turned and looked at her. "You're so lucky you're driving. I might have hit you for that comment. Besides, you sound like my mother. You two are so great for my self-esteem. If I didn't have any issues with my physical appearance—and who doesn't, by the way?—I sure do now."

Muriel smiled at me. "You're beautiful. You just refuse to see it because you're incredibly humble." I snorted at that. "Okay, make that half humble and half stubborn. So, you're having nightmares, huh?"

I nodded. "Occupational hazard," I mumbled.

"I know, right? So, do you want to go to the mall after school for some retail therapy? We could ask Jen and Shayla to come with." Muriel stopped at a red light and looked at me. "You can buy the place out."

"I won't be buying it out too much since I'm officially unemployed. Except for the wicked deal I struck with my dad. He felt guilty about making me quit the bakery, so he's paying me to do stuff around the house." I grinned at Muriel.

"Geez, Milayna. You could sell a dentist a lifetime's supply of candy if you tried. How do you do it?"

"I say please?" I shrugged. "Anyway, what about Lily?"

Muriel made a face. "She has to work." I waited for the rest of the story, but she didn't give it up.

I poked her thigh with a pencil. "What's with the look?"

"What look?" Muriel didn't look at me.

"When I asked about Lily, you made a face. What's going on?" I braced my ring finger against my thumb and put it near the side of her ear. "I'll flick your ear if you don't tell me, woman!"

Muriel raised her shoulder to protect her ear. "Okay, okay. She's just been weird lately."

"How so?"

"I don't know—she's just been weird." Muriel shrugged. "Kind of standoffish."

"Well, we should ask her anyway so she doesn't feel left out. Even if she has been weird, the group needs to work together and we can't do that if we aren't getting along. So let's be the bigger people and invite her." I sat back in my seat.

Muriel made another face and glanced at me, "We all know she's the bigger person." She cupped her hand under her chest and raised an eyebrow.

I looked at her for a few beats before I burst out laughing. Muriel and I laughed for half of the short drive to school.

Muriel pulled into a parking space and threw the car into park. "Ugh. I really wanna go home and go back to bed."

"Pssh, I hear that." I pushed my door open, forcing myself out of the car and into the school building.

We got to our lockers. Pulling out my two-ton chemistry book, I shoved it into my messenger bag. I started to turn to go to class but stopped, picking at the chipping blue paint on Muriel's locker door. The skin between her eyebrows was furrowed, and her face strained.

"Muriel?" She glanced at me and smiled. "If there was something wrong, you'd tell me, right? Because not telling me everything didn't work out so great last time, remember?"

"Yeah, I'd tell you," she said quietly. And for the first time since we were kids, I knew she was lying to me. I wondered if that was what my dad meant when he said I'd be able to feel the thoughts of other people. But that was humans. Did it work on DAs, too?

"Okay. See you in calc." I hoofed it toward chemistry. I felt a little flutter in my stomach. Chay would be there. I wasn't sure if the flutter was because I was looking forward to seeing him or because I dreaded it.

I walked into the room. His chair was empty. I felt a twinge of disappointment.

"Geez, you're slower than an old woman. Move already," he said so close to my ear that my hair fluttered from his breath.

I looked over my shoulder. "Were you following me?"

"Yes. You can't be alone. That means walking to and from classes." We walked to our table and sat down.

"Do you follow me to every class?" I asked, perturbed. I didn't like him stalking around in the shadows, following me all day.

"Not every class. Sometimes Jake watches you, sometimes Jen or Muriel. It depends on whose class is closest to yours." He shrugged and threw his bag on the table.

"I don't like being followed," I grumbled.

"Well, get used to it, princess," he said. "You have your very own version of the DA Secret Service." I glanced at him. He winked, and my heart did a somersault.

I decided that the flutter in my stomach at the thought of seeing him was most definitely dread. He was so infuriating. How could it be anything else?

"You really need to get some sleep. You look like—"

"Don't say it." I glared at him. He smiled, and my damn stomach did the little fluttering thing again.

Muriel and I were sitting in our usual spot at lunch. We were laughing at something that happened in calculus when a tray slammed on the table next to me. I jumped and looked up.

"Oh, it's you." I continued spreading peanut butter on my apple slice. "Don't you have someone else to bug?"

"Nope. I cleared my calendar just for you," Chay murmured.

"Gee, I feel so flattered. Wait, flattered isn't the word... um... irritated. Yeah. That's the word. Go away, Chay. We can't make fun of you if you're sitting next to us." I narrowed my eyes at him. Muriel laughed.

"Nope. The others will be here soon, too. So plaster on your pretty smile and try to act friendly for a change."

"Act friendly? I am friendly. You're the one who walks around with a scowl on his face, grumbling all day."

He smiled at me. "Better?" he asked. I couldn't answer. The fluttering in my stomach was moving up my throat.

Geez, he has a great smile. Plump lips, but not so much that they're feminine, over straight, white teeth. Why does he have to open his mouth and ruin it?

"I guess it'll have to do," I said and turned my back to him. Maybe if I didn't look at him, I could forget he was sitting right next to me. But he was so close I could feel his body heat, and every time he moved, I got a whiff of his cologne. There was no ignoring Chay. He had a presence about him. When he was near me, every nerve tingled, and I hated every single second of it. Right? "So," he said, "I hear we're all going to the mall after school."

I swung my gaze between him and Muriel. Chay grinned, and Muriel gave me her *I'm-so-sorry-please-don't-hate-me* look. "He invited himself. What could I do?"

"Of course he did." I gave Muriel my best *I'm-gonna-kill-you-later* glare.

I watched the black hands on the clock hanging over the classroom door. It was the last class of the day. As the minute hand moved closer to three o'clock, another butterfly threatened mutiny in my stomach.

The mall. Why does he have to go to the mall? Guys don't even like the mall—do they?

I dreaded it, and I hated that I cared he was going at all. I didn't like Chay. At least, that was what I kept telling myself. He was irritating and commanding, and I wasn't into guys like him.

So why is he all I can think about? Jake hasn't even crossed my mind all day, but he's the kind of guy I'm into. Right? I think.

The final bell rang. I grabbed my stuff and cursed.

How can I have retail therapy with Chay there? This was supposed to be Muriel and me. Girls' day. Trying on ridiculously expensive clothes and every pair of shoes in the store. Stuff no guy, especially Chay, wants to do. I want to stomp my feet and scream. No wonder little kids have tantrums. I think one would actually feel good right now. Huh.

I walked slowly to my locker, wondering who was following me. The second I turned, I spotted his eyes and watched as a slow grin slid across his face. I sighed.

I got to my locker and threw my crap inside, slamming the door. He stood on the other side, his hip leaning against the lockers. He looked completely relaxed, while I had butterflies the size of softballs bouncing around in the pit of my belly.

"Let's go." He pushed off the lockers.

"Wait. Where's Muriel?"

"Outside."

I followed Chay to the parking lot and stared in disgust at what I found. Muriel's car was full. Drew was sitting in the front seat next to her. Jen and Shayla were crunched in the backseat with Jeff. Steven and Jake were at football practice and Lily was working, so I couldn't hitch a ride with any of them.

I looked slowly to my left. Chay held his car door open for me with a raised eyebrow. "Are you going to stand there all day or are we gonna get the torture over with?"

"Which particular torture are you referring to?" I walked slowly to his car.

"The mall. What else?"

Uh, how 'bout having to ride with you?

I slipped in the passenger's seat. He shut the car door and walked around the front end toward the driver's side, twirling his keys around his finger. I looked for an escape route, but Muriel had already pulled out of the parking lot. I was stuck with Chay.

You are so gonna pay for this, Muriel.

He was quiet on the way to the mall. The only sound was the hum of his car's engine and the frantic beating of my heart. We'd just pulled into the parking lot when he looked at me.

"Your name's really pretty."

"Oh... um, thanks." I looked at him for the first time since leaving the school and gave him a small smile. He had an odd look on his face. "Your name is... different."

81

Michelle K. Pickett

"Yeah."

"I mean it's unique," I said quickly.

"I know what you meant, Milayna." One side of his mouth lifted in an amused grin. He reached out and gently tugged on a piece of my hair before sliding it behind my ear. It sent shivers down to my toes.

Whoa. What the hell was that?

He dropped his hand and flung open his door. "Let's get this over with."

Having Chay spend the afternoon at the mall with us wasn't the catastrophe I thought it'd be. He was actually fun to be with when he wasn't in a mood. The group had a great time laughing with and teasing each other.

We sat in the food court in the middle of the mall and watched the people pass by. Potted palm trees hung over us, strung up with paper lanterns. After-noon light shined down on us from the skylights high in the second-story ceiling, making Chay's dark hair glossy. I tried not to notice. I hated that I kept looking.

"No, no, look at this one," Drew said behind the napkin he held in front of his mouth. He laughed so hard it was hard to understand him. "But, Mom, I don't want to get a haircut. The frizzy perm look is in this year." He pointed at a mother pulling her teenaged son into a barbershop by the collar of his plaid button-down. His hair sprung in all directions and could definitely use a good conditioning.

"Wait, check out the red-headed guy's T-shirt," Jen squealed.

"Feed a starving artist… buy my book," I read and laughed.

"Yeah, he doesn't look like he's missed too many dinners, and he has an ice cream cone. I want ice cream," Jen said wistfully, smiling.

Chay pointed to a little girl crying; her mom pulled her behind her. The little girl held a Barbie doll in one hand and every so many steps she took, she'd look at it and start crying harder. The screams filled the food court, and I wanted to plug my ears.

"But Mom, I didn't want the Barbie. I wanted the Spiderman doll." Chay shook his head and chuckled.

I narrowed my eyes at him. "That's so sexist. I have a Spiderman action fig-ure. He stands watch on my bedside table." He stared at me, looking as though he was at a complete loss for words. I started laughing, and his lips twitched to hide a grin.

We sat at the table, eating nachos and making up stories for the people who walked by, laughing like kids.

Drew stood and brushed tortilla chip crumbs off his shirt. "I'm going to GameStop. Anyone up for it?"

Jeff stood up. "Lead on."

I looked at Jen and Muriel. "I say we go find out what Victoria's Secret is." I arched a brow.

Jen giggled and grabbed her things. Muriel jumped out of her chair so fast it fell over.

I started to stand when Chay put his hand on my arm and leaned in to me.

His lips were against my ear, moving over them in a fiery caress. "We need to leave," he murmured. .

"Why?" I wasn't ready for the day to be over. I was having fun, even with him there. Amazing.

"Because I think you're gonna have a vision."

"How do you...?" My stomach clenched so hard that I doubled over. He grabbed my elbow to steady me. Of course he knew. With his ability to know when a team member was in trouble, he saw the vision coming before I did.

He told the others to stay put in case the cause of the vision was in the mall. "We'll keep in touch with our cells."

Chay helped me outside. My head had started to pound, and the blood pulsed behind my ears so loud that I struggled to hear him.

"I'm gonna be sick," I whispered. He steered to me a wastebasket, and I heaved the nachos I'd just eaten.

Well, that's attractive.

We made it to his car, and I fell onto the passenger's seat. I sat sideways, my legs outside the door. Chay handed me a napkin, and I was wiping my mouth and hands off when the vision knocked into me. I pressed the heels of my hands to my eyes and tried to relax.

Lily. Red faces. Fat bodies. Hobgoblins.

I dropped my hands from my face. "It's Lily," I whispered. I was sure she needed our help. We needed to get to her. Protect her. My hands started to tremble, and I willed the vision to give me more. I needed more information so we'd know how to help Lily.

"What do you see?"

"I just see her with the hobgoblins." I closed my eyes and concentrated.

Laughing. The hobgoblins are cackling. Lily is... laughing. That's wrong. Her shoulders are shaking and the skin is crinkled at the sides of her eyes, but her mouth is covered. Crying. She must be crying. No tears. She's not crying. Laughing, then.

"She's... laughing." I opened my eyes and looked into Chay's. "What's going on?"

He opened his mouth to answer and then clamped it shut again. His lips pressed into a thin line.

A searing pain burned through my head, and I screamed and clutched it in my hands. It pounded and pounded, over and over, like someone was hammering out a rhythm on a drum. There was no time between beats, and soon the individual pounding turned into a constant pain so intense that my jaw ached from clenching my teeth against it.

She's shaking hands. A pale, white hand inside a large, gray one.

My right hand started to burn. Jerking it away from my head, I looked at it. I expected to see burn marks, but there was nothing.

I looked at Chay again. He seemed resigned. His lips were pressed togeth-

83

Michelle K. Pickett

er and his hands were laced behind his neck. "I knew it was coming. I hoped I was wrong, but I knew it was coming." He shook his head, a scowl marring his features. "Damn it!"

"What's going on?" He turned his face from me, not answering. I reached out and pulled his chin toward me. "What's going on?" My teeth clenched against the pain from my twisting stomach and throbbing head.

His eyes turned dark, like storm clouds moving across the sun; the blue and green swirled together. Reaching up, he pulled my hand from his face, looking at it for a long minute before turning it over and pressing his lips to my palm. It was incredibly sensual and took me totally by surprise. My body was singing inside. I could feel every breath, every heartbeat, every nerve ending. I had no idea what to say or do in response, so I slowly pulled my hand from his and fisted it in my lap so he couldn't see it shake.

"Chay, tell me what's going on. Shouldn't we be going to Lily? She's alone. She'll need the rest of us for strength," I said, my voice barely above a whisper.

"She doesn't need us. She's made her decision."

"What are you talking about?"

He ran a fingertip across my forehead and to my temple, moving it over my skin in slow, soft circles. "Is the vision gone?"

I tried to concentrate on the vision and not the feelings his one finger was pulling from me. "Yes." I watched him, confused. "Why didn't we have to step in? Oh no—are we too late?" I grabbed his arm.

He studied where my hand touched him, a strange expression on his face. I couldn't decipher his looks. He had so many. I let go and slid my hand between my thigh and the car's seat.

"Yes, we're too late, but not in the way you think."

I waited for him to continue. When he didn't, I slammed both palms on the dash in front of me. Leaning forward, my head dropped between my arms, I let out a frustrated growl and pushed myself back into the seat. "Damn it, Chay! Stop talking in riddles and tell me what's going on!" I fell silent and tilted my head to the side. A thought ran through my head. I turned to Chay. "She crossed. Didn't she?"

Chay licked his lips and scratched his eyebrow with his thumb. He opened his mouth to answer when we heard Muriel yell to us.

"She crossed, didn't she?" Muriel called, hurrying toward the car. "I've been picking up bits and pieces in visions today."

I waved my hand in the air. "Hey! Am I ever going to get a straight answer?"

"Yeah," Chay answered Muriel.

"Does she know yet?" Muriel asked.

Chay ran his hand up the back of his head. "She suspects."

"Hello? I'm sitting right here." I raised my hand above my head and pointed down at myself.

"She crossed," Muriel told me.

I nodded. I really didn't know what to say, so I said nothing.

"She's an Evil now." Jen's voice trembled. "She's working against us."

"Oh... wow. I didn't see that coming." I put my hands on the sides of my neck and massaged.

"There's no way you could've," Chay said quietly.

"You did."

"Because I'm more attuned to what is going to hurt the group. I've been seeing her in my visions for a few days."

"So you were aware that she was going to hurt herself," I said.

"No, I was aware that someone was going to hurt the group. She isn't part of the group anymore. But her absence makes us a little weaker, and it makes Azazel's team a little stronger. Not much, and it's nothing we can't handle, but a little stronger."

"Then why did I have the vision? If there was nothing for me to correct, if there was no one for me to help, why did I have a vision?"

"She's underestimated your abilities. They're getting stronger every day. Your vision wasn't meant for you to step in and protect a human, it was meant for you to protect our group," Muriel answered.

"So what happens to her now?"

"Who knows?" Drew shrugged a shoulder.

"Who cares?" Chay answered.

"I care!" Shayla cried, her hand on her chest. Her eyes wide, she took us all in. "She was one of us. We should all care what's going to happen to her."

"She isn't one of us anymore. Now she's an enemy. We don't have the luxury of caring." Chay turned his back to Shayla and looked at me. "Let's go." He waited until I was settled in the car and closed the door. I waved at everyone through the window. There were no smiles or happy waves. Just somber faces and eyes mirroring betrayal.

Chay got in the car and drove toward home. "There's nothing we can do?" I asked.

"About?"

I sighed. "Lily."

"Yeah. Watch our backs."

85   *Michelle K. Pickett*

12

First Fight

I BAGGED UP THE GARBAGE, SET IT ON THE KITCHEN FLOOR, shook out a new bag, and stuck it into the trash bin. "This is when it would be nice if you were old enough for chores," I grumbled to Ben. He smiled and shrugged before running down the hall with his arms stretched out, making noises like he was flying an airplane.

I think there's something seriously wrong with that kid.

Hefting up the full bag, I walked out of the side door and screamed. The bag dropped onto the paved drive, and garbage spilled out of a ripped seam.

My heart was racing, pumping adrenaline through my veins like I was a junkie. I slapped my hand over my mouth and took two deep breaths through my nose.

His shoulder was leaning against the house and his finger was hooked around his belt loop. "You scream like a girl," he drawled.

"I am a girl," I said from behind my hand.

"Yeah, I've noticed." A ghost of a grin touched his lips, and my heart started racing for a completely different reason than him scaring me half to death.

"What the heck are you doing here, Chay?"

"The others will be here in a minute. I imagine your dad will be out here, too."

"All right, that's great. We'll have a reunion. But while we wait, could you please answer my freakin' question?"

"What are you trained in? Judo, Jiu-jitsu, Tae Kwon Do?"

"Tae Kwon Do, Krav Maga, and a little bit of everything else. Why?" I asked slowly.

"Because you're about to get a chance to use your skills. Lily and her new posse are on their way over. She thinks she can talk you into switching sides." Pushing off the house, he walked to me. He stood so close our toes almost touched.

"You know, I never really liked her. I should have trusted my instincts."

Chay laughed. The light over the door cast his face in odd shadows. He looked almost sinister. If I didn't know better, I'd have thought he was the one I needed to be afraid of, but at that moment, there was nowhere else I wanted to be, and that feeling confused me. Well, that wasn't exactly true. I didn't want to be where Lily was, but that, it seemed, was going to be unavoidable.

"Are you scared?" he asked, studying my face.

"Yes," I breathed. "Are you?"

"Yeah, but not for the reason you think."

Always with the riddles.

"Why, then?"

He cleared his throat and lifted his hand toward my hair. And my insides went nutso. I wasn't sure what the heck they were doing. I just knew, in that second, on my driveway with spilled garbage around our feet, I pulled my bottom lip between my teeth, held my breath, and willed his hand to keep moving.

"Hey," Muriel called, jogging up the driveway.

Chay dropped his hand and turned away. "Where's everyone else?"

Great timing, Muriel. Just perfect.

"Right behind me."

"Good. Lily is almost here." He ran his hand across the back of his neck. *Sulfur. Screaming. Fighting.*

I put my hand over my ears. "I can't have one now!"

Chay pulled my hands away. "Listen to me, Milayna. This is one vision you have to fight—"

"But I can't fight them." I started to panic.

"You have to try. The hobgoblins and Lily are coming to force you into a vision. They know if you're having a vision, you're at your weakest. They also know you're our strongest member of the group."

"But I've never—"

"Listen to me! No one is going to get hurt here tonight. There is no reason for the vision. You can fight it." Chay still held my hands. He gave them a small squeeze before letting go.

"He's right, honey," my dad said, walking outside and standing next to me. "This isn't a vision for you to help a human. They are forcing you into your vision state by creating a false sense of danger. There's nothing they can do to us."

"Okay. Okay, I'll try."

"Good girl." My dad gave me a quick kiss on the forehead just as the other members of our group walked up the driveway.

Michelle K. Pickett

Sulfur. Lily walking toward us.

"Argh, it won't go away," I said, cursing violently—things I'd never said in front of my dad, and I felt my face burn with a blush. He didn't seem to notice, or he didn't care. My heart raced and sweat pooled at the base of my back.

"What do you see?" Chay asked.

"She's coming. She's just a few houses away. She's alone."

Why is she alone? Where are the others?

"Yeah, the hobgoblins are in the backyard," my dad said.

My head jerked up. Only Chay and dad stood in the driveway with me. The rest of the group was in the backyard. I could hear the high-pitched voices of the hobgoblins followed by the muted voices of the others.

Chay. Gray face. Sulfur. So hot.

"Chay," I whispered. I didn't know I'd said it out loud until he turned his head and peered into my eyes.

"What?"

"You're going to get hurt if you stay out here." I grabbed his arm and pulled him toward the door. "Go inside."

"Bumps and bruises, that's all. We'll all get knocked around a little."

"No." A searing pain burned the back of my eyes. I squeezed them shut, tears springing to life behind my eyelids. I pressed my fingers to them, shaking my head. "No, no, the vision is for you. They're here for you."

"The hobgoblins—"

"It's not them," I yelled. "It's something else. Go in the house. You can't be out here."

Sulfur. The smell of burning meat. Ash floating in the breeze. Chay.

I heard his name. Just a whisper. I ignored what my dad and Chay told me. I focused on the vision instead of fighting it. Something was wrong. They thought it was Lily coming to convince me to join Azazel. But she was just a diversion. They were really after Chay. Until I turned eighteen, Chay was the highest-ranking DA in the group. He was the strongest, and he gave the members of our group a unique advantage, an advantage Azazel wanted to dispose of. Getting rid of Chay would weaken the group and make it easier for Azazel to pick us off one by one until we were all dead or converted.

I dropped my fingers from my eyes, the tears rolling down my cheeks. "Please trust me. You can't be here."

My dad clamped a hand on Chay's shoulder. "It's all right, son. We have to protect each other. If Milayna is sure you're in danger, you need to listen."

Chay walked in the house, slamming the door behind him. I heard him slide down the door and sit on the kitchen floor, a string of profanities spewing from his mouth. As soon as he was safely inside, the vision dissolved.

"Stubborn, isn't he?" Dad asked with a chuckle.

"You have no idea." I looked up and saw Dad's face set in hard lines.

I tensed and turned in time to see Lily walk around the evergreen tree and start up the driveway. "Hi, Milayna."

I took a step toward her. "You're not welcome here, Lily. Leave."

"I'm not welcome? This isn't like in the movies where you can keep the vampires away by not inviting them inside." She laughed. The sound was garish and ugly. I stared at her. "Where's Chay?"

"He's not here."

"You know, Azazel and his demons can tell when you're lying."

I shrugged a shoulder. "Good for Azazel. Color me impressed. My answer is still the same. Chay's not here."

"Too bad. I was hoping he'd come out and play."

"I guess you'll have to settle for me," I said with a lot more bravado than I felt.

"You think you're ready for me, Milayna?"

"The question you should be asking yourself is—are *you* ready for *me*?" I smiled. "Because you'll have to go through me to get to Chay."

Lily rushed me with a scream. Her face turned almost as red as the hobgoblins. I stood my ground. Partly because I didn't want to give her the satisfaction of seeing me run and hide, of knowing how scared I really was, but mostly because I needed to prove something to myself. That I was strong enough to fight Azazel and his demons. That I was worthy of being a demi-angel.

Lily threw a jab. I blocked it, knocking it away. She kicked. I grabbed her ankle and jerked her toward me, jamming the heel of my hand into her nose. Thick, foamy blood oozed from her flaring nostrils, and a look of shock registered on her face. Before she could regain her composure, I kneed her in the gut and pushed her away. She stumbled down the driveway before falling backward and hitting her head on the concrete. It took her a moment to stand. When she finally stood, she held her head, looking dizzy and disoriented.

I immediately wanted to go to her and check her injuries. Make sure she wasn't hurt too badly. Ask her why she betrayed the group and tell her it wasn't too late to change her mind and come back. Then she opened her mouth and my hopes of her returning to us died.

"You'll be sorry, Milayna," she said, wiping the blood from her nose with the back of her hand. "This isn't over." She glared at me before stalking off into the darkness.

With a new sense of strength, I walked into the backyard. The hobgoblins were scurrying around, swinging on the swing set, climbing the fence, shimmying up the clothesline poles, and sliding down the ropes like a zip line. They acted like a bunch of demonic toddlers hyped up on too much sugar.

I looked at Muriel. She sat with her elbow on the picnic table and her cheek in her hand, watching the hobgoblins run through the yard. The rest of the group had similar looks of boredom on their faces.

"Milayna," one of the fat, red goblins said in a singsong voice. "You've come to play with us."

"Why haven't you dealt with them?" I asked the group sitting at the table.

Michelle K. Pickett

"You try to catch them," Drew snapped. "Sometimes, we just have to sit and wait for them to get bored."

I walked into the middle of the yard. Three of the five goblins ran over to me, chanting my name in their screeching voices. The other two were trying to figure out how to get down from the clothesline.

"Would you please get them, Jake?" I pointed at the two pitiful excuses for goblins hanging by their hands from my mother's clothesline, their feet kicking in the air as they cackled with glee.

Jake plucked them from the clothesline, knocked their heads together, and dropped them to the ground. They disappeared with two small *pops*. All that was left was a circle of white smoke blowing in the breeze.

"Where's Chay?" one hobgoblin asked, looking at me with its big eyes. A tuft of black hair stood straight up on top of its head.

I'd think they were cute if I didn't know what they are.

"He's not here."

"Chay, Chay, Chay," they chanted. "Come play with us."

"I told you, he's not here." I picked up one of the goblins and dropkicked him across the yard. He disappeared in midair, leaving nothing more than a puff of smoke and a violent curse behind.

The last two grew angry. Their faces changed from soft little creatures to the hard, menacing demons they were. Their eyes turned black, and a snarl tore from one's throat.

"You'll be sorry you pissed us off, Milayna. He's coming for him," one red midget said, "and then you're next."

"I'm shaking in my shoes. Get out of here before I dropkick you like I did your brother."

Drew walked up behind the two goblins and picked them up by the scruff of their necks. He walked to a black hole in the far corner of my yard. I didn't see it until he dropped the goblins down it and kicked the dirt back in place. It fused together, closing the small tunnel leading to the goblins' home down south.

I stared at him, and he shrugged. "There's always a portal somewhere. We just have to find it. I happened to spot that one."

"Where's Lily?" Shayla asked.

"She left."

"Good riddance."

We walked into the house through the patio doors. I saw Chay sitting with his back against the side door, still mumbling under his breath.

"Sleeping on the job, Chay?" Drew drawled.

"Sidelined. Bummer," Jake said, laughing.

"Shut up." Chay got up and walked to me. I braced myself for the yelling to start. Instead, he brushed the hair out of my face and gazed into my eyes. "Are you okay? Did she touch you? Because if she touched you, I swear—"

"I'm fine," I whispered.

He seems upset, and not just because he had to sit out the fight, if that's what it was, but because I might be hurt. Because he cares?

"It's not just me he wants." I twisted the sleeve of his shirt in my fingers and held it firmly. "You have to be careful. Promise me."

He let the knuckles on one hand slide down the side of my face, and I tried really hard not to lean into it. I mean, my crush was Jake. Not Chay. I tried so hard to pull away. I did. But my eyes closed, and I leaned into his hand. "I know. I heard." His voice glided over me like silk. Soft and husky—and so damn sexy. Liquid fire moved through my body.

I heard Muriel's small chuckle from somewhere in the room. It couldn't have said, "I told you dark and brooding was your type," any louder if she'd screamed it. Forcing my eyes open, I cleared my throat. "Lily's eighteen, right?" I asked.

"Yeah, we all are, except you," Chay answered. His hand rested lightly on the curve of my shoulder, his thumb rubbing my neck.

"Then why did she change? I mean, I thought we were immune to Azazel when we turned eighteen?" I moved away from Chay and reached into the refrigerator. Pulling out Cokes, I handed them to everyone. Chay's fingers moved over mine when he took the can from me. His gaze never left mine.

"No, you're immune because of your higher rank. The others gained some strength when they turned eighteen, and the group as a whole will be stronger when you're eighteen, but they'll never be immune." My dad took a long pull on his Coke. "But any one of us can turn at any time. It's a personal choice, regardless of age or rank."

"Oh."

Crap. There's so much to learn. This is worse than studying for the SATs.

"Another thing I don't understand—why don't our neighbors hear or see what's going on? I mean, we just had five fat, red goblins running around our yard, squealing and acting like a bunch of brats who OD'd on Red Bull and Fun Dip candy, but no one seems to have noticed."

"Well, it helps that the lots in this subdivision are an acre each and the perimeter of ours is mostly wooded," my dad said, easing into a chair. "But the truth is, most people are blind to otherworldly things. What you see and hear as a demi-angel is much different from what their minds are capable of understanding.

"That's one reason we can keep Ben from being tainted by what we see and do. His mind isn't ready to accept the situation. But the closer to the age of accountability he gets, the more he'll understand, and the more he'll see.

"Demons are around us every day, but people don't see them. It's the same when they're here. We can have all the fury of Hell in our backyard, and the neighbors won't see it."

Chay took a drink of his Coke and wiped his mouth with the back of his hand. "We probably will."

A frown pulled at my dad's mouth. "True, this is going to get ugly."

91   *Michelle K. Pickett*

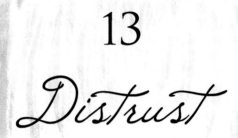

13

Distrust

Compared to what was happening in my life, school was even more of a bore than usual. The visions took over. I had them at school, at home, and anywhere I happened to be. If there was a human in danger and I could step in, I had to. I was learning to let the visions have their way. It became easier with each one. Not fun, necessarily, but easier. I'd do what they wanted me to, and then go about my life like normal. Because it was normal. At least for me.

The only bright spot in my school day was Chay. Jake had become a distant memory. Oh, he was still gorgeous and charming, but he wasn't Chay... who also happened to be gorgeous but was definitely not charming most days. He had his moments, though, and I was beginning to think more and more about him and less and less about Jake. That made me feel off-balance. I knew where I stood when it came to Jake, which was nowhere. He had Heidi, the cheerleader. *Rah-frickin-rah.* I wasn't in the picture.

But with Chay, I had no idea where I stood. Did he have any feelings for me beyond our duties as DAs? If so, he didn't make it obvious, but he did flirt subtly— or maybe I read into things because that was what I wanted. *Crap*! Relationship stuff sucked. I wanted to go back to first grade when we just wrote, *'Do you like me? Circle yes or no.'* on a piece of paper. Things were simpler then.

A large book bag slammed on the tall, black table next to me in chemistry. I didn't bother looking up. I knew it was him. I could smell his cologne. I could feel his presence. And then, I could hear his mouth.

"You look better today. Not like you usually look." He slid onto his chair next to me and started pulling his book and supplies out of his backpack.

Was that supposed to be a compliment?

I sighed and turned toward him, drumming my pen on my thigh. "How do I usually look?"

"Tired and crappy. But not today. You took the sleeping pill Jen's dad left for you?" he asked, sifting through his notes.

"Yes. Wait, how do you know about that?" I gave his shoulder a shove. "Do I have no privacy whatsoever?" My face heated, not from a blush, but from anger. Who did he think he was interfering in my life? Demi-angel business, fine. The rest of my life he needed to stay the hell out of!

He rolled the shoulder I shoved, and one side of his mouth tipped in an amused grin. "We all need to know what's going on. The pill interfered with your ability to function. You weren't one hundred percent physically. We had to make sure we were."

"Well, excuse me for sleeping."

He looked down at his notes and shrugged. I had no idea what he was thinking. Jake was a shallow pond. You could see right to the bottom. A person could decipher every thought, snide comment, or joke. Not so with Chay. Compared to Jake, Chay was the depth of an ocean. Deep and dark. There was no way to decipher him. At least, I hadn't found one. I needed a secret decoder ring.

Class started, and Chay and I worked silently on the assigned lab. He added the chemicals, and I wrote down the results. I reached for the lab slip and turned the page in the packet when he said something that threw me even more off-balance than I already was.

"You smell good today." He tilted his head and watched closely as he poured chemicals into the beaker.

My heart did a little flip right before it tap-danced around my chest.

Why do I care what he thinks?

My hand stilled over the paper I recorded the results of our lab on. "As opposed to what? Do I smell bad most days?"

"No, you always smell good. Apricots."

"Huh?"

"Your hair. You must use apricot shampoo. I like it." He glanced at me then. Just a quick look out of the corner of his eye.

"Um, thanks. You smell good too," I said, cringing when my voice came out strained and weird sounding.

He nodded once in acknowledgement. He didn't speak, only winked, and one side of his mouth lifted slightly in a grin. He continued with the experiment, leaving me to wonder what the heck just happened.

"Done." He flipped the book closed. "You should leave."

"Why?"

"You're gonna have a vision."

Michelle K. Pickett

"How do you do that? How do you know I'm going to have a vision before I know?" I shut my chemistry book harder than I meant to and glared at him.

"Sometimes I have visions of you having visions, not always, but sometimes. Actually, they're more glimpses than full visions like yours. It's odd, if you think about it. But there you go. Anyway, like I said, you should leave."

"No. I can't have one now."

He shrugged a shoulder.

My stomach clenched, and I narrowed my eyes at him. I pushed my chair back. The feet screeched across the tiled floor. I walked to the front of the room and asked my chemistry teacher to be excused. With each passing second, my stomach twisted tighter. It felt like the time I got my hair stuck in the fan when I was a kid. It wrapped around the fan blades so tight that I thought it'd pull from my scalp.

"Is your assignment finished?"

"Yes, sir."

"You can wait until the bell rings. It's only fifteen minutes," he said, not looking at me. I hated when people didn't look at me when I was speaking to them.

My stomach squeezed harder, pushing the breath from my lungs, and I wrapped one arm around my middle and held on to the desk for support with the other.

"I really need to go to the bathroom," I insisted. When I saw he was going to say no, I blurted, "I'm going to puke. I really need to go, and like, right now!" His face scrunched up in a disgusted look, and he nodded for me to leave. I hurried out of the room and down the hall.

I tried to think of somewhere private. I couldn't have a vision in the middle of the hall while people pushed and shoved their way from class to class. Ducking into the bathroom, I locked myself in a stall. It smelled of urine and stagnant water. Wet toilet paper stuck to the puke-green floor. I stepped around the mess and leaned in the corner of the stall, my arms wrapped around my stomach like they could shield it from the searing pain shooting through it like missiles. My head pounded in time with my racing heart.

My vision started to fade, like someone was dimming the lights. The room turned gray, and then was cloaked in darkness. When all I saw was black, images started scrolling through my mind like credits after a movie.

Lily talking to Jake. Jake laughing. Hobgoblins watching from the rafters in the school's ceiling, watching between the cracks in the tiles.

"Lily. What about her? Come on, come on," I whispered.

Chay. Lily. Chay's angry. Lily laughs and walks by, her finger trailing across his shoulders.

She's trying to recruit the team one by one.

I flew out of the bathroom and skidded to a stop, my sneakers squeaking across the floor.

"What are you doing here?"

He's blocking the bathroom door like a bodyguard... or a prison guard.

"Waiting for you. What does it look like?" Chay answered. He stood with his feet spread and his fingers hooked around the belt loops of his jeans. "What'd you see?"

"Lily talking with Jake. They were laughing about something she said. And..." *Lily talking with you.*

"And what?" He arched a brow.

"Nothing. That's all." I wasn't sure why I didn't tell him I saw her talking with him, too. It just didn't feel right. Maybe I didn't want to hear the answer confirmed. Of course she'd talk to him. The real issue was what the conversation led to.

Would he switch sides? It would be a big win for Azazel if he did.

"I'll talk with Jake and see what he has to say. She's gonna try to convert us, you know. That's her job," Chay said with a shrug.

"I know."

But who will she manage to get to switch? That's what worries me.

We walked toward my locker just as the bell rang. I saw her walking toward me, a sneer on her face. It was becoming a permanent fixture.

"Milayna," she said and shouldered me hard. I took a few steps backward to steady myself, my eyes never leaving hers. A burst of heat bloomed in my chest, bringing with it a longing for vengeance for her betrayal, but also patience. If she wanted to get a rise out of me, it wasn't going to happen. Yet. But her time was coming. "Hi, Chay." She smiled as she walked past him.

I looked at him through my lashes. His face was blank, unreadable. Was he hiding something or keeping his emotions in check in front of Lily? My stomach twisted in response. I wasn't sure what it meant, but I didn't like it.

"You can't read minds, but you will develop the ability to feel what people are feeling, their emotions, and even what they might do just before they do it," my dad had told me.

But I felt loyalty. Commitment. I didn't think Chay would switch sides, but how could I know for sure? I didn't want to be suspicious of him—the emotions filling me bounced off each other like bumper cars. I couldn't focus, and felt confused and unsure. But I had to trust someone, and I desperately wanted that someone to be Chay.

We walked down the hall to calculus. Banners hung from the ceiling, painted in bright colors, announcing the football game the following night against our biggest rival. We had two high schools in the same school district, one on the south side of town and one on the north. The annual football game was a big deal—whoever won got bragging rights for the year, rubbing the other school's nose in their victory and flying the victor's flag for the year, declaring themselves the best in the district. My team, the South Bay Cougars, had lost seven years in a row. It was our year to win.

I stopped at my locker to grab my calculus book. Chay leaned his shoulder against the locker beside mine and watched me.

Michelle K. Pickett

"What?"

"Just looking."

"At what?" I glanced around, expecting to see something interesting. Lily, a goblin, a fight, a couple making out—you never knew what you'd see in school. It was like living in a reality television show. "I don't see anything."

"That's because I'm looking at you," he said slowly. He reached out, touched a curl in my hair, and rubbed it between his fingers. "Your hair's pretty. I can see why Joe liked it so much." It tickled when he brushed the curl behind my ear, and I rubbed my shoulder against my ear, giggling.

I'm giggling like a little girl. Get a grip. Geez, you're losing it.

"You're ticklish. That's cute." He smiled.

Is he flirting with me? 'Cause it's so working.

"Where's Chay?" I tilted my head and touched my fingers to my lips. Chay's forehead wrinkled and his brows knotted over his eyes. I smiled. "What have you done with the sour-faced, grumbling idiot I've come to know?"

He laughed. The sound was like a warm melody washing over me. I wanted to do something that would make him keep laughing. "Yeah, I guess I deserve that."

I gave him a quick smile before looking down the hall. "I wonder where Muriel is. We always meet and walk to calculus together."

I sucked in a breath and froze. Muriel and Lily were walking together, laughing and talking. When they walked by my locker, Muriel looked at me and smiled, waving with a wiggle of her fingers.

What is she doing? No, no, no! Okay, wait. She must have a reason for hanging around Lily. A perfectly logical explanation. Like, she's gathering information! Yeah. That's it. Because Muriel would never turn. She wouldn't. Not Muriel.

"Like I said, you don't know who you can trust." Chay glanced over his shoulder at Muriel and Lily.

"How can we do our job if we are all wondering if the other has switched sides?" I squeezed the strap of my messenger bag until my fingers ached.

"It makes it difficult."

"That wasn't an answer, Chay."

"That's because I don't have one," he said, looking down at me.

"And you?"

"Me what?"

"Are you trustworthy?" I pulled my bag against my chest.

"You don't know who you can trust, Milayna. Remember that. Once a demi switches sides, it hurts the entire group."

I didn't point out to him that he didn't answer my question. Or maybe he did. He told me to trust no one. Him included.

I skipped swim practice that afternoon. I didn't want to see Muriel, and since she gave me a ride to school, I was forced to ride the bus home. I hated the bus. It smelled of rotten lunches and body odor, with vomit thrown in to round it all out. I walked toward the dingy, yellow bus when he called to me.

"What are you doing, Milayna?"

"I'm not going to swim practice today. I'm catching the bus home."

"I can see that," Chay said. "But why?"

"Muriel was my ride."

"Ah. C'mon." He motioned with his head. "I'll give you a ride." My heart started thumping. *Yes, please!*

"Are you getting on or not?" the bus driver yelled over the rumbling engine.

I shook my head. She closed the door and gunned the engine. The gears groaned when she shifted into drive and slowly pulled away, leaving Chay and me standing in a cloud of gray exhaust.

"I thought I wasn't supposed to trust you," I said, following him from the bus line to the student parking lot. There were just a few cars left. His yellow car stood out like a beacon. It almost glowed in the afternoon sun, and I had the stupid thought that it was the perfect car for a demi-angel. It looked almost like a halo.

"I said you don't know who you can trust. I didn't say you couldn't trust me. Let me have that." He lifted my messenger bag off my shoulder. I grabbed it by instinct. He tapped my hand on the strap with his finger and grinned. "I'm just going to carry it to the car. You don't have to worry about me stealing your chemistry homework." He chuckled. "I have my own."

I smiled and let go of the strap. "Sorry, reflex. I'm not used to having people carry my things."

"Jake doesn't carry them for you?"

I laughed. "You're the spy; you tell me."

"Spy?"

"Following me around."

"Ah. I don't follow you all day. I have other people to watch." He grinned, and the sting of jealousy hit me. Who else was he watching? A girl? Why did I care?

I don't care. He can watch a hundred girls… it doesn't matter to me.

Yeah, keep lying to yourself, Milayna.

"No, Jake doesn't carry my books. He carries Heidi's."

"The jock and the cheerleader, typical. But you like him." Chay spun his keys around his finger.

"What?" I wanted to cover my face with my hands. I could feel the heat of a blush crawling up my neck to my face and burning my ears. Blotchy red face, red hair… not a good look with fair skin. If Bozo the Clown had a daughter, I'd be her.

"You like Jake. It's obvious by the way you look at him."

I'm that obvious? I wonder if I was that obvious to Jake.

"He's okay," I said, trying to think of a way to change the subject.

Michelle K. Pickett

Chay snorted a laugh. "Just okay?"

"Yeah. Since we're being so nosy today, who do you like? Whose books do you carry around during the day?"

"Yours, evidently." He smiled at me, his blue-green eyes twinkling.

"Other than right this minute, whose books do you want to carry during the day?"

He shrugged a shoulder and looked straight ahead, not answering.

"Fair is fair, Chay. You know my secret crush, or, well, not-so-secret crush according to you. Now you have to tell me yours."

"I'm not one of your girlfriends spending the night playing truth or dare. I don't have to tell you shit," he snapped.

I laughed. "That bad, huh?"

"No. Actually, she's amazing." There was that green-eyed monster again, smiling at me, taunting me. Jealousy raced through my veins, dragging knives against the sides, cutting me open. I cursed myself for asking. I didn't want to know, because I was beginning to see the truth. My crush on Jake was over. There was another guy in town. *Chay.*

He held the passenger door of his car open for me. I slid in. Throwing my bag in the backseat with his, he closed the door and walked around to the driver's side. I watched him move. So graceful—an odd way to describe a guy. I never thought of one as graceful, but Chay's movements were fluid, easy. He seemed comfortable in his own skin, at ease with himself and who—what—he was.

He climbed into the car, and I immediately wished I'd taken the bus home. Even though it reeked, it was better than the smell in Chay's car. It was all him. His clothes, his hair, his cologne. I was hyperaware of him. My breathing sped up, and I gripped the armrest so tightly my fingers ached.

Trying to distract myself, I looked around the car. Pop cans and burger wrappers were thrown haphazardly on the floor in the backseat. Piles of folders and papers were stacked on the seat. CDs and his iPod were stuffed in a cubbyhole in the dashboard, and his cell phone was dropped in a cup holder. When I looked up, he was watching me.

He grinned. "I know—it's a sty."

"I didn't notice it when I rode with you to the mall." I laughed.

"That's because I cleaned it out." I raised an eyebrow and stared at him. "Okay, I threw everything in the trunk, but it was clean in the car."

Wait. He cleaned it? Did he plan for me to ride with him?

Chay's car rumbled to life. He shifted into drive, sat for a moment, and then shifted back into park.

"You wanna go get something to drink? You don't have to be home yet, do you?"

"Um, sure. We can go somewhere and get something." My heartbeat increased even more, though I didn't think that was possible. I was sure it was going to give out from exhaustion any second. There was no way it could keep beating that fast and not suffer irreparable damage.

"What do you feel like?"

Kissing you. I paused and bit the corner of my bottom lip. *Whoa!* "How about a milkshake?" I said, and then cringed.

A milkshake? A milkshake, really? How nineteen-fifties can I get? Geez, way to wow him with your über sophistication, Milayna.

He smiled. "I knew I liked you for a reason. I love milkshakes. Well, ice cream in all forms. And I know just the place to get the best milkshakes in town."

Wait, he likes me? Like, he likes me, likes me or just likes me? "Okay, let's go."

He shifted into drive and pulled out of the parking lot. I looked out of the window as we drove through town and forced myself to watch the buildings pass by instead of staring at him. According to him, I wasn't able to keep my crushes a secret, so I decided looking at him would be a mistake, because I was pretty sure I was crushing on the guy.

Unfortunately, my eyes had a mind of their own and traveled to him more than once. And occasionally, I'd catch him glancing quickly in my direction. Neither of us spoke, but we couldn't help the tentative smiles that touched our lips. When the corners of his mouth lifted in a grin, my toes curled and my stomach felt like it was free falling.

We pulled into the parking lot of a little ice cream shop. He got out and jogged around the car to open my door. The awkward feeling was back. No one had ever treated me that way, carrying my books and opening doors. Even past boyfriends hadn't done that.

Chay held the door to the ice cream shop open. It was a simple place. The back wall, the first thing I saw when I walked in, was lined with a counter-high freezer full of dozens of flavors of ice cream.

"Some of them are made here. You can't get them anywhere else," Chay told me.

"Wow, Ben and Jerry's better watch out, huh?"

At the front of the store were booths and tables, all done in red vinyl and shiny metal. The floor was black-and-white checkered tile. There was a jukebox to my right. Nineteen-fifty's nostalgia hung from the walls and neon signs directed you to the bathrooms, the cashier, and proclaimed *Uncles* the best ice cream in Michigan. It was the coolest place I'd seen.

An older man behind the counter greeted Chay. "It's been a couple of days since your last ice cream fix. I was worried something was wrong. You here for the usual?" A broad smile broke out across his face.

"Hey, Uncle Stewart. Yeah, hook me up with the usual, please. How are things?" Chay asked with a grin.

"Good, good. How are things with you?" He lifted one bushy eyebrow and his gaze darted in my direction. "Who's your friend and why is someone so beautiful hanging around with the likes of you?" he teased.

99

Michelle K. Pickett

"Uncle Stewart, this is Milayna. Milayna, this is my Uncle Stewart. He owns the place."

"Hi." I reached out to shake his hand.

"It's a pleasure," he said, turning my hand over to kiss the top. I felt a blush crawl across my face, and Chay's uncle smiled. "Call me Uncle. Everyone does. Now, what can I get you?"

"A chocolate milkshake, please."

"Well, now, that's Chay's pick, too."

Smiling, I felt the blush grow deeper.

I watched as he mixed the milkshakes, squirting lots of whipped cream on them and plopping three cherries on top of each.

"Here we go. Two chocolate milkshakes, extra whipped cream, and three cherries, because Chay is spoiled." Uncle grinned, and I laughed. Chay rolled his eyes. I took out my wallet to pay, and Uncle just stared at me. "Family doesn't pay here, dearie."

"But I'm not—"

Family? He's an angel. But how did he know I was a demi? Do I put out an aura or a beacon? Does he have angel radar? Is that even a power?

"Yes, you are." He winked. "Enjoy your milkshakes."

"Thank you." I smiled, and Uncle gave me a wave.

"Let's sit outside." Chay held the door open to the patio area.

We walked to the white café tables at the side of the building. They were shielded from the sun by cheery, yellow-and-white striped umbrellas. When Chay pulled my chair out for me, I decided he was really starting to freak me out. He had this whole *Invasion of the Body Snatchers* or *The Stepford Children* thing going on.

"You don't need to pull my chair out and open doors for me."

"Yes I do." He sat across from me, stretching his long legs out. They brushed against mine, and I gripped the Styrofoam cup so hard that I had to force my hand to relax before I crushed it.

"It's not like we're dating."

"That's just how I was taught."

Oh. Of course he's doing it because that's how he was raised. Why else?

"Your uncle is nice." I stirred my shake with the straw.

"Yeah."

"He's one of us, isn't he? An angel. That's why he called me family," I asked quietly.

"He's a demi."

"Oh. So... " Silence stretched between us, and I fumbled for something to say to fill it. "Tell me about yourself."

He looked at me and quirked an eyebrow. "Why?"

He's perfected the art of one-word answers.

I shrugged one shoulder. "Just trying to start a conversation, and it seemed like the thing to ask."

"Do you always have to talk?"

I sighed. "Never mind." I took another drink of my shake.

"Only child. My dad's an angel, my mom's not." He shrugged. "That's about it."

"Wow. You really have a thing about answering questions with as few words as possible." He glanced at me, and I smiled.

"So? What about you?" he asked.

I managed to keep a straight face when I said, "Oh my gosh, you started a conversation. I should probably look for aliens. They may have probed you and pushed the words right out!"

Chay snorted a laugh, and milkshake bubbled over the rim of his paper cup. "Okay, I admit I don't have the ability to talk nonstop like some people." He wiped milkshake off his hands with a napkin.

"Ah, is that so? I hadn't noticed," I said. He smiled around his straw, and I had to hold back a sigh. "Okay, well, I have a younger brother Benjamin. My dad's the angel. He's a police officer, and my mom's an accountant."

"Yeah, I knew your dad was with the police department. So is mine. There are a lot of angels and demi-angels who are on the force. That's why we can call the police when there's a fight with the Evils or demi-demons and they don't get suspicious—a lot of them are angels, too."

"You've fought a lot?"

"Too much."

We fell silent, drinking our shakes. I watched the cars drive past, counting them—anything to distract me from staring at Chay. When I glanced at him, he was staring at me.

"Good milkshake," I said, scooping the last few drops out of the cup.

"Ready?"

"Yeah, I need to get home. Lots of chemistry homework to do."

"He really piled it on today, that's for sure." He ran his hand through his hair. "If you need a study partner..."

"Sure. Um, if I get stuck, I'll text you."

He nodded and smiled. "Yeah. That's what I was gonna say."

We were quiet on the drive home. Chay broke the silence when he pulled into my driveway and slipped the gear into park. "I want to have another group meeting. Can you come over tonight?"

"Yeah, why?"

"I just want to see what the general feel of the group is about Lily," he said "How 'bout six?"

"Okay, I'll see you then." He walked around and opened the car door for me, grabbing my bag out of the backseat.

"Thanks for the milkshake."

"Sure." His eyes followed his movements as he slipped the strap of my mes-

101 *Michelle K. Pickett*

senger bag up my arm and settled it on my shoulder. When his fingertips slid over the side of my neck like a feather, I sucked in a sharp breath. His gaze shot to mine.

I wrapped my fingers around the strap of my bag. "Thanks." I gave him a shaky smile. "I'll see you later." Turning, I walked up the path to my door.

At six o'clock, my dad drove me to Chay's. He wouldn't let me walk alone, and Muriel wasn't home. He dropped me off and waited, watching me through the windshield as I climbed the porch steps and walked to the door. I pushed the doorbell, smiling when I heard the University of Michigan's fight song start to play. *Go Wolverines!*

Chay lived in a beautiful home with a wraparound porch and baskets of ivy hanging over the bannisters. The front was lined with bright fall mums; their smell hung in the air. I was admiring the flowers when the door opened.

"You must be Milayna," a man about my dad's age said. He was tall like Chay and had the same dark hair. It was even cut the same—short on the sides and a little longer on top.

"Yes, sir."

"Well, come on." He smiled and opened the door wider so I could pass through. He waved to my dad before closing it after me. "They're all in Chay's room."

Chay's room! Oh, no, no, no.

My heart beat a little faster. I followed his dad through a large room full of overstuffed chairs and comfy-looking couches. A large flat-screen television, tuned to a classical music channel, hung on the wall.

"Chay!" his dad yelled down a hallway. When there wasn't an answer, he looked at me and rolled his eyes. "Last door on the left."

"Thanks." I walked slowly down the hall. The walls were filled with family photos. I saw Chay as a baby and toddler, as a boy with his dad on fishing trips, his school portraits—the kind that always turn out horrible but parents displayed them anyway as their little way of torturing us. I stopped to look at a photo of him and his uncle at the ice cream shop when I saw a photo of our dads together. There was also a picture of them with Uncle Rory. I was looking at them when I heard a door open behind me.

"Like what you see?" he drawled. He leaned against the doorjamb, one arm stretched above his head.

"I'm amazed is all."

"Amazed?" His eyes twinkled. They looked more blue than green just then.

"Yeah, I wasn't sure you were capable of smiling until I saw the photographic evidence."

"Ah." He pursed his lips to hide a grin. "C'mon. Everyone's in here."

I followed Chay into his bedroom, which was actually two rooms. The wall had been knocked out and a wicked cool archway with built-in bookcases on either side was put in its place, combining the two bedrooms into one large room. On one side of the archway was his bed—somewhere deep inside my stomach a huge butterfly staged a rebellion at the sight—and dresser. On the other side was a couch, some waffle chairs, and an entertainment center with a huge television where the guys were already engrossed in a video game. Their little avatars ran around the screen, battling aliens.

I expected posters of sleek cars or rock bands. But his walls were mostly bare. Painted a silvery gray to complement his maroon bedspread and curtains, it was sophisticated. And it fit Chay perfectly.

"Nice room."

"Thanks." He turned and led me to the couch. "Move," he said and knocked Steven's foot off his knee. "Get up and let her sit there." Steven rolled his eyes but moved to a beanbag.

I sat where Steven had been, and Chay eased himself down next to me. Leaning over me, he flicked open a door on the table next to the couch. "You want a Coke?"

"Sure." He pulled a pop out of the little table. Sitting up, he handed it to me. "Thanks." I bent forward and studied the table, which was actually a small refrigerator. "I so want a room like yours." I laughed.

He smiled, slow and sexy, and my heart melted little by little. "Or you can just come visit me." And there it went. My heart officially melted into a puddle of goo. While I was trying to recover from his comment, Chay turned toward the room.

He put his palms on his thighs and yelled to be heard over the commotion in the room. "Okay, everyone! I want to get right to the point of why we're all here so we can get on with the pizza and fun stuff. So, who has Lily talked to?" Everyone stopped what they were doing and stared at him. Most had odd expressions on their faces. No one said anything. That was when I noticed Muriel wasn't there.

"Come on, I know she's talked to some of you," Chay said with an exasperated sigh. "She's talked to me."

I looked at him. I wasn't sure why, but I was angry that he didn't tell me.

Slowly, everyone in the room raised their hand. Lily had talked with everyone there. Except me. Lily didn't make a secret out of the fact she didn't like me much. But her job as an Evil was to recruit demis for Azazel and from what I understood, I was at the top of his Christmas list. So I couldn't get my mind around why she wouldn't approach me. Unless... she planned to use the team members against me.

"Milayna?" Drew asked.

"No. She hasn't said anything to me. I wonder why?"

"Who knows? Maybe Azazel wants to turn everyone against you and force you to choose sides," Chay answered. "Is anyone having any trouble with her

Michelle K. Pickett

other than her talking to you?"

Everyone answered in the negative.

"What about Azazel's team? Has anyone had any contact with them?"

Everyone raised their hand except Jen and Shayla.

"You?" I asked Chay.

"Yes." He didn't elaborate, but I didn't expect him to. He was stingy with his information.

"Did anyone have any problems with the goblins? Since you're here, I'm going to assume you didn't take them up on their offer."

The room erupted in a flurry of "*no*," "*no ways*," and a few curses.

Chay smiled. "Good. Let's have some pizza."

"You have pizza in here, too?" I opened the door to his private refrigerator and peeked inside.

He laughed. "No, it's in the kitchen."

Everyone got up and raced down the hall to the kitchen. I grabbed Chay by the arm and waited until the last person left the room. "Why didn't you tell me you talked with Lily and had a visit from the little red imps?"

"Imps?" He arched a brow and pursed his lips.

"It's faster than hobgoblins. Just answer my questions. Why didn't you tell me?"

"I warned you, Milayna. You don't know who you can trust."

Ugh, you keep saying that. I got it. I got it. I wonder where Muriel is?

14

Football

FOUR WEEKS, FOUR DAYS UNTIL MY BIRTHDAY.

Muriel left early that morning. She didn't tell me beforehand that we wouldn't be riding together, or I would've had Jen pick me up. Instead, I had to find my own way. Faced with riding the bus, I prayed to the car gods that my old beater would start. Thankfully, it roared to life—probably waking all the neighbors—and I drove myself to school.

"What happened this morning, Muriel?" I slipped into my seat next to her in calculus.

"I'm sorry. I forgot to tell you I had a make-up quiz to take in one of my other classes. I wanted to take it this morning, so I wouldn't be rushed tonight for the game."

"Where were you last night?" I clicked my pen open and shut, open and shut, open and shut.

Muriel snatched the pen out of my hand and gave it a disgusted look. "I had some errands to run for my mother."

"Oh." I didn't mention that I saw her car in the driveway all night. Chay's warning kept repeating in my head.

I saw Chay looking at us from the corner of my eye, but I ignored him. I didn't believe Muriel, my best friend and cousin, would switch sides. It just wouldn't happen. If she said she had other things to do, I believed her. Chay's warning be damned.

Michelle K. Pickett

It was Friday, the night of the big game between the South Bay Cougars and the North Bay Cowboys. The group was going to the game together.

Chay followed me home from school that afternoon. "I'll pick you up tonight," he said when we got to my house and he walked me to the door.

"That's okay. I can ride with Muriel."

He drummed his fingers on the car door and shook his head once. "I'll pick you up."

I sighed. I hated his moody, *I-know-it-all-and-you'll-do-it-my-way* side. He'd been that way all day. He stalked back to his car. Revving the engine once, he backed out of the driveway and headed toward his house.

"I'm surprised he didn't want to walk me inside," I muttered. Then I looked up and knew why. My dad was waiting at the door. "Hey, Dad."

"How's it going? Everything good?" He clamped a hand on my shoulder as I walked by him into the house.

"Yeah, why?" Goose bumps ran up my arms and the hair on the back of my neck did *the wave* like people in a stadium watching a game.

Great. What big surprise is he gonna spring on me now? I'm not sure I can take anything else. No more demi-angel stuff. Enough is enough. And I think I'm at a full tank.

"You didn't ride with Muriel today." He followed me inside.

I let out the breath I was holding, my cheeks puffing out. "Oh, that. Yeah, she had a quiz to make up before school. She left before me."

"Ah."

We walked into the kitchen, and I dropped onto a chair. He poured us two glasses of milk and rattled around in the pantry until he found my mom's hidden Oreo cookies.

"Ooh, living on the wild side, huh? Dipping into mom's private stash of cookies. Dangerous." I grabbed a cookie and dunked it in my milk. "Mm, yum. Hey, Dad? How do you know Chay's dad?" I asked around another bite of milk-soaked Oreo.

"Hmm?" He was focused on twisting apart his cookies and scraping out the frosting centers.

"I saw a photo of you and him at Chay's house last night. You've never mentioned you two knew each other. There was one of you and him with Uncle Rory, too."

"Oh, hmm, I didn't know he kept those old things after he moved." He shook his head and chuckled. "We used to work the same beat in the department years ago. Lots of good memories." He stared off in space for a few seconds before he pulled his attention back to the present and smiled at me.

"He moved?"

"Mm-hmm." My dad sat his glass of milk down and wiped his mouth. "After Chay reached the age of accountability, his dad took a job with another department. But there weren't many demi-angels in that area. So they moved back as soon as a position opened here." My dad stuffed his mouth with another Oreo and talked around it. "That's how I initially met Chay's dad. Uncle Rory and I teamed up with him to make sure the three of you were safe before you reached the age of accountability."

"Is that why everyone lives so close together? Because you teamed up to protect us when we were kids?"

"Yeah, and because demi-angels don't just draw physical strength from each other, but also mental strength and comfort. Haven't you felt a difference when you are with other demis?"

I tipped my head to the side and thought about his question. "Yeah. I didn't think about it until now, but yeah. I feel calmer, more at peace. I have a sense of belonging. Not to just the group, but to something bigger. It's hard to explain."

"Demis naturally gravitate to each other. It isn't a conscious decision—it just kinda happens. Our group found each other to keep you kids safe. Now you're able to fend for yourselves for the most part. It's time we step back and let you make your own decisions."

"What do you mean—our own decisions? You mean to take sides? About joining with Azazel?" I spun the Oreo like a top and glanced at him through my lashes.

He leaned back in his chair and stretched his legs out in front of him, crossing his ankles. "That would be one decision, yes." He tried to seem relaxed, but I could hear the tension in his voice and see it in the way his neck muscles bunched around his shirt collar.

"And the other is to remain a demi?"

"Yes." His tone was just a little too sharp and when he put his glass down, it hit the table just a little too hard. Most people wouldn't have noticed.

"But those are the only two? I mean, we can't renounce our status, can we, Dad? I can't walk away from being a demi?"

My eyes were trained on my dad, waiting for an answer and hoping it was one I wanted to hear. I gripped my cookie so hard that it broke and the pieces plopped into my milk. I ignored it.

"Not that I'm aware of. I've never heard of it happening before. The only way would be to join with Azazel and transfer your powers to him," he said, a grim look on his face.

"And that's what Lily did." Tears sprung to my eyes.

"I know."

I sniffed and wiped my tears away with the back of my hand. "Sorry. I don't know why I'm crying." I tried to laugh, but it came out as a sob. "I barely know her, and she doesn't even like me."

He sat up and leaned toward me in his seat. "It doesn't matter how well you

Michelle K. Pickett

knew her. She betrayed you. She betrayed the entire group. It's okay to feel sad and angry about that."

"Dad? If there were something going on, you'd tell me, right? I mean, if you knew someone was thinking about changing sides, or if they already have, you'd tell me? Because I don't want to find out like I did with Lily if someone I really care about decides to betray the team."

He tilted his head to the side and studied my face for a beat. His brows furrowed over his eyes. "Of course I'd tell you, Milayna. Is there something you should tell me?"

"Nope. Everything's good, Dad." I stood and grabbed my things before giving him a kiss on the cheek. "I gotta get ready."

"Oh right, the big game is tonight. Let's see," he scratched his eyebrow with his thumb, "we want the Cowboys to win, right?"

I rolled my eyes. "You make the same joke every year. Maybe if you'd stop, we'd actually win a game."

He made an overly innocent face. "I guess I jinxed you for another year."

"Thanks for the cookies, even if you did commit petty larceny by taking them. And make no mistake, Mom will press charges if she finds out."

"Yeah, yeah. When your mom notices they're gone, we'll just blame it on Ben." My dad grinned, and I laughed.

Chay picked me up at exactly five o'clock. The game didn't start until seven.

Chay held the car door open for me, and I slid in. "Why do you want to go so early?" I asked.

"My Uncle Stewart sets up an ice cream truck every year at the game. I help him. You don't have to help if you don't want to. I just couldn't—"

"I'll help."

"I'm sure there'll be a free milkshake in it for ya," he told me. He looked over and smiled.

"I'd do it even if there wasn't. I don't mind helping."

And you'll be there. Enough of a reason for me.

"I know you would. You're a nice person, Milayna." He shifted the car into drive and maneuvered through the streets of our subdivision.

"Oh, ah, thanks," I said, feeling my face warm. "You can be nice, too, when you try really hard."

He laughed and nodded his head. "Yeah. I've been told that before."

"I can believe it."

The ride to the school was short. It was only a few—silent—minutes later when Chay parked. We walked to the field and found his uncle's ice cream truck. "Hey, Uncle Stewart, what do you want me to do?" Chay called.

His uncle stuck his head out of the door and smiled. "Hiya, Chay. Hiya,

Milayna!"

"Hi, Uncle." I lifted my hand in a wave.

I dropped my things on the ground next to the truck's opening. "What can I do to help?"

"You're helping me? Well, ain't that sweet of ya!"

"Hello? Your nephew over here is helping, too." Chay waved his hand in his uncle's face.

"Yeah, but she's sweeter than you. C'mon, Milayna, I'll show you what needs doin'."

I smiled over my shoulder at Chay and followed Uncle Stewart inside the truck.

Uncle Stewart showed me how to mix the malt base and the ice cream base for the machines. Then I was given the extra hard job of putting out the toppings. I had a suspicion that he was giving me all the easy jobs. Chay was washing down the truck from ceiling to floor, making sure everything sparkled before it opened.

I was filling the cherry container when Chay grabbed my wrist. Two cherries dangled by their stems between my fingertips. He looked in my eyes as he guided my hand to his mouth. He ate the cherries one by one, his soft, full lips brushing against the tips of my fingers, eyes, more green than blue just then, locked on mine.

My wrist burned where he touched it. My eyes were transfixed on him, his mouth, his lips, his tongue. I parted my lips and tried to remember how to breathe normally. Time seemed to slow, and the blood in my veins turned to molten lava. As it made its way languidly through my body, it seared me, burned me from the inside out with an exquisite pain that only his touch could quench.

My heart screamed with pleasure when he reached around my waist and pulled me to him. "Oh," I gasped. I dropped the cherry stems on the floor and put my hand on his shoulder, stifling a moan at the definition I felt there.

"I just swept that floor," he murmured with a crooked grin.

I looked down at the floor. "Sorry, I'll—"

"Milayna." I looked up at him. His eyes darkened. His hand let go of my wrist and skimmed up my arm and around the back of my neck, gently nudging my head toward him. My lips parted, and I leaned into him. He dipped his head… and I screamed.

I dropped my hands and held my head. The pain was searing. I heard Chay's uncle run into the truck. He took one look at me and closed the doors and windows.

"She has visions?"

"Yes," Chay answered. His arms tightened around me. He sounded so far away, the sounds in my head drowning him out.

Football field. Concession stand. Orange rope.

"What do you see, Milayna?" Chay's voice.

109   *Michelle K. Pickett*

"A concession stand. An orange rope."

A woman wearing a blue apron. Picking up the rope. No, not a rope. An extension cord.

"It's an extension cord." My vision cleared, and I whirled around to the window and tried to unfasten the locks. "How do I open it?" I yelled. Chay reached over, unlatching the window, and I peered out. My gaze searched the growing crowd for the concession stand and the blue-aproned woman in my vision.

A force jerked me backward and slammed me against the back of the truck. I squeezed my eyes closed and watched the vision scroll through my consciousness.

Black rope. No, another extension cord. The wires are exposed. Water.

"She's going to electrocute herself! We have to find her." I ran to the door. "Go that way, and I'll go there. Blue apron and blonde hair in a black hairnet. She'll be behind a concession stand. Go! Go now!"

I turned when Chay grabbed my arm. "You can't go by yourself, Milayna."

I jerked free of his grasp. "This is what I'm supposed to do," I yelled. "This is why I am what I am! I can't stand by and let her get hurt... or worse." I jumped down from the truck and ran into the growing crowd before he could stop me.

"Show the stand. What does the concession stand look like? Show me something to help me find her!" I mumbled to myself, begging the vision to give me more information. There were so many people and it seemed like the crowd was growing by the second, swallowing me. Keeping me from my purpose.

I looked for the woman's concession stand, but I didn't have any distinguishing landmarks to use to help me find it. And there were so many little stands set up that it was a never-ending maze. It was the biggest game of the season next to homecoming. Little buildings and trailers filled the space, selling everything from sweets to foam fingers.

I ran between the vendors, looking left and right for a woman in a blue apron. I was out of breath, struggling to breathe from running and the thought of not finding the woman in time. My lungs burned, and my stomach clenched like someone was wringing it out like a wet dishrag. I doubled over and rested my hands on my knees.

She's picking up the cord.

I ran around a small cotton candy stand and came face-to-face with the woman, the orange extension cord in her hand.

"Hi," I panted. I motioned for her to wait a second while I caught my breath. My foot ground the end of the black cord into the dirt, filling the receptacle end with enough dirt to make it unusable. "I'm sorry. I'm so out of breath. I ran over here. My brother is crying for some cotton candy. Are you open?"

"No, sorry. I haven't gotten the machine hooked up yet. But if you come back in about ten minutes, I should have some ready."

"Oh, okay. No problem." With one final twist of my foot, I stepped away. The vision cleared, and the excruciating pain in my stomach eased.

"Darn it," I heard her say over my shoulder. "I need another cord," she yelled to someone in the small building.

I smiled. It felt good to help. The feeling was indescribable. I was still smiling when Chay found me and grabbed me by the arm, yanking me toward his uncle's ice cream truck. I tried to jerk my arm free, and he tightened his grip.

"Let go," I ground out through clenched teeth. "What the hell's the matter with you?" I jerked my arm again, but his grip was too tight. His fingers dug into me.

"I'm not letting go until you're safely in the ice cream truck. You seem to have a problem with running into crowds alone." Chay's tone was flat, emotionless.

When we reached the ice cream truck, his uncle took one look at us and warned, "Chay—"

Chay didn't stop. He jerked me into the truck and slammed the door. "Don't. Ever. Do. That. Again!" he yelled.

I flinched. "But I had—"

"I could have done it, Milayna, if you would have just waited instead of running into the crowd, putting yourself in danger!"

"Chay," I started in a calm voice, "you had to check the other side of the field. There's no way you would have gotten to her in time. I barely got there."

"You can't run off by yourself like that! I lost you in the crowd. Anything could have happened to you. Don't you get that?" He jammed his hand through his hair with a growl of frustration. "You have to be more careful," he said softly. Gripping my upper arms, he pulled me to him.

I sucked in a breath when he pulled me against him. My eyes didn't leave his. I was breathing in short, shallow gasps. Chay's breathing mimicked mine. Moving my arm, Chay let it slip from his grasp. I moved my hand next to his head and hesitated for a few beats, my hand trembling. But the urge to touch him was too strong to deny. My fingers moved slowly over his hair. When he didn't stop me, I grew bolder and delved my fingers in the dark, silky strands, letting them flow between them before sinking my hand in his hair again.

His hand skated down and rested on my lower back. He let go of my other arm and slid his fingers up, across my shoulder, along the side of my neck, to cup my jaw.

My heart was speeding in my chest. Adrenaline filled my bloodstream... and something else. Alarm? Longing? Arousal? I wasn't sure. I'd never had feelings that strong for another person before. All I knew was when he touched me, fire burned through me, and I had to remind myself to breathe. I moved my hand to the back of his neck, and I felt more than saw him lean into me. I closed my eyes and lost myself in him—

"Chay, your friends are here," his uncle yelled from outside.

"Damn it." He let go of me and brushed by so quickly that I stumbled forward. "Let's go."

Wait. What happened? He went from boiling to freezing in a second flat.

Michelle K. Pickett

I walked out of the truck and looked around. The group, minus Lily, was there.

"See ya, guys. We gotta gear up." Jake pointed between him and Steven.

"Good luck," we called.

"Yeah, we're gonna need it," Steven muttered.

Uncle Stewart made us all milkshakes, and we went to grab seats. Chay, Jeff, and Drew climbed to the top of the bleachers. Jen, Muriel, and I stared at them.

Jen shook her head. "We don't do heights."

"It's the only way to see everything." Chay rolled his eyes. He walked down the steps and narrowed his eyes at me.

"What?" I put my straw in my mouth and raised an eyebrow at him.

"You can walk up a flight of stairs and sit on a damn bleacher," he snapped.

"I could. But I'm not going to." He glared at me, and I whispered, "What if I have a vision up there? Huh? I don't imagine falling would help anything."

He sighed and looked at the bleachers. "Probably not. How about halfway?"

I looked at Jen, and she shrugged. "Okay, halfway." I brushed past him and plopped on a bench.

We sat behind two students with their dyed black hair, black clothes, and black fingernails. They both had black eyeliner thickly outlining their eyes.

If Azazel's demi-demons would just dress like that, it would be so much easier to pick them out.

A mother of one of the football players sat behind us. Every time a play was made or a referee called a foul—or whatever they have in football—she'd scream or swear.

For the first half of the game, Jen, Muriel, and I giggled at the people around us. The preppy kids to our right who were more worried about getting their clothes dirty from the bleachers than the actual game. The mother screaming behind us. Drew, Jeff, and Chay yelling at the players—like they could really hear them. They were all infinitely more interesting than the game.

"It's intermission?" I asked when the teams left the field and the marching band pranced onto the field.

"No." Chay rolled his eyes. "It's halftime."

"Same difference." I waved my hand in the air. "Let's go visit your uncle."

"You want another milkshake, don't you?" He grinned.

Jeff looked me up and down. "Where do you put them all? Most people would weigh three-hundred pounds if they ate like you." He was staring at my legs. Chay elbowed him hard in the side and glared at him. Jeff held out his hands in surrender. "Sorry, sorry." He laughed.

I looked between the two and decided I didn't have enough energy to try to decipher the teenage male brain. "I want to make sure he doesn't need any help." I lifted my chin and pursed my lips together, trying not to smile. "My need for a milkshake fix has nothing to do with my visit to the ice cream truck. Much."

"Sure." Chay gave me a half grin. "Anyway, he'll be fine. My cousins will be there helping."

"I want to check just to be sure." I stood and started down the bleachers, Chay following me.

"Don't you trust me?"

I looked at him over my shoulder and winked. "You're the one who told me I didn't know who I could trust, Chay."

He rolled his eyes and chuckled. "Whatever."

Chay was right. His cousins were there to help, but his uncle gave us ice cream cones for checking on him, so it was worth the trip. Jeff was right. If I hung around Uncle Stewart too much, I was going to gain fifty pounds—all in ice cream.

When halftime was over, Chay decided to spend the rest of the game teaching me the finer points of football. He pointed at the players running back and forth on the field. I tried to listen and learn all the different plays and rules he explained, but by the time the game was over, I didn't know any more about how the game was played than when I got there.

But I did know I liked it when Chay leaned his head down to mine, when I felt his breath skim across my cheek as he talked. I liked the warmth of his thigh against mine, and the smell of his cologne swirling in the air when he gestured with his hands and pointed at the players. Yeah, I learned a lot of things, none of which were related to football.

The best thing I learned was that I loved how it felt when he took my hand in his and laced our fingers together. He didn't ask, and it wasn't awkward. Chay just picked up my hand, looked at it for a beat, threaded his fingers with mine, and continued explaining the game.

Jen looked at us with a raised eyebrow. I shrugged a shoulder. I had no idea what the hell was going on in his head. But secretly, I relished the feeling that not only was he holding my hand, he also didn't care who saw.

We were all having a great time, talking, cheering, joking—and for once, our team was winning. It was wonderful until my stomach started to twist. I ignored it.

It's just all the junk food I ate. It'll go away. Please, let it go away.

But when my head started to pound and a fine sheen of sweat covered my face, I couldn't hide it any longer.

"What's wrong?" Chay whispered in my ear.

"Nothing." I bit the inside of my check. If Chay hadn't sensed I was going to have a vision, it must not be anything bad—so I lied.

Not now. Please, please, not now. I'll just wait it out. I'll be like a woman in labor and breathe through my pain. Except I don't know how to do that. Shit! My stomach is on fire.

"A vision?" His mouth was so close to my ear that I felt his lips moving.

"No," I whispered. It was the only thing I could manage to say in a somewhat normal voice. He still hadn't sensed my vision. He was just guessing. I could wait

Michelle K. Pickett

him out. A pain shot through me like an arrow. I bent forward and lay on the tops of my thighs, my arms wrapped around my knees.

"But it's coming." This time it wasn't really a question, and his blue-green lasers burned into my eyes.

"Mm-hmm." My breath came in small pants. It felt like someone was sitting on my chest. I couldn't get enough air, and my lungs burned.

"Let's get down before it hits. We'll go to the ice cream truck." He helped me up.

"What's wrong?" Jen asked. Muriel leaned forward in her seat and looked at me.

"Vision," Chay mouthed. "We're going to get some ice cream," he said aloud. The people around us must've thought I lived on ice cream.

We climbed down the bleachers and had just rounded the corner when I doubled over and threw up on the ground.

"I'm so sorry." My face burned from embarrassment.

"It's okay." Chay ran his hands over my hair and gently held it back. "C'mon, let's get to my uncle."

We barely made it to the ice cream truck when the vision hit me full force, knocking me backward into Chay.

Sulfur. Heat.

I could smell the sulfur. It was as if the source of the stench was in the truck. It burned the back of my throat and stung my nose.

"Could I have something to drink, please?"

"You can have whatever you want, darlin'," Chay's uncle told me. "Whatever you want."

"What do you see, Milayna?" Chay popped the tab on a Coke and held it out to me.

"Nothing really. I smell sulfur, and I feel heat. But I don't see anything yet." I took a big drink of Coke.

Football field. Lily. Hobgoblins.

"It's going to happen here. I see the field. The stands are empty. Lily." I spat her name; it was so repulsive to me.

"Okay, Evils, what else? Demi-demons?" Chay rubbed his thumb over the back of my hand.

I shook my head. "I don't... how do I tell?"

"There'd be a group, like ours."

"I don't know. It's gone. Can't you tell? Aren't you getting a sense that there's danger?" I looked at him and took another drink of my Coke. The carbonation bubbled back up, and I hiccupped. "Oops, excuse me." I let out a giggle and felt my face warm.

"Even your burps are cute," Chay said with a chuckle. "Anyway, mine aren't as reliable as yours. You're sure the stands were empty?"

"Yeah."

"So we stick around until everyone is gone and see what happens. Maybe you'll see more between now and then."

"Yeah, maybe." I didn't really want to see more. The visions drained me. If we were going to have a fight on our hands, I needed to conserve my energy.

It wasn't long after Chay and I went to the ice-cream truck that the game ended. The stands started to clear and students filed out of the parking lot. They honked their horns and shouted out of their car windows. South Bay had finally won a game.

While we waited for everyone to leave, we decorated our car windows with South Bay blue and gold window paint—declaring our victory. Not just any victory, either. It was a freakin' blowout. Or, at least according to Jeff and Chay. I just agreed with them like I knew what they were talking about.

"No. Way."

"Um, Yeah." I took the cap of the big marker and moved around Chay.

He grabbed me around the waist, picked me up, and deposited me away from his car. "No writing on my windows."

Putting my hands on my hips, I closed my eyes. I stood there so long that he asked me if something was wrong. "Yes," I answered, not opening my eyes. "I'm having a vision."

"What do you see?" He rubbed his hand up my arm.

I pushed him hard in the chest, catching him off guard. He stumbled backward, confused. I ran around the other side of his car and started writing on the back window.

"My vision was that you'd let me decorate your windows and you'd even like it." I said, laughing. He stalked toward me.

"Write fast, Milayna!" Jeff yelled.

"Muriel, help me!" I said. I was laughing so hard I was surprised anyone could understand me.

"Uh-huh. Nope and no way." Muriel shook her head.

Chay grabbed for me, and I darted around him to the other side of the car.

"You know you like it!" I said. "Just let me finish this side so it'll be balanced." I pointed the blue marker at him.

He shook his head, laughing, and waved his arm at his car. "Continue your coloring project."

When we'd finished writing our bragging rights on our car windows, we went back and sat on the bleachers.

The concession stands closed, and the people locked up and went home. The football players had changed out of their gear and left for one of the after-game parties. Steven and Jake hurried back outside to meet the group. Soon it was just Uncle Stewart and us.

The field was dark and ominous, eerie without the bright spotlights. We all sat in a row on the bottom bleacher. Drew's knee bounced up and down as we waited. Chay's uncle called our parents; they were arriving when the first

Michelle K. Pickett

hobgoblin showed up with a small puff of white smoke. The smell of sulfur filled the air as several more goblins popped out of their portal like little, red hand grenades.

They were in their mischief mode. Running back and forth on the field, screeching and laughing in their banshee-like voices.

It was only minutes later when Lily showed up followed by a group of teens I'd seen around school.

"Chay," she purred.

"Lily."

"I see the gang's all here," Lily said with a sniff. "I'm surprised your girlfriend let you fight this time."

"I don't have a girlfriend."

I rolled my eyes.

What an ass. He nearly kissed me twice and held my hand during most of the football game.

"Who are your new friends?" Drew asked from the bleachers; his knee still bounced up and down. I didn't know if it was nervous energy or if he was scared. Either way, the knee bobbing got on my nerves.

I was so fed up with the whole thing already. The visions zapped my energy. I could have laid down in the middle of the football field and taken a nap... while the fight was going on, if I wasn't so scared. That was the only thing keeping me on my feet.

"Oh, you know. Some family from down south."

"Demi-demons," Shayla whispered to me.

I swatted her away. "I know."

"Well, I suppose we should get on with things." Jeff kicked his toe in the sandy ground. A cloud of dust billowed around us. "Let's see. You're gonna ask us to side with Azazel and turn Milayna over to you. We're gonna say no. You're gonna get mad, your friends are going to get mad, and the fat hobgoblins over there are going to get mad. That's gonna make us mad, and we'll all end up fighting in the end. So we might as well just get on with the fight now and save our breath." He walked to stand in front of Lily. "No sense screamin' and yel—"

Lily round-kicked him in the face. He spat out a mouthful of blood and smiled, his teeth stained pink. "Fighting it is then. You know, Lily, I never did like you much. It doesn't surprise me that you turned. You're just that big of a bitch."

Lily screamed and threw a punch at Jeff's face, but he easily deflected it. "I really don't like hitting girls, even if they are Azazel's flunkies, but if you keep throwing punches, I will defend myself."

Lily threw a kick aimed for Jeff's crotch. He caught her foot in midair, twisting it around until she face-planted in the dirt. "I told you. Stop while you're ahead. Or at least fight another girl. After you turned traitor on the group, I'm not above smacking you around a little."

"Bite me." Lily pushed off the ground and wiped the dirt from her face with the back of her hand.

"Oh, for goodness sake," I said, shaking out my arms and rolling my shoulders, "if she wants to fight, let her fight." I took a fighting stance. "C'mon, this is what you're here for right? To have another go at me? You're jealous—"

She swung, and I blocked the blow easily. "I'm not jealous of you."

I made a quick jab. I knew I connected with her face when the familiar pain of a successful hit spread through my hand. She glared at me and spat a wad of mucus next to my foot. I made the mistake of looking at that grossness and not watching Lily. She got a fairly good hit in. I flicked my thumb over my lip to wipe away the trickle of blood.

"Oh, Lily, yes you are jealous." I feigned a right and landed a left. "You're afraid Chay likes me a little too much. I've seen the way you look at him. Looks like yours only mean one thing—you've got it bad, don'tcha?"

Lily screamed and landed a nice roundhouse to the side of my head. I stumbled, taking a second to shake it off. She came at me with a jab to the abdomen. I blocked it with a grunt.

I swept her feet out from under her. She fell on the ground. One knee in her back, my head down as I tried to catch my breath, I panted when I spoke, "All those months of secretly wanting him and he never noticed you. Now the new girl is hanging around, and you're jealous." I stood and kicked the dirt wet with her mucus at her. "You know what? You should be jealous."

Lily stood and stepped to the side. I mimicked her movement. My gaze stayed locked on her. We circled each other like a pair of those wind-up ballerinas in a cheap jewelry box. I waited for her tell. I knew she'd make her move soon. I just had to wait her out. Out of my peripheral vision, I saw my group lined up in front of the group that came with Lily. Yeah, they had my back.

"He'd never touch you," she ground out between clenched teeth.

"Oh, but you're wrong." I pouted. "Poor Lily. He has touched me, and now that you're out of the picture for good, I'm gonna get everything you wanted."

She started to circle faster. Her eyes darted from my eyes to my side and back again.

Yeah. Go for it.

She screamed and threw a kick at my right side. I sidestepped, but I still caught some of the impact. It was enough to make me eat dirt. I rolled and scissored my legs, knocking her legs out from under her. She fell next to me with a grunt. We recovered and jumped to our feet almost simultaneously. She threw a jab. I blocked it just before I made contact with a palm-heel strike to the head, knocking her on her ass, dazed.

"Milayna, if you keep knocking that poor thing on the head, you're gonna give her permanent brain damage," my dad called as he and Chay's dad walked toward us from the parking lot.

"Dad…" I threw my arms out at my sides before letting them drop and smack against my thighs. "She doesn't need a brain to work for Azazel."

117 *Michelle K. Pickett*

He shrugged. "True."

"Damn, girl. What are you, a black belt?" Jeff looked at me with wide eyes.

"Brown." I smiled at Jeff just as a flash of blinding white light lit up the football field. I shielded my eyes with my hand. "What was that?"

"Just Azazel having a little temper tantrum, that's all. We might have a demon or two show up," Chay's dad said behind me. I glanced at him over my shoulder. His hands fisted at his sides.

"Great. I can't wait." Goose bumps broke out across my skin, and I shivered.

He looked at me and smiled. "No worries."

"Well, since I'm new at this stuff, what do we do now? Do we fight? Do we run?" I looked at the group of teenagers that arrived with Lily.

One burly boy with fists the size of Christmas hams gawked at me and smiled. "We fight until you give up and join us. Azazel needs you."

"Then I guess it's going to be a long fight." I opened my mouth to say something else, but the ham-hand guy punched me. If Chay hadn't knocked into him, I'd have been laid out next to Lily in the dirt.

Oh, is this over yet? Can we just agree to disagree and go home? I want to curl up in bed and forget all about this. I already hurt. I'm such a baby.

That one hit was all it took to start things, and for a second, I froze. It wasn't at all like the small tiff I had with Lily. Nope. They didn't fight one at a time. A tangle of arms and legs kicking and punching covered the football field. The hobgoblins ran with glee through the maelstrom, cheering the demi-demons on.

Oh crap. I'm so not ready for this shit. Remember my training. Empty my mind. My body knows the moves. Let it take over. Don't overthink. React. Protect. And get the hell out.

My brain stopped working. There was too much. Where did I go? Which person did I fight? Who did I help first? There were too many thoughts... too many bodies tumbling over each other... blood, grunts, the sound of flesh hitting flesh. I swallowed down the bile that rose in my throat.

Get it together. Your group needs you. You can't stand here like a wuss. Do your job.

And then she walked up to me with her pretty, blonde hair and a small smile. I couldn't believe someone who looked as sweet and innocent as she did could be one of Azazel's army... until she launched a round-kick to my head that sent me to my knees. My ears rang from the hit and the side of my face throbbed. I decided she didn't look so sweet and innocent, after all. Anger bubbled from a place deep in my belly. I shook my head once and forced myself to move. Swinging my arms, I jumped to my feet.

Once I was standing, I didn't waste precious seconds returning her kick. She fell back a few steps before advancing again. I deflected two of her strikes before she landed another across my jaw. I was all at once thankful for the years my parents forced me to take Tae Kwon Do and every other type of martial art instead of the piano lessons I wanted to take.

The next time she tried to kick me, I was ready. I grabbed her foot and yanked her forward, knocking her off-balance. As she fell toward me, I landed an uppercut to her nose, knocking her backward. Blood spurted, and she screamed in pain. I winced. I really disliked physical violence, but I wasn't going to stand on principle and get my butt handed to me either.

I looked to my side and saw Jen had her fight under control. Shayla seemed fine too. I turned in a circle, looking for Muriel. I couldn't find her and worried she'd gotten separated from the group and needed help, but I couldn't go look for her.

I saw my dad get hit so hard that he fell to the ground. A huge guy bent over and hitched him up by the arms, holding him for a second guy—who was built like a model for a bodybuilder magazine—to land another hit.

Dad! Two against one. I'm coming. Hold on... hold on.

Anger shot through my veins, and I sprinted toward him. Heat ran through my body. I could feel the map of my veins as my fiery blood shot through them. But a weight sat in the middle of my chest, heavy and painful. As hot as my blood was shooting through my veins at an inhuman rate, the rock in my chest was just as cold, freezing the area around it, constricting the tissue, hardening the muscle it touched. But it was there, from my ice-cold center, that I tapped into the rage that zinged down each nerve, turned my sight red, and cleared my head of everything but the fight and protecting my group—my family.

My dad's attacker's back was to me. When I kicked my foot up between his legs, he crumpled to the ground.

Doesn't matter how big they are. A swift kick to the frank and beans does the trick every time.

"I didn't think you'd be the one saving me," my dad said with a wry smile. His lip was already swelling, blood trickling from the side of his mouth and a cut high on his cheekbone. The demi-demon still held him from behind. "This is gonna hurt," my dad muttered before he bent his head forward and threw a wicked head-butt into the guy behind him.

"Think of it as teamwork." I threw a jab at the guy still holding my dad and his hold loosened enough that he slipped from his arms.

"Milayna!" my dad yelled, his eyes wide.

A pair of strong arms wrapped around me from behind and lifted me off the ground. Helpless, I watched as the two much younger demi-demons regained their strength and attacked my dad, throwing punches and kicks so quickly and often that my dad wasn't able to keep up. His knees crumpled beneath him, and he collapsed against the sandy ground.

I struggled against the person that held me. I kicked and screamed, but my arms were pinned and my feet didn't connect. I tried to head-butt him, but he anticipated the move and kept his head tilted and out of reach.

I looked around the football field. Everyone was in the middle of their own fight. I was alone with the kid, locked in his iron grip. He dragged me to the

Michelle K. Pickett

middle of the field and tossed me down on the grass. The hobgoblins ran over, jumping up and down on their short, stumpy legs.

"Milayna," they called. "Finally, you've come to play."

I looked around, frantic. "Chay!"

"He's busy. It's just you and me." The gigantic boy smiled and rolled his shoulders.

I screamed again. But no one could hear me over the noise of the fight.

"Come with us, Milayna, and all this ends. Your friends walk away and live normal lives. We'll let your parents live in peace, and Azazel will treat you like a princess. You just have to say the word."

"Go to Hell," I whispered.

"You first."

The earth started to shake, and the ground vibrated under me. I'd have thought it was an earthquake if we'd lived in California, but we didn't get many earthquakes in Michigan. The ground swelled beneath me, and I tried to pull myself to my feet. The boy grabbed me by the hair and kneed me in the stomach. The breath rushed out of my lungs, and I fell to the ground on my hands and knees, coughing and gasping for air.

What the hell is going on? Doesn't anyone else see this?

The earth moved, dipping and rising, tossing me to and fro like the tilt-a-whirl ride at a carnival. I tried to steady myself, but the rippling movement grew larger and more intense until the earth caved in, like a sinkhole. A yellow light shone from the bottom of the crater, piercing through the darkness.

I screamed and tried to scramble away. The boy tried to kick me back toward the hole, but I grabbed his foot and yanked as hard as I could. He lost his footing on the unsteady ground and slid down into the gulley, disappearing into the hole. I cringed at the sound of his screams.

I pushed up from the ground and crawled on all fours away from the hole. The ground was still rippling, like clothes hanging in the wind, and I slid backward. Desperate, I grabbed for whatever I could get my fingers around. I hitched my arm in a deep crevice. My arm stretched down and dug into the packed dirt. I held on, hoping the dirt wouldn't give way and send me sliding down the side of the bowl-like depression and into the glowing hole at the bottom—and straight to Hell.

I just have to hold on until someone can help me. Chay or Drew… somebody.

Then I saw the shadow, and I knew my time had run out. I wasn't sure if Chay or anyone else could get to me in time. I'd seen the glowing yellow light before. I'd smelled the sulfur. I knew what the shadow was before I looked over my shoulder. I'd seen them all in a vision. The woman in the parking garage. The yellow light, the sickening smell of sulfur, the gray-faced demon grabbing her. I remembered it all.

"Chay!"

Milayna   120

"Milayna," it hissed. "It's time to come home."

I looked over my shoulder and saw one long, gray arm clear the pit's opening. It reached for me. Kicking, I flung my legs out of reach. I tried to hitch my legs up far enough to climb out of the large dip in the earth, but my feet couldn't find enough leverage to push me up and over the side of the gulley. If the ground I held gave way, I'd have tumbled right into the hole.

My heart beat furiously in my chest and my breathing came in large, deep gasps. My vision was wavy, like it was rippling with the earth. Fear coated me in a sheen of sweat, stained with the soil I was rolling in. I reacted to the situation more than thought of what was happening. There wasn't time to digest what was happening. Fear and the need to survive. That was what drove me.

I used my arms to pull myself to the top of the growing crater. Almost perfectly round, its concave sides made it nearly impossible to hoist myself over the rim. My muscles burned from the effort. I was tired from my visions earlier in the day and from the fight. I struggled to grab on to something, but the earth crumbled and I slipped down the side toward the hole, the demon's arm getting closer and closer. Its fingernails cut along my ankle; I screamed when they drew blood.

Grunting and straining, I pulled myself up again, out of the demon's reach. I was just throwing my arm over the lip of the opening when a shoe nudged my arm. I looked up, eyes wide and panic burning through me. "I think you're going the wrong way, Milayna." An ugly smirk spread over Lily's face. "Haven't you heard? In near-death situations, you're supposed to follow the light." She waved her hand at the yellow, glowing hole.

"Screw you," I bit out between gasps.

"Big talk considering your position. Here, let me help you." Lily squatted next to me. She put a hand on my arm and bit her bottom lip. "Hmm, nope, can't do it. See ya, Milayna."

She pushed my arm off the ledge. It didn't take much effort, really. My muscles were burning. My body was tired, at its limit. I held on to the rim of the crater by my fingers. They screamed in pain. I closed my eyes and tried to muster enough energy to pull myself up one more time, but it wasn't there. I was drained. Done.

And that was when the block of ice in my chest exploded. The heavy heat of Hell melted the ice and heated it to the point it burned me from the inside out as it flowed through my veins.

The tips of Hell's flames called to me, singeing me with the sting of failure. The searing sizzle of fear. The twisting pain of the unknown, of what would happen when I let go. I felt a warm tear burn down my face. What was at the other end of that hole? It looked innocent enough: just a hole with a warm, yellow light shining from it. But... the smell, the screams of the damned, and the unbearable heat. It was far from innocent, and I didn't want to take the slide to the bottom.

I'm so scared. Oh shit, my fingers are slipping. No, no, no. Not yet. I'm not ready. Not yet.

Michelle K. Pickett

Small pieces of earth broke under my fingers and fell to my face. I tried to adjust my hands to get a better grip, but I slipped closer to the edge. More earth rained down on me. I turned my face from it. I heard scuffling and grunting. Someone's head peeked over just as my fingers gave way and I started sliding down the side of the crater.

"Grab my arm, Milayna," I heard someone shout above me. They lay on their stomach and reached down to me. Two things happened simultaneously—I grabbed the arm reaching out to me, and a demonic hand wrapped around my ankle. I winced when its unnaturally hot flesh touched my skin. The person above me tried to pull me up. The demon below jerked me down. It became a very deadly game of tug-o-war, and I was the rope.

I gritted my teeth against the pain of being pulled in two directions, hanging in midair for what seemed like an eternity. I didn't know how the person above me was going to pull me to safety. I knew the demon wasn't going to let go, and no one could climb down into the crater to help me or they'd slide into the pit. For a brief second, I thought about letting go before the person helping me was pulled down with me. I couldn't damn someone to eternity in Hell because they were trying to help me. I had to let go. I was just about to release my grip when I saw a body hurl over the mound of dirt and into the hole, taking the demon down with it. It lost its grip on my leg, and I slammed against the side of the crater with a grunt.

The dirt started to cave in quickly. I kicked my feet, freeing them from the falling dirt. I used the person above me as leverage to climb up the curved and crumbling sides. When I finally reached the top of the mound, I looked up into the face of my rescuer. I expected to see Chay or my dad.

"Uncle Stewart?"

"Yeah, I figured since you helped me so much with the ice cream truck today, the least I could do was give you a hand in return." He helped me up and away from the earth moving to fill in the remaining gap. The pudgy hobgoblins jumped into the hole just before it was swallowed up by the last of the dirt

I turned to Uncle Stewart and buried my head in his soft, red flannel shirt. "It's okay, Milayna, it's okay," he soothed, patting my back awkwardly. "Are you hurt?"

"No. Well, not really."

"Well, your jaw looks a little bruised, and I imagine your ankle is burning up right 'bout now. Those suckers have hellfire for skin, ya know. Well, yeah, I guess you do know, don't ya?"

"Is it over?" My words were muffled against his chest. He was warm and solid, and I felt so cold. So, so cold.

"Yeah. All but a few stragglers. Your group's none the worse for wear. Those kids can hold their own in a fight."

I pulled back to look at him. "My dad?" I fisted my hands in the front of his shirt.

"Fine, fine. A little dazed, but nothing serious."

"Thank you. I..." I bit my lip, new tears forming. My throat was so tight with them that it was hard to swallow.

"Sure thing. Come by the shop tomorrow, and we'll have ourselves a celebratory milkshake." He smiled down at me.

I felt a hand on the small of my back and turned. Chay's eyes searched mine. "Milayna," he murmured.

I turned from his uncle and walked into Chay's arms. He was sweaty and there was blood on his face and shirt, but I didn't care. I stood on my tiptoes so I could wrap my arms around his neck. He wound his hand through my hair and held my head against him while I cried. He didn't say anything—there really wasn't anything to say. He just held me until my tears faded. And there wasn't anywhere else I wanted to be. He didn't make me feel weak for crying. He just held me and let me soak up his comfort. It was a part of himself he didn't offer often, and I was overwhelmed he gave it to me. I lifted my head from his shoulder and looked at him.

"You're hurt!" I reached out to touch a cut just under his eye, but curled my fingers and let my hand fall away, still unsure of where the lines of our relationship were drawn. His gaze held mine.

"Nah, just scratches mostly. The other guy looks much worse." His fingers moved in circular motions over the small of my back.

"That wouldn't have been the guy that went crashing down on the demon's head, would it?"

"I wouldn't know anything about that." The corner of his lips tipped up.

Michelle K. Pickett

15
The Date

I sat at the kitchen table with my parents the next morning. It was Saturday, our weekly family breakfast. My dad made blueberry waffles, or at least, he tried to. All he actually made was a mess, so I took pity on him—and us because we had to eat them—and made the waffles.

"The waffles are good, Milayna." He winked at me. Or tried to. His eyes were swollen and looked like a patchwork quilt of blues and purples.

"Yeah, thanks for the help, Dad." I rolled my eyes and squirted a pool of syrup on my plate.

"I'll make it up to ya. I'll clean up," he said around a bite of waffles.

I let my shoulders sag. "Thank you." I sighed. "I have a ton of homework."

"May I have more syrup?" Ben asked and pointed at the bottle with sticky fingers. "Please?"

"That was a very nice way to ask, Ben." My mom smiled at him. "But no."

"What? Why? Milayna has a lot!" He pointed at my plate and glared at me like I'd stolen the world's last syrup stash.

"Milayna doesn't get it in her hair."

"Yeah, frog freckle." I smiled and stuck my tongue out at him.

"Mom! Milayna stuck out her tongue!" Ben pointed at me with his fork. A piece of waffle plopped on the floor.

"Ben, let's try to keep the food on the table." My mom sighed. "Milayna, keep your tongue in your mouth."

My dad spotted something on the television in the other room and laughed out loud. Jogging into the living room, he turned the sound up.

I looked up when I heard the broadcaster mention something about vandals at the high school, giggling at what I saw. It was a photograph of the high school's football field.

"The newscaster said the authorities think it was students from the other team in retaliation of our win." My dad laughed.

I smiled and looked over at my mom. My breath hitched in my throat. She had a strange expression on her face that I couldn't read. "What's wrong, Mom?"

"I can't believe you two were in that mess. It's a little... frightening." My mom twisted the collar of her shirt around her finger. Her voice came out in barely a whisper and sounded small.

I looked back at the television and tried to view the picture from my mom's perspective. There were large ripples in the earth. Patches of sod had been burned away, leaving black trails in the otherwise green field. The scoreboard lights had been shattered and glass covered the ground. I hadn't noticed how bad it was the night before. I was so relieved to get away from it that I didn't pay attention to the damage Azazel's team had done.

"It looks worse than it was," my dad told my mom, patting her hand before taking it in his.

She jerked her hand away. "Don't patronize me. It looks bad. I'm sure it looked worse last night with demons crawling all over it. Look at you! Your face looks like it went through a meat grinder," she yelled, making my little brother cry. She stood so quickly that the table rocked and her chair fell over backward.

"But we're all okay, Mom." I ran my fingers through Ben's hair and squirted half the bottle of syrup on his plate to calm him.

"Yeah, this time." She stalked from the room. I watched her leave and wondered what things looked like through her eyes.

That afternoon, I sat on my bed, reading my chemistry book and hating every second of it. My cell phone was lying next to me. Every few minutes, I'd glare at it, waiting for it to deliver a text from Muriel. She hadn't texted me back after I'd texted her earlier in the day. Friday at the football game was the last time I'd seen her. I didn't see her after the fight. In fact, I didn't remember seeing her during the fight, either. She got home okay because her car was parked in her driveway when my dad and I got home. Besides, if she hadn't, my Uncle Rory would have called looking for her.

My cell vibrated. "Finally, Muriel, geez," I grumbled.

I grabbed my phone and clicked to read the text, but it wasn't from Muriel. When I saw who it was from, I just stared.

Chay: Wanna get out of the house for a while?

Michelle K. Pickett

Me: Maybe. Where?

Chay: I dunno. We'll figure something out.

Tapping my fingers on my bottom lip, I couldn't help the smile that spread across my face. I tried to warn myself that it probably had something to do with the group, a meeting or something, but part of me hoped it was more than that. I took a deep breath to calm my nerves.

I typed quickly before I lost my nerve. The thought of spending time alone with Chay was both exciting and unnerving at the same time.

Me: Kay. When?

Chay: I'll be there in five.

Me: Make it ten.

Chay: Fine.

I jumped off the bed and ran to the top of the stairs.

"Mom? Is it okay if I go out with a friend?" I yelled.

"Who?"

Geez, I was hoping you wouldn't ask that. "Chay," I said as normal as I could. Smooth. No big deal.

She didn't answer. Seconds later, she materialized at the bottom of the stairs. "Is there something you want to tell me?" She smiled and quirked an eyebrow.

And the third degree begins.

"We're just friends." I could feel my cheeks heat.

"Okay. Where are you going?"

"I don't know. He didn't say. Can I go?"

"Have fun," she said and walked away. I tried to hold in a squeal as I turned with a jump and ran to my bedroom to change.

Ten minutes… hair, a little makeup, crap! What do I wear? Where are we going? I can't do this. I think I'm getting an ulcer.

After empting my closet, I finally decided on my favorite pair of distressed jeans and a lavender cashmere sweater that fell off one shoulder. I put on a little makeup, enough to highlight, but not to look like I was trying too hard. Exactly ten minutes later, the doorbell rang. I could hear my dad and Chay talking in the foyer. I finished buckling my boot, grabbed my cell phone, and ran out of my bedroom door. I had to force myself not to skip down the hallway.

What is the matter with you? He just wants… what does he want? Do I care? Nope.

"Hey." I made sure I took the stairs one at a time.

"Hi."

I was so nervous I had to concentrate on my breathing so I didn't hyperventilate or hold my breath and pass out. Either one would've been wicked embarrassing. It was bad enough I'd already puked in front of the guy. Twice.

Chay seemed completely at ease, as always. He stood with his thumbs hooked through his belt loops, looking amazing. His jeans rode low on his hips, and his blue T-shirt was snug in all the right places.

Stepping down from the last stair, I looked at Chay. I waited for him to clue me in on what we were doing.

"Well." My dad leaned back on his heels before rocking forward on his toes. "You two have a nice afternoon." Whistling, he walked away.

"Ready?" Chay asked.

"That depends." I looked up at him.

He flipped his keys around a finger. They jangled when they hit his palm. "On?"

"What we're doing," I answered.

He chuckled. "How about a movie? Can you handle that?"

Oh, crap, I don't know if I can or not. A dark theater? Close seating? Sounds like torture.

"I think so. What's the occasion?"

"A break from chemistry homework. I've had enough studying for one day."

Oh. Of course, a break from studying.

"Sounds good." I shrugged a shoulder.

He opened the front door for me, and I walked by him, holding in a groan. He smelled too good to be legal. I knew sitting next to him in his small car was going to be torture. At least the theater would have popcorn to mask his gorgeous smell.

"So, which movie do you want to see?" He slid the key into the ignition and started the car.

"This was your idea. I thought you had a plan." I glanced at him as I clicked my seatbelt in place.

"Nope. Just wanted to get out of the house." He shrugged a shoulder. "Besides," he continued, "if I keep you out all day, you won't have time to finish."

I angled my body toward him. "You don't want me to finish my homework? That's why you called and asked me to go with you?"

"Partly." He grinned. I wasn't sure what there was to grin about.

"Why?" He was so confusing. It was almost exhausting being around him. My heart did funny things, it was hard to breathe, and my head spun trying to keep up with the asinine remarks he made.

"Because I thought you were going to text me to work on our chem homework together. When you didn't, I decided to take things into my own hands and remove homework from the equation."

"Why?"

He sighed and jammed his fingers through his hair. "Because I wanted you to text me, and you didn't."

He wanted me to text him?

"You told me to text you if I got stuck on something. I was doing fine."

"Exactly."

"Exactly? You know, I have absolutely no idea what you're talking about."

127

Michelle K. Pickett

We pulled in to the movie theater, and he parked the car. Turning in the seat, he looked at me. "I wanted you to text me. I didn't care about chemistry."

"Oh." I looked out of the window at the people walking through the parking lot. "You know, last I checked, cell phones worked both ways." I shrugged a shoulder. My sweater slipped over it and his eyes followed, lingering there for a few beats before moving to my gaze. I gave him a quick smile. "Just sayin'." I opened the car door and slipped out.

He seemed to mull over my answer, a grin on his face. "Well... then I guess I should have texted sooner."

I bent down and stuck my head in the car. "Yes. You should've. Now, let's go. I want some popcorn."

He got out of the car with a laugh, and I bit my bottom lip to keep a stupid grin off my face.

We picked a horror movie. A lovey-dovey chick flick didn't seem his thing, and I wasn't into the military, bomb-throwing action movies that were playing. So we settled on a horror film we both wanted to see.

"You really don't need to pay for all the popcorn and Cokes," I said, standing at the concession stand with him. The smell of buttery popcorn filled the building. Buzzers and alarms sounded in the arcade next to the concession stand and made it hard to talk without yelling. "We can split the cost."

"It's good. I have it," he said close to my ear. His breath skated down my neck, sending ripples of warmth through me. He bought our popcorn and Cokes from the concession counter. "Butter?" He looked at me.

"Stupid question. Popcorn has to have butter. I think it's a law somewhere," I said, guiding him to the butter station.

"A law, huh?" He watched me put the popcorn bucket under the butter spray. "I hate the butter pumps. It gets the top corn all buttery, but when you get to the bottom, it's like eating paper," he muttered.

"I'll show you how to get the butter down to the bottom. But if you tell anyone my secret, I'll have to kill ya."

He laughed. "Okay, show me your skills."

I grabbed a straw next to the fountain drink dispenser. I stuck one end on the nozzle of the butter dispenser and the other down in the popcorn tub. "Now push the plunger."

He pumped the butter, and I moved the tub of popcorn around, shifting the straw up and down in the tub.

"Okay." I shook the popcorn around to get it all gooey with hot, melted butter.

"Pretty slick trick." He winked at me and grinned.

"Shh." I put my finger over his lips. "Our little secret." I watched his eyes darken and let my finger slip away with a shy smile.

I'm so totally flirting! I'm not good at flirting. Am I doing it right? I wish I could text Muriel and ask what to do! Oh, wow.

Chay wrapped his arm around the bucket and carried it and his pop in one arm. He held my hand with the other, and he didn't let go until we were in the theater trying to get situated in our seats. As soon as we sat our things down, he threaded his fingers with mine again.

He squeezed my hand gently. Something bloomed in my chest, releasing hundreds of colorful butterflies. Their wings fluttered against my ribs, tickling my insides in a weird, but oddly pleasant way.

We sat silently watching the previews play. His thumb gently grazed across the top of my hand. He held my hand throughout the movie, his thumb caressing my skin, leaving a trail of fire.

Halfway through, I dug deep for all my flirting prowess—which was virtually none—and lifted the armrest between us. I scooted close to him and laid my head on his arm. He tensed and I bit my lip, waiting for his reaction, but he settled back into his seat and wrapped his arm around me, pulling me close.

I was sure that was what heaven felt like, because nothing had felt so good or so right in my life before.

"Did you like it?" Chay asked when we walked out of the theater.

"Yeah. It was scary." Truthfully, I couldn't remember much about it.

"You jumped a few times." He chuckled.

"No, I didn't."

"Liar."

"Okay, maybe a couple times," I admitted with a grin. "You jumped once too." I pointed at him and let my finger run down his chest, wrapping his T-shirt around it.

He laughed and put the back of my hand to his lips. I sucked in a breath when his lips caressed my skin. His eyes found mine and he smiled, unlocking the car door and opening it for me.

The night was rainy. Black clouds blotted out the moon, and fat drops of cold water pelted the windshield of Chay's car. The raindrops covered the glass like a film, hiding us inside. I shivered.

"So." Chay slid in the car next to me. "How 'bout that chemistry homework?"

"What about it?"

"Tomorrow? We could work on it together. I could come over or..." He looked at me with a lopsided grin.

"Sounds good." A finger of anticipation ran up my spine.

He blew out a breath like he'd been holding it, waiting for my answer. "Good. It's a date, then." He tilted his head to the side. "Milayna..."

"Hmm?" I answered with a smile, and my insides swirled. "Oh!"

"A vision." He cupped the side of my face in his hand.

My stomach twisted in a knot.

Oh, not now, please not now.

My head started to pound, and I put my fingers to my temples. I could feel my heartbeat thudding against them.

Go away!

129　　Michelle K. Pickett

My vision blurred. With a sigh, I gave in and let the vision take over my senses. I closed my eyes and waited for the images to scroll through my consciousness.

Cherries.

Cherries? That was random.

A hand. Big… a man's hand. It's digging. No, no, it's scooping something.

My eyes flew open, and I grabbed Chay's arm. "How far is your uncle's ice cream shop from here?"

"Around the corner a little way. Why?" His mouth dipped in a frown.

"Go." When he didn't move, I yelled, "Go now!"

"What did you see, Milayna?" Chay asked, alarm in his voice.

"I don't know. I don't even know if it's your uncle, but I saw cherries and ice cream."

A piercing wail. A constant screaming. Not a person. An alarm.

And then I smelled it. Smoke.

"Ooh, hurry, Chay." I squeezed my eyes tighter, trying to see the vision and hear the sounds more clearly.

It's hot. Flames lick the walls. There's a sign. Uncle's Ice Cream.

"Drive faster!" I grabbed my cell phone and dialed 911. "What's the shop's address? Chay! What's the address?"

"I don't know. It's on West Chestnut, that's all I know."

"911. What's your emergency?"

"There's a fire at Uncle's Ice Cream Shop on West Chestnut." I pinched my eyes closed with my forefinger and thumb to ease the pounding behind them.

"Is there anyone in the building?"

"I think… I think so."

Chay's tires screeched as we took a corner too quick. I had to hold on to the dash to steady myself. My phone dropped between the center console and the seat. I wiggled my hand between the seat and the console, but the phone was wedged in place.

"Are you sure?" Chay asked.

"Yes, I saw the sign." I was thrown back and forth as Chay weaved in and out of traffic. His car fishtailed several times, hydroplaning across the wet pavement. Cars honked as we flew by.

"I need your phone."

"In my jacket pocket."

I leaned over the center console and fished his phone out of his pocket. Scrolling through his phonebook, I found the number to his uncle's shop. I pressed call and waited for someone to answer, biting my nails.

"Is he there?"

"He's not answering."

A searing pain exploded in my head. My lungs burned when I tried to breathe. I coughed and gagged, my hands at my throat.

Milayna

A body on the floor. Flames surrounding it.

"You have to hurry," I choked out between coughing fits.

I heard sirens. Climbing up on the seat to look out of the back window, I half expected to see a police car. There was nothing. I turned around and saw the large truck barreling toward us.

"The firefighters beat us," Chay said with a relieved sigh.

Water. Smoke billowing. A man lying on the floor.

"It hasn't changed," I whispered.

"Damn it." He smacked the wheel with the heel of his hand.

The tires squealed when he took the turn into the parking lot too fast. The firefighters were already working. One tried to stop us from getting out of the car.

Chay strained against the firefighter blocking him. "My uncle's in there!" Chay yelled. His face was red and his neck corded with muscle as he tried to push his way to his uncle.

"You're sure?"

"Yes. He's behind the counter!" I looked at the flames reaching out of the windows of the shop like they were waving at us, taunting us.

Please get to him in time. Hurry.

"We've got at least one person inside," the firefighter shouted.

We watched as they broke through the door, and two men disappeared into the smoke-filled building. An ambulance turned into the parking lot just as the firemen pulled Chay's uncle through the door.

The EMTs hauled a gurney out of the back of the van and loaded Uncle Stewart on top of it. They strapped him down, put an oxygen mask over his mouth and nose, and inserted an IV in his arm.

I stood next to Chay, the cold rain pelting down on us. Absently, I rubbed my chest with my hand. I didn't notice until he mentioned it.

"What's wrong? Why are you rubbing your chest?"

I blinked. I hadn't noticed until he mentioned it. "It hurts to breathe. It burns." My eyes watered, and I sniffed as I watched the EMTs work on Uncle.

Both of Chay's hands were on top of his head. His dark hair was spiky from the rain. His skin was cold and drained of color. Only his eyes were sharp, watching everything. His gaze never left his uncle and the paramedic squeezing air down to his lungs. "Has the vision changed?"

"Yes." I didn't say anything else, and Chay didn't ask for details. I was thankful because although the vision had changed, I wasn't sure if it was for the better.

131 *Michelle K. Pickett*

16

Apologies

MY LUNGS ARE BURNING. **A** HOSPITAL BED. **B**EEPING. **D**OC-tors and nurses work on Uncle. Heart monitor. My heart skips a beat, a stab of pain sizzles through my chest, stealing my breath.

I tried to keep my eyes open as the images scrolled through my mind, not wanting Chay to know I was seeing them. I didn't know what they meant, and I didn't want to upset him more than he already was.

Chay sitting on a bench. His head in his hands. Shoulders slumped.

"We're taking him to St. Mary's," an EMT yelled, climbing into the ambulance. It sped away, sirens blaring.

"C'mon." We got into Chay's car, speeding to keep up.

"Chay, slow down. Uncle wouldn't want you to get in an accident."

Chay's foot eased off the gas pedal, and he rubbed the back of his head. "I need to get there and make sure he's okay."

I grazed the backs of my fingers over his cheekbone. "I know. Me too." I held up my phone. "I'm going to call our parents."

Chay nodded absently. He was silent the rest of the drive.

The hospital smelled like disinfectant and sickness. I hated the smell. The walls were painted a muted sage, and the floors carpeted in beige. A vase of flowers sat on a small table. A painting of a flower-lined creek hung on the wall behind it. It was all very pretty, but it didn't change where we were—a hospital ER waiting room. The place people waited to hear if their loved one was... well, a place people didn't want to be.

We'd been there for three hours. My dad and Chay's parents arrived shortly after we had. I stood in the hallway across from where Chay sat with his head in his hands, just like in my vision. I watched him, biting my nails. He hadn't said more than a few words to me since we'd arrived, and I didn't know what to say to him.

I hadn't had any more visions. I tried to reassure him, telling him that was good.

"Nothing about this is good," he'd snapped, and then sat silently.

"Dad," I whispered. "Do you think this has to do with the Evils or demi-demons?"

"Probably." He didn't say more.

What is it with the men in my life and one-word answers? It really pisses me off.

I blew out a breath. "Why'd they do this to Chay's uncle instead of one of us?"

"Retaliation." I jumped at the sound of Chay's voice.

"For what?"

"Saving you. He stopped the demon from pulling you into the pit. Azazel's retaliating." His voice was hard, hateful.

"Son—"

Chay waved his dad away and stood. "What? It's true." He turned his back to me and stalked down the hall.

I didn't see Chay again that night. Minutes later, the doctor gave a report on Uncle Stewart. He'd suffered smoke inhalation, a concussion from hitting his head on the counter when he fell, and what they suspected was a mild heart attack—but more tests were needed to confirm that diagnosis. Still, the doctor expected a full recovery. My dad and I left after that.

I was relieved that Uncle would be okay.

I was devastated that he almost died because he'd saved me.

I was shattered that Chay blamed me.

I lay on my stomach across my bed. My chemistry book and notepad were opened beside me. But instead of working on the assignment, I drew circles across the page. I couldn't forget the hateful look Chay gave me at the hospital or the cruel way he said I was the reason for the fire.

The doorbell pealed through the house. With a sigh, I tossed my pencil down, shoved my books away from me, and crawled off my bed. The doorbell rang a second time while I was walking toward the stairs.

133   *Michelle K. Pickett*

"I'm coming." I jogged down stairs and pulled open the door. My limbs turned stiff, and my blood chilled. "What are you doing here?"

Next time, I'll use the damn peephole.

"We have a date, remember?" My gaze locked on his. It looked friendlier than the night before, but I remembered the accusation I saw there, and it still stung like a stream of angry hornets flowing through my body.

"Really?" My hand on my hip, I narrowed my eyes at him. "I was sure it was cancelled. How's your uncle?"

"He's good. The doctor was right; he did have a mild heart attack. They're putting a stent in, but he's gonna be fine. He said to tell you *'thank you'*."

"I was only returning the favor. See ya, Chay." I started to push the door closed. Chay's arm shot out and blocked it.

"Milayna," Chay murmured. My name dripped from his tongue like decadent chocolate. "I'm sorry." He started to reach for me, but he hesitated.

I watched his hand and wished I had laser beams for eyes so I could zap him and cause a tiny bit of the pain he'd caused me. I stared at his hand for a beat before my gaze traveled to his. "Accepted," I said in a clipped tone, hoping it was it clear I was finished talking. "I have to go. See you in class." I started to close the door.

"Wait, Milayna—" He stuck his foot between the door and the jamb.

"What?" I made an exaggerated sigh.

"What about chemistry?" He held up his book bag and eyed me. His expression was open, vulnerable, and I almost caved. I wanted to. I wanted to grab him and squeeze him against me. But he'd hurt me and I wasn't real amenable to a repeat. So I kept my bitch wall firmly in place.

"I've already finished." I almost choked on the lie.

"Fine." He turned and walked away. I slammed the door behind him.

Jerk.

After Chay left, I sat on my bed thinking.

I thought I was supposed to help people with my visions—to set wrongs right and protect humans from the evil around them. But I nearly got Chay's uncle killed. How's that helping?

I grabbed my purse, scrambled off my bed, and ran down stairs. "I'm going to Grandma's," I called to my parents and rushed out of the door before they had a chance to ask me why or tell me I couldn't go.

I sped all the way to my grandma's apartment, lucky there were no cops around. I was doubly lucky that my beater made it in one piece. It shook and shimmied all the way there. The old motor groaned and coughed.

I pushed through the heavy glass doors into her building, waving at the little old lady behind the reception counter. She had a beehive hairdo that was as tall as she was, but she was nice and had the sweetest smile.

I hurried through reception and into the great room. It was full of chintz chairs and over-stuffed couches. It had a huge stone fireplace separating it from the dining hall, where Mrs. Richardson sat eating dessert with who I guessed were her grandkids.

"Hello, Milayna. I didn't know you were visiting today," she said around a bite of lemon meringue pie. Meringue stuck to her upper lip.

"I'm surprising Grams."

"Well, take her some pie, dear." She scooped out two big pieces and placed them on a paper plate. I didn't have the heart to tell her that neither of us liked lemon meringue.

"Thank you, Mrs. Richardson." I smiled and waved as I walked toward my grandma's apartment.

I rang the bell when I reached her door. I heard her call out, asking who was there.

"It's me, Grams!" I pushed open the door.

"Milayna!" She wheeled her chair and peered down the hall. "What are you doing here? Is everything okay?"

"Everything's great. I just wanted to visit." I lifted the plate of pie. "I also have this." I wrinkled my nose.

"Oh, that must be from Trudy. I told her earlier I didn't like lemon meringue. She's gone senile." I almost laughed out loud. "Well? Come here and give me a kiss," Grams said.

I dropped the pie on the kitchen counter as I walked by. Leaning down, I kissed Grams' cheek, giving her shoulders a squeeze. I breathed in her perfume. It reminded me of spending the night with her when I was a little girl. The pillowcases on her bed always smelled of the same perfume: lavender-something, clean and fresh. It brought back so many happy, peaceful memories.

"So. What's up?"

"Not one for small talk today, huh?" I asked, smiling.

"Not when I can tell something is bothering you."

"I need to get rid of it, Grandma," I blurted, then cringed and wished I could suck the words back in. I'd meant to ease into the conversation.

"Milayna." She sighed and rubbed her forehead. "We've been through this."

"No. There's a way, I know it." I sat on the purple couch I loved and leaned in close to Grams.

"Yeah, okay, you can turn." She swung her arm in the air. "Flip sides. That'll get rid of it," she snapped, her voice rising.

I flinched and scooted away from her. "You know I don't want to do that," I whispered.

"Then what?" Her graying eyes bored into mine.

I looked down at my lap, twisting my fingers. Shrugging a shoulder, I puffed out a breath to calm my nerves. "It's hurting the people I love."

"Tell me what happened, child." She took my hand in both of hers.

"There's this boy—"

"Why do all stories start that way?"

Michelle K. Pickett

I laughed. "Be serious. This boy... I like him a lot, Grams." I looked in her eyes, hoping she'd see the truth in my next words. "I like him a lot. And I think he likes me. He's a demi-angel, too, so he knows what it's like."

She hummed her agreement. "It does help to have someone understand." Leaning back in her wheelchair, she got comfortable.

"Well, I met his uncle, who's a demi-angel, and he's a really nice guy and he was so sweet to me, and..."

My tears started to flow and nose run. I sniffed loudly. My grandma made a face and handed me a tissue. "Keep going."

"Well, there were some demons at the football game Friday night. Actually, just one demon, but that was enough."

"Yeah, you don't need more than one to ruin a perfectly good evening," she said matter-of-factly, like we were talking about a bad dinner guest.

"Anyway, the demon got a hold of my foot, and he was dragging me—"

She bolted up in her chair. "Are you all right? What happened? Does your father know?" She fired questions at me, not giving me time to answer.

"Grams, I'm fine. Yes, Dad knows. He was there. And I'm trying to tell you what happened, but you keep interrupting me." I smiled at her

"Well, you can't just go around telling an angel that demons are grabbing people and not expect them to get riled up, especially when it involves my grand-daughter. Hmph."

"So this demon gets a hold of me and is dragging me toward a pit straight to, well..."

"Yeah, yeah." She waved her hand in the air. "Hell. I've heard of it once or twice." She rolled her eyes, and I had to bite my lip to keep from laughing. "So? You're on your way to Hell and...?"

"Well, I'm sure I'm toast. Everyone else was busy fighting, and the demon was so strong I couldn't fight him off by myself. So this boy's uncle stepped in. He saved me. Well, he helped hold him off until Chay—that's the guy—could help."

"So? I don't see the problem. A demon is a menace, that's for sure, but you said yourself you're okay." She leaned back in her chair.

"The problem is the next night the uncle's ice cream parlor burned down for no apparent reason. He was inside. He almost died from smoke inhalation and a heart attack."

"But he's all right?"

I flung an arm out from my side. "Yeah, now."

"It's upsetting, but I still don't see what this has to do with you." Grams shrugged a thin shoulder.

"Ugh, Grams! I caused it." I slapped my chest with the flat of my hand.

"The fire?" She arched a brow at me.

"Not directly, but I caused it just the same. If he hadn't helped me, he wouldn't have almost died."

She tilted her head to the side and considered what I said before answering,

"Eh. Maybe."

"Maybe? Grams, don't you think it's a little coincidental? He saves me from a demon the night before his business becomes an inferno?"

She bounced her index finger against her lips before she asked her next question. "Let me ask you something, Milayna. Who saved the man?"

"What?" I wrinkled my forehead.

"How did the man get rescued? Was there another person in the building with him?"

"No." I skimmed my fingers over the couch.

"So how? Did someone see the fire?"

I picked at the hem of my shirt and cleared my throat. "What do you mean by *see*?"

"That's what I thought. You had a vision. Right?"

"Yes."

"And that vision saved the man."

"Yes, but—"

"So isn't it logical to assume if you hadn't had the vision, your guy's uncle would be dead?"

I sighed and squeezed my eyes with my thumb and index finger. "I don't know. Maybe. Probably."

"And you want to believe you caused the fire?" She tsked. "You saved his life. End of story." She flicked her hand in the air like she was sweeping the whole mess away.

"But if he hadn't done what he had, it never would have happened."

"Maybe." She shrugged and twisted her lips. "But if you had given up your power, he'd definitely be dead."

I let out a breath and nodded. "So you won't help me?"

"There's only one way to get rid of your demi-angel status."

"How?" I leaned forward, my forearms on my thighs.

"Give it to Azazel. I won't help you do that, Milayna. I'll do anything for you, you know that, but I won't stand by and watch you sign away your soul."

I stood by the front door with my mom Monday morning, waiting for Muriel to pick me up for school. "Muriel and I haven't talked since Friday night at the game," I told her as we watched Muriel pull into the driveway.

"Really? You two are always talking or texting. What's up?"

"I don't know." Muriel honked her horn. I gave my mom a quick kiss. "See you later."

"Milayna?"

I stopped and turned toward my mom. "Yeah?"

"I love you." Her eyes were glassy, like she was trying to hold back tears.

Michelle K. Pickett

I smiled at her. "I love you, too, Mom. I'll see you tonight."

I ran down the driveway to Muriel's car and slipped into the passenger's seat, pulling the door closed behind me. "Hey! How was your weekend?" Muriel asked as I buckled my seatbelt.

"Fine. You do anything?"

"My mom and I had a girls' day out on Saturday." Muriel told me all about her day out with her mom in mind-numbing detail: how they got their hair done, their nails done, and went clothes shopping at the mall. "We bought out the entire place," she gushed. I only half listened. My mind was on chemistry and who would be there.

I got to class before Chay. I sat at our assigned station and waited, although I didn't particularly want to see him. The final bell rang and class started, but Chay didn't show. I knew he was at school. His car was in the student parking lot when Muriel and I drove in. The huge, yellow beacon in the middle of a sea of drab clunkers and muted sedans was kind of hard to miss.

Class seemed to last forever. I wasn't able to complete my lab for the day because I never finished my homework. After Chay had left on Sunday, he was all I could think about. I'd hoped he'd done the homework so we could do the lab. Since I couldn't do the in-class portion of the assignment without the homework, the instructor gave me the option of making up the lab after school the next day or taking a zero. I took the zero. I didn't care. I had bigger things to worry about— like demons and other hellish things.

When the bell finally rang and the torture of chemistry was over, I bolted out of the classroom. That was when I saw him. He stood across the hall in front of the door, hip leaning against the wall and his thumb hooked through a belt loop on his low-riding jeans. He looked amazing, and my heart stuttered in my chest.

"Skipping class?" I asked with an arched brow.

"Only the ones with hostile classmates."

I snorted a laugh. "Whatever."

He followed me to calculus. Out of the corner of my eye, I could see him watching me. I didn't stop, and I didn't talk to him. I walked straight to class and to my seat. He didn't follow me in.

Muriel came in a few seconds before the bell rang. "Where's Chay?"

I rolled my eyes and blew out a breath. "How should I know?"

"I saw him in the hall." Muriel looked back at the door.

"He's skipping." I doodled on the tabletop. "He skipped chem class, too."

"Really? Why?" Muriel looked at me with her eyebrows raised.

"He's mad at me," I said quietly.

"Pssh." She waved him off. "He's always mad about something."

"Yeah. What'd you buy at the mall?"

Not that I care. I just want to change the subject. I'm thinking about Chay too much. I don't need to talk about him too.

The group ate lunch together like always, but Chay didn't show. He wasn't around the rest of the day. I didn't know exactly how I felt about that. Probably because I didn't know how I felt about him. No one had ever stirred the emotions he had in me—good or bad. When I was happy, I was beyond deliriously happy. But when I was mad? It didn't even register on the Richter scale. But there was confusion and disappointment swimming in there, too. They muddied the water even more, until I didn't know what I felt. I just knew I didn't like being mad at him because I didn't like being away from him. It felt... wrong.

Just before I climbed into bed that night, my phone vibrated. I pushed the button to read the text.

Chay: Can we talk?
Me: Now?
Chay: Yeah.

"Ugh, call me," I said as I typed. My finger hovered over the send button. I didn't really want to talk with him. Instead of hitting send, I deleted the message.

Me: No.

I put my phone on my nightstand. When it vibrated again, I didn't look at it.

Why... why... why am I so stubborn? I want to talk to him. So why didn't I say yes?

Four weeks until my birthday.

I was supposed to ride to school with Muriel that morning. It was Tuesday, and we had swim practice that afternoon. I loved to swim. I loved the water, the feel of slicing through it as I did my laps. And I was looking forward to the physical exertion. It was a great stress reliever.

I walked through the door on my way to Muriel's and stopped midstride with one hand on the bannister, one foot on the first step, and the other behind me still on the porch. I stared at it.

What's it doing here?

A bright yellow Camaro that reminded me of Bumblebee from Transformers sat in my driveway. Chay's car. He wasn't inside it. In fact, I didn't see him anywhere.

I started across the street when I saw Muriel, sitting in the driver's seat of her car with the window rolled down, talking to Chay. She laughed at something he said, rolled up the window, and backed out of her driveway.

"Muriel!" I called after her as she drove away.

Either Muriel forgot I was riding with her or Chay convinced her to leave me behind. Either way, they're both gonna pay. Painfully... slowly.

"Want a ride?" Chay called as he sauntered across the street. A small grin pulled at his lips.

"No."

Not when I'm being coerced. I'll take my own car.

139 *Michelle K. Pickett*

"Looks like you need one."

"I can drive myself."

"C'mon, Milayna. Let me give you a ride. If you drive, I'll follow you anyway. You can't be alone, remember?"

I knew I was fighting a losing battle. I reached for the handle. He beat me, opening the door for me. I could smell his cologne and feel his warm breath skim the side of my neck as I slid onto the passenger seat. A little shiver passed through me.

He climbed into the car and turned his body to face me. "Milayna, I'm sorry I was such an ass at the hospital. Are you gonna stay mad at me forever?"

"We don't have time for this, Chay. I don't want to be late."

In other words, please just drive so I can get out of here.

"For chemistry?" He snorted. "You probably don't even want to go after yesterday—"

"What about chemistry? And if I'm not supposed to be alone, why did you skip class and leave me there by myself?" I glared at him.

"I was around."

"Around. Good, that makes me feel so much better. You were around. Great, Chay. You have about two seconds to start driving, or I'm getting out and driving myself." I turned my head and looked out of the side window. The sky was gray with ugly clouds swirling and blotting out the sun. My mood was just as ugly.

"You're impossible to deal with. I'm trying to apologize."

"And I told you Sunday your apology was accepted. So drop it."

His hands dropped on the steering wheel. "Then I'm confused. What's the problem?"

I'm falling for you, and I'm afraid you're going to hurt me.

I sighed and looked at him. "There's no problem. Let's just go."

"Fine." He threw the car into gear and hit the gas a little too hard.

"Fine," I repeated with the same amount of sarcasm he used.

We drove to school in silence. It was a long, awkward, uncomfortable silence. I rolled the hem of my shirt around my fingers and looked out of the side window, watching buildings and other cars pass, but not really seeing them. Chay drummed his thumb against the steering wheel, his eyes super-glued to the front window.

When we got to school and Chay pulled into a parking spot, I was out of the car before he put it in park. I hitched my bag over my shoulder and hoofed it toward the building.

He quickly caught up and walked next to me. We were about halfway from Chay's car to the school when he reached out and took my hand, threading his fingers between mine. I jerked my hand away and glared at him.

"What?" He flung his arm up in the air and let it fall against his thigh. "You said you accepted my apology and there was nothing wrong." His voice got louder with each word.

"Don't." I bit my bottom lip to keep from saying more.

"You didn't mind it Saturday." He moved closer. I put my hand on his chest to stop him. He dropped his backpack, put his finger around my belt loop, and pulled me closer. I felt his heartbeat beneath my hand. It was strong and... fast. It increased the closer we came to one another. My heart was racing, my breathing quick and shallow. His matched mine. It was the first time I realized I had the same effect on him that he had on me. Our gazes locked. Warmth grew in my chest and spread through my body.

"You're so beautiful," he murmured and leaned in closer still. His thumb caressed my lower lip, pulling it from between my teeth. An avalanche of butterflies tumbled in my stomach. I couldn't contain my small sigh.

The student parking lot grew crowded. The buses had arrived, and students walked around us, bumping and pushing past, as we stood toe-to-toe.

Chay's hand cupped my cheek, his thumb under my chin. He angled my face upward and let his gaze roam across my face until he came to my lips. His gaze darted quickly to mine before he looked at my lips again. He tilted his head.

A group of giggling girls bumped into us. "Oops. Sorry!" one called as they were swept away in the crowd.

Chay cleared his throat, dropped his hand, and jammed his fingers through his hair.

"Chay... we really need to get to class."

"Yeah." His voice sounded strained. He gave his head a shake and flexed his fingers. "Here, give me that." He slipped my bag off my shoulder. Grabbing his bag, he threw both over his shoulder, and we walked toward the school.

I slid into my assigned seat in calculus later that morning. "Pretty dirty trick this morning."

"Yeah. Sorry, but he knew you wouldn't ride with him any other way." Muriel shrugged a shoulder and doodled in her notebook.

"Ever think there was a reason for that?"

"Have *you* thought there may be a reason he wants to spend time with you?" She stopped doodling and chewed on the end of her pen. All her pens had teeth marks. She was like a puppy with a chew toy.

"Yeah, I'm not supposed to be alone," I grumbled and had the fleeting thought that I sounded like Ben when he acted bratty. I decided not to examine that too closely.

"No. If that were it, he'd have let you ride with me. Give him a chance, Milayna. He seems like a great guy, even if he's the dark and brooding type." The cap of her pen pressed against her full bottom lip as a slow smile curved her mouth.

"Oh, shut up." I couldn't help my giggle. I was still pondering the potential awesomeness of a relationship with Chay when Muriel's elbow jabbed me in the

141   *Michelle K. Pickett*

ribs.

"Ow! What?" I snapped.

"I asked for your answer to number three of yesterday's homework assignment, Ms. Jackson," my calculus teacher said in his annoying, nasally voice.

Aw, really? Dude, I have demons after my soul. Can't I get out of homework for, like, ever?

17

Muriel

THREE WEEKS, SIX DAYS UNTIL MY BIRTHDAY.

I bolted upright in bed, covered in a cold, clammy sweat that made my pajamas stick to my skin. When I started to climb out of bed, my cell phone vibrated, skidding across the nightstand. I caught it just as it fell from the table.

I looked at the screen and smiled, pushing the button to read his text.

Chay: Are you okay?

"Yes," I said as I punched in the letters and hit send.

Chay: Then why are you awake?

Me: Why are you?

Chay: Nightmare, huh?

Me: Yes.

Chay: You wanna talk?

I surprised myself when I answered yes, almost dropping my phone when it rang seconds later. I answered before it woke my parents.

"It's three o'clock in the morning, Chay. I thought you meant text, not actually talk on the phone," I whispered.

"But then I wouldn't hear your voice," he said simply. My insides melted into goo.

"Um." I had no idea what to say to that. "Why do you want to hear my voice?"

"I like it." His voice melted over me, relaxing muscles I hadn't realized were tensed.

I sighed and looked at the ceiling. "That's not an answer."

143   *Michelle K. Pickett*

"Yes it is."

"Okay. Fine." There was no use in prodding for more information. He probably wouldn't give it, and I'd probably end up saying something embarrassing.

"Can I pick you up tomorrow?"

"Yes." I picked at the edge of my blanket. "I was hoping you would."

"Hmm, that makes two of us. Goodnight, Milayna."

Oh, wow. Really? I like that. A lot.

"Goodnight."

I clicked off the phone. "Yeah. Like I'm going to sleep now," I grumbled and got out of bed, wandering downstairs to the kitchen. I looked out of the window over the kitchen sink. Every few minutes, I was certain I saw a little red menace running through the moonlight.

Grabbing the ice cream and a word search, I sat down at the kitchen table. I was half done with the word search and completely full of ice cream when my cell rang. Jumping, I snatched it up. "Chay, stop calling. You're gonna wake my parents."

"Sorry. How long have they been out there?"

I didn't bother asking who he was talking about. "I've been watching them for about an hour."

"Why didn't you call?"

"Because they aren't doing anything except pulling up my mom's plants and running through the yard. Besides, they can be entertaining... until I think of what they are."

His low laughter made me smile. "Yeah. Too bad all demons aren't like them."

We fell into an easy silence. I couldn't hear him on the other end of the phone. I'd just decided he'd fallen asleep when he spoke.

"I really am sorry, Milayna."

"I know."

"I shouldn't have... it wasn't your fault."

"You don't have to keep apologizing. You were upset. It's okay, really."

He let out an unsteady breath. "I'm... what are you doing for your birthday?"

What was supposed to come after the 'I'm?'

"Apparently, I'm going to be fed to the hounds of Hell on my birthday," I said, only half joking.

"That's not going to happen," he murmured. "So, after the official time of your birth and all this is behind you, what do you have planned?"

"I don't know. I don't think I have any real plans." I pushed the word search away.

"What about your parents?" I could hear Chay moving in bed, the blankets shuffling, and butterflies started darting through my chest. I tried hard, really hard not to think of him in bed. I really did. It didn't work. "Milayna?"

Crap... What? Oh, right. Birthday. Focus.

"We'll probably have dinner with family, but that's it. Unless you know something I don't."

Please, not a surprise party. I just want to forget about this birthday.

"No, I don't know anything." He didn't sound like he was hiding anything.

"Really? Because even though I don't think they would, I can't put it past my parents not to throw a surprise party. And I'm just not up for it. I just want this birthday over so I can forget about it. So if you know something, tell me so I can prepare myself." I stood and wandered through the house.

"Geez, you're a real party animal." He laughed. "I don't know anything. I swear. I have a feeling your parents want your eighteenth birthday to be over and done with as much as you do. So if this whole *hounds of Hell* thing doesn't work out, you want to go out to dinner with me?"

Right then, my toes curled and my heart did a cartwheel. "Yes. I think I do."

A date. He asked me on a date! Not... I think I do. I do. I really do. "Good, it's a date."

"Huh."

"What?"

I looked out of the window overlooking the front lawn. I could see Muriel's house across the street. "Muriel's car is gone. I know it was there when I went to bed."

"Any visions today?"

I thought back over my day. I didn't have any major visions; those were hard to forget. But I hadn't had any minor flashes either. "No."

"Not even now? With the hobgoblins running around?"

"Ugh, those pipsqueaks. But no." I wrapped my shirtsleeve around my fingers and stared at the empty space where Muriel's car should've been.

"Then it's probably fine. Doesn't your uncle go into work early? Maybe he took her car," Chay said.

I sighed. "Probably." Then my heart sank. "Their kitchen light just came on. He hasn't left yet."

Chay was silent. It stretched between us. I knew what he was thinking. I was thinking it, too. Lily had switched sides. It wasn't beyond any of us to get sucked in by Azazel's lies.

"I'm sure it's nothing." His tone was flat, expressionless.

"No, you're not."

"You're right. I'm not. Remember, Milayna, we don't know who we can trust."

"What do you mean '*we*'? Before, you told me I didn't know who *I* could trust."

"You can trust me," he said quietly.

Isn't that something a person I couldn't trust would say?

"Where were you last night?" I asked Muriel in calculus. "I looked out of the window at four this morning and your car was gone." I pulled my calculus book from my messenger bag.

"Spying on me?"

"No, I couldn't sleep and was walking through the house. I happened to look out of the window and noticed it missing."

"I had to babysit for the Jenkins' kids. The mom works nights, gets home around five." It made sense. Muriel babysat the Jenkins' kids a lot. But I couldn't shake the feeling she was lying. "I didn't know I needed to punch a time clock. You can check with my parents if you want." She tapped her pencil on her book.

I glanced up from my homework and turned to her. "Why would I do that?"

"I don't know, Milayna. Why would you?" She arched a brow.

"I wasn't trying to be nosy, Muriel. I was worried."

She sighed and tossed her pencil on her book. "Sorry. I didn't mean to get bitchy. I'm just keyed up with everything going on."

"I know. Everyone is."

Class started, and Muriel and I fell silent. The teacher was babbling when I texted Muriel.

Me: Who follows me after calculus?

Muriel: What do you mean?

Me: Chay told me someone from the group is always around between classes. You and I have different classes next period, so do Chay and I. So who follows me to history? I don't see Jen until I get to class, so it isn't her.

Muriel: Chay.

I read her text and leaned back in my chair. Doubt bombarded me like a Kamikaze pilot. Why hadn't he told me he followed me after calculus? Why didn't he just walk with me to class?

When the torture of calculus was over, I gathered my things and told Muriel I'd see her at lunch. I was halfway to my next class when I turned and leaned against a locker. I saw him instantly, trailing six or seven people behind me.

"Don't you want to carry my books?" I called. When he was closer, I asked, "Why didn't you tell me it was you?"

"I was going to—"

"Really?" I crossed my arms.

"After Saturday, I wanted to tell you. I mean, I wanted to walk with you, not seven people behind. But then Saturday night happened and you were so angry with me, I decided it wasn't the best time to bring it up."

"Hmm." I tapped my finger on my lower lip. "What about yesterday when you drove me to school? What about this morning when we were on the phone?"

"Okay, I know this is going to sound bad, but it's the truth. I was going to tell you today. I follow you to all your classes. I always have. Even when you're walking with Jen or Shayla. And I planned to tell you today because I don't want to follow you. I want to walk next to you and hold your hand like Saturday at the movie and, yes, carry your books for you." He leaned his shoulder against the locker next to me. We were so close that we brushed against each other.

"And I should believe you?"

"Well... yeah." He looked shocked that I wouldn't.

"Okay, fine."

"You believe me? That easily after all the warnings I've given you?"

"Yes." I pushed off the locker.

"Why?"

"Because my books are heavy. It will be nice not having to lug them from class to class."

Chay laughed and took my bag from me. "So do I get to hold your hand?"

"Let's see how the book thing works out first. Then I'll let you know."

He chuckled, a low rumbling deep in his chest that warmed me to the core, and I couldn't help but smile.

Oh, I'm such a goner. He is so gonna break my heart.

After history was over, I walked into the hallway and turned left toward my next class. I jumped when I came face-to-face with Chay, who leaned against the wall next to the door.

"Hi. Give them to me."

"Hi back." I handed him my books, and we walked to my next class. When I sat down in my seat, he hooked the bag over the back. His hand grazed my back and arm as he walked away, leaving goose bumps on my skin and a fluttering deep in my belly.

"See you after class," he murmured.

I smiled as he walked away.

"What's going on?" Shayla asked with a crooked grin.

"Oh, he's just walking me to and from classes. You know, I'm not supposed to be alone and all that crap."

"Mm-hmm." She winked at me.

And I'm pretty sure it has something to do with me falling hard for Chay.

The first one came at lunch. It started the same as always, but it wasn't a bad one. Only Chay knew I was having it. I looked down at my plate so no one else could see my face. Chay reached for my hand, giving it a small squeeze.

Gray hands. Person in a black hoodie.

Just as quick as it came, it left, leaving me with an uncomfortable feeling that someone was making deals with the other side.

I concentrated on the image, trying to see who was in the black hoodie. Whoever it was, they'd just shaken hands with a demon. The last time I had a similar vision was when Lily jumped sides. I looked around the table. No one was

147 *Michelle K. Pickett*

wearing a black hoodie. Then it hit me.

Muriel is wearing black. Was it a hoodie?

"Where's Muriel?"

It was unlike her not to tell me when she wasn't going to be at lunch, when she was going to babysit, or when we weren't going to drive to school together. And not only was she not telling me things, we didn't talk as often. We always talked every day, usually more than once, and we always texted each other. But I couldn't remember the last time we talked on the phone, and she rarely texted me.

Stop it! She would not turn.

"I don't know," Drew answered. "She didn't mention missing lunch."

"Yeah, she didn't mention it to me either." I chewed on my lower lip. "I guess I'll find out at swim practice."

I looked around the lunchroom for Lily. I held my breath, hoping she'd be wearing black. My eyes traveled over the long, rectangular tables filled with rowdy students until I found her. She sat at a table on the other side of the room, laughing with her new group of friends. She wore yellow.

Damn.

Muriel didn't show for swim practice.

Chay surprised me and stayed for my practice, which was good since Muriel, who was my ride, didn't show. I was self-conscious with him watching me, but we were racing other teammates. The competitive nature in me took over, and I almost forgot Chay was there. Almost. He wasn't someone a person could forget for long.

"You're good," he told me as we walked to his car after practice.

"Thanks."

"You looked good too." He grinned.

"Yeah, I looked awesome in my swim cap and no makeup," I said with a laugh.

He grabbed my hand and pulled me around to look at him. "You looked awesome."

I looked down, embarrassed. "Thanks."

He held the passenger's door open for me. I had one foot inside the car, my hand holding the door for support, when the second vision hit without warning.

Hot. Sulfur. Glowing hole.

I sucked in a breath. It felt like Friday night at the football game all over again. The demon, the glowing hole, the unbearable heat, and the disgusting smell.

Black hoodie. A creamy, white hand enclosed in a gray one.

My head started to pound. I rubbed my temples, trying to ease the relentless waves of pain crashing into me.

Painted fingernails.

"Oh, no," I whispered.

"What's wrong, Milayna?" I jumped at the sound of Chay's voice. I was so engrossed in the vision I'd forgotten I wasn't alone. He wrapped his arm around me and helped me into the car.

"I had the vision again. Someone's definitely turned." I put the heels of my hands to my eyes and rubbed.

"You're sure it isn't Lily you're seeing?"

"Yes... no... I mean, I don't think it's her. The person in the vision is wearing a black hoodie. The hood is up, hiding their face. I saw them shaking hands. It's a girl."

"How do you know if their face is covered?" He smoothed a curl behind my ear that had come loose of the messy bun at the nape of my neck.

"Her nails are painted." Closing my eyes, I remembered Muriel telling me that she and her mother had their nails done over the weekend.

A lot of people have painted nails. And not just girls. But what about my nightmare... she's been in them. She held me for the demon. No! Those are just silly dreams.

"If it's a girl, then maybe it just has to do with Lily," Chay said.

"No." I shook my head and rubbed my temples. "I can't explain it, but I have a feeling it's someone else."

"Who?"

"I don't know," I lied.

My best friend and cousin, for one. And I'm a horrible person for suspecting her.

Michelle K. Pickett

18

Again

THREE WEEKS, FIVE DAYS UNTIL MY BIRTHDAY.

Listening to music, I hummed along while I put dishes in the dishwasher. I glanced out of the window over the kitchen sink. It was sitting on a swing in my backyard. I dropped my head on my arm leaning on the counter and cursed.

Great. Another night with the demon imp patrol.

I watched it swing, kicking its fat little legs in the air and cackling in its irritating, high-pitched squeal. A second hobgoblin marched across the yard. It glared at me through the window. I put the last of the dishes in the dishwasher and reached for my cell phone. It rang and I jumped, dropping it on the floor. I snatched it up, hitting the answer button.

"You see them," I said.

"Hi to you, too." I could hear the smile in his voice, and I laughed. "Yes, I see them. What are you doing?"

"I'm watching one stare at me through the window."

"Hmm. Whatcha wearing?" His voice was low and lazy.

"Huh?" He'd never asked me anything like that before. He didn't seem like that kind of guy… whatever that meant. I wasn't sure. "Geez, stop playing around, Chay." But something about the question, the thought that maybe he'd really want to know, heated my blood.

"I like you in purple," he murmured. It was almost a quiet growl.

"How do you know I'm wearing purple?"

"Because I'm watching you," he said behind me.

I jumped and turned, letting out a small scream. "Crap, you scared me! How'd you get in here?"

"Your dad." He laughed.

"I didn't hear you ring the bell."

"How could you over your music?"

"Ugh. How long have you been here?"

"Long enough." He grinned. I rolled my eyes. "The question is—how long have they been here?" He nodded toward the window.

"I just noticed them."

"Well, why don't you go out and see what they want?" He shooed me with his fingers.

"Alone? You're going to let me outside without a security guard?" I teased, pulling my hoodie on. I froze.

A black hoodie. Just like my vision.

Chay watched me look at my hoodie. "It doesn't mean anything."

"Sure." I smiled at him, trying to hide my panic. But I wasn't sure. I'd like to think I wouldn't turn, but I was sure Lily didn't think she'd turn either. But I was wearing a black hoodie like the traitor in my vision and my fingernails were painted. Pretty damning evidence.

I went outside and walked around back. "Hi, guys," I said, looking at the little red goblins. The smell of sulfur swirled around me.

"Milayna," they squealed. "Swing with us."

Sighing, I sat on the swing next to the more sociable of the two goblins. "Why are you here?"

"We want to play."

I sighed and dropped my head in my hands. "I'm not playing tonight. Tell me what you want so I can go inside and go to bed. I'm tired."

"No. First, you have to play." It jumped off the swing and ran in front of me.

"I'm not playing." I stood up and turned to leave.

"I wouldn't do that," they growled, and I knew the mischievous, happy little goblins had just turned into their demonic counterparts.

I stopped with my back to them. "Then tell me why you're here. Otherwise, I'm leaving."

"We're supposed to tell you that she's changed sides."

My body started trembling and blood rushed behind my ears. First, I had one thought. If she'd already changed, it wasn't me. Dodged a bullet there. But that still left Muriel. "Who?" I asked the goblins.

"That's no fun. You have to guess," one said in a singsong voice.

"I already know Lily changed sides."

"You know nothing," Scarface growled.

"Whatever." I walked toward the gate when Scarface ran between my legs, tripping me. I fell with a grunt. Turning over, I sat cross-legged on the grass. He walked up to me, sticking his face near mine.

Michelle K. Pickett

"He's coming for you."

"He's coming for you. He's coming, he's coming," the other goblin sang, jumping up and down.

"Tell him to come on, then. I'm getting tired of waiting." I leaned closer to its face and lowered my voice. "He doesn't scare me."

"He should."

"He's a coward." I waved my hand in the air. "I'm not afraid of cowards, no matter what their name is."

"Azazel won't like this."

"Tell him to get over it." I got up and brushed the dirt from my jeans. "Go back to Hell where you belong."

With one final glare, there were two small *pops* and they were gone, leaving just the slightest smell of rot and burning flesh.

I opened the gate and rolled my eyes. "I should have known you wouldn't stay in the house."

"I came out when it tripped you," Chay said.

"I'm surprised you didn't come bursting through the gate like a lunatic." I smiled up at him.

"I would have, but you sounded like you had it under control. You know, I don't think antagonizing him is the best way to handle this." He reached out and wrapped a piece of my hair around his finger.

"You and I both know this isn't going to end without a confrontation. I'd like to have it sooner rather than later."

And I want to see how I fare… what side I end up fighting for.

"What are you thinking?" Chay studied my face.

"Hmm?"

"Your brows are furrowed, and the corners of your mouth are turned down." He rubbed his thumb across my bottom lip. The motion sent a tingling sensation through my body, and my lips parted.

Lifting my chin, he gazed into my eyes. He dipped his head and tentatively touched his lips to mine. When I fisted my hand in his T-shirt and pulled him closer, his mouth moved over mine with more intensity. His tongue slid across the seam of my lips, and I opened for him. The tips of our tongues touched, and I sighed in pure bliss at the feel of him. He dropped one hand to my hip and cupped the other around my neck.

"Look at the lovebirds," Shayla said, walking up the driveway.

"Damn it," Chay said, pulling away. He ran his hand through his hair. "Will I ever get to kiss you without someone interrupting?"

I smiled, but it died cold when I looked at Shayla. Wearing a black hoodie and standing next to Lily, she wore an arrogant smile. I looked at her hands—painted nails. I immediately felt guilty for suspecting Muriel.

"Ladies," Chay said.

"Chay." Lily walked to him and tried to wedge herself between us.

Milayna

"Shayla, I thought you were stronger than this. Although, I should have known. You might be stronger than Lily, but you definitely aren't smarter." Chay wrapped his arm around my waist, cutting off Lily's attempts to separate us. I gave her a smug smile.

"I'm smart enough to know when to cut my losses." Shayla glanced at me before appraising Chay. "You should listen to his side of things."

"Shayla? What are you thinking?" I looked at her, dumbfounded.

Someone barreled through the gate from my backyard, knocking into my shoulder. I turned, expecting to see a grotesque gray face.

"Jake. How'd you get back there?" I rubbed the welt forming on my arm.

"Jumped the fence. Steven and Jeff are on their way," he said, looking at Shayla and Lily.

"How'd you—?"

"I called him," Muriel interrupted. She and Drew walked up behind Shayla and Lily.

I looked toward Muriel and saw Steven walk toward Shayla and Lily through my front yard. Jeff came from the opposite side, creating a circle around them.

"Just go. You two make me sick." I waved Shayla and Lily away with a flick of my hand, turning from them.

"We have a message for you," Shayla called.

"What?" I stopped with my back to them.

"Azazel is growing tired. This isn't going to end well for you, Milayna. You might as well switch now before it's too late. Or too late for the ones you love."

I looked over my shoulder at Shayla. "I'm not changing sides. I'm not a traitor. Tell Azazel that his warnings don't scare me, especially coming from the two of you."

"What about us?" A group of people pushed through and gathered around Lily and Shayla. All dressed in black hoodies—demi-demons. They looked like the same bunch from the football game. I started counting. Twelve of them and eight of us. Not the greatest odds.

"What about you?" Chay asked.

"Milayna, change. Make things easier on yourself and just end this now," one said.

"No. Thanks for askin', though."

Then it happened. I wasn't sure who threw the first punch, or maybe it was a kick, it didn't matter. Fists were flying, legs were kicking, and blood was dripping. There wasn't time to think, only react.

A girl who stood about a head taller than me, and looked like she should be on the cover of a bodybuilding magazine, rushed me. I panicked.

"Oh shit," I muttered, just before she barreled into me. My back hit the garage door—hard. The breath whooshed out of me, and it took a second for me to recover. That was all she needed. She kneed me in the gut, and I had the stupid thought that at least it wasn't my face.

153   *Michelle K. Pickett*

Pain radiated out from my center to all parts of my body. Burning, breath-stealing, mind-numbing, pissing-me-off pain.

I had to get her off me. She was pinning me against the garage, giving me very little room to maneuver. My foot came down hard on her instep and her grip on me loosened. I took advantage of the distraction and elbowed her in the jaw. She stumbled backward from the force, and I moved away from the garage. Now I was in my element. I could get the leverage I needed to defend myself.

My martial arts training was extensive. My first instinct was to go all out and kick some ass, but I held back. I didn't want to hurt anyone. I just wanted to defend myself and the rest of the group.

I saw Jen trying to ward off two of the demi-demons. I ran to help her, kicking one guy in the side, before moving to his front and kneeing him in the crotch. "Don't. Hit. Girls," I bit out as he fell to the ground.

As quick as the fight began, it ended. The demi-demons took off down the street and the group filed into my house.

I stood in the driveway, watching the other group run down the road. Drew grabbed me under the arm and dragged me into the house with the rest of our group.

"What happened?" I panted. "Why'd they leave?"

"What, you want to keep fighting?" Jake asked with a laugh.

"No, but they took off so fast... we're done?"

"Someone called the police. That's how these fights generally end. Someone sees a bunch of teenagers throwing punches and they call the cops." Jake shrugged.

"Don't worry, they'll be back," Chay said. I looked across the room where he sat.

"You're hurt," I said more to myself than him.

"Nah." He wiped the blood from a cut over his eye with the back of his hand. "It'll be fine."

"I'll get the first aid kit. Muriel, will you get some ice?" She didn't answer. I looked around the room. "Where'd she go?"

"I dunno. I was kinda busy. I didn't take attendance." Jeff threw a Coke across the room to Jake.

"Huh." I shook my head and tried to remember if she was there when the fight started.

Jen interrupted my thoughts. "I'll get the ice, Milayna. And stop Jeff from using the Coke as missiles."

"Thanks. I'll be right back." Running upstairs to the bathroom, I grabbed the little first aid kit my mom kept there. I replayed the night in my head.

Was Muriel there? Yes, she called Jake. But I don't remember seeing her after the fight started. Maybe she left and called the police. But why isn't she here now? Why do I feel this way? It's Muriel. We're like sisters. I know her. It's fine. She's fine.

I jogged down the stairs and lay the kit on the table. Jake took a peroxide pad and wiped it over a gash on his leg. I took some gauze pads, a cleansing wipe that wouldn't sting his eyes, and some butterfly bandages to Chay.

"Let me clean your cut." I expected him to tell me he could do it himself. I was surprised when he moved closer to me in the chair, lifting his head so I could clean the blood from his face.

I stood between his legs and wiped the cloth over the cut, dried the area with the gauze, and got a bandage ready. Chay rested his hands on my hips, and my hand stopped in midair. It sent chills up and down my body, and although my gut hurt where I'd been kicked, it warmed and fluttered.

I cleared my throat and forced myself to focus. Pressing one piece of tape on one side of the cut, I felt his thumbs graze the skin under my sweatshirt. I sucked in a breath. Goose bumps immediately spread over my body. My hands shook, and I didn't think I'd get the second bandage on with his thumbs caressing my bare skin.

"Uh, there."

"Thanks." He stood and looked down at me. His fingers gripped the waistband of my jeans, and he pulled me closer. For a second, we just stared at each other, and then he tilted his head to the side and lowered it to mine.

I stepped back. Not because I didn't want him to kiss me. Oh, I did. In the worst way. But I didn't want an audience. I turned and looked around the room to see who noticed. It was empty.

"They went out to deal with the hobgoblins." He pulled me gently to him. I took a step, falling into him. He put his hands on my waist to steady me before sliding his hands up my sides and cupping my face. Angling my face upward, he lowered his lips and brushed them gently over mine. Just a caress. My eyes fluttered closed, blocking out everything but him—the feel of his mouth on mine, his tongue sliding along mine, his taste, the way his muscles flexed under my hands. I was wrapped in a whirlwind of Chay. Nothing registered except him.

He lifted his head and looked at me. "Finally. A kiss that wasn't interrupted."

"Do it again," I whispered.

He smiled and lowered his mouth. His lips touched mine softly, his tongue swept over my lips, and I parted them. His tongue dipped into my mouth, and I moaned. Wrapping my arms around his neck, I ran my fingers through his silky hair. I felt a trembling inside. More than just a fluttering or butterflies. No, this was deep within me. Electrical currents ran up and down my spine, and my fingers tingled where I touched him. I'd never felt anything so... beautiful.

He grabbed my hips and yanked me against him, closer, and then closer still, until every inch of me touched him. His lips moved from my lips to my neck, and I gasped at the sensation. A vase of flowers lifted from a table, flew across the room, and shattered against the floor. We broke apart, shocked.

"Whoa." He looked at me. "Telekinesis?"

"I don't know," I said, breathless. I pulled him back to me. "It was ugly any-

Michelle K. Pickett

way. Don't stop."

Chay grazed his lips up the side of my neck. He kissed the hollow behind my ear before sucking gently on my earlobe. I sucked in a breath, breathing his name. Squeezing his biceps, I could feel the muscles under my hands flexing as he moved his hands over my shoulders and delved his fingers into my hair. He pulled it gently, guiding my head back and exposing my throat, kissing and nipping at my skin.

I let my hands move over his shoulders and down the hard planes of his chest to his waist. I hesitated briefly at his waistband before gliding my hands under the hem of his sweatshirt. He stiffened, raising his head, and his eyes locked on mine. I ran my fingernails lightly over his skin. My heart felt like it had wings fluttering in my chest when goose bumps covered his skin under my touch.

Chay ground out a curse and pulled my lips to his, kissing me hard and deep. His lips moved over mine fiercely. My hands moved from his chest to his back. He let one hand glide from my hair, over my shoulder and down my side. When he reached the hem of my sweatshirt, he slipped his hand beneath and ran his fingers along my spine.

He swallowed the moans that his touch pulled from me. My breathing was quick and shallow; his kisses went on forever. I felt like I was suffocating. I couldn't get a breath. My chest burned, and my head started to swim. My fingers curled into his chest, and I thought that if I suffocated from kissing Chay, it was surely the best way to die.

"Well, they're gone." Jake stomped into the kitchen like a moose. "Whoops." He looked between Chay and me with a grin. "I'll tell the others we gotta go. You two just... well... yeah." He backed out of the door, closing it hard behind him.

"I should go, too." Chay held my hands in his, looking at them. Then he kissed the palms one at a time. I moved my hands from his and cupped his face, pulling him to me. It didn't take much effort. He came willingly. Standing on my tiptoes, I kissed him.

"I'll see you tomorrow," I said when I pulled my lips from his.

"Yeah. 'Bye, Milayna."

"'Bye."

18

Fire

THREE WEEKS, FOUR DAYS UNTIL MY BIRTHDAY.

So, I had demons who wanted to drag me to Hell where their leader could suck the life out of me. And somehow, Chay managed to overshadow that tiny detail when we'd had our first uninterrupted, mind-blowing, goose bump-inducing, toe-curling kiss. Possibly the best first kiss in the history of first kisses. At least in my history of kisses. Which, admittedly, wasn't a lot of history, but still, it was a pretty damn awesome kiss.

I dreaded seeing him in chemistry class. Sitting next to him, smelling him, knowing I couldn't tackle him and spend the rest of the day kissing him. Of course, we'd both need some Carmex when the day was done, but a small price to pay.

He slid into his seat next to me just before the bell rang. "Hey." He leaned over and placed a gentle kiss on my mouth. When he pulled back, my fingers touched my bottom lip.

Oh, holy Hell's bells, he just kissed me in front of everyone! Ha!

He gazed into my eyes. "Milayna. Move your hand." I let my fingers fall away from my mouth, and he replaced them with his lips. This time, the kiss wasn't so gentle. I wrapped my hand around the back of his neck and curled my fingers in his hair.

When he pulled back, my breath came in pants and my heart pounded so hard it hurt. "Hi." My voice came out breathy and soft, and Chay gave me a half grin. So cocky.

Michelle K. Pickett

I sighed and wished it were a lab day so we could spend the hour talking, but there wasn't one scheduled. Chay reached under the table and threaded his fingers with mine as we waited for the teacher to begin his lecture. When he didn't, I looked up and my heart lurched. It was the next best thing to having a lab—it was movie day!

As soon as the movie started playing, Chay and I scooted our chairs as close as possible and whispered throughout the entire DVD.

"Well, I hope none of that is on the next exam." I shoved my things in my bag when class ended.

Chay chuckled. "Yeah. That'd definitely suck." He glanced at me, and one side of his mouth tipped in a grin. "But so worth it."

"You can be charming when you want to be." I kissed him quickly before we walked toward calculus.

I'd barely gotten in the door that afternoon after school when my phone rang.

"Hey, Muriel." I held the phone between my cheek and shoulder, lugging my school things upstairs. "I meant to ask you earlier. Where'd you take off to last night after the fight with the asshat demi-demons?" I threw my bag on the floor inside my bedroom.

"I was there."

"I saw you at first, but you disappeared. You didn't come inside with everyone else."

"Yeah, I ran home to let my parents know everyone was okay. I was going to come back across the street and stay with you guys, but a hot shower and my comfy yoga pants were screaming my name." I heard the microwave ding through the phone.

"Well, after the fight, everyone went outside to deal with the goblins except Chay and me. And he kissed me."

"Oooh, nice."

"Yeah, it was great. He was great. It was our first real kiss. I mean, he'd been trying for a couple of days, but something always interrupted us. This was the first real, uninterrupted, full contact, pure bliss kiss." I flopped on my bed.

"Wow," she said around a mouthful of whatever she was eating. Knowing Muriel, it was probably a cheese quesadilla. "Not to take the focus off Chay's kissing prowess, but the reason I called was to tell you the goblins are in your backyard."

"Great." I pinched my forehead between my thumb and fingers. "Just what I need. I'll talk to you later." Ending the call, I braced myself to face the red imps.

I grabbed a jacket and went outside to see what the little creatures from Hell wanted. Of course, I got the same answer they always gave.

"We want to play," the friendly one said, swinging from my mom's clothesline.

"But this time, it isn't going to be fun," Scarface warned.

"Uh-oh, no fun, no fun," the other chanted in its high-pitched, screeching voice. "No fun, no fun."

Scarface held up a stumpy, red finger. The tip was on fire.

My stomach clenched.

Oh crap. The real fun is starting.

My head started to pound, and my vision faded in and out. My only thought was that I couldn't have a vision. Not when they were there. Not when I was alone.

"I'm here, Milayna," Muriel said behind me. She placed her hand on my shoulder.

Thank God for Muriel. I needed someone to watch my back. I was going to have a vision. If the pounding in my head was any indication, it was going to be a big one.

My sight flickered in and out. It was like a television alternating between a picture and static. I couldn't see the vision, and I couldn't hear it either. I made myself relax and concentrate, willing it to show me something.

"What's going on?" Chay. I'd recognize his voice anywhere. He must have sensed danger. That caused sweat to bead on my forehead and the back of my neck. If Chay sensed danger, this wasn't one of their ordinary trips to pull up my mom's flowers.

"I think they're trying to force a vision," Muriel said.

"Fire," the friendly one said. Scarface stood still, holding his finger out for us to see.

Fire. Big wheel bike. Lawn mower. Gas cans.

"He's going to set my garage on fire," I whispered.

Scarface held out his finger and a fireball shot from the tip, hitting the side of our detached garage. A second fireball flew through the air. The garage went up in flames.

Fire trucks. Sirens.

"I'll call the fire department." Muriel started toward the house.

"No! Not yet," I yelled. "The vision isn't gone."

A man. Burning. Falling beam.

I could see it all. I could smell the smoke, the burning flesh of the firefighter trapped under the beam. I squeezed my eyes closed, willing the vision to leave. It was horrible. The man's skin blistered and bubbled as the flames ran up his arms and to his face, turning the skin red and then black as it peeled away from the bone.

"They're here," Chay said.

159   *Michelle K. Pickett*

Muriel turned to Chay. "Who?"

"Demi-demons."

"Chay." I grabbed his arm. "There are gas cans in my garage."

"Where?"

"In the far right corner." I wrapped my arms around my waist. My head was pounding in sync with my heart and my teeth were chattering.

Why are my teeth chattering? Does that happen when you're in shock? Or just freaked out? Or scared?

Chay ran to the garage and pulled open the door. The air spurred the fire, and flames darted out in front of him.

"Chay!" I screamed and grabbed his shirt, pulling him back. "It's too late." I let go of his shirt and rubbed my temples. "It's spreading too fast." I shook my head. Tears zigzagged on my face.

"I need to call the fire department." Muriel bounced on the balls of her feet.

Not yet. The man will still get hurt. We can't call yet.

"Oh, I already did that," Lily said.

I swung around and shoved her shoulder so hard that she stumbled backward into one of her demi-demon freak friends. "You didn't."

Lily looked at me with wide eyes. "Yes, I had to report a burning building. You wouldn't want the fire to spread?"

Fire. Unbearable heat. A man. A beam. Pain. Fear. Nothingness.

I squeezed my eyes closed and rubbed my temples. "My vision hasn't changed. There's going to be an accident. A firefighter." Before anyone realized what I was about to do, I raised my head, pulled back my fist, and landed a hit across Lily's jaw. Pain radiated up my arm from the impact. I hoped that meant it was a good hit on her end.

"Do you know what you've done?" I screamed. My gaze darted around the group. "Do any of you realize you've probably just killed a man? Each and every one of you deserves to burn in Hell with Azazel."

I could hear the sirens in the distance. They were close. My stomach churned and bile rose in my throat, burning it.

Jake and Steven ran up the drive, shouldering through Lily and Shayla and knocking them out of the way.

"What's going on? Did someone call the fire department?" Jake looked from me to Chay.

"Yeah, but one of firefighters is going to get hurt." I bent at the waist and rested my elbows on my thighs, my head in my hands. I was dizzy, so dizzy, the effects of the vision starting to overwhelm me. I tried to keep functioning, to keep talking and telling the others what needed to be done, what was going to happen, but the vision was strong.

Stop it. Burning. Pain. Stop it.

The images and sensations were washing over me like waves in a hurricane. Everything played behind my eyes as though it were a movie...

The firefighter walks to the garage door. He breaks through with an ax. Something catches his eye, and he steps inside. Black smoke fills the garage. Red-and-orange flames roil across the ceiling above his head. The man looks up. He sees the ceiling... he knows. I feel his panic. He turns toward the door, but it's already too late. The beam collapses. It hits him in the head and knocks him to the floor, landing on top of him. I feel his bones crack when the beam lands on his chest, hear his scream of pain.

"Milayna." Chay pulled my face to him. "Open your eyes." His voice was smooth and soft.

I opened my eyes and looked into his blue-green stare. He was blurry. Watery. I didn't realize I'd been crying until then. "I'm okay. I can't stop... I can't stop shaking." I wiped my eyes with my fingers. As soon as I closed my eyes, the vision started to play...

The heat is suffocating. I can feel it crawling down my throat and into my lungs with every breath the firefighter takes. His mask was knocked off when he fell. His arms are pinned. He can't reach his breathing apparatus. Every breath he takes is a deadly mixture of smoke, and blistering heat burning away delicate tissue.

Pain! He kicks his feet back and forth. He's lying in a puddle of fire. His suit isn't on fire... but the heat... the heat is too much. He starts to feel lightheaded; the room tilts to one side and then the other. He tries to scream, but only manages a croak. He looks at the door and sees another firefighter coming to get him. He has a moment of peace... 'I'm going to be okay.'

And then the flames reach the gas cans.

The blast blows the man at the door backward. It rains fire down on the man under the beam. Pain. He screams and thrashes under the flames eating his flesh like worms boring into his skin. Pain. His hair is scorched and burned away, and the flames begin their assault on the flesh below. Pain. It crawls over him like it's a living thing enjoying the torture it's exacting. The man is still screaming, but his voice has long since quieted. Pain. His lips are gone. His face is bubbling and turning black as the fire continues its feast. Pain. His skin begins to flake and float away like ash. Pain. Pain. Pain. Then nothing. The man is quiet. He's gone.

The vision ended. I sucked in a deep breath and opened my eyes. "We need to stop him from going into the garage." I grabbed Chay's arm. My hands trembled, and my eyes were full of tears. "He's going to die if we don't stop him." Bits and pieces of the vision began replaying in my mind.

Burning flesh. Explosion. Gas cans.

"Which one?" When I didn't answer, Chay shook me. I closed my eyes so I could concentrate. "Which one, Milayna?"

I opened my eyes and looked around, trying to find the man. "I don't know. I... in the vision... his face... it's burned... I can't tell! I can't tell! What

Michelle K. Pickett

if I can't find him in time? What if—?"

"Listen! Focus on his face. Concentrate. What does he look like before the flames reach his face?"

"Him!" I pointed at a man with an ax.

Chay took off. He ran smack into the man who was walking, ax in hand, toward the blazing garage.

"Sir, that group of kids over there started this. We saw them in the yard just before the fire."

"Son, tell it to the police. Move out of my way."

"But, by the time the police get here, they'll have taken off. Can't you do some kind of arrest?"

"No. I'm only going to ask you one more time to move."

"But—"

The fireman pushed Chay out of the way and walked toward the garage. He was just a foot away when the roof collapsed. The fire hit the gas cans, and an explosion knocked him backward.

"It's gone," I whispered, pressing the palms of my hands over my eyes to block out the memory of seeing the man burn alive, his skin bubbling and turning black, hearing his screams pleading for help. The feel of life draining from his body.

The group of demi-demons took off before the police arrived. We were interviewed and, of course, lied to the police. Somehow, we didn't think they'd buy a story of fat, roly-poly demons with burning fingers throwing fireballs at the garage. So we told them a group of kids started the fire. No, we didn't know why and no, we didn't know who they were.

"I better call my dad," I said after I talked to the police. Thankfully, the garage wasn't attached to the house, so it wasn't damaged. Dazed, I walked inside. I didn't make it to the phone. I slid down the wall to the floor and started crying. The vision was horrible. The worst I'd had. I could almost feel what the man felt, the pain from the flames licking at his flesh and the smoke choking the air from his lungs.

Chay walked in and sat next to me. I turned to him.

"A bad one, huh?" I nodded. "They're getting worse." He put my hair behind my ear. "It's okay to be upset, Milayna. I haven't had visions like yours, but judging by the few I've had, I can imagine they're terrible."

I looked at him, tears flooding my eyes. He wrapped his arm around my shoulder and pulled me against him. Burying my face in his neck, I cried. He held me silently. Muriel came in and called my parents. Chay sat on the hard tile floor in my kitchen holding me until my dad got home. He ran his fingers up and down my back; occasionally, he'd smooth my hair back from my face, placing it gently behind my ear. He didn't talk. There was nothing to say.

When my dad pulled up, Chay kissed me softly on the forehead and eased himself up. He went outside, told my dad what happened, and then went home.

My dad helped me up from the floor. "You want to talk about it?" His voice was soft and his eyes full of concern and love.

I shook my head. "No. Not now."

"Okay. When you do, I'm here to listen." He put his hands in his pockets and rocked back on his heels.

"Thanks, Dad. I'm so tired. I think I want to lie down for a while."

"Okay. Let me know if you need anything. I'll be right outside, dealing with this mess."

I climbed the stairs, each one an effort. I was always tired and weak after a vision, but after that one especially. Maybe because it was such an emotional one. Maybe because the images were so vivid... so grotesque. I wasn't sure. All I wanted was to fall into bed, pull my soft comforter over me, and block out the world.

Just a few hours. That was all I needed.

Then I'd be ready to fight back.

Michelle K. Pickett

20

THREE WEEKS UNTIL MY BIRTHDAY.

Monday, I overslept. I was standing over the kitchen sink, gulping down cereal, when my dad walked in.

"I have to stay home to meet the insurance adjuster about the garage. You want to cut school and have lunch with your old man?"

"I probably should go to school… but yeah, I don't want to. I'd rather have lunch with an angel."

My dad laughed. "Good. It's a date."

After the adjuster came, looked around the garage, and asked a million and one stupid questions, it was one o'clock. My dad took me to my favorite restaurant for lunch. They had the best hamburgers in the state.

"How come the demons never try to come into the house?" I took a bite of my olive burger and groaned. It was so good.

"Our houses are protected from them."

"Like with a magic spell?" I looked at him over the rim of my milkshake. The restaurant might have the best burgers, but the milkshakes weren't nearly as good as Chay's uncle's were.

"Yeah. They can come into the house, but they lose their powers. That's one reason the demi-demons and Evils are always starting fights." He took a big bite of his fried-egg burger, and the yellow yolk oozed between the slices of bun. I almost gagged. Ick.

"I don't get it. What does fighting have to do with our houses being protected?"

"If they can pull us away from the house long enough, they might be able to find a way to break through the protective barrier." He took a swig of Coke and stole an onion ring off my plate.

"Makes sense, I guess. You said that was one reason? What else?"

"Well, they use the fights to distract us and give the demons a chance to grab the person they're after—"

"Yeah, I remember from the football game." I shuddered.

"And they fight to weaken the group. Between the constant fights and the visions, the emotional and physical stress starts to take its toll and you become weaker. And that gives them an opportunity to complete their first objectives—break the protective barrier and grab their target." He took another bite of his disgusting egg-covered hamburger. Yellow slime dripped onto his plate.

"Hmm, they're busy bastards, aren't they?" I cringed as soon as the words left my mouth. I just swore in front of my dad... so not cool. He cocked an eyebrow at my slip. "Sorry."

"Eh, that's okay." He waved off my words with a flick of his hand. "I was thinking the same thing."

"Dad, I need to tell you... I... um, I'm sorry I got so mad at you about this whole angel thing. I love you, even if you are a freak." I smiled at him, and he laughed.

"I love you too. And I'm sorry it was sprung on you the way it was. I was hoping to ease into it, but things started moving too fast."

"It's okay. We're good, right?"

"Of course we are," he said with a nod. "A little thing like a pack of demons isn't going to come between us."

"Nope, no demon is coming between us, but if you don't leave my onion rings alone, we're gonna have some major trouble," I said with a laugh when he stole another ring.

When we got home after lunch, I went straight to my bedroom and crashed. He was right. The constant visions, fights, nightmares, and stress were taking a toll. I was exhausted, physically and emotionally.

I slept until my mom woke me up for dinner that evening.

By Tuesday, I felt better and that afternoon, I let out more stress and frustration at swim practice. I swam as hard as I could. I loved how it felt when my body sliced through the water, how my muscles burned when I pushed myself to go faster, farther. I beat my best time. I guess swimming when demons were chasing me was good for my game.

When practice was done, I stayed in the pool, floating, listening to the whooshing the water made when it filled my ears. Flipping my swim cap

165   *Michelle K. Pickett*

off, I let my hair float around me, closing my eyes and relaxing my muscles. I wanted to stay there forever, or at least until the Azazel crap was over.

"Outta the pool, Jackson," my coach yelled just before she started flipping the lights off.

"Want to stake out the clearance racks at the mall?" Muriel asked when I walked into the locker room.

"Sure," I said, but I was starting to feel lightheaded. The room started to tilt, and the lockers spun around me.

"Milayna? Are you having a vision?"

"I don't know. I think so. It's... different."

I wasn't sure what was happening. I felt sweat mix with the pool water and snake down my back. My hands were slick with it. It broke out on my forehead, running down the side of my face.

Muriel's voice sounded distorted and far away. I braced a hand against the lockers to steady myself. The room faded even more, and then the vision broke through.

A man. His back is to me. A gray figure laughing.

I pressed my fingers to my temples and massaged them, willing the vision to give me more information. Show me more of the person.

Shaking hands. One white, the other a sickly gray. The sound of laughter.

My head pounded and my hand burned as if I were the one touching the demon.

Dark hair. His shoulder leaning against the wall and his finger hooked in his belt loop. The demon laughs. Lily sidles over, and the man kisses her.

Slowly, the room righted itself. The lockers stopped spinning and my vision returned to normal, but my stomach still cramped. I sat and bent forward on the bench, wrapping both arms around my middle. I gritted my teeth against the intense pain, not sure why my stomach still hurt. Usually, when the visions ended, so did the physical effects.

End it, Milayna. Or I will.

"Oh!" I jumped up, nearly falling backward over the bench.

"What?" Muriel stood next to me and looked around. "What happened?"

"It's like Azazel was talking to me."

Muriel and I gathered our things and hurried out of the locker room. I wanted to get home. The vision turned my blood to ice. I couldn't stop shaking. I needed to go home where I felt safe. But I wasn't safe anywhere. None of us were. Not really.

Two weeks, four days until my birthday.

We sat at our usual table at lunch Friday afternoon. Drew's mouth was stuffed full of fries when he asked, "Hey, who wants to go out for a movie tonight?"

"Me," Muriel said a little too fast. I smiled to myself. They were so into each other.

"I'm up for it." I looked at Chay.

"I can't." Chay shook his head. "I have a project due in American History."

"You waited until now to start that? That's a third of our total grade, Chay." I looked at him with wide eyes.

"Yeah. I've been procrastinating."

I snorted a laugh. "Ya think?"

In the end, it was Drew, Muriel, me, Jake, Jeff, and his girlfriend Trina who went to the movie and out for burgers. "What's up with you and Jake?" Muriel looked in the bathroom mirror and rubbed on some lip gloss with the tip of her pinkie.

"What do you mean?" I looked at her, my brows drawn over my eyes.

"He's being awful attentive tonight," Muriel said and looked at me sideways.

"Really?"

Muriel shrugged, and I followed her out of the bathroom and to our restaurant booth.

We went out to dinner at a local diner. It was going fine. Everyone seemed to be having fun, joking and telling funny stories that took our minds off everything happening in our lives.

A man. Gray hand. Shaking hands.

It was just a flash, not a full-blown vision, but a flash of images scrolling through my mind, gone as fast as it came. I tried to shake it off without anyone knowing anything was wrong.

"Are you okay?" Drew asked.

"Yeah, why?" I pulled a fry through my puddle of ketchup.

"You zoned out for a minute."

"Sorry." I smiled at him.

Everyone started talking at once. Conversations overlapped and I tried to focus. I laughed at jokes, answered questions, and joined in telling embarrassing stories about people. Drew was in the middle of a story about our horrendous English teacher when I happened to look over his shoulder and spot Jeff walking back to our table from the restroom.

He stopped at a table and smiled wide at whoever was sitting there. Drew was blocking my view. Jeff talked for a few seconds, then pulled out a chair and sat down. He talked and laughed for a little over five minutes before he returned to our table.

Michelle K. Pickett

When the group got up to leave, my gaze landed on Jeff's mystery table. I sucked in a breath and could feel the color drain from my face. Lily and Shayla sat at the table, eating burgers and fries. And Jeff stopped and talked with them like nothing was wrong.

What's going on? This is exactly what Azazel wants. I'm starting to doubt everyone.

My mind kept going back to the images and the warning Chay gave me. You don't know who you can trust, Milayna.

After dinner, we all went to a movie. The girls and guys argued over what to watch, gory versus lovey. Finally, we settled on horror. In the middle of the movie, another flash of images passed in front of my eyes.

Gray hands. Gray face with a grotesque smile. A man with his back to me. Burgundy Abercrombie hoodie and black boots with silver buckles.

Cold panic stabbed me. Jake was wearing a burgundy Abercrombie hoodie. I couldn't remember what type of shoes he had on. I peeked at the floor, but the theater was too dark for me to see.

My hands started shaking, and bile rose in the back of my throat.

My dad said demis feel calm around each other, that being together was soothing. I don't feel that with Jake. I feel unbalanced, not at all calm. Chay warned me. I don't know who I can trust. Why didn't I listen?

I couldn't concentrate on the movie. I thought about Jake's shoes, picturing him at the restaurant, in the movie theater's lobby, but I couldn't remember them. I twisted my fingers together in my lap for ninety-three minutes—I know because I counted every one—before the movie finally ended.

"You want to go get some dessert or something?" Jeff suggested as we walked out of the theater.

"Um." I looked down. White Nikes, not black boots. But still, Jake was wearing a burgundy Abercrombie hoodie, and I couldn't shake off the funk I felt being around him.

"This has been great, but I need to get home," I said.

"Okay, I guess that's my cue." Muriel gave Drew a small smile.

"No, no, you guys are still having fun. I have to get up early for practice anyway. I'll take Milayna home." Jake fished his keys from his pocket.

Muriel looked at me and raised her eyebrows. I rolled my eyes at her.

"Thanks, Jake," I said.

"No problem." Jake drove me home, talking and joking during the ride. I tried to keep up with the conversation, but the only thing I could think about was his damn hoodie. A few weeks ago, I would have been trying to figure out how to get it off him. Now I just wanted to get home as fast as possible.

As soon as the car rolled to a stop in my driveway, I opened the door to get out when Jake said something that made my heart jump—and not in a good, swoony way.

"Do you ever think of changing, Milayna?"

Milayna   168

The hairs on the back of my neck stood on end. "No. Never."

"Even if it meant you'd save your family?"

I turned to him. "My family wouldn't want me to change, no matter what happened. Do you think about it?"

"Hell no!" He shook his head and drummed his thumbs on the steering wheel.

"Then what's up with the questions?" I narrowed my eyes and studied him.

He rubbed a hand over the back of his neck and shrugged. "You know, Lily and Shayla are going to try to get to all of us. Just got to keep tabs on everyone."

"Yeah." I shot him a quick smile.

Gray hands, burgundy Abercrombie hoodie, and black boots.

My hands shaking, I shot out of the car and up the walk to the house. Jake followed me. My insides were swirling like someone took an egg beater to them, and Chay's warning swam in my mind.

Stupid, stupid, stupid. I should've been more careful after Lily and Shayla.

"Thanks for bringing me home. It was a lot of fun being out with the group." I tried to sound normal. My throat was so tight, I was sure my voice sounded strained. I wished he'd stayed in the car instead of walking me to the door. It wasn't like we were on a date.

"Maybe we could do it again?"

"Yeah. The group definitely needs to get out and do fun stuff together. Stuff that doesn't include demons," I said with a nervous laugh.

"Well, yeah. But that's not what I meant." He skimmed his hand up my arm to my neck. I was in too much shock to really follow along with what was happening. It wasn't until his hand curved around the back of my neck and he leaned in, saying, "I was thinking next time it could be just me and you."

Oh please, don't kiss me.

I was never very lucky when it came to guys. Jake's lips touched mine. I suppose it was a nice kiss. It was soft and sweet. But, it wasn't Chay. His were perfect. The kind of kisses that made my heart fall into my stomach and my toes curl—a kiss that created warmth in all the right places. They threw me off-balance in a way that I never wanted to end. The kind in romantic movies when the gorgeous guy kisses the girl, the music swells in the background, and you think, 'Yeah, that doesn't happen in real life.' But when I kissed Chay, it was as though it did happen. I heard music in my head. Our own symphony. Okay, totally too corny. But true.

Yeah, Jake's wasn't like that.

Jake rested his hand on my waist and started to deepen the kiss when I took a step back. "Um, that's nice, but I'm with Chay. I really need to go…" I motioned to the house.

169 *Michelle K. Pickett*

There was no way in Hell, or, preferably, out of it, we'd go on a date together.

"Yeah. Okay." He frowned. "I'll see you Monday. That's if we don't have any trouble over the weekend."

I laughed. It came out too loud and shrill, and I cringed. "Yeah, we don't want any trouble."

"Right. 'Bye, Milayna." He lifted his hand in wave and walked away, watching me as he went.

He's gonna change. Maybe he has already and that's why I felt so weird around him.

"'Bye." I made myself stand still for seven seconds. I ticked them off in my head. Okay, I was going for ten seconds, but I didn't make it. I wanted away from him.

I all but fell into the house. I tried not to slam the door closed—I forced myself to push it closed gently, but as soon as it latched, I threw the deadbolts. Letting my purse fall to the floor, I leaned my forehead against the door, sucking in a deep breath to calm my nerves.

My hands were still shaking. My entire insides felt like they were shaking. I was James Bond's martini: 'shaken, not stirred.' Of course, that was said in the delicious Scottish Sean Connery's voice, because everyone knew he was the best James Bond. Yeah, I totally watched too many of those old movies with my dad.

"Milayna." I flinched at the sound of my dad's voice coming from the living room. "How'd it go?"

"Uh, okay, I guess." My face was still buried against the wood door.

I'm never moving from this spot. As long as I stand right here forever, my life can't get any weirder and I can't screw it up any more than I have already.

"Did you have fun?"

Jumping, I slapped my hand over my mouth to hold in a squeal. I turned and let out a breath, dropping my hand. "Chay. What are you doing here? Aren't you supposed to be slaving over your project?"

He slipped his fingers in his pockets and shrugged. "I should be working on my project, but there was something more important I needed to do."

We seemed to move in concert. He slid his hand under my hair and cupped the back of my neck, and I leaned forward and fisted my hands in his hair, pulling him to me. I tilted my face up to him, and he lowered his lips to mine. I lost myself in his slow, tender kiss. Fingers of warm electricity made its way through my body, sparking off the sides of my veins like the stars of sparklers, and I moaned into Chay's mouth.

When he broke our kiss—because, hey, we had to breathe sometime—I said, "Chay, not that I'm not thrilled you're here, because I am. Beyond thrilled, actually. But, why are you here?"

Milayna   170

"Look in the backyard." He jerked his head toward the back window.

I rubbed my temples where an ugly migraine was building. "Ugh, again? How many of them? Just the two?"

"Nope. Six."

"Six. Wonderful," I sighed. I wasn't planning to deal with the little red goblins when I got home. "What do they want?"

"You. I've been sitting out there with your dad for an hour. They ignored us. They're running around like normal, digging up flowerbeds, swinging, trying to climb trees. Someone should really explain that their legs are too short for that." He chuckled.

"Let me change clothes, and we'll go see what they want."

"Can I come?" Chay winked.

I stopped halfway up the stairs and looked down at him with a smirk. "My dad likes you, but I think that would definitely put you on his shit-list."

"You're probably right. I'll just stand here and enjoy the view."

That doesn't make me feel self-conscious at all.

I hurried up the stairs, stripped out of what I was wearing, and into my favorite faded jeans and a sweatshirt.

"'Kay. Let's go see what the imps want tonight," I said when I got back downstairs.

"I like you like this better." Chay looked me up and down.

"Like what?"

"Faded jeans, your favorite sweatshirt." He wrapped a finger around one of my belt loops and pulled me to him.

"How do you know it's my favorite sweatshirt?" I laid my hands on his chest.

"You wear it a lot on weekends." He kissed the hollow behind my ear. I curled my fingers into him and sighed his name.

"Mm. Wait, how do you know?" I pulled back and looked at him.

"I see you. I live behind you, you know."

"Hmm, I don't know if that's sweet or creepy." I raised an eyebrow.

He kissed the tip of my nose. "Sweet, definitely sweet."

I laughed. "Okay, whatever you say. Creeper."

"The only thing I don't like is this." He reached behind me, took the clip out of my hair, and ran his fingers gently through the wavy strands. "You should wear it down."

My voice stalled. I let my gaze roam over his face. I drank in his features, his odd-colored eyes that looked more green just then than blue, his strong jaw that had a day's worth of stubble, and full lips—the bottom just a little fuller than the top, giving him a natural pout that was too damn sexy to be legal and begged to be nibbled on, his dark hair cut short on the sides but left longer on the top, giving him that natural bed head look that was hotter than hell itself. I reached up and smoothed back a lock of hair that had fallen over

Michelle K. Pickett

his forehead. "Okay," I whispered when I found my voice.

Chay tilted his head and looked at me. "What?"

I shook my head. "Nothing. I'm just glad you're here."

"Me too." Turning me around, he threw me over his shoulder. I giggled as he carried me into the backyard. Chay put me on the edge of the deck and sat next to me, his arm wrapped around my shoulder.

"Milayna's here," one of the hobgoblins cheered, smiling wide.

"Yeah, I'm here. What are you doing here?" I rolled my eyes and buried my face in the curve of Chay's neck. I was so over the pipsqueak duo.

"Did you have fun tonight?"

Burgundy hoodie. Black boots.

"I had an okay time, why?"

"Because Azazel said to tell you—"

I jumped off the deck and kicked the goblin. He rolled head over butt in the air, cussing the entire time. I turned to Chay. "I need to talk to you." When he didn't move, I grabbed the sleeve of his suede jacket. "Now."

"What's going on?" he asked when we were in the house.

"I was going to text you when I got home. But then you were here and you started kissing me, and you really know how to use your lips." I reached out and ran my fingers over his bottom lip. "I mean, geez. How's a girl supposed to think?" His teeth bit into his full bottom lip to hold back a grin, and my eyes stalled on the sight. "Really? Like that's helping."

"Sorry." He laughed and wrapped his arms around my waist so tightly a whisper couldn't have squeezed between us. "What's up?"

"Jake is changing. Or maybe not. I don't know for sure." I put my hand on top of my head. "I just had some flashes of a vision tonight, and I think the person in them was Jake. But, then, I'm not sure." I flung my hand from my head out to my side. "I think they could be someone else. But part of the vision was definitely about Jake. But the other part wasn't. I think. I don't know." I dropped my arm and my hand slapped against my thigh.

"Milayna, slow down." Chay cupped my face. "Start at the beginning."

"Okay. I had a vision of a gray hand and a burgundy Abercrombie hoodie and black boots with a silver buckle. You know, like motorcycle boots? So I know someone is going to change. Jake was wearing a burgundy Abercrombie hoodie—"

He threw his hands in the air. "Damn it, Milayna!"

I put my hand on my hip. "Let me finish. But he wasn't wearing black boots. He had white Nikes on. So I don't know if it's him or not. I'm not sure what the vision meant. If it was about Jake or someone else. If it was about someone turning... who is it? The person in the hoodie or the boots?" I pinched the bridge of my nose between my thumb and forefinger. "I can't focus. There's too much floating in and out of my brain."

I grabbed Chay's arm. "Oh, I almost forgot. When we got here, he asked me the oddest questions. Like if I ever thought of changing or if I would change if it meant saving my family. So I asked him if he'd changed and he said, 'Hell no.' When I asked why he was asking me if I would change, he said he was just 'keeping tabs' on everyone." I let out a breath. It felt good to tell someone else. The weight of the visions were crushing.

Chay's face turned hard. "I knew we couldn't trust everyone in the group. But Jake?" Chay shook his head. "He's one of our strongest. I just never thought he'd switch sides. You're sure?"

"No. I mean, I'm sure that someone is switching, but I don't know who."

"Shit." Chay rubbed his hand up and down the back of his head.

"Yeah. Come on. Let's go see what the goblins want before they tear the whole yard up." I pulled him by the arm toward the back door.

"Okay, guys," I said when I walked into the backyard. "Let's play."

They hopped up and down, clapping their fat little hands together. "Yay, Milayna's playing. Azazel will be happy."

"No, I'm not playing with him. I'm playing with you. What's your game?"

"He said to tell you that he hopes you had a good time tonight," Scar-face said.

My stomach sank.

Chay threaded our fingers together. "Tell him I did, thanks for asking." I smiled at the goblin.

"And Azazel wants you to know that the two of them will be good workers." The friendly goblin smiled at me. He squeezed his hands together so tightly that the tips of his fingers swelled and looked like little red balls.

"What two?"

"Nope, that's no fun! You'll have to wait and see," the goblin sang before he popped out of sight, followed by his red, pipsqueak posse.

173   *Michelle K. Pickett*

21

Chay

My phone rang at eight o'clock Saturday morning. I pulled my comforter over my head. "Go away," I mumbled into my pillowcase.

It could be Chay.

I snatched the phone off the table. "Hello?" My voice was still raspy from sleep.

"Good morning, beautiful." His voice sounded like decadent chocolate drizzled over plump, ripe strawberries. So very sexy.

"You're up already? You know, we actually get to sleep in on Saturday mornings." I stretched in the warmth of my bed.

"I want to see you."

"When?" I tried to hold back a yawn.

"Now."

I laughed. "Now? Are you kidding?" The phone disconnected, and the doorbell rang.

Pulling my hair into a ponytail, I bounded down the stairs. I opened the door and there he stood. Tall, ripped, and every girl's dream of handsome.

And he's mine, mine, mine, I sang in my head.

"Chay," I said, laughing. "What are you doing here?" I tilted my head to the side and touched my fingers to my parted lips. Oh my. He sure beat the hell out of sleeping in. There was a feeling of weightlessness in my chest, a fluttering deep in my belly, and I knew I was in so deep with him.

"I told you, I want to see you."

"Are you in your pajamas?" My breath hitched in my throat thinking of him sleeping… in bed.

"Sweats and a T-shirt… yeah. So are you." He grinned in a lazy way that sent my heart galloping.

Ohmigosh. Hormone overload. He slept in those clothes. And his hair is still messy and he hasn't shaved and…

"Who's at the door?" my dad called.

"Chay," I hollered over my shoulder, my voice a little breathier than usual.

"Is he having breakfast with us?"

Turning to Chay, I licked my lips and tried to smooth a stray lock of hair behind my ear. "Um, do you want to have breakfast with us? We have breakfast as a family every Saturday."

Chay looked at the ground and shook his head slowly. "I don't want to crash your cereal party."

I laughed. "He wouldn't have asked if he didn't mean for you to stay."

He looked at me through his impossibly long, black lashes. "And you?"

"I always want you," I whispered. "Always."

His lips twitched and he gazed into my eyes. "Then I'd love to have breakfast with you, Milayna."

Geez, he looks way too good for this early in the morning.

"Okay, I'll be right back." I started to close the door and then remembered he was still standing on the porch. Grinning, I opened it and rolled my eyes. "Come in."

I started toward the stairs when he caught my hand, "Don't get dressed. I'd feel awkward sitting at your table in my pajamas."

"I won't. I just gotta, you know… " I made brushing motions in front of my mouth. "Teeth. Dragon breath and all." I ran upstairs to my bathroom, brushed my teeth, splashed water on my face, and ran wet fingers through my ratted hair, leaving it down like he liked. I walked to the stairs and smiled when I heard him and my dad talking in the kitchen. I wasn't the only one who liked him.

"Milayna?" my mom called quietly from her bedroom down the hall. I turned. "Your guy's here?" She tilted her head toward the stairs, a gleam in her eye.

"Yeah." I couldn't help the smile that stretched across my face.

She smiled back and winked. "I guess we'd better get breakfast going."

"Oh, it's my week to cook." I rolled my lip between my teeth.

"I'll do it. You two go do whatever it is people do this early in the morning." She stifled a large yawn.

"No, that's okay. I want to." I hurried downstairs.

Michelle K. Pickett

"Hey." Chay held his hand out to me.

"Hey." I slid my hand in his and he pulled me to him, kissing my temple. His lips were soft and warm, and I had to concentrate on what I was going to say. "Uh, I forgot this is my week to cook, so we can talk in here." I pulled him behind me to the kitchen.

"Wherever is great. I could help."

I turned to him. "You want to?"

"Sure, what are we cooking?" Looking around the kitchen, he picked up an egg-shaped timer. He turned it over in his hands like he'd never seen one before.

"Well, what do you like?"

"You."

I bit the corner of my bottom lip to hold back my smile. I lost the war—I looked up at him and smiled. "I like you too." I bumped my hip into his. "But, what would you like for breakfast?"

"I like anything."

"Banana pancakes?"

"You know how to make banana pancakes? I knew I was fallin' for you for a reason."

I think my heart just stopped. He just said that out loud with my dad in the room!

I cleared my throat. "Ah, well, you haven't tasted them yet."

Chay and I cooked breakfast together. Banana pancakes and fruit with fresh-squeezed orange juice. He was in charge of the fruit and orange juice. He didn't know the first thing about cooking, so I made the pancakes.

By the end of breakfast, he'd sufficiently charmed my parents into thinking he'd hung the moon. When he asked if he could borrow me for the day, they didn't hesitate.

"Sure," my mom said. "Just have her back by tomorrow morning."

Chay stopped with his glass of orange juice halfway to his mouth and stared at my mom with a dumbfounded look. I snorted a laugh and nearly choked on a piece of cantaloupe.

My mom chuckled. "Midnight," she clarified.

Chay sat his glass down and let out a big breath. "Right. Of course." He nodded. "I'll pick you up in an hour, Milayna?" At my nod, Chay rinsed his plate at the sink before walking toward the door. "Thank you for breakfast, Mr. and Mrs. Jackson."

"Anytime. See ya, Chay," my dad said, waving over his shoulder when Chay walked by.

"See ya, Ben."

"Later, dude," Ben said around a mouthful of pancake and fist bumped Chay.

Milayna   176

Exactly an hour later, his yellow Camaro pulled in the driveway. He walked to the porch; I opened the door before he rang the bell.

"I would've come out if you'd honked," I said.

"Honked? My dad would kill me. You don't honk for a lady, you walk to the door."

"I think I like your dad." I reached up to push a curl behind my ear. Chay's hand beat me. He twisted the red strands around his fingers before sliding them behind my ear. My breath stalled in my lungs. Every time he touched me, I was afraid to breathe, to move, to speak. I didn't want to do anything that would break the spell—make him stop. He let the strands sift through his fingers as he trailed the tips of his fingers down the side of my neck, across my shoulder, and down my arm until he reached my hand and threaded his fingers with mine.

"So where to?" He looked at me, his face relaxed and his expression open. It was something I rarely saw on him and I would've gone to the moon and back just to keep that look on his face.

"Me? You asked me out, remember?"

"Okay, I pick whatever you pick." He grinned.

"I hate that. Tell me what you want to do and I'll tell you what I want to do. And then we'll pick."

He turned to me and took a step, forcing me to take a step backward. I felt the smooth metal of the car behind me. Chay splayed his hands on each side of me, boxing me in. He leaned in close, but he didn't touch me. I could feel the warmth of his body, smell his scent, and remember his taste. "I don't care what we do, Milayna. I just want to spend time with you." He shifted his weight and wrapped an arm around my waist.

There goes my heart again—doing all kinds of funny little tricks.

"We have all day, right?"

"Every second." He nodded.

"The zoo."

"Sounds great." Chay pushed off the car and opened my door for me.

"You're really okay with the zoo?" I asked once we were in the car, afraid he'd think it was boring or childish.

"Yeah, I haven't been since I was a kid. It'll be fun."

We drove to the zoo without one quiet second between us. We talked about everything, except who—what—we were. We didn't bring up the subject of demi-angels or demi-demons. There was no mention of demons or hobgoblins. Azazel's name was never uttered. It was glorious.

177   *Michelle K. Pickett*

We were at the big cat exhibit when I sucked in a breath and doubled over, dropping the slushie Chay had just bought me. The red liquid spewed across the pavement like the iced blood running through my veins.

"C'mon." He guided me to a bench. I sat down, leaned forward, and wrapped my arms around my knees. "A vision?"

I nodded.

"Why didn't I see this coming?" Chay said through clenched teeth. "You're in a lot of pain?" He looked miserable. "What can I do?"

"Nothing," I whispered. I wasn't even sure I said it loud enough that he could hear. "When the vision is over, it'll go away."

"The pain never gets better. I thought it'd lessen as you got used to them."

"No, it's not better." I pressed the thumb and index finger of one hand against my eyes to ward off the pounding growing in my head. It felt as if a person were inside my head, banging against my skull trying to break through. The other hand gripped the bench so hard my fingernails bent. My breath hissed through my clenched teeth as my insides squeezed together like they were in a vise, then stretched out of shape, all the while they burned and burned. I could almost taste the char in the back of my throat.

I tried to keep my breathing even and focus on the pictures that started to scroll in front of my eyes. Deep breath... in and out... in and out...

A little girl. A stuffed bear. Falling.

"A little girl with a stuffed bear."

Chay blew out a breath. He put both hands on his head and turned in a circle. "You just described half the kids around us."

"That's all I see," I snapped. Anger buzzed through my veins like a hive of angry hornets. The vision was only giving me glimpses of the problem. I needed the whole picture. My heart galloped in my chest. I didn't know how much time I had. I couldn't fail again. I couldn't.

Come on, come on! I need more. Give me more!

"I'm sorry," he said, rubbing my back.

I concentrated on the vision, trying to block out everything around me and just see the images in my mind and listen to the sounds.

Pink shorts. Pigtails. The bear is falling.

I focused harder, rocking back and forth on the bench, my hands pressed to my eyes.

A tiger. The stuffed bear. Falling.

"Oh!" I dropped my hands and sat up. "She's wearing pink shorts and pigtails. Her father has on a blue shirt and jeans. They're either by the tiger exhibit or they're on their way."

"I see them."

"Stop them! Stop them now! They can't get to that exhibit." I stood and bounced on the balls of my feet, my hands on the top of my head. My insides quivered like the nasty, green Jell-O they served at school.

"How?"

I can't think. I can't think of a way. The vision, it won't stop playing. It won't let me think!

I held my head. "I don't care! Just stop them or that father is going to fall into the pit with the tiger. She's going to drop her bear into the grating between the rock fence and the drop-off. He's going to try to climb over to get it, and he'll fall."

"I know what to do." Chay ran to a nearby kiosk gift shop and bought two stuffed bears. He ran back to me and grabbed my hand. We made it to the tiger exhibit just as the little girl dropped her bear over the fence. She started to cry. The father let go of her hand and braced himself to jump the fence when Chay stepped in.

"Sir, please don't do that. It's dangerous, and you have a lot of kids watching. You wouldn't want one of them trying it." He knelt down in front of the little girl. "We have two bears just like yours. How about you take one of our bears, and we'll let the zoo keepers have your bear as a surprise?"

She wiped her eyes with the back of her hand. "Okay." She took the bear Chay held out to her.

"Thank you," the father said, taking his little girl's hand and letting her pull him to the next exhibit.

"Better?" Chay looked at me and cupped my cheek in his hand. I leaned into him.

"Yes, but I don't want to leave while that bear is still there. Another parent might get some crazy idea or, God forbid, a kid. Will you stay here while I go get an attendant to fish it out? I won't feel good until it's gone." Chay waited at the fence while I found a zoo employee to get the bear so no one else would be tempted to try and grab it.

"Here." Chay held out the second stuffed bear when we walked away from the tiger exhibit. "This one is for you."

"Really? Thank you." Hugging the bear to me, I looked up at Chay. I pulled the bear back and looked at it, straightening its bow and smoothing the fur from its plastic, blue eyes. "This is…"

No boy has ever giving me anything like this before. What's it mean? It's just a bear, but what if it's not just a bear? What if it means something more to him? I think I'm going crazy. This love stuff is so hard to figure out. Wait. Love?

Chay tilted his head and looked at me. "What?"

I decided to go the bold route. Slipping my hand behind his neck, I pulled him to me. His lips fit mine perfectly. When I pulled back far enough to speak, I said, "Thank you. I love it."

"Damn, Milayna, if I'd known you liked teddy bears that much, I'd have been buying them for you every day."

179 *Michelle K. Pickett*

I sat down on a bench and settled my new stuffed friend in my lap. "Listen, I know we haven't been here that long, but do you think we could go?"

"Sure." Chay's brows knitted together. "Did I do something wrong?"

"No! You... You've been great. I've had a, um, it's been really nice being with you." I gave him a small smile and fidgeted with the bear in my lap. "It's just... the visions really zap my energy, and I feel so tired afterward. I don't want to ruin the day."

"Would eating help?" At my nod, he said, "How 'bout we get something to eat and see how you feel? If you still want to leave, we can. If you feel better, we can stay and see the rest of the zoo."

"Okay." I really wanted to go home and take a nap. A nap with him wouldn't have been too bad.

"Do you want to eat out here? We could get some burgers and sit on the lawn."

"Are your parents home?" I looked down at the toe of my shoe when I asked. When he didn't answer, I looked up through my lashes.

He was watching me with his blue-green gaze that seemed to see straight into me and read all my secrets. He cleared his throat. "Unfortunately, yes, they are."

I nodded and kicked at the ground with the toe of my shoe. "So are mine." I looked over my shoulder. There was a long stretch of crisp, green grass. Large oaks and sugar maples surrounded the area. The autumn sun warmed the air and shone through the brightly colored leaves like a stained glass window. "So, let's lie in the grass."

He smiled. "Okay, pick a spot, and I'll grab something to eat."

I found a place close to a tree and eased myself down onto the cool grass, watching him in line at the concession stand. Actually, I watched the other girls watching him, gloating when he didn't notice their attempts to attract his attention.

He paid for our food and brought back two burgers and every imaginable condiment. "I didn't know what you liked," he said with a shrug.

We made our burgers and ate in silence. I watched people walk by and listened to the birds in the tree above us.

"You're still exhausted." Chay's gaze trailed over my face.

"No, I feel better."

Sort of. I'm so tired, but I don't want our day to end. I want every second I can have with you.

"Let me take you home."

"No! I mean, are you ready to go home?" I held my breath, waiting for his answer.

"No, but I don't want you to be miserable. Here, lay your head in my lap. Rest for a while and see how you feel."

I hesitated.

My head in his lap. Oh, man. That is so not going to help me relax.

"Um, okay." I lay my head in his lap, my hair fanning out over his legs. He ran his finger down the side of my face and smiled down at me, twirling my hair around his fingers. It felt so good when he ran his fingers through my hair. It tickled throughout my body, like a feather was fluttering just beneath my skin. My muscles felt like jelly, and my eyes grew heavy.

I'll close them just for a minute. Then we'll get up.

Chay continued running his hand through my hair and down the side of my face. My body felt weightless, like we were floating away. Just him and I. As I snuggled closer, he pulled me to him until there was no space between us, just a beautiful sensation of perfumed peacefulness. It pulled me to it. I heard Chay's warm voice urging me to go, and with a contented sigh, I gave in.

Opening my eyes, I blinked a few times. I looked around before looking up at Chay. He was leaning back on his elbows, looking into the distance, my head still in his lap.

I pushed my hair out of my face. "I fell asleep. I'm so sorry. How long have I been sleeping?"

And, ohmigosh, did I snore or drool?

"About an hour or so, not too long." He sat up and looked down at me. "Feel better?"

"Yeah, but I'm sorry I made you sit here." I started to sit up, but Chay pushed my shoulders down, keeping me in place.

"You didn't make me do anything. I'm right where I want to be." He framed the side of my face with his hand. "What do you want to do now? Do you feel like doing something or should I take you home?"

I covered his hand with mine. "I don't want to go home."

"Then what do you want to do? We'll do whatever you want."

"How about the gardens?" I sat up. Chay's hand followed me, never leaving my hair.

"Whatever you want." He wrapped his hand around the back of my neck and pulled me to him. His lips were firm, moist, and molded to mine perfectly. The kiss was soft and slow. He lifted his head, and his gaze held mine. "You're beautiful." I felt a blush heat my cheeks. I looked at the ground, turning my face from him. He cupped my cheeks and pulled my face back to his. "Why do you do that? Why do you look away?"

"It's, um... I'm not..." I dropped my gaze from his.

No one's ever told me I was beautiful except family and they don't count, and you're... like... uh, freakin' amazing. How could I ever be beautiful standing next to you?

"Look at me, Milayna." I lifted my gaze to his. "You're beautiful." He kissed me gently.

"Thank you," I whispered around the lump squeezing my throat closed.

Michelle K. Pickett

I remembered back to when Muriel and I called Chay the hottie. It definitely fit. He was a stone-cold fox. I couldn't figure out how I measured up. It wasn't like I was a hag, but I didn't look in the mirror and see someone beautiful looking back at me.

"Let's go find these gardens you want to see."

We strolled through the gardens hand in hand for the rest of the after-noon until it was too dark to see and we were forced to go home.

"It's almost tomorrow," he murmured against my ear as we swayed in the swing in my backyard, watching the stars glimmer against the velvety black sky.

"I know."

"Think your mom and dad would let me bring you back the day after tomorrow?"

I smiled. "Somehow, I doubt it. Besides, aren't you tired of me yet?"

"I don't think I'll ever be tired of spending time with you." He ran his finger down the side of my face, across my jaw and to my lips.

My body instantly reacted to his touch. I could feel myself being drawn into him, like an invisible string was pulling me. His lips replaced his finger, moving softly over them. I leaned farther into him, urging him to take the kiss deeper. The air around us grew heated. My heart thundered in my chest. My breath came in small gasps when his mouth moved from mine to travel along my neck and across my collarbone. I sighed.

A ball Ben left in the yard jumped in the air, bouncing against the side of the house.

Chay lifted his head and grinned. "Telekinesis."

"Yeah. Kiss me again and let's see what else we can make bounce around."

He laughed and lowered his lips to mine.

22

The Vision

Two weeks, two days until my birthday.

Sunday morning at nine o'clock, I dialed the phone. I listened to the ringing on the other end, tapping my fingernails on my bedside table.

"'ello," Chay answered, his voice gravelly.

"Rise and shine," I chirped.

"What time is it?" I could hear his blankets rustling through the phone.

"About an hour later than you let me sleep yesterday," I told him.

"Don't you know weekends are for sleeping in?" Chay asked.

"I want to see you." I held out my hand and looked at my freshly painted fingernails.

"Isn't that my line?" he said and yawned.

"Yeah, but it works both ways. I'll pick you up in an hour."

He laughed. "Okay, if I have to."

"You do."

"I can't wait," he said, and I grinned like an idiot.

An hour later, I rang the doorbell at Chay's house. A pretty blonde answered the door. "Hi, Milayna. Come in."

"Hi, Mrs. Roberts."

She wasn't at all how I expected Chay's mother to look. She was a pale blonde with fairer skin, and a few freckles dotting the bridge of her nose. He and his mother shared the same unusual eye color, though.

"Chay will be right out. Have a seat." Mrs. Roberts perched on the

183   *Michelle K. Pickett*

arm of a chair and folded her hands in her lap. "You and Chay are in classes together?"

"Yes, ma'am. Three."

"That's great. You two seem to be getting along quite well."

Smiling, I nodded. I could feel a blush fingering its way up my neck toward my face. Nerves made my breakfast roll over in my stomach and play dead.

"So." Mrs. Roberts smiled and slapped her palms on her thighs. "Do you want to see some baby photos?" I almost laughed. I couldn't tell if she was serious or not. I mean, my mother liked to pull out the baby albums, but she at least waited until the third or fourth date.

"No, she does not." Chay jogged into the room, wearing a pair of distressed jeans and a T-shirt that knew all the right places to hug him. "Hi." He leaned over and kissed me.

When he lifted his head, I put my fingers to my lips and glanced quickly at his mother. She didn't seem the least bit concerned, but my face was burning.

"Oh, you embarrassed her." Chay's mom tsked and waved a hand at him. "Don't worry, Milayna, we know you kiss. It's nothing to be embarrassed over." She smiled and winked.

"But you'd embarrass me with baby photos." Chay laughed.

"Of course. I'm your mother. That's my right after twelve hours of labor and a nine-pound baby."

Chay rolled his eyes and made a blah, blah, blah motion with his hand, but smiled at his mom. "Are you ready?" he asked me.

"Yes."

"Where are you two off to?" Mrs. Roberts looked between us.

"I don't know. It's Chay's pick today. I picked yesterday."

"Dear, let me tell you a little secret. Don't let Chay pick. You'll find yourself spending the day at the go-kart speedway."

"That's okay; he spent the day at the zoo with me." I looked up at him and grinned like a moron.

"I'm just sayin'. I'd rather spend the day at the zoo than riding go-karts and picking gnats out of my teeth." She shuddered.

I tilted my head to the side. "Huh. Good point."

"Okay, see you when you get home." She kissed him on the cheek and then patted it. "Behave."

"I always do."

She snorted a laugh. "It was nice meeting you, Milayna."

"You, too, Mrs. Roberts."

We walked outside, and Chay looked around. "Where's your car?"

"My car isn't in the best working condition. I was hoping you'd drive."

"No problem. Wait, how'd you get here?"

"I walked."

"From your house? You walked around the block? Alone?" His voice rose with each syllable.

"Like my parents would ever let me do that. My dad drove me. I walked up the driveway alone."

"Don't do that!"

"What?" I could tell by his voice I'd upset him. Not the best way to start the day.

"Scare me like that." He blew out a breath.

"I'm sorry—"

He interrupted my apology with a kiss. Not the chaste schoolboy kiss he gave me in front of his mother, but a long, wet, stomach-fluttering, kiss.

"Hasn't your mother taught you not to interrupt?" I asked when he lifted his head.

"I think she mentioned something about it one day, but I interrupted her." He grinned at me.

"Cheesy, Chay." I smiled at him, and he shrugged a shoulder. "So, where are we going?"

"Wherever you tell me to drive." He opened the car door for me.

"Oh, no. It's your turn to pick."

"And if I said I wanted to go fishing?"

"I'd say we'd need to go by my house so I could get my rod and fishing license," I answered.

"Really?" He made a face.

"What? Girls can't fish in your world?" I stowed my purse in the back-seat.

"No, that's great. I love that you'd go fishing with me. It's just that you're the only girl I've dated that would."

"Is that what we're doing?" I slid into the car. He jogged around the back of the car and jumped in the driver's side.

"What? Fishing?" He slid the key into the ignition.

"No. Dating." I bit the corner of my bottom lip. My heart hammered in my chest as the seconds ticked by, and he didn't answer.

"Hmm." He cleared his throat and rubbed the back of his neck with one hand. "I—"

"Sorry, I shouldn't have said anything. I don't want to make the day weird." My knuckles cracked, and I realized I'd been twisting my fingers in my lap. I forced myself to relax my hands.

"Well, if you wouldn't interrupt me..." He leaned over and kissed me softly. "I was going to say I hope that's what we're doing. Dating, not fishing."

I let out a breath, and a huge smile spread across my face.

"Does the smile mean you're happy with the answer, or are you trying to figure a way out of dating me?"

185   *Michelle K. Pickett*

"The smile says I was hoping that would be your answer. I can't stop smiling, actually." I laughed. Twisting my fingers through his hair, I pulled his lips to mine. We were both still smiling and our teeth hit when we tried to kiss. Looping my arms around his neck, I pulled my face from his, buried it in the curve of his neck, and breathed him in.

He kissed the side my temple. "Now that we have the logistics of our relationship figured out, where do you want to go?"

I pulled back and looked at him, shaking my head. "Oh no, it's still your day to pick. This is an equal opportunity relationship."

"How about the mall?"

"The mall." I made a face. "I think you're trying to get me to forget it's your day to pick."

"What? Guys can't like the mall in your world?"

"You don't," I said, holding my breath against the pain building in my chest.

"Well, if you can like fishing, then I can like the mall. Besides, I'm thinking about the mall and then maybe the shops at the Waterway." Chay looked at me, and his brows pulled down. "What's the matter?"

I pinched the bridge of my nose with my fingers. My head started to pound.

Chay. His car. A bicycle.

"Don't back up," I said.

Chay dropped his hands from the steering wheel and brushed the hair from my face. "Tell me when it's safe," he said quietly.

Three little boys on their bicycles rode behind his car. The boys were laughing and goofing off, doing all the things boys do. What they weren't doing was watching for cars.

"Okay?" he asked, and I nodded. Chay put the car in reverse and slowly backed out of the driveway. "You know, you're as good as having one of those back-up sensors," he said with a chuckle.

I tried to give him a stern look, but failed and smiled. Reaching over, I pinched his side lightly. He laughed and brushed my hand away.

"Oh," I raised my eyebrows, "you're ticklish. That's a good thing to know."

We drove carefully up beside the boys riding their bikes, and Chay rolled down his window. "You guys start watchin' for cars or you're gonna get hurt."

The boys looked over at Chay with wide eyes before turning their gaze back to the road. Like a flock of geese, they swerved their bikes to the left and into the bike path in synchronization.

I would've thought after spending the entire day with him the day before, we'd have run out of things to talk about, especially since before we knew each other, he never seemed to talk in more than monosyllabic answers. But it seemed the opposite was true. The more we talked, the more we found to talk about. It seemed Mr. Dark-and-Brooding was long gone.

We started our day at the mall, laughing our way through the shops, looking at ridiculously priced clothes and shoes. Chay was a good sport about tromping through the stores with me. Even though going was his suggestion, I wasn't convinced he was all that interested in mall hopping, so I made it a quick visit. A few stops at the clearance racks, the bookstore, and the music store for Chay.

We were coming out of the music store when I tugged on the belt loop of Chay's lower-than-legal jeans. "Hey. Isn't that Jeff?"

He leaned in front of me to get a look, cupped his hands around his mouth, and yelled, "Jeff!" But Chay's voice was swallowed by the sounds of the shoppers coming and going.

"Who's he with?" I stood on my tiptoes to get a look.

"Trina? Is that her name?" Chay shrugged and looked at me. "Some blonde who's not nearly as beautiful as you." He brought my hand to his lips and kissed the inside of my wrist.

I tilted my head and looked at him. "Huh. That one was just on the okay side. I've definitely heard better lines. You need to work on your game, Victor." I patted his check and walked around him. He grabbed me from behind and tickled my side.

"Work on my game, huh?" He laughed.

"Yes," I giggled. "Hold the cheesy stuff."

"Okay, I'll keep that in mind."

"Let's go into Victoria's Secret." I had to bite the inside of my cheek to keep from laughing at the pink staining his high cheekbones. "Don't you want to see what all the fuss is about?" He cleared his throat, sticking his fingers in his pockets. I wrapped a lock of his hair around my finger. "Aren't you curious to know what the secret is?" I murmured.

His lips parted, and he wet them with his tongue. "Milayna..."

I took pity on him and pulled him past the store. "Okay, let's get out of here."

He blew out a breath and gave me a grin. "Hungry?"

We left the mall for an early lunch at a small café on the Waterway, an area next to the river full of art galleries, over-priced shops and street vendors, and every type of restaurant imaginable. We ate outside, watching the boats float lazily down the river.

"Let's take a boat ride tonight," Chay said.

"I'd love to take a boat ride! Why not after we eat?"

"It's prettier at night when the lights are lit. Haven't you seen them?"

Michelle K. Pickett

"Nope. Never been past the mall." I sipped my frozen lemonade and my mind wandered to Chay and me on a boat drifting down the river, engulfed in a coat of darkness. Alone, but for the gentle waves lapping at the side of the boat. My heart started to speed up, and my breath came in small gasps. Oh, hells yeah. I wanted that boat ride.

"A boyfriend has never brought you here?"

"Hmm?" Chay's question interrupted my semi-naughty—on its way to very naughty—daydream. "Oh. Not until today." I didn't mention the fact that I hadn't had too many boyfriends, and none that lasted more than a few weeks. My heart had always been saved for another. I'd thought it was Jake, but now I knew it was Chay.

"The boat ride is great at night. There are different colored lights lining the water. All the shops and restaurants are lit up, and the boat plays music and has a small dance floor. It's all very..."

"Very what?" I asked when he didn't finish.

"Romantic."

"Romantic, huh? Hmm. Are you trying to seduce me?" I teased. Sort of teased, really. He had me in knots. I wouldn't have minded a little seduction. Or a lot.

Chay put his mouth next to my ear. His breath skimmed across my skin, pulling goose bumps from it. I felt his lips move when he spoke, and I shivered. "No. What I'm trying to do is romance you."

Oh, wow. He has invaded me. Completely inserted himself into my life, my thoughts, my heart. He doesn't need to romance me. I'm his. Already his.

"Uh-oh. Did I just hear you right? You're a romantic?" I leaned closer to him. Our mouths were a fraction a part. Not touching, but hovering next to each other, our breaths mixing.

"Why is that so hard to believe?" He pulled back and looked at me.

I sighed. "You were kind of... well, distant and closed off when we first met." I swirled my fork in my pasta. "Muriel called you dark and brooding. I wouldn't have pegged you for the romantic type."

"Huh." He picked up his cup and took a drink of Coke.

"What?"

"You were talking about me to Muriel," he said with a lazy grin.

"Don't get an inflated ego."

When we finished eating and left the café, we walked past a street vendor selling handmade jewelry. Chay picked up a hammered silver cuff bracelet with a heart engraved on it. He paid the vendor and slipped it on my wrist. I sucked in a breath as his warm hands slid the cool metal against my skin.

Surprise and happiness stole my words. I licked my lips and a small, tentative smile touched them. My hand shook when I reached out to trace the heart engraved in the silver. My heart swelled to the point that it pressed tears at the back of my eyes. "A souvenir of your first trip to the Waterway," he murmured, kissing the hollow behind my ear.

"I can't... it's too expensive."

"I want you to have it."

I still looked at the bracelet, moving my finger over the heart again and again. "Thank you. It's beautiful, but it's not a souvenir of my trip to the Waterway." He gave me a puzzled look. "It's a reminder of my day with you."

He pursed his lips to hide a grin and looked down at the ground. "I like that." He took my hand and kissed the palm before threading our fingers together, pulling me toward a large, metal sculpture. Situated around it were benches and large containers overflowing with fall foliage and brightly colored flowers.

"What are we doing?" I asked when he stopped and stood staring at the ground.

He held up a finger for me to wait. "We are waiting for... that." He laughed when I jumped as geysers of water shot out of the cemented area around the sculpture and created a screen between us and the visitors on the other side. Colored spotlights shone on the water, creating a rainbow.

I stuck my hand into one of the water walls surrounding us. "Wicked cool."

"If you think that's cool, wait until tonight." One side of his mouth tipped up in a grin. "You want a better look?" he asked quickly.

"No!" Letting out a small scream, I fisted my hand in the front of his shirt just seconds before he pushed me into the cold spray. I pulled him in with me.

We stumbled over each other's feet, trying not to fall and embarrass ourselves, all the while laughing loud and unrestrained. I loved seeing the openness on Chay's face, hearing his deep laugh, seeing the skin crinkle at the sides of his eyes.

"You weren't supposed to get me wet too!" he said, still half laughing. He pulled me against him and kissed me quickly.

"You didn't think I was going to be the only one walking around in uncomfortable, wet jeans did you?" My jeans made a sucking sound when I pulled them away from my skin.

"I didn't think you'd know what I was going to do in time to grab me."

"I saw your tell." I shrugged.

"My what?"

"Your tell. The slightest movement a person makes just before they do something or when they're lying."

"And what's my tell?" he asked, looking at me. The water still sprayed around us, soaking us both.

"Depends on what you're going to do. Just now, you shifted your

189   *Michelle K. Pickett*

weight. I knew you were going to push me in because your shoulder tensed and your weight shifted to give you leverage."

"So what are my other tells?"

I looked down, spreading my fingers over one of the colored lights, watching the water and light dance on my skin. "Your eyes darken just before you lean in to kiss me." I tried to keep my voice from quivering like my insides were. Goose bumps covered my skin, and I hoped he thought they were from the cool water splashing over us rather than me thinking about how his kisses made me feel—all warm and gooey and like my world had tipped. "That's my favorite." I looked up at him, and his eyes darkened. "Yeah, just like that," I whispered as his lips lowered to mine.

Chilled from the cool water, we climbed a grassy hill in a park near the water sculpture. I squeezed as much water from my hair and clothes as I could and stretched out on the lawn to let the sun dry them. We lay in the grass with the large autumn sun beating down on us and talked. And laughed. And talked some more.

Once we were dry enough that our shoes didn't make squishing noises when we walked, we spent the rest of the afternoon wandering through the small art galleries and shops.

"What are you doing?" I giggled at the look on Chay's face as he regarded an abstract painting in one of the upscale art boutiques. He tilted his head from one side to the other, studying the random shapes and colors.

"Honestly?" He stepped closer to the painting and narrowed his eyes. "I'm trying to figure out what it is."

"It's abstract. You aren't supposed to know what it is." I nudged him with my shoulder.

He laughed; the sound bounced off the walls of the mini gallery, echoing in the sparse space. "If I'm going to pay that kind of money for something, I want to know what it is."

"So you're the type of guy who likes velvet paintings of dogs playing poker?" I teased.

"Something like that. I wouldn't mind a photograph or two."

"There are some really pretty prints a little further down." I took his hand and pulled him to the photographs on display.

Chay gave them a cursory glance and shook his head. "Nah, not for me. Maybe if I did this." He placed his hands on my upper arms and guided me in front of the photographs. "Yeah, that's a photo I could get used to." He snapped a quick photo with his cell phone.

I could feel my insides melt at his words. "Be serious," I said on a laugh.

Is he being cheesy or is he really this romantic?

When the sun started to set, we found a bench overlooking the water and sat to watch. The sky was streaked with magnificent colors of red and gold shining through puffy, white clouds.

"It's pretty here. Thank you for bringing me."

"I can't believe you've lived here all your life and you've never come until today." Chay looked at me and ran a finger up my arm.

"I know. We always travel to another city or state to do the touristy things. I never thought there were places to go right in my own hometown. I'm glad I've never been here before, though. I liked seeing it for the first time with you."

He cupped my face with his hands and kissed me as the last of the sun's rays slipped behind the horizon and the Waterway lit up around us like a Christmas tree. It was beautiful. The multi-colored lights made the water look like a floating rainbow.

"Now we take the boat ride I promised you," Chay said, pulling me gently to the dock.

We boarded the boat and found a spot next to the railing away from the other passengers, watching the lights as we floated down the river. A band played in the small dance area and music filtered outside, the sound mingling with the gentle lapping of the water and the far-off conversations of people walking along the water's edge.

"You're right. It's beautiful," I told him.

He leaned forward and touched his lips softly to mine, running his fingers through my hair. I wrapped my arms around his neck and pulled him closer. He kissed me as soft music carried on the breeze from the dance floor.

Pulling back, he looked at me and smiled. "Let's dance."

"That's okay. I'm not much of a dancer."

Dude, give me a reason to press up against you and I'm there. But dancing? I'd trip and take us both down like the Hindenburg.

"You'll be fine." Chay gently tugged on my hand. "I'll show you how. As slow as the songs are, you'll only have to sway." He pulled me to him. His gaze held mine, expression serious. "Dance with me, Milayna. I want to hold you. Feel you against me. Whatever you're afraid of, whoever you're afraid of, I'm here. I'm not letting you go. Please." He placed his lips against my temple before leading us into the cabin.

His words reached down and wrapped themselves around my heart and, at that moment, I was sure there wasn't anything I would have denied him. I followed him to the dance area. It was a small room, with large windows giving a view of the water and the lights twinkling on shore. The band played slow instrumentals. The floor was full of couples dancing close, murmuring to each other as they swayed in time to the music.

Chay led me to the small, wooden dance floor and wrapped his arms

Michelle K. Pickett

around my waist. I circled his neck with my arms and breathed him in. We moved to the music, looking at each other, not speaking. It was intimate and sensual, being so close to him. His hands moved slowly up and down my spine, and I threaded my fingers through his silky hair.

"What are you thinking?" he asked quietly.

"That it's been a perfect day. And that I don't want tonight to end," I whispered. "What are you thinking?"

"That I can't remember when I've been this happy." He ran a finger down the side of my face.

We danced until the boat docked an hour later. We would've stayed and ridden again, but we'd been on the last boat ride of the night. The shops on the Waterway were closing. Slowly, the lights were flickering off, taking some of the magic with them.

Chay and I walked hand in hand down the cobblestone lane to the parking garage where Chay's car was parked when a stabbing pain in my stomach doubled me over. Then my head started to throb.

Not now. Not tonight. Please, just one normal night.

But the feeling didn't go away. It intensified. The stabbing pain spread like a rash, blanketing my body in unbearable pain that took over my senses until that was all I could focus on. My fingers pushed on my temples, trying to push away the searing pain in my head. I tried to relax and the let the vision take over, but I was in too much pain. I tensed against it.

"You're having a vision?"

I nodded, still clutching my head. It felt like someone was inside my skull with a blowtorch.

Red light. Water. Woman.

"What do you see?"

I shook my head. The pain was too intense to speak. The twisting in my stomach squeezed the breath from my lungs, and the burning in my head and across my skin was almost unbearable. My vision jumped in time with my heartbeat, which was speeding at an incredible rate.

Water. Blood. Woman.

Concentrating on the images, I tried to block out the pain. I rolled my head and shoulders to relax my neck and back muscles. Chay guided me to a bench and I sat down and bent forward with my arms around my knees, while he gently massaged my shoulders.

Tour bus. Woman. Blood. Bridge.

The images were coming too slow. They weren't giving me enough information.

"A woman and a tour bus," I said through clenched teeth. "I don't know if she is getting on the bus or is already."

"What does she look like?"

"Brown hair and glasses. She's wearing a green blouse. That's all I can see."

"Okay, what's the tour bus look like?"

"Like a bus!" I yelled. "Sorry." I rocked back and forth on the bench, my arms still wrapped around my knees. My stomach felt like it was tied in knots. I could taste the metallic taste of blood in my mouth where I'd bitten my cheek to keep from crying out. Bile rose in the back of my throat, burning it.

There were a lot of tour buses. The Waterway was a huge tourist attraction. The streets were crowded, full of groups of people boarding their buses and strolling down the cobblestone streets to their cars.

Bridge. The woman. Headlights. Squealing tires.

"The bridge. Something is going to happen to her on the bridge."

Falling. Water bubbles. Blood swirling.

"C'mon." Chay pulled me off the bench. I stumbled forward. I could feel her falling, feel the sting of the water when she hit it. See the blood swirling, mixed with the air bubbles in the water. I shook off the feelings and followed him.

"I can feel it," I panted, trying to keep pace with his longer strides. I pushed through the pain of the vision. It was so intense that I wanted to lie down on the cobblestone and curl into myself.

"What?"

"What she's gonna feel if we can't find her."

We ran toward the bridge. I stumbled several times, trying to keep up, when hot, searing pain stabbed through me, stealing my breath.

The sidewalk was crowded, and we were running against the flow of traffic. We were jostled and pushed. Some people looked at us in surprise, and some got angry and yelled for us to slow down. We kept running as fast as we could through the throng of people.

I lost my grip on Chay's hand. Panic swallowed me as he disappeared into the crowd. I had no choice but to keep moving in the general direction of the bridge. My eyes darted from person to person, searching for Chay, but I didn't slow down to look for him. The images screamed through my head, pushing me. The urge to find the woman was too great. I had to get to the bridge before she got to the tour bus.

I continued running, pushing my way through the people coming at me. Trying to move against the flow of people did nothing but push me backward, wasting precious seconds. Finally, after what seemed like hours of pushing my way along the crowded sidewalk, I saw the bridge. The lights shone brightly against the darkening Waterway. I stood on my tiptoes to get a better look, straining to find the woman. I didn't know where to look. The vision replayed the same images in my head over and over, never adding anything new.

I couldn't hold my position through the mass of people walking toward me. I darted into the street, where there was less foot traffic and a better

193 *Michelle K. Pickett*

view. Trying to ignore the pain that still ravaged my body from the vision, I ran faster toward the bridge, dodging cars and buses, the image of the woman fused into my brain. I scanned the crowd for a green shirt. I'd never noticed how common the color was, but it seemed like every woman at the Waterway that night was wearing some variation of green.

When I reached the foot of the bridge, I saw her. She walked on the side of the bridge toward me. I scanned the area. There was no tour bus. I heaved a sigh of relief and tried to push my way to her.

I heard it before I saw it. The engine too loud. It barreled down the bridge too fast. Her back was to it as she walked alongside the row of parked tour buses, looking up at their route signs. I watched in horror as the bus slammed into her. Her body flew into the air like a rag doll. She bounced off the concrete guardrail and fell over the side of the bridge. I heard her hit the water with a sickening slap.

I stopped running. The vision was gone. I stood in the middle of the road and stared at where the bus hit the woman. I'd been just seconds away from reaching her. If I could've gotten to her... if I'd seen the bus... if... if... if. I put my hands on top of my head and squeezed to block out the person screaming next to me. My lungs burned, felt deflated like balloons, and the back of my throat was scorched in an itchy sort of way. I sucked in a large breath and let it out. My neck muscles strained, and my head throbbed—it was then I realized I was the person screaming.

I fell to my knees. My screams turned to tears. It was done. The vision hadn't done its job. I failed. I was positive the woman was dead. I could feel it. My fingers and hands turned cold, and my toes felt like leaden ice cubes. An icy wind whipped through my hair, stinging my face where it smacked against it. My blood was like slush slogging through my veins.

People ran to the side of the bridge and looked over. They knocked into me as they passed. I sat motionless in the middle of the road. I wondered why they were running. There was nothing to do—it was over.

Someone grabbed my arm and jerked me off the ground. I screamed. Then I saw his face.

Chay crushed me against him, turning me away from the bridge. "C'mon," he murmured close to my ear. His breath was warm on my frozen skin.

I let him guide me to a small café table outside one of the shops we'd walked through earlier in the day. I could hear sirens in the distance. They grew louder and louder until their piercing wails were so loud that I had to put my hands over my ears. The red and blue flashing lights cast everything in odd shadows. They were nothing like the beautiful lights of the Waterway just minutes earlier.

I buried my face in the curve of Chay's neck and cried. Every few seconds, I'd lift my head and look toward the bridge. Chay would cup my face

Milayna   194

and guide it back to him. Finally, he unzipped his jacket and pulled my head to his chest. He wrapped his jacket around me like a blanket and shielded me from the ugliness on the other side.

And for just a moment, it was enough.

It was almost one o'clock in the morning when we gave our statement to the police. Chay had called our parents and explained why we missed curfew. I sat and stared straight ahead. I couldn't get the image of the woman's body bouncing off the front of the tour bus and over the side of the bridge out of my head. Sometime during our wait, the coroner drove slowly through the remaining crowd of people.

"I knew she was dead," I whispered. They were the first words I'd spoken since Chay and I gave our statement to the police.

"This isn't your fault." He threaded his fingers through mine before kissing the inside of my wrist.

I shrugged a shoulder and looked away.

Yes, it is.

"You're freezing." He frowned and placed his jacket over my shoulders. I stuck my arms through the sleeves. His jacket was soft and warm and when I breathed in, I could smell his cologne lingering in the fabric.

"Can you take me to my grandma's? I'll call my parents from there."

"Whatever you need, Milayna."

We were quiet on the way to my grams' apartment. I looked out of the passenger's side window while Chay drove through town. The lights whizzed by and melded into one multi-colored rope rolling past the window. I watched it wind its way around the car through my watery gaze. I wasn't sure when I started crying. Maybe it was while Chay and I were sitting in front of the darkened shop, or when the police interviewed us, or maybe I'd been crying all along.

When we reached Grams' apartment, Chay walked me inside.

"Go lay down, child," Grams said as soon as she saw me. I crawled onto the purple couch I loved and pulled one of her soft, patchwork quilts over me. I still couldn't get warm. "You must be Milayna's Chay," I heard Grams say.

"Yes, ma'am."

She tsked. "Call me Grams. All the family does."

"Okay," he said, looking over her head at me. I tried to smile at him, but I couldn't get my lips to form it.

"A bad vision?" she asked Chay.

He nodded. "A bad outcome."

"Ah. Well now, that is an unfortunate turn of events. She was just

Michelle K. Pickett

coming to terms with everything." Grams looked over at me. "She's strong. Stronger than she thinks. She'll be all right."

"If you don't mind, I'd like to stay with her for a little while. Please."

My grandma studied Chay so long that I didn't think she was going to answer. "I don't see the harm in that," she said finally. "I'll call her parents. How much do they know?"

"Everything. I called them."

"Good, they can fill me in." Grams wheeled her chair into the other room to use the phone.

Chay sat on the floor next to the couch. He reached out and smoothed the hair from my face. "How are you feeling?"

"Fine."

Chay sighed and looked at me. His eyes were full of emotion. The blue and green seemed to swirl. "Milayna, you've given me the same answer for the last two hours. Tell me what you're really feeling."

"Like I failed."

Again. I failed again. But this time, I let someone die. What kind of demi-angel am I? Maybe I'm no better than Azazel.

"You didn't fail. You did everything you could do, everything and more. No one thinks you've failed."

"I do." I felt hot tears streak down my face again and wondered if I'd ever stop crying.

Chay kissed me lightly on the mouth before brushing my tears away with the pads of his thumbs.

"I'm going to go change. I'll be right back." I eased away from Chay and off the couch. I shut the bedroom door softly behind me before digging out a pair of black yoga pants and a long, purple T-shirt from the drawer of things Muriel and I kept stashed at Grams'.

I went into the bathroom and washed off what little makeup was left on my face and changed into the clean clothes. Wrapping myself up in Chay's jacket and my grandmother's quilt, I went back into the living room.

"Milayna, why don't you go lie down? You look exhausted," Grams said.

"'Kay." It didn't matter where I was. Couch or bed, my thoughts would follow me.

"I'll see you tomorrow." Chay gave me a small kiss before turning toward the door.

"No, Chay, wait. Sit with me until I fall asleep?" I didn't want to be alone. The memories wouldn't go away. The images from the night played over and over in my head. But I felt safe in Chay's arms. He understood like no one else could. I needed him.

He looked quickly at my grandmother. At her slight nod, he smiled at me. "Sure."

Milayna   196

I climbed onto Grams' four-poster bed. Chay sat up beside me, his back against the headboard and his long legs stretched out in front of him, my head laying on his chest, and his arm around my shoulders. I listened to his heart beating, strong and alive. We lay like that, unspeaking in the darkness, for a long while. I didn't even feel myself get sleepy, but then it was morning and the sun streamed through the windows into my eyes.

I heard my parents talking to my grandma in hushed tones from the living room. Crawling out of bed, I walked by a mirror. I was surprised I was still wearing Chay's jacket, and I wondered vaguely what he'd worn home. When I smoothed my hand over the soft suede, something shiny caught my eye. I looked at my wrist in the mirror and saw the bracelet he'd bought me. I wasn't sure why, but it brought tears to my eyes.

I was crying when I went to bed, and I'm crying when I wake up. All I do is cry.

"Hey, honey," my dad said when he saw me.

My mom put her arm around my shoulders and guided me to the sofa. Turning, I buried my head in the side of her neck and sobbed. I cried so hard my entire body shook. My mom sat quietly and let me cry, smoothing my hair down my back. She didn't say anything until my sobs turned to hiccupped sniffles. "It's okay, Milayna," she whispered.

I shook my head. It wasn't all right. Not for me. Not for the woman at the Waterway.

"Things like this are going to happen. Sometimes, the visions fail us." My dad reached out and patted me on the knee.

"Then why have them?" My words were muffled against my mother's shoulder. "Why did I have the vision if there was nothing I could do to stop it?"

No one answered me.

"I want to get rid of it." I heard my dad's quick intake of breath and felt my mother tense. "How do I get rid of this... whatever it is? Power? Sixth sense? I want it gone."

I was done. I'd tried it. I'd given being a demi-angel a chance. The visions controlled my life, and I let them, doing what they told me to. But it was obvious I wasn't cut out for the demi-angel gig. First, the girl at school, and now, the woman at the Waterway. I'd failed them both. And one died because of it. Because of me. No. I wasn't going to do it anymore. I didn't want the job in the first place. There had to be someone else I could give it to. Someone who'd do it better.

"Milayna—"

"Dad, there's gotta be a way. I can't watch something like last night again. Knowing I could have stopped it if I had only been quicker. Gotten to her faster. Knowing that it's my fault." I started crying again.

"It's not your fault, Milayna. You did what you could. You did everything right," my dad said calmly.

Michelle K. Pickett

"I didn't do enough!" I yelled and balled my fists.

My mom pushed me gently away from her and looked into my eyes. "Stop it," she chided softly. "This isn't your fault."

"But if I—"

"You had no chance of saving that woman." My dad leaned forward on the couch and let his hands drop between his knees.

"But I was right there. I was almost to her. If I'd gotten there sooner, she'd still be alive. I failed her, and she died because of it. I'm not cut out for this demi-angel shit. I'm supposed to help people, not kill them!" My voice rose on the last few words until I was almost screaming. Hot tears seared my skin as they ran down my face.

Why can't they see what's in front of them? I'm a failure. Just let it go. Accept it and move on. Oh. I get it. I'm an embarrassment to my dad. That's it. A failure and an embarrassment.

He sighed. "No, she wouldn't. This vision was intended to teach you a lesson."

When my dad's words finally registered, I raised my head and looked at him. "What do you mean?" I asked slowly. A small burning began deep in my stomach.

"Azazel did this, Milayna. If you'd gotten to the woman, he would've used someone else. He knew you'd have a vision if he put someone in danger. He used it to show you he can get to people—strangers, friends, family. He's trying to scare you into giving in to him."

I shook my head and held my hand up in front of me. "He killed her for no reason? Just to prove a point?" The burning grew. My stomach was consumed in fire. I could feel the flames licking at my lungs, stealing my breath. My head emptied of all thought but that of Azazel and the evil he brought down on innocent people.

My dad nodded. His lips were mashed so hard into a thin line that they were white.

"You're sure there's no other way to get rid of this? I can't transfer it to another group member? Give it to them?"

My dad shook his head. "No. It's yours alone."

I nodded my head. "Right. Okay." The images of all the visions I'd had ran through my memory. With each one, my muscles tensed until they were so taut it felt like they'd snap. My teeth clenched until my jaw ached. Still I watched the visions replay in front of me. The little girl who'd have been violated by the pervert in the park. The woman on the street who'd have been attacked by the serial rapist... on and on until it ended with the night before at the Waterway.

No! He can't do that! Someone has to try and stop the demon bastard. If I can't get rid of this demi-angel shit, then...

"I'm not giving it to him. There's no way he's going to be allowed to do things like this without paying. He may have thought this would break me, but he's just made one helluva enemy. I'm gonna fight him until I take my last breath. That's what I was born to do."

I was tired of being scared. Of worrying when I'd see another demon. When Azazel would show his face. He used that innocent woman's death as a way to break me. I sat on my favorite purple couch and knew...

He'd just made me stronger.

Michelle K. Pickett

23

Steven

TWO WEEKS UNTIL MY BIRTHDAY.

I'm drowning.

My lungs burn from lack of oxygen. I try to hold my breath, but the need to fill my lungs causes me to open my mouth and inhale. Water fills my lungs, my head pounds, and my chest burns. My body tries to rid itself of the offending water. I cough and suck in more.

I'm dying.

I start to convulse. My body jerks and shakes. I'm writhing in pain. And through it all, I hear a voice. Not my mother's voice telling me she loves me. Not my fathers or my grams'. Not Chay's.

"This could have been avoided, Milayna, if you'd only sided with me," it says.

I bolted upright in bed and rubbed my chest, looking from side to side. I was in my bed at home. There was no one there. I was safe.

I let out a breath and climbed out of bed, walking to the window. A shadowy figure stood on the sidewalk in front of my house. I jerked backward, tripped over my feet, and fell on my butt. Slowly, I crawled to the wall beside the window. I stood up, peeking out from behind the curtain. The figure stood in the same place.

My heart began to race, blood rushed behind my ears, and beads of sweat ran down my back.

Who is that?

I dropped to all fours and crawled to my bedroom door. Opening it, I made my way into the hallway. Standing, I bolted for my parent's room.

"Dad!"

"We see," he called from downstairs. I ran down the stairs and peeked around the corner. He sat on the couch, looking outside.

"Hey, beautiful." Chay smiled and motioned for me to come to him.

"What are you doing here?" It was the first time I'd seen him since the Waterway. We'd talked on the phone and texted each other, but I hadn't been ready to see anyone, not even him. He shrugged a shoulder. "Oh. You sensed trouble. Why didn't anyone tell me about the little party with shadow man out there?" I sat on the couch between Chay and my dad.

"No need to wake you," my dad said. "You haven't been getting enough sleep as it is. Why are you up now? A nightmare?"

I nodded. Chay wrapped his arm around my shoulders, pulling me to him for a quick kiss. I snuggled against him, resting my head on his shoulder.

"Who's our mystery guest?" I said around a yawn, waving my hand at the window.

"Not sure. Probably a demi-demon," Chay answered.

"What's he doing out there?" I snuggled closer to Chay, feeling safe in his arms, against his warmth. My stalker friend didn't exactly fill me with warm fuzzies—more like a glass of ice water. The hair stood up on the back of my neck, and I scooted even closer to Chay. He squeezed me against him.

Chay shrugged. My head bobbed up and down with the movement of his shoulders, and I smiled. "My guess is he's trying to scare you."

"I don't know if I'm scared or just creeped out." I reached for the phone. "Did you call the police?"

"Your dad did. You should really go upstairs and try to sleep," he whispered close to my ear, sending jolts of adrenaline-filled electricity through my bloodstream.

"Like I can sleep with Peeping Tom out there." I shuddered and snuggled closer to Chay, soaking in his warmth.

The three of us sat quietly in the darkened living room, waiting for the police. Chay put his hand under my hair and massaged the back of my neck.

Just minutes later, a spotlight pierced through the darkness and illuminated our stalker. There was a blip from the siren, and the red and blue lights started flashing. They gave everything an eerie glow. Mr. Peeping Tom looked menacing as the lights scrolled across his skin. The car pulled up to him and stopped. He and the officer exchanged words before the officer guided him into the back of the police cruiser, and it drove away.

"Well, that was interesting," I murmured. "Did you recognize him?" I looked up at Chay.

"Yeah. His name is Edward. A real pain in the ass." Chay coughed and looked at my dad. "Sorry, sir."

Michelle K. Pickett

My dad smiled. "Aren't all demi-demons a pain in the ass?"

Chay picked me up for school later that morning.

"Morning." He stood on the porch with his hands in his pockets. His arms were straight, making his shoulders rise.

"Hi." I stood on my tiptoes and kissed him.

"Get any sleep after I left?" His arm snaked around my waist for another kiss.

"Not really."

"What's wrong?" He pushed me away from him and studied my face. "Have you been crying?"

"Not much." I cried for the woman who died and for my friends and family, who I was afraid would die, as well. Grief mixed with fear was a constant weight on my shoulders. Every day it got a little heavier, harder to carry. I felt like I'd snap under the pressure.

After the shock of watching the woman get killed, I decided to fight Azazel. To use my power against him. And I was determined to do it, too. But I was still scared, especially of what he could do to the people I loved.

Chay hugged me and ran his hand up and down my back. "I'm sorry."

I buried my face in his shoulder and inhaled his scent. His touch and his smell calmed me. I lifted my head, blew the hair out of my face, and smiled at him. "Let's get this over with, huh?"

The school day dragged on and on. I thought the last bell would never ring so I could go home. I hated being in the same place with Shayla and Lily. And now that they'd shown themselves, I had to see the other Evils as well. Chay walked me to and from every class, and every time, we'd see an Evil or a demi-demon.

"Just ignore them," Chay told me when he walked me to history class.

I picked at the cover of my notebook. "Yeah. That'll be easy."

"They can't do anything to you at school. They're just trying to scare you."

"It's working." I eyed one of them as we walked by.

Finally, the last bell of the day rang. Desperate to get out of that building, I dashed to the door and out of the classroom. The walls felt like they were closing in on me and everywhere I looked, I saw one of Azazel's groupies. I needed out. I was almost to my locker when I felt a hard tug on my backpack. I thought it was Chay. He'd be mad I didn't wait for him. Turning, I flinched at the ugly sneer marring the face that glared back at me.

"Lily." I tried to sound unaffected by her presence.

"Milayna…" She slowly pulled out the syllables of my name. "Where's your bodyguard?" She looked around and arched a perfectly shaped brow.

"I don't have one. Where's your malevolent posse? Oh, sorry." I tapped my finger on my lips. "Do you need me to define 'malevolent?' It has more than two syllables." I tilted my head to the side, my eyes wide.

"Funny. They're around," she said, inspecting her French-tipped nails. "We're always around."

"Good to know." I shouldered past her, knocking her backward. My heart was drumming double time.

Chay walked toward me, looking at the ground, shaking his head. A ghost of a grin touched his delicious lips. "Not smart."

"I figured it was better than cowering in fear in front of her."

"Probably. Next time, wait for me." He reached out and lightly pulled on a lock of my hair before pushing it behind my ear.

Muriel flopped backward on my bed with a huff. She'd come over after school to do homework, which took about a minute to do. "We should do something. I'm bored."

I looked at her from across the room where I was hanging up my clothes I'd thrown around that morning looking for something to wear. "You're always bored. I swear, you're hyper. You need some Ritalin."

"Hey! Where'd you get that top? That's straight-up sexy. You need to wear that tonight, and we need to go somewhere." She climbed to her knees in the middle of my bed.

"Why do I want to go out with you and wear something sexy? I was kind of saving this for Chay." I looked at the pale pink, silk tank top. The front collar was a little lower than I was used to, and the back plunged, fabric cascading in delicate folds, the two sides held together by a thin band of silk across the back.

"Yeah, Chay's coming too. We'll all go. Movie and dinner, huh? Sounds good, right?" She was already sending the text to the group. She tossed her phone on the bed and smiled at me. Two seconds later, my phone chimed.

Chay: Are you going with Muriel tonight?
Me: Might be fun.
Chay: 'Kay. I'll pick you up.

At six o'clock, Chay pulled into my driveway. We drove to the movie theater to meet Muriel, Drew, Jen, and Jeff. Steven and Jake had football practice.

"Hey, guys!" I skipped to catch up with Muriel, towing a less enthusiastic Chay behind me.

Muriel turned and tugged on Drew's sleeve to get his attention, and they met us in front of the ticket booth. "Hey! Crazy crowded tonight."

"I know, right? We're parked in the last row of the back lot."

Michelle K. Pickett

"I think we're just two or three rows from you. I've never seen it this busy."

Drew looked over my head at Chay. "Hey, man."

"Drew, how's it going?" Chay fist bumped him over my head. I was starting to get a complex. Either I was short or they were grotesquely tall. Or maybe just gorgeously tall... yeah.

"It's all Channing Tatum, you know." Muriel looked at me and grinned.

I smiled and winked at her, but I didn't say anything.

Chay buried his face in the curve of my neck and planted soft kisses up to my ear. "Channing Tatum, hmm?"

I shrugged and looked at him wide-eyed. "I don't even know who that is."

Chay laughed, picked me up, and swung me onto his back piggy-style. He carried me to the door of the theater before he set me down. Muriel rolled her eyes. "You two are sickening."

We met up with Jen and Jeff in the arcade before buying our popcorn and going into the theater.

"Let's see some shit get blown up!" Jeff threw a piece of popcorn in his mouth and smiled.

"Let's see Channing Tatum blow shit up while he's naked," Jen corrected.

I choked on my Coke.

It was late when the movie ended and we'd eaten. We walked across the back lot to our cars when they stepped out of the shadows of the dumpsters.

I turned and framed his face with my hands. "Be careful."

Chay pulled me closer and kissed me gently. His hands tangled in my hair. "You too."

Muriel shook her head. "Geez, I hate this," she muttered. "It's so gonna hurt."

"Hiding out in the dumpsters with the trash? Just where you belong," I yelled to the group of Evils and demi-demons standing in front of us.

Chay blew out a breath, ran his hand up the back of his head, and let it rest on top of his head. "Milayna, please don't antagonize them. 'Kay?"

I looked at him and shrugged.

"He wants you," one of them called back.

"He's a fool and a coward. And he doesn't know when to take a hint. I've already said no. More than once. Does he need me to draw it in crayon?"

I heard Chay groan behind me and mutter something about 'not keeping my mouth shut.'

The Evils and demi-demons moved closer to us. One guy stood in front of me. He was half a head taller than me, but as thin as a rail.

I can take string bean, here, easy.

I rolled my shoulders and shook out my arms.

"What did you say?" the guy asked.

"Milayna," Chay warned.

I was way too stubborn to listen to Chay's subtle warning. Instead, I continued egging the demi-demon on. Taunting him. "I said, Azazel. Is. A. Fool. And. A. Coward." I over-enunciated each word to make my point. I was tired. Irritated they were ruining our night. And I wanted to go home. Plus, if we ended up fighting, they were going to ruin my brand new, sexy, silk shirt. And that pissed me off.

He reached out and slapped me hard across the face. My head snapped to the side from the force. My skin burned, and I was sure if I looked in a mirror, I'd see a perfect, red handprint.

Whoa. Should've been paying attention. I didn't see that one coming.

Chay tried to push past me. I held my arm out to stop him.

"It's okay." In my mind, I was visualizing hitting the idiot that slapped me. I turned quickly, hit the guy under the chin with a palm-heel strike, kneed him in the balls, and pushed him away from me.

He lay on the ground, holding his crotch. I walked over to him and crouched down.

"Don't ever touch me again," I whispered.

"You're either fearless or a badass," Drew said from my side when I'd stood. I didn't have time to answer. The rest of the demi-demons rushed us.

Before I could turn around, one had me in a bear hug from behind. I elbowed him in the stomach. He let go and I turned, kicking at his balls—always my favorite move on a guy—but he caught my foot and twisted it. I landed on my stomach with a grunt—the concrete ate away the flesh at my elbows.

I pushed myself off the ground and punched behind his knee. He fell next to me. I landed an uppercut. I could feel his teeth clamp together when the hit connected, sending jolts of pain through my hand.

He looked at me with such hatred that I flinched. He got one good backhand to my face in before I rolled, jabbed him in the side, and swung my arms, jumping to my feet.

I was fighting off my doofus of a demi-demon when a heard a commotion to my left. Shouting, scuffling, Chay cursing a violent string of words, a grunt, and then nothing.

The guy I was fighting took advantage of my distraction and got a good hit to my head. I shook off the stars I saw floating in front of my eyes just in time to block his next blow. He threw another punch, and I ducked. He hit nothing but air. It threw him off balance enough that two good kicks had him

Michelle K. Pickett

lying on the ground.

I ran to Chay. There was a group of demi-demons, and I only saw Drew and Jake fighting them, but I knew Chay was in the mix. I'd heard him.

What's Jake doing here? He had football practice tonight.

The closer I got to the group, the stranger I felt. My stomach swirled like someone was using a hand mixer in it. Around and around it went, scraping the sides of my body. A heat built in my chest and radiated through my body down to my fingers and toes. I looked at my fingers. They looked the same, but they tingled, like how it felt after I'd slept on my hand, when it prickled and tingled.

Pushing my way through the group of demi-demons, I braced myself for them to fight, but they ignored me, too preoccupied by the show in the middle of the circle. When I broke through the circle of people and saw what had their attention, my breath stalled and I was frozen in place. My eyes refused to translate the image I saw to my brain.

Then Jake hit him again and blood flew out of Chay's mouth and splattered on my leg.

I pushed off as hard as I could and barreled into Jake. He was huge. A football player, he worked out in the weight room regularly. I knew I didn't have a chance in hell against him, so I was counting on the element of surprise. I barely budged him, but I prevented him from landing another hit on Chay.

"What the hell are you doing?" I screamed.

"Fighting with my team." He gave me one of his movie-star-handsome smiles.

"Your team? Since when do you fight against us?"

"Since I joined with Azazel." I just stared at him. Another demi-demon came close and assumed a fighting stance. Jake waved him away. He stepped toward me and cupped my cheek. "Don't look so surprised." His body almost touched mine. Not quite, but I could feel his heat. His hand still held the side of my face, and his thumb rubbed over my cheek. "Come with me. You'd have everything you've ever dreamed of." He leaned forward, and his lips skimmed mine. "We'd be good together, Milayna."

What in the ever-loving hell is going on? Jake, what have you done?

Jake leaned in to kiss me a second time, and I spat in his face. With a growl of disgust, he pushed me away so hard that I landed on my butt—not really a place you wanted to be in a fight. Jumping to my feet, I had just assumed a fighting stance when I heard sirens in the distance. I knew they were coming for us. The demi-demons scattered, disappearing into the night.

I scrambled toward Chay, who was lying on his side on the ground, and Drew, who was facedown a few feet from him. I came to Drew first. For a second, I was paralyzed with fear at what I might find if I touched one of them. I could feel the tears building in my eyes and a ball of pain gathering in my chest. I placed my hand on Drew's back and let out a huge breath when I felt it move up and down.

Breathing. Good. That's good.

"Muriel! Jen! Hey!" I motioned them to Drew.

I knelt down to look at what I could see of Drew's face and jerked back.

Oh no, no! Get someone. Ambulance...

My hands shook as I pulled my cell phone out of my pocket. I pushed the button for emergency and slid it across the pavement to Jeff. "Jeff! Ambulance." He grabbed my phone and gave me a thumbs-up.

Drew. Okay, Jen has him. Chay.

I hurried to Chay. I put my hand on his chest and let out a half laugh, half sob when my hand moved up and down with his breaths. "Chay?" I smoothed his soft, dark hair off his forehead and replaced it with my lips. "Can you hear me?" My breath came in small pants, and my heart thundered in my chest so hard I thought it would burst free.

Please, please be okay.

"Yeah," Chay muttered.

Okay, okay, he's talking. That's good. It's even a one-word answer. That's so typically him. So we're good. Okay.

"Where are you hurt?"

"I hurt friggin' everywhere. Help me up." Chay started to push himself into a sitting position.

"No, no. I think you should wait for the ambulance before you get up."

"Crap, Milayna, tell me you didn't call an ambulance." He let out a frustrated breath and ran his fingers through his hair.

"Well, I guess you're not hurt too badly. Your pissy attitude is still intact. And, yeah, Jeff called an ambulance because while I'm over here talking to you, everyone else is over there, trying to get Drew to wake up. He hasn't regained consciousness."

"What?" Chay jumped up. "Whoa." He held his hands out from his sides. I grabbed him around the waist to support him. "The ground is moving."

"See, you need to go to the hospital and get checked. You're dizzy. You might have a concussion."

"I'm not dizzy. My feet are just wobbly."

I rolled my eyes. "Whatever, Chay." I knelt next to Drew. The ambulance had just pulled into the parking lot, and the EMTs were unloading their equipment. "Is he awake?" I looked at Muriel. Her mouth was turned down.

"He answered some questions when we asked him, but he didn't open his eyes."

"Move out of the way, kids. Let us through." The medics shouldered through us.

Muriel, Jen, Jeff, and I watched while the EMTs loaded Chay and

Michelle K. Pickett

Drew into the ambulance.

"What hospital are you taking them to?" Muriel asked.

"St. Mary's." The EMT got into the ambulance and it drove out of the parking lot, lights flashing.

We followed the ambulance to the hospital. We weren't allowed to see Drew or Chay because we weren't family. Pacing the emergency room waiting area, we raided the vending machines and waited, not too patiently, for news. Drew and Chay's parents met us there and kept us updated on their condition.

It didn't take long for the doctor to finish his assessment of Chay. He told Chay's parents that his head CT scan was clear, and his ribs weren't broken like they feared, but if they wanted to be cautious, the hospital would admit him for a twenty-four-hour observation period, but he really didn't see the need. I was sure it had more to do with Chay's unbearable attitude and the doctor's eagerness to get away from him. Mr. and Mrs. Roberts took Chay home, making me promise to keep them updated on Drew's condition.

Drew's parents rarely left his bedside. He still hadn't opened his eyes, although he would respond to some stimuli. When we asked what was wrong, the nurses would only say a doctor would have to determine his diagnosis. I didn't like that answer. Around midnight, Drew's parents sent us home, promising they would contact us as soon as they knew something.

"Now what?" Jeff asked.

We stood in the hospital parking lot, frozen. We didn't talk, move, I wasn't sure we even saw what was in front of us, but rather the images of Chay and Drew beaten, bloodied, and unconscious on the ground.

Head trauma. That was what the EMT said in his little walkie-talkie attached to his shirt. I kept hearing it over and over. Head trauma.

I balled my fists at my sides and clenched my teeth so hard that my jaw hurt. One name came to mind when I thought about Drew. And it wasn't the name people might've assumed. It wasn't Azazel I wanted to see beaten and cowering at my feet. No, it was someone else. Someone we trusted. Someone we thought had our back. Someone who'd pay for this.

Jake.

It was no surprise that Drew didn't make it to school the next day. It was during calculus that my phone vibrated. I dug it out of my pocket and read the text message.

Drew: Sprung! Yay! No more barrel-butt nurse wanting to

know how much I peed.

Me: TMI, Drew.

Drew: Yeah, well, it was creepy.

Me: It's creeping me out thinking about it now.

Chay: I'm not sure I like knowing my friend is talking to my girlfriend about peeing.

Me: I didn't know this was a three-way. Wait, that came out wrong.

Chay: Ha!

Muriel: It's a four-way.

Me: And things get even creepier. How long have you been in the convo?

Muriel: Since measuring pee. By the way... gross.

Me: Second that.

Chay: Yeah. Gotta say I could have gone without knowing that.

Drew: Yeah, well, there isn't much to keep you entertained there.

Me: Everyone want to come over for pizza tonight?

Drew: Yup.

Muriel: Yes. Gotta go.

Chay: Yes. Why?

Me: Good. TTYL.

I clicked out of the conversation. I knew Chay would interrogate me the first chance he got. He was so predictable. As soon as calculus was over, he leaned his hip on the locker next to mine and drummed his thumb against his books. "What's up with the pizza party tonight?"

"I just want to have a meeting and see how everyone is doing now that Jake's turned. I worry about Steven." Shutting my locker, I turned toward Chay.

"I know." His voice sounded strained, and the skin between his eyes wrinkled. "Me too."

I pushed off my locker. "You sound funny. Why? Did something happen with Steven?"

"No. Not that I know of, anyway. You have the visions—you tell me." Chay placed a quick kiss on my nose, and we started toward our English class.

"I haven't had another vision about anyone turning."

"So, see, we're fine. When do we meet at your house?"

"Around six." I had a nagging feeling in the back of my head that I was missing something. It felt like a brick had fallen into my stomach. And the harder I searched my mind for whatever was nagging at the fringes of my

Michelle K. Pickett

memories, the farther it moved from my reach.

The group filed into my house at six o'clock on the nose. When pizza was involved, they were all over it.

"Can we eat and talk? I'm starving," Steven said, walking through the door.

I smiled. He seemed like his normal self. And I hoped Jake's turning didn't affect him like I worried it would.

"It's on its way. So we have to talk first."

Steven gave me a disgusted look, and I laughed. Yes, definitely his normal self.

We all sat in the living room. The room was full of noise from everyone talking at once. I stood and cleared my throat—no one paid any attention. "Hey!" I called. No one even glanced in my direction.

"Maybe if we start making out, they'll pay attention," Chay said with a chuckle. I rolled my eyes. His answer to everything, although I was usually more than willing to oblige. "No?"

"No. The only person's attention you'd get is my dad's."

"Hmm, okay." Chay let out a loud whistle, and everyone turned and looked at me.

I didn't waste time on small talk. There was only one question I needed the answer to. So I asked it. "I've had another vision. Who's changing?"

No one answered. I didn't really need them to. I was gauging their expressions, watching their body language. I couldn't always see what I was looking for, since some people had a more pronounced tell than others.

As I looked around me, studying each face and body movement, I felt a current of electricity sizzle through the room. It seemed to stretch from me and touch everyone in the room. A wave of panic washed over me, and I stumbled backward a step. Chay's arm darted out and steadied me.

The electrical impulse didn't hurt, and I forced myself to take two deep breaths to calm myself. When I started to relax, I remembered what my dad had told me: 'You can't read minds, but you will develop the ability to read people's emotions and perhaps even know what they might do just before they do it.'

"Jake, Lily, Shayla. Who's joining them?" My eyes roamed over everyone in the room. The electrical current seemed to follow my gaze. It touched each person as I looked at them, flowing from me to them. It created a bridge, of sorts, between us.

What is this? What am I supposed to do with it... another power to add to my freakishness? How am I supposed to know how to work it?

Then I had an idea. Turning, I looked at Chay. He leaned back in his chair and looked back at me with a raised eyebrow, but he didn't say anything. The current poked around, like an eleventh finger. It roamed around Chay's face and neck, touching him. I felt nothing and was just about to give up on the whole thing—chalk it up to another bizzaro freaky demi-angel thing—when I looked into Chay's eyes.

The current followed and as soon as it touched Chay's eyes, I was hit full force with his emotions. They came at me so hard that I took half a step back. The current acted like an extension cord and plugged me into him. His emotions flowed right into me. I felt everything he felt. Saw it through his eyes.

He was full of questions. The strongest was what was going on with me. Yeah, I seconded that. But I also felt a sense of calmness. A bond. A strong tie of strength and protectiveness, and the word 'mine' was repeated. I sucked in a breath at the last feeling. Love. Strong, undeniable, unbreakable… love. My heart stuttered at the realization, and the current zipped up my arm, making the hair on the back of my neck stand up like little Roman soldiers.

I blinked and broke the connection. I turned to Muriel. "What?" she asked. I didn't answer. I just looked in her eyes, and she squirmed in her seat. "Milayna?" Even with her nervousness and discomfort from me staring at her like a lion stalking its prey, I felt calmness when the current touched her, but she still worried. She was scared. Not just for her, but for me too. There was a definite bond between us. Love. Different from Chay's. A familial love. But there was something else. Something I couldn't reach. It was like she'd locked it in a closet. Hidden it from me.

I moved my gaze to Steven's. He looked at me for a few seconds. The current locked on him, and the feelings that traveled over the bridge worried me. There was no calmness. He felt uneasy. There was no bond. He felt like an outsider in our group. There was no tie… he abruptly looked away and broke the connection. The current roamed over him. It didn't stop moving, poking, searching. But Steven wouldn't look me in the eyes.

The room erupted. I jumped and lost my focus. The crazy current fizzled. What had seemed like minutes for me and my freaky emotional zapper had really only been seconds. I was thrust back into real time. Everyone talked over each other. They all denied they were having thoughts of changing sides. All but one.

Steven.

I stared at him, waiting for him to say something. He looked at the toe of his shoe. I figured it would happen. He was Jake's best friend. Of course Jake would try to convince him to change sides, but I had hoped he was stronger. That he'd come to the group for support instead of betraying us and turning traitor.

"If anyone is thinking about switching sides, do it now. The group doesn't need you. We'll fight on our own. And we don't have a problem fighting you." My gaze lingered on Steven, who still hadn't looked up.

Michelle K. Pickett

The doorbell rang. "Pizza's here," I said with a smile.

I paid the delivery guy and turned to take the pizza into the kitchen, stopping short when I came face-to-face with Steven. "Oh. I didn't hear you walk up." I backed up and hit the door behind me.

"Sorry, Milayna. I forgot I have somewhere I'm supposed to be. I'll catch ya next time." He hunched his shoulders and shoved his hands in his hoodie's pocket. His voice was flat, just like the look on his face, emotionless, empty.

"Sure." I moved out of his way, watching him walk out of the door and down the drive. He looked over his shoulder at me, his expression grim. Then I noticed them. Black boots with silver buckles. Just like in my vision the night the group went to the movie. "Chay, look at his boots."

Chay took the pizza boxes from me. He didn't say anything. There was nothing to say. Steven had already switched sides.

24

The Store

ONE WEEK, SIX DAYS UNTIL MY BIRTHDAY.

It became a daily ritual at school. Lily walked by me in the hall and shouldered me. The harder the better, it seemed. Well, I'd had enough. I saw Lily and Shayla walking toward me, the ever-present sneer on their faces. Lily shouldered me like I knew she would. I stuck my foot in front of her. She landed facedown on the pile of books she was carrying.

"You're in way over your head, Milayna," Shayla said, helping Lily gather her things from the floor.

I couldn't help the small smile on my lips. It felt so good to watch Lily sprawl out on the dirty floor. I wished I could've rewound time and watched it again.

"I'm not the one on my knees, Shayla." I turned on my heel and walked away, but not before I saw someone in my peripheral vision bend down and help Shayla. I looked over my shoulder and saw Jeff.

Chay walked up beside me. "I swear, Milayna, if you don't start waiting for me after class, I'm gonna—"

"What are you gonna do?" I interrupted and smiled up at him.

"Tell your dad," Chay finished.

I burst out laughing. "You're gonna be a tattletale?"

"This is serious," he said quietly.

"I know. I'm sorry. Next time I'll wait, but you have to be on time, Chay. You were late today."

Michelle K. Pickett

"Geez, nagging me already." He lifted my book bag off my shoulder and swung it over his.

The school day flew by. I was in and out of classes quickly, and for the most part, painlessly. Except for calculus, where we were given three pages of homework. Three freakin' pages! There should be child labor laws for homework.

The last bell rang and we all hurried from our seats, grabbing our books and running toward the door before the teacher could pile on any more homework.

"Can you believe the calculus homework?" I complained to Muriel.

We were walking down the hall to the gym. We had a swim meet that afternoon. I had to grab my bag out of my gym locker on the way to the bus. I hated riding the bus, with its awful smell and sticky floors. But it was school policy that students ride the buses to and from sporting events. Bonus.

We grabbed our swim bags and walked toward the grime-covered, faded yellow bus.

Crap, I forgot my swim cap on the bench in the locker room.

I turned and jogged back to the school. "Save me a seat," I yelled over my shoulder to Muriel.

"Why? What are you doing?"

"I gotta grab my swim cap."

"Milayna! Wait for me. You shouldn't go alone."

"I'll be fine. I'm right behind you."

I ran through the gym and into the locker room. After grabbing my swim cap, I hurried back through the gym. I was halfway across the room when the door swung open and I realized I had a problem. A big one.

Butterflies the size of birds swarmed my stomach, and a lump in my throat sealed them in. So much adrenaline mixed with my blood that it made me dizzy and a little queasy.

Stupid, stupid! Why am I so damn dense sometimes?

He advanced on me. I backed up until the back of my knees hit the bleachers, falling with a grunt. He smiled. His face was so beautiful. If I didn't know what lay behind those denim-blue eyes, I would've bent to his every whim. But he wasn't the good, hometown boy everyone thought he was. He was evil.

I couldn't believe I'd once thought we belonged together. Now, I could see evil running through his veins. Evil that Azazel let loose when he turned. No, we didn't belong together. Azazel and Jake belonged together. They were the perfect match.

"Come with me, Milayna. We'll be great together. It's so much easier on this side." Jake spread his hands out at his sides, palms up.

I shook my head once. "Nothing is easy."

"This is. It's perfect."

"Nothing is perfect," I bit out.

He leaned over me. His face was so close I could feel his warm breath moving my hair. It smelled like a combination of the corn dogs served for lunch and breath mints. I wrinkled my nose and turned my face from the smell.

I shoved him as hard as I could, trying to move him enough to pass by. I needed out of the gym. It wasn't safe to be there alone with him. It wasn't safe to be there alone, period. One of his new friends could show up any minute.

What was I thinking coming alone?

I wasn't. But pushing him did nothing. He didn't even flinch. I might have been the highest demi-angel at our school, but I wasn't Superman. Or Wonder Woman. Whatever.

I heard them before I saw them. Their grunts and groans were audible before their grotesque bodies materialized. I saw the smoke in the corner of the gym, smelled the sulfur. They were coming for me.

Damn. I wish I had wings.

"Okay, okay. Call off your goons." I sighed, feigning resignation.

With a snap of his fingers, the smoke billowing in the corner disappeared. The groans of Hell went with it.

Perfect, my butt. They don't sound like they're having a party down there.

"What do you want me to do?" I narrowed my eyes at him.

"Tell him you'll side with him and he'll do the rest." He shrugged one shoulder. "Easy."

The door banged against the gym wall, and I jumped. I was sure Azazel was there, and I was finished. I'd failed.

"What are you two doing in here?" Coach Johnson bellowed.

My breath rushed out of my lungs. I'd never been so happy to see grumpy Coach Johnson, with his perpetual case of halitosis. I could have kissed him, stinky breath and all.

"I was just leaving." I pushed Jake away.

He stood and gave one of his dazzling smiles, holding his palms out in front of him as if in surrender. "Have it your way, Milayna," he whispered.

"What's burning? Have you two been smoking?"

"No, sir," I answered, looking Jake in the eyes. "Jake was just asking me to senior prom."

"Oh, well, you two have at it then." He grinned and winked at Jake— his star football player.

"No, no, that's okay. I told him I already had plans for that night. I can't

Michelle K. Pickett

go with him." I stood and stepped around Jake, walking quickly toward the door before Coach Johnson left.

I ran down the hall to the doors and pushed through them so hard they smacked against the doorstops. I ran until I reached the bus and let out a huge breath when I sat on the ugly, green vinyl seat next to Muriel. Looking down, I realized my hands were shaking. In fact, it felt as if my whole insides were shaking.

"Milayna, what's wrong? You're shaking." Muriel grabbed my hands.

"I ran into Jake." My voice quivered and I couldn't say his name above a whisper, like it was some kind of horrible curse word.

"Crap, what happened? Are you okay?" She squeezed my hands and pulled me toward her.

"Yeah." I nodded. "Coach Johnson walked in and I was able to get out of there, but it was close."

"You can't go anywhere without someone with you. You can't take a chance something like that will happen again." Muriel's tone was firm. She almost sounded like my mother. I would have laughed at the thought if I wasn't still reeling from my near date to Hell with its newest golden boy, Jake.

I let out a long breath—my cheeks puffed out. "I know."

Even with the scare from Jake, the day didn't end all bad. We won our swim meet.

After the swim meet, Chay was at the school to pick me up. I saw him through the window as we drove into the school's parking lot, and I could tell by his face that Muriel had already texted him. His feet were planted shoulder width apart, his hands were clasped behind his back, and there wasn't a trace of a smile on his lips anywhere.

Damn it!

"Thanks a lot, Muriel." I glared at her.

"I thought maybe he could talk some sense into that stubborn brain of yours." She shrugged a shoulder.

He met me at the door of the bus. As soon as I stepped out, he grabbed my bag, slung it over his shoulder, and stalked away. I followed close behind him. He opened the passenger's door of the car for me to get in, shut it after me, and stalked around to the driver's side.

Great. Just friggin' wonderful. I don't think he's blinked since he's picked me up.

"What the hell were you thinking?" Chay yelled as soon as he got in the car.

"I was just grabbing my clothes. I didn't think—"

"Crap, Milayna, you can't go running off like that. Why do you think everyone is going out of their way to make sure you aren't alone?"

"Well, I didn't ask them to," I shot back. It wasn't like I wanted everyone to have to wait on me, to interrupt their life and make me the center of it. "Wait. Everyone?"

"Yeah."

"So that's what you're doing? Going out of your way to make sure I'm not alone?"

Not because I want to be with you, but because I have to rearrange my schedule to babysit you. Nice.

"Yes... No... that's not what I meant." I started to get out of the car. "Where are you going?" he called to me.

"To ride with Muriel." I jerked my bag out of the car and slammed the door.

Jerk.

I jogged across the parking lot to catch Muriel before she left. She jumped when I yanked open the door of her car and slipped in, slamming it behind me. "Oh. Hi." A frown pulled at her lips. "Everything okay?"

"Let's just go home." I forced a smile.

"What happened?" Muriel looked over at me when we were stopped at a red light. I ticked off the seconds in my head until it turned green. I just wanted to go home.

I sighed. "Nothing I want to talk about."

"You're mad at me."

"No." I let out a huge sigh. "I don't know what I am." I dropped my head in my hands.

"Okay. Well, what happened?"

"He basically said he was spending time with me because I wasn't supposed to be alone," I blurted.

Muriel snorted. "You know that's not true, Milayna."

Yeah. So why am I making an issue of it? Ugh. Sometimes, I don't understand my own brain.

My stomach clenched and twisted. I gritted my teeth and hit the dashboard with my fist. I didn't want a vision now, but my head started to pound and my eyes saw images of things that hadn't happened yet.

"Muriel, I'm gonna have a vision." I blew stray hair out of my face before cursing violently under my breath.

Come on. Give me a freaking break, please.

"Now?"

"Yeah."

A gas station. No, a convenience store. A woman.

I concentrated on the store. I strained to see the name. Bob's... something. I couldn't make it out.

A woman. Spilled pop. A crushed bag of chips. A gun.

Michelle K. Pickett

"Muriel, look for a convenience store called Bob's."

Gunshots. Blood.

"Hurry, Muriel." I gripped the door handle so hard that my fingers ached. The tension snaked up my hand and my arm to my neck, where it slithered around and started tightening.

My insides were churning. I could feel my lunch swirl in my stomach, threating to make a repeat visit. I couldn't help thinking of the Waterway. What if we didn't get there in time? What if we didn't find the woman?

Blue T-shirt stained with blood. A bloody hand.

"I see it. Hold on." Muriel made a U-turn, earning several honks and a few fingers. She pulled into Bob's Convenience Store's parking lot.

"There, the blonde in the pink dress walking toward the door. We gotta stop her from going in the store."

"Here." Muriel pulled her wallet out of her purse and hurled it on the ground behind the woman.

I jumped out of the car. "Ma'am? Is this your wallet?"

The woman turned around, looked at Muriel's neon green wallet, and shook her head. "No, that's not mine." Leave it to Muriel to have the ugliest wallet in history. The woman could tell right away it wasn't hers.

The vision hadn't changed.

Gunshots. Blood. The woman.

I took two steps toward her, the wallet in my outstretched hand. "Are you sure? I'm almost positive I saw it fall out of your bag."

"I'm positive. My wallet isn't that color," she said, an amused look on her face.

"Oh, you wouldn't happen to know whose it is?" I stepped in front of her when she tried to sidestep me.

"Why don't you look inside and see if there's any ID?"

Crap. The vision hasn't changed, and I can't get her to stop going into the store.

"Muriel!" I called, my voice quivering and an octave higher than normal. I didn't have a good feeling about this vision. No matter how I played it out in my head, it didn't change, at least not for the better. Butterflies started to swarm my stomach and my blood felt like goo oozing through my veins.

"Yeah?"

"Call the police. Now!"

"'Kay."

The woman stopped and looked at me with wide eyes. "What do the police have to do with the wallet?"

"Nothing. There's a robbery in progress. I need to report it."

"Where?" she asked, panicked. She looked around, turning in all directions.

"Here."

That wasn't exactly true. The robbery hadn't taken place yet, but it was the only thing I could think of to keep the woman out of the store and keep her alive. The vision had changed, but my stomach was still tied in knots and the blood rushing through my veins was full of adrenaline. Something wasn't right.

Blood. Glass. Bloody blue T-shirt. Stop it.

"Muriel, get down!" I screamed at the same time I tackled the woman. She fell on her hands and knees just as the bullet soared through the front window of the store.

Glass covered us. My hands were sliced and bleeding. Shards of razor-sharp glass were everywhere. The woman had a bad gash on her right cheek, but otherwise, we were both fine.

Slowly, the twisting in my stomach eased and fear slithered from my neck as the images faded. I could hear the far-off wail of sirens. They wouldn't get here in time. The man had already run from the building.

The store clerk hurried to the door. "Are you okay?" He helped us up, picking the large pieces of glass out of our hair and off our clothes.

"We're fine." The woman sounded a little dazed. Her eyes were wide and she wobbled when she walked, like a little girl wearing her mother's high heels.

I sat on Muriel's car's bumper and waited for the police. The sensations of the vision slowly dissipated and were replaced with the normal reaction of scared shitlessness a person would have after having a bullet soar over their heads—vision or no vision.

The police wanted a statement of what happened. After they interviewed the store clerk, they interviewed the woman. She said she hadn't seen anything, but I'd saved her life when I pushed her to the ground.

Great. Thanks, lady.

"Miss, what happened?" a police officer asked. He had kind eyes and reminded me of my dad.

"I happened to look through the window and saw the man with the gun. I panicked and pushed the lady down." That was mostly the truth.

"How did you see the gun?"

"Through the window," I repeated.

"The window is covered in posters and signs."

"Well, some of the window is uncovered or I wouldn't have been able to see through it." I tried not to sound annoyed.

"Did you see the man?"

"His back was to me."

"What about when he ran out of the building?" The officer took notes in his little notepad.

"He was holding a gun. I tried not to look at him."

"Why?"

Michelle K. Pickett

Just drop it already!

"Why? Because I didn't want him to start killing the witnesses!" I said, my voice rising. I tried to sound hysterical. I was sure I came pretty close since I was borderline hysterical by that point. The reality of what happened had started to sink in. One of us could have been shot. Killed, even. Yeah, hysterical seemed to sum up my emotional state. And even though I was only a few weeks away from technically becoming an adult, I wanted my mom and my grams' purple couch. That always made me feel better.

"I'd like you to come to the station and look at some mug shots anyway, just in case something jogs your memory."

Muriel and I drove to the station. She was quiet, and the silence made me uneasy.

"I'm sorry," I said, smoothing out a piece of tape holding gauze on my hand.

"For what?" Muriel glanced at me.

"Making you go with me."

"Milayna, you probably just saved my life. Here I thought the group was trying to keep you alive, and you just saved that woman's life and probably mine too. Thank you."

She reached out, grabbed my hand, and held it a little too tight considering I'd just had half a plate glass window pulled out of it by the EMTs, but I held on to her just as tightly.

We were one bullet away from possibly losing one another. Demons, Azazel, now freakin' bullets flying around. It's too much. Too many things threatening the people I love and I don't know how to protect them from it all.

"It was nothing. All in a day's work." I smiled. Muriel squeezed my hand before letting go. She didn't smile back.

We called our parents and told them what happened. Then we spent the next four hours of our life looking through picture after picture of criminals along with the store clerk.

"I couldn't believe how many there were," I said as Muriel and I walked out of the police station. Goose bumps broke out on my skin thinking about it.

"I know, right?" Muriel muttered. "It would have been nice if the surveillance cameras," Muriel made air quotes around the words surveillance cameras, "were actual working cameras and not just empty boxes put up to deter crime. 'Cuz, guess what? It didn't work."

My lips twitched. "Yes, that would have definitely been helpful." Muriel had been bitching about the cameras since the store clerk told the police they weren't real working cameras. She'd bitched to me, the police, and the store clerk, who really got a dose. "I just wish I could have given them something useful to work with. But I didn't see the guy long enough... Anyway, that's four hours of our life we won't get back." I sighed.

Milayna   220

"Yeah. I'm just happy we had four hours of life left." Muriel unlocked the car, and we climbed in to go home.

My dad met us at the car when Muriel pulled into her driveway. "Are you okay?" His face was pinched with worry.

"Yeah."

We walked across the street to my house. As soon as I opened the door, I smelled him. He waited in the foyer, his hair mussed from running his hand through it. My heart lurched when I saw him, and I reminded it we were supposed to be mad at him for the idiotic thing he said. But somehow, it didn't seem like such a big deal anymore. And I didn't want to spend my life choosing to be angry.

He walked to me, cupped my face in his hands, and kissed me hard and deep. My father cleared his throat. Chay kept kissing me, and I kept kissing him back. I wrapped one arm around his waist, the other around his neck, and cradled the side of his head. I held him tight against me, until not even a whisper could fit between us. And still he was too far away. I felt so safe in his arms that my heart hurt. I didn't realize I was crying until I tasted my salty tears on our lips.

"Okay then. Ignore the father." My dad walked away.

"I'm sorry about what I said, Milayna. It came out all wrong—" He wiped my tears away, kissing each spot. "Don't cry. I can't stand to see you cry."

I waved off his words and shook my head. "It's okay."

"Your hands. What happened to your hands?" He looked at the bandages the EMTs had applied.

"Just some glass. It's nothing."

He kissed me again. It was a slow, make-your-toes-curl-and-insides-swirl kiss, and my heart drummed against my chest. I leaned into him, urging him to take the kiss deeper.

"Chay, would you like to stay for dinner?" my mother called.

He lifted his head and grinned. "Yes, ma'am."

"And that's how you get their attention." I heard my mom tell my dad in the kitchen.

I giggled and walked toward the smell of food. I was starving. When I walked into the kitchen, I froze. The large window behind the kitchen table was right in front of me. Through that, I could see my goblin buddies waiting for me in the backyard.

"Oh, yeah, I meant to tell you. You have some little red visitors." My dad dished up some of the casserole my mom sat on the table in front of him.

I watched them run through the yard. "How long have they been

Michelle K. Pickett

here?" A weight fell onto my shoulders and pushed the air out of my lungs. I closed my eyes briefly and covered my face with my hands.

"About five hours."

I let my hands fall slowly from my face. "About when the robbery happened," I whispered.

"Yeah."

"I'll go out and see what they want so they'll go."

"Eat first, before it gets cold. They've waited this long. They can wait until after dinner." My mom sat down at the table and patted the chair next to her.

Chay pulled out my chair, and I sat down. Throughout dinner, my parents and Chay asked me a million and one questions about the vision I'd had: what had happened at the convenience store, what the police said, how my hands felt, and on and on. By the time dinner was over, I felt like I'd been interrogated again, only my family was more insistent than the police officer had been.

After dinner, Chay and I sat on the deck and waited for the mini-goblins to reveal the purpose for their visit. I lay sidewise, my head in his lap. His arm was like a steel band around my waist, holding me to him. After the day I'd had, I welcomed the sense of protection he offered.

"Milayna's here!" Friendly said in a singsong voice.

"It's about damn time. I was getting bored," Scarface said.

There were seven hobgoblins running amok in my backyard. I knew two of them. One I'd named Scarface and the other Friendly, based on his personality. They usually always came to bug me. It was like they were my personal demon buddies. The others I'd never seen before, although they all looked alike, so it was hard to tell.

"What are you doing here, guys?" I let out an exasperated sigh. I was drained from the vision and the hours I'd spent at the police station. I just wanted a quiet, peaceful evening so I could sleep.

"Did you like our game?"

My heart slowed. I could hear it plodding along in my chest, squeezing the blood through my veins. "What game?"

"The store. That was a close call with the bullet," one of the hobgoblins said, its eyes wide.

"How do you know about that?" I pulled myself up to a sitting position. My knees were pressed against my chest and my arms wrapped around them. Chay wrapped his arm around me and scooted me close to his side.

"'Cause we did it. It was easy convincing the guy to rob the place. Just a few subliminal suggestions and he was all set. Of course, he thinks it was all his idea, but that's okay. Whatever gets the job done, right?" The demon's lips pulled over his yellow, chipped teeth in what I guess was intended to be a grin. It looked more like a snarl, so maybe that was what he meant it to be.

Who knew with them?

"You don't know anything," I bluffed, cringing when I heard the slight tremor in my voice.

"You're wrong, you're wrong," Friendly chanted. "It was fun, fun, fun." The red imp twirled around, tossing colorful fall leaves into the air.

"We know you saved that woman from the bullet Azazel meant for her. We know the window exploded over you and that's what cut up your hands. We even know you've spent the last few hours at the police station," Scarface said, ticking off each item on his stubby, sausage looking fingers.

"How do you know?"

"I told you, we did it. Wasn't it fun?" This from Friendly again. I was beginning to think he was a little dense. He twirled a red-and-orange leaf between his fingers before holding it out to me.

I batted his hand away. "No." My insides shook. I wasn't sure if it was fear or rage. Another innocent victim. Azazel tried to kill another innocent human. The trembling inside my body spread until my entire body trembled, inside and out. A mix of emotions tumbled in my head like a cement mixer churning them over and over.

"She didn't like our game." Friendly's eyes turned black and his face distorted. "We planned that especially for you. You should be polite."

"Azazel is irritated. He wants an answer. You either give it up or die. That bullet could have fired a second sooner and we'd be having this conversation in the afterlife, you know." Scarface made a show of picking something furry and bloody out of his teeth. He'd probably found a squirrel for dinner, or a neighbor's cat. My stomach turned over, and my dinner splashed around. I was afraid I would hurl it on the little demon's feet.

"Tell Azazel that this is the last time I'm going to answer him. It's becoming redundant. No." My body started to heat from the inside. A tingling heat fingered its way through my veins and muscles. I shifted on the deck, letting my legs fall and dangle off the side. I didn't recognize this sensation. It was new, and I felt off-balance. My breathing started to quicken and was shallow. The earth started to slow, and I felt sluggish.

I remembered the woman and the store clerk. Both could have died today. Muriel, too. Flashes of the glass showering over us, of the man running from the scene, of the EMTs pulling glass from the woman's and my cuts, ran through my mind, and my vision clouded. Blood pounded behind my ears. Rage raced through every molecule.

Scarface's demeanor changed from the moody hobgoblin to a demonic irritation from Hell. "He won't like that answer." He stood in front of me with his feet planted apart and his hands on his hips. When he leaned his head toward me, his butt stuck out in the back. He looked hilarious. Any other time, I would have laughed at the sight. But not then. Then, I wanted to pick him up and snap his neck. I couldn't get to Azazel, so the goblins would

Michelle K. Pickett

have to do.

"You know what, guys? I really don't care," I whispered through clenched teeth. Jumping off the deck, I grabbed for Scarface. He jumped out of reach of my hand—but not my power.

The tingling in my fingers increased to an uncomfortable level. Lifting my hand, Scarface rose off the ground. I squeezed. His eyes widened, and he gasped for breath. I waved my hand toward me and Scarface followed, floating in the air. I pulled him eye to eye with me. I could feel the heat radiating off his body and smell the rot and singed flesh. With every pant, I got a whiff of his halitosis.

"I'm tired. I'm cranky. I'm downright bitchy. So go to hell, and make sure you tell Azazel to screw himself."

Pulling back my arm, I swung. I watched the red body fly across the backyard until it disappeared with a pop. One by one, little pops sounded until there was nothing left but seven little puffs of smoke and the fading smell of sulfur.

Chay looked at me. His mouth was open and his eyebrows were raised. "Um, that was interesting. When did you learn that trick?"

I shrugged and shook my head, rubbing my chest with the palm of my hand. "I don't know. It just... it just came to me."

"Well, now things are going to get really interesting," Chay said.

25

Suspicion

ONE WEEK, THREE DAYS UNTIL MY BIRTHDAY.

The dream was back. Well, the nightmare. I'd been having it since the night of the football game. The night I first saw the demon. The night I first saw the glowing embers of Hell, Azazel's home.

I crawled out of bed and walked into my bathroom. Sweat snaked down my back, and an icy, cold lump formed in the pit of my stomach, weighing me down.

I looked at my reflection in the mirror. Dark circles framed my green eyes, either dull from not enough sleep or too much crying. Maybe both. Who the hell knew anymore? "Pull it together, Milayna," I whispered.

I heard my cell phone vibrate, the metal banging against the nightstand. Running into the other room, I grabbed it, flipped it open, and clicked the button to read the message without looking to see who it was from.

Muriel: What are you doing up?

Me: Hey. Just another nightmare. What about you?

Muriel: I saw your light. Why? Were you expecting someone else? Hmm? Maybe Mr. Hottie?

Me: LOL! Nah.

Muriel: Gonna be able to go back to sleep?

Me: I don't know. Probably not.

Muriel: Wanna talk about it?

Me: Not really.

Michelle K. Pickett

Muriel: Well, if you do, text me.
Me: I will. G'night.
Muriel: Night.

Two seconds later, my phone rang. I cringed and snatched it up, pressing talk before my parents heard.

"Hello?"

"Hey," a voice smooth as the most decadent chocolate said in my ear. "Another nightmare?"

"Yeah." I lay back in my pillows and closed my eyes, pretending he was next to me, not houses away.

"You wanna talk about it?" Chay asked.

"You know, I really don't... Wait, yes I do." I needed to tell someone. I couldn't carry around what I learned in my dream alone. And I could trust Chay.

He chuckled on the other end of the line, and I smiled at the sound. "Is that a yes or a no, Milayna?"

"It's a yes under one condition."

"And what's that?"

"This is you and me talking. It isn't for anyone else's ears. Okay?"

"Okay," he said slowly. "But if this is something that affects the group—"

I sighed. "Never mind." I couldn't believe that my boyfriend put the group before us. I needed to talk to him, just him. But he couldn't keep it between us. He had to involve the others. Pssh, whatever.

"Fine. It's just you and me."

"I think someone else is going to betray the group," I blurted. "I keep having this dream, and it's someone in the group making a deal with Azazel, but it's different from when the others turned. They're talking about what a big surprise it'll be and that no one will see it coming, things like that. I'm sure someone is going to betray us."

"Who?"

"Well, if I knew, it wouldn't be a surprise betrayal." I rolled my eyes. "Anyway, I can't see them in the dream."

"Is it a male or female voice?"

"I don't know." I sighed, frustrated. "It's distorted. Like it's synthesized."

"You're right. We can't tell the group. We can't let on that we know."

My blood ran cold. It felt like someone had just run an ice cube up my spine.

I drove myself to school the next morning, Chay's warning still ringing in my ears. I could see his yellow car behind me, and Muriel's car was in front. I was sandwiched between the two of them. Protecting me, they'd said. Except one might work for the enemy. How was I supposed to feel protected?

As soon as we'd parked, Chay was at my car door. He reached out and lifted the strap of my book bag off my shoulder.

Schooling my features to show no emotion and keeping my voice neutral, I said, "Thanks, but I've got it," and held the strap in place. I stepped back and rolled my shoulder out of his reach. A knot formed in my chest when I looked at him.

Chay gave me an odd look and took a step back. "It isn't me."

I narrowed my eyes as him. "Isn't that something a person would say who was trying to fool the other?"

He laughed, bent down, kissed me. "You know it isn't me." His lips skimmed against mine when he spoke. He kissed me again. Reaching for my book bag, he slipped it off my shoulder. I let him. I was too mesmerized by his kiss to stop him, or even care. He lifted his head and locked his gaze on mine. "Trust your instincts, Milayna. You know it isn't me or you wouldn't have told me." He gave me a little tug. "C'mon. Chemistry waits for no one."

We walked into the building, and Chay stopped so fast that I walked past him and had to double back to see what was wrong. "They're here," he said.

My adrenaline spiked, and the hairs on the back of my neck stood at attention. "Who?" I looked over my shoulder, expecting to see a group of demi-demons or the hounds of Hell.

"The hobgoblins. They're watching."

I chuckled and started walking toward class. "I know. They've been here every day this week. They hide behind the ceiling tiles."

He turned and glared at me. "You didn't tell me?"

"What difference does it make? Besides, I thought you already knew. Why? What do you think it means?"

"Nothing good. They're watching someone. I'd say it's you, but considering what you told me last night, it could be any one of us." He wrapped his arm around my shoulders and pulled me close to him.

A chill ran through me. If Chay was right and they weren't watching me, then my dream could be a premonition. We had a snitch in our group. That was worse than someone changing outright. Now we'd be suspicious of each other. It could break the group apart.

That afternoon when I got home from school, the two hobgoblins, Scarface and Friendly, were waiting for me in my backyard. I sat on the swing on the back deck, watching them run around the yard, singing. Considering they were minions from Hell, I wasn't sure what they had to sing about. But they were.

I saw Chay jump the back fence and smiled. The red imps ran over to him, asking their usual question.

Michelle K. Pickett

"Play with us?"

"Nope." He kept walking with barely a glance at the short, red goblins. He jogged up the deck steps and sat next to me on the swing. We swayed softly, waiting for the goblins to run out of energy. It could be minutes or hours, but eventually, they'd grow tired of the game and tell us why they were there.

"I figured I'd be seeing you," I said and scooted next to him.

He wrapped his arm around me and pulled me close. "I've been watching them. Have they talked yet?"

"Nah, they've been singing."

He laughed. "Singing? About what?"

"I have no idea. It's in a different language." I shrugged. "Don't really want to know, either."

"Probably not." Chay moved his fingertips in circles over my shoulder, sending shots of white-hot electricity through my arms and straight to my lungs, which were quickly becoming incapable of taking a normal breath.

"Milayna," one hobgoblin sang in its shrill voice. "Did you have fun at school today?"

"Not particularly. Did you?"

"Yes." It swung its arms back and forth like a kid. It was so cute just then. It looked like a stuffed animal—like one of those Troll dolls. I wanted to rip its head off, it made me so mad.

"Good."

"Don't you want to know why we were there?" Scarface asked with a wicked smile.

"I know why. You like to watch." I picked at an invisible piece of lint on my jeans.

His smile widened, his fat lips thinning across his face. "But you don't know who."

I tilted my head to the side and looked at him. "Yes I do," I said as if it should be obvious.

"It's coming for you tonight, tonight, tonight," Friendly chanted.

"Really? What is it? Tell me what the big occasion is so I know what to wear." My heart sunk like an albatross was attached to it. What next? They'd proven they could cause mischief, life-or-death situations. What did they consider a big occasion if shooting at a woman at a convenience store is just a game? I knew I certainly didn't want to be around to see it.

"We'll never tell," he said with a self-satisfied smile before they disappeared with a pop and plume of white smoke.

At nine o'clock, I heard glass shatter. I walked to the front door and flipped on the porch light. Nothing. I flipped the switch again. Nothing. And I knew the demi-demons were there.

At five after nine, Chay jumped the fence and let himself into the house.

"What took you so long?" I looked at him with a hand on my hip.

He leaned down and kissed me. "I was putting on my lip balm and brushing my teeth."

"You always do that just before a fight?" I teased.

"No, I always do that just before I do this," he murmured before kissing me again.

"Let's get this over with," I said.

"I hate this part," Jen and Muriel said at the same time, walking into the room from the kitchen.

Me too.

I walked out of the front door with more boldness than I felt. My insides were shaking and sweat was pooling at the base of my back. I hoped they weren't like dogs or bees and could smell fear, because I was stinkin' of it.

I saw Lily and Shayla first. No biggie. I could take either one of them. Then I saw Jake and next to him was Steven. My heart dropped. Both were football players. I wasn't sure I could take either one of them. I didn't particularly want to try. Even though my training taught me how to use an attacker's weight and strength against him, I wasn't ready to test it out on Jake.

There were eight Evils and six of us. That wasn't too bad. When a demi-angel switched sides, they lost some of their strength. Six of us could take on eight of them and do fine. It was the demi-demons that stood behind them that posed a problem. Their powers were fairly matched with ours. Taking on eight Evils and four demi-demons would be difficult. Very difficult.

I was relieved when I saw my Uncle Rory walk across the street. My dad came out of the house, followed closely by Chay's dad, who, like his son, jumped the back fence. With the three of them, our odds were a little better. Not great, but better.

"Let's see." Jake tapped his bottom lip with his finger. "We ask you to surrender. You say?"

"No." I tried to sound bored.

"We ask you to join with Azazel, and you say?"

"No."

"So that only leaves one thing," Jake threw the first punch. Chay deflected it.

This is so stupid. What good does it do?

One of the female demi-demons charged me. I braced myself for what I suspected was going to be a hard hit. And, damn, I hated it when I was right. She lunged at my midsection, knocking us both to the ground. I hit my head hard on the cement front step. Stars floated in front of my eyes.

Michelle K. Pickett

She took advantage of my daze and landed a hard punch to the side of my face. I could feel her ring dig into my skin and the warm blood trickle down my cheek. I felt a second blow to my chin. My teeth clacked together, and pain ricocheted through my head like a metal ball in a pinball machine. It bounced from bumper to bumper, burning into my skull with each hit.

"Milayna, get up!" Jen yelled. She had pulled the demi-demon off me and was holding her in a bear hug from behind.

Slowly, I managed to pull myself from the ground, looked at the hulking girl, and landed an uppercut to her chin followed by a jab just under the rib cage.

"No fair, two against one." Jake smiled at me.

I followed him as he circled me. My mind raced. The best I could hope for was that Jake wouldn't hit a girl. When he threw his first punch, I knew that wasn't the case. I easily deflected his second and third jabs. His arms were longer, but I was quicker and missing a hit was more tiring than landing one. If I could keep him entertained long enough, maybe my dad or Chay would be able to help.

It happened so fast. First, I was on my feet holding my own against the much larger and stronger Jake, and then he feigned a jab to the right. When I moved to avoid contact, he kicked my feet out from under me. For the second time that night, I was lying on my back with stars dancing in front of my eyes. I didn't recover as quickly from his blow, however. My head pounded and my sight blurred.

Jake's blurry face leaned close to mine and smiled. "Say goodbye, Milayna," he murmured. Picking up my ankle, he dragged me from the front porch to the side yard. My head bounced against the cement walk and then the ruts and stones in the grass.

He pulled me along the side yard and into the back. Blinking to clear my vision, I saw the stumpy legs of the hobgoblins running around and smelled their ever-present odor of sulfur. It wasn't until I saw the glowing hole and smelled rotting, charred meat that I realized what was happening.

I kicked at his hand with my free foot, trying to sit up and claw at his arm. He pushed me back. Jake was big. He was built, solid, packed muscle. But I fought him. I kicked. I scratched and clawed at his hand. I grabbed at anything I could reach and hung on. If he was going to drag me to hell, he was damn well working to do it.

"No, no, no," I screamed.

"Yes. You had your chance. Now Azazel will take what's his, with or without your consent."

He pulled me closer to the hole. I could feel the heat radiate from it and smell burnt flesh and sulfur. Bile rose in my throat, and I gagged.

The groans and shrieks of the damned channeled upward from the hole like a sharp wind and smacked me in the face. I did not want to meet the same fate, and I twisted and clawed at the ground for something to hold on to. My nails dug into the grass, leaving gouges as Jake pulled me across it.

I screamed. When no one came, I screamed again. I wasn't sure if I screamed a name, or a word, or if it was just a piercing sound. I just remember screaming and knowing if someone didn't help me, I would be doomed to that pit with the rest of the damned.

I arched my back, taking in another breath to scream when I saw two feet. "Help me!" I screamed at the person.

I strained my head to see who was watching Jake drag me closer and closer to Hell. When they didn't help, I was sure it was another Evil or a demi-demon.

It was Muriel.

"Muriel! Help me!" I reached out to her.

She stood motionless and watched Jake inch closer to the hole. Her eyes were wide and her lips slightly parted. She stood with a blank stare and watched. We were almost to the pit. The heat became unbearable. Sweat covered me. It dripped from my hair into my eyes, and I could taste the salty droplets when they landed on my lips. The smell emanating from the pit was revolting, and the sulfur fumes stung my eyes and the back of my throat.

This is it. I have to do something now or I'm done. I took a deep breath and channeled a motto from one of my many self-defense classes. I control my actions. I control my pain. It doesn't control me. I am strength.

I gritted my teeth against the pain I knew was coming, swung my arms, and jumped to my feet. The movement took Jake by surprise and his grip loosened on my hair long enough for me to duck and jump to the side. My head throbbed from bouncing across the ground, the hits, and from the chunk of hair Jake yanked out that still hung in his hand like a souvenir.

"Not tonight, Jake. Sorry." I took a fighting stance and watched, gauging his next move.

Jake smiled and let his body relax. "Milayna—"

I bolted. I wasn't sure I could take Jake in a hand-to-hand fight. I turned the corner of house, but he'd already caught up to me. He grabbed my arm and jerked me against him. I threw an elbow to his gut. He grunted, tightened his grip, and started dragging me toward the pit a second time.

I twisted to the side, trying to punch his face and land an elbow to the ear. But my position was too awkward to connect with any force. I pulled my head back and landed a hard head-butt against his nose. Blood gushed, thick and dark, from Jake's flaring nostrils.

"Damn it, Milayna! Why are you making this so hard?" He jerked me hard, and I stumbled and fell.

I saw feet round the corner of the house. I pushed up on my elbows and watched through a haze of sweat-soaked hair as Chay ran across the yard toward us and plowed into Jake. He hit Jake repeatedly in the face and

231   *Michelle K. Pickett*

gut.

"That's enough. Son, he's done. You need to stop." My dad pulled Chay off Jake. His voice was soothing and calm.

Sirens blared in the distance. Jake rolled to his hands and knees, pushing himself off the ground. Smirking at me, he flicked the blood off his lower lip with his thumb and chuckled. His teeth were tinged red from bloody saliva. "This isn't over," he said.

It took Jake three tries to jump the fence, and each time, he doubled over in pain. When he finally was able to climb over, I heard him hit the ground hard on the other side, grunting with the impact.

The ground began to move beneath my feet. I backed away from the pit, and kept backing up until I reached the back deck of my house. Collapsing halfway up the stairs, I laid my head on the step. My breathing was ragged, and my heart raced painfully against my ribs.

Chay sat next to me and whispered in my ear. I wasn't sure what. I only knew it was over. They were gone, and I was safe.

Until the next time.

26
Coals from Hell

ONE WEEK, FOUR DAYS UNTIL MY BIRTHDAY.

I skipped school Friday. Well, actually, my parents let me skip. My face was a beautiful shade of black and deep purple that no amount of make-up was going to cover. Since the bruises would be hard to explain, I was given a free pass to stay home and watch cheesy soap operas all day. I loved those things.

The bad thing about staying home was that it gave me too much time to think. I thought about the pit, the sneer on Jake's face when he dragged me toward it, the sounds of the suffering and smell of rot and decay.

But mostly, I thought of Muriel. Why didn't she help me? Why did she stand there, watching? Why didn't she scream or run and get someone? When I confronted her later that night, she said she was too afraid. That she was immobilized by her fear of Jake and what lay waiting in the glowing pit. I wasn't sure if I believed her, and I hated that. And while the rest of the group bandaged and iced their wounds, Muriel only had one little bruise. That made me question her actions even more.

She should've had my back. There shouldn't have been any thought involved. If she'd needed help, I'd have been there for her. Period. The two of us could have taken Jake. I can't trust her to help me in a dangerous situation. I always thought I could trust her with my life. Now I know that's definitely not true. Talk about a slap in the face.

The best thing about staying home was that Chay stayed home, too.

Michelle K. Pickett

Of course, with both my parents working, I needed a babysitter. What better person than him? Too bad he had to watch me from his house. My parents weren't stupid enough to leave two horny teenagers alone for the day. Oh, the trouble we could cause. And would.

So Chay sat at his house covered in cuts and bruises, and I sat in my house covered in the same. We texted to keep each other company.

Chay: I hate this.
Me: What?
Chay: Texting.
Me: You don't want to text me?
Chay: No.

My phone rang, making me jump.

"Hello."

"That's better," he murmured, his voice washing over me like a balm, easing my pain.

"What's better?"

"I can hear your voice. I couldn't hear your voice through text messages."

I smiled. "And why do you need to hear my voice?" I snuggled deep into the quilt I was wrapped in.

"Because it's beautiful, like you."

I felt a blush heat my cheeks, which was silly since I was the only person in the room.

"Your voice isn't so bad either," I said, grinning like an idiot. "The guy it's attached to will have to do, I guess," I teased, closing my eyes and picturing him.

"Oh really?" he said with a chuckle. "Gee, don't stroke my ego or anything."

I sighed. "I can't stop thinking."

"About?" I could hear him rustling through the phone.

"It's almost here."

"What?"

"November first. My birthday." I picked at my quilt.

He let out a breath. "I know. All Saints' Day."

"Ironic, isn't it?"

Monday, I was forced to go to school. I spent the weekend holed up at home. It wasn't all bad, though. Chay spent most of the weekend with me. He came over Saturday morning for our traditional family breakfast. I was sure I charmed my parents more every time they saw him. Of course, it helped that he saved my life Thursday night.

When Chay wasn't at my house, I was at his, usually looking to see what goodies he had stocked in his personal refrigerator. He was so spoiled. But so was I. He made sure it was stocked with all my favorites. Peanut butter M&Ms could ease a world of hurt, and it just happened that Chay seemed to have an unending supply of them—and they were my favorite candy. Coincidence? I didn't care. I just wanted the candy.

But Monday dawned a beautiful fall day, and makeup covered most of the horrendous bruises on my face, so off to school I tromped under extreme protest. My parents were unmoved. But it turned out to be an okay day. Chay picked me up in his bright yellow Camaro. We sat together in AP chemistry and texted each other during calculus. We held hands while we ate lunch with the group, and sat together in English class. Yeah, my days were becoming gauged on how often I saw, touched, and kissed Chay Roberts. All three of which I seemed to be doing more and more.

The only down side to school was Muriel. It was the first time we'd spoken since Thursday night.

"Hey," Muriel said when I sat down in calculus.

"Hey back." I didn't look at her. My emotions were still bouncing back and forth. I wasn't sure how I felt about her excuse for standing around during the fight with Jake. It just didn't ring true, and I couldn't shake it off.

"How was your long weekend?"

"Pretty good. Yours?"

"Horrid," she said, her voice catching.

"Why? What happened?" I turned to her then. Her eyes had dark rings around them, and her normally silky black hair looked like she hadn't washed it in days. She looked terrible.

Muriel put her hand on her chest, and she shook her head while she spoke, "I feel horrible about Thursday night. I don't know what happened. I just froze."

Waving her words away with my hand, I instantly felt horrible that I doubted her.

She wasn't the person in my dream. She wouldn't betray the group, betray me. She just got scared. I was scared. I mean, we're all scared, right? She's always been there for me. And I'm doubting her for one mistake. That's not fair... although it was a pretty big mistake. Something just isn't right.

I didn't want Muriel to know I doubted her. I didn't want anyone in the group to know I suspected anyone of being a traitor, so I blew it off. "Don't worry about it. It can happen to any of us."

I looked to the front of the class where the instructor had started his lecture. Chay watched us, his full bottom lip turned down in a frown.

"You don't trust Muriel, do you?" I asked Chay on the drive home from school that afternoon.

"I've told you, we don't know who—"

235 *Michelle K. Pickett*

"Yeah, I heard you the first fifty-eight times you've told me. We don't know who we can trust. But we have to trust someone, Chay. Otherwise, how can we function as a group?"

He drummed his thumb on the steering wheel. I didn't think he was going to answer, but he finally said, "No, I don't trust Muriel."

I shifted toward him in my seat. "Then who do you trust?"

"I trust you." He looked at me for a few beats before returning his gaze to the road. "I trust you with my life. With... " He cleared his throat and looked out of the side window for a second. "Um, Jen seems fine. I guess I trust her. Jeff was quick to help you Thursday night, but he and Shayla used to date. So, I don't know how that figures into things." Chay shrugged.

What I want to know is what was supposed to come after 'with' before you changed the subject. And Jeff and Shayla? Huh, I need to get on the gossip hotline more often.

"But not Drew or Muriel?"

"No. Muriel stood watching Jake pull you toward that hole. I don't buy the story that she was so scared she froze. We've been doing this a long time, since before you came into the group. She's never frozen before. As for Drew, he has a thing for Muriel. If she flipped sides, I can't be sure he wouldn't follow. That makes him a wild card." Chay looked at me and abruptly changed the subject. "Hey, you wanna get a milkshake?"

"Where?"

"My uncle's."

"But I thought his shop was closed." *Because of me,* I thought. Flashes of Chay's face at the hospital ran in front of my eyes, and I flinched. The pain echoed through my body.

But he doesn't really blame me. Neither will Uncle. And I really want to see Uncle Stewart.

"Yeah, but he makes them at home, too."

I laughed. "Yeah, I could go for a milkshake with extra whipped cream and three cherries."

One week until my birthday.

Chay picked me up for school Tuesday morning. I ran down the stairs, grabbing a piece of toast and kissing my mom on the cheek before running to the door. He was there waiting for me, as usual.

"Good morning," he said lazily, bending for a quick kiss.

When he lifted his head, I licked my lips, touching them lightly with my fingers. "Yes, it is." He smiled and threaded his fingers with mine.

When we reached the car, he held the door open for me to get in. I was beginning to like that. He walked around front of the car to the driver's side, swinging his keys around his fingers. Sliding in the car, he leaned over and kissed me again. This time longer... deeper... and, yes, toe curling. I loved that.

"Have the dream again?" he asked, pulling out of my driveway.

"Yeah."

"Were you able to see any more of the person?"

I shook my head, frustrated with myself. "No. If my subconscious knows someone is going to betray us, then it should know who. Or I should at least feel it when I'm around them like I did with Steven."

"Maybe. It won't be too much longer until we find out."

"That's what I'm afraid of." My birthday was inching closer each day and with it, the fight of my life. For my life. I wish I could rewind time. Like the movie Groundhog Day. Just keep living the same day over and over and not have to worry about my birthday. Maybe I'd replay the day at the zoo. That was a good day for the most part.

School went by in a blur. I thought I made all the right comments, turned in my homework to the correct classes, and went to swim practice, but my mind was preoccupied. I couldn't stop thinking of the dream. I tried to put the pieces together, but I just came up with one jumbled mess of a picture—I had no idea who the traitor was.

I was spread across my bed doing calculus homework when I smelled it. The unmistakable odor of sulfur. My stomach dropped and my heart yo-yoed in my chest. The smell of sulfur never brought good things.

I pushed aside my books and hopped off the bed, jogging down the stairs and out of the door to the backyard.

Empty.

I didn't have the same sense of when another group member was in danger that Chay had. None of us did. But the sulfur smell was stronger. There was definitely something going on somewhere.

I fished my cell phone out of my pocket and called Muriel. I started talking as soon as she picked up. I didn't even give her a chance to say hello. "Start the phone chain. Something's happening. Get everyone together."

"I don't see anything," Muriel said.

"It's not here. I'm not sure where it is yet, but the sulfur smell is burning the back of my throat it's so strong. Something is going on somewhere."

"Got it." Muriel hung up. She'd call and text the next person on the phone chain and they'd do the same and so on until everyone was notified.

Except... Chay usually started the phone chain because he usually

237 *Michelle K. Pickett*

sensed the danger. Chay!

I ran to the back fence. The closer I got, the stronger the sulfur smell. "Shit."

I ran back to the house, dialing Muriel at the same time. As soon as Muriel picked up, I yelled, "They're at Chay's!"

"Got it." Muriel's voice was all business. She clicked off the line.

"Dad! Dad!" I screamed.

He ran out of the back door and grabbed my arms. "Milayna, what?"

"They're at Chay's. Can't you smell the sulfur? They're at Chay's. I have to go..."

And then I was running, my dad keeping in step with me. We jumped the fence and zigzagged through yards, around swing sets and kiddie pools, until we reached Chay's.

I walked to Chay and stood silently next to him. He reached for my hand. Our fingers intertwined in silent reassurance. I kept my expression neutral, showing no emotion in front of the other group. What I really wanted to do was grab Chay, hug him, kiss him, and make sure he was all right. But I forced myself to stand stoically by his side.

It wasn't long before the rest of the group showed up. Jeff from behind, Jen and Drew from the sides, and Muriel hopping the fence with my Uncle Rory.

The two groups stared at each other. I wasn't sure how long we stood silently staring at each other. It could have been seconds—it could have been minutes. It seemed like hours. The longer we stood there, the bigger the lump in my gut grew. Something was going to happen. I could feel it. It swirled in the air. A whispered threat. A promise. And the most worrisome, it showed on Chay's face. He knew. He could feel it. His arm and neck muscles were corded, and tension rolled off him in waves.

My heart was skipping every other beat. It was almost like it had forgotten how to beat. I felt hollow. The beats of my heart echoed against the empty walls of my chest.

I saw it. A pretty blonde shifted her weight. Her tell.

They ran all at once. We braced ourselves and readied for the attack. They came at us in a "V" formation or what looked like an arrow. It wasn't a random free-for-all like usual, but a planned attack—with a specific goal.

"What the hell are they doing?" Chay yelled.

Jeff watched them and shook his head. "Dunno."

They got closer and closer, still in formation, running at us in eerie silence. They ran across the sidewalk and on to the yard.

"Get in front of Milayna!" Drew yelled.

Chay didn't question Drew's order. He reached out and pulled me behind him just as the lead demi-demon, Edward, plowed into him. They both landed hard on the ground, fists flying.

The second line of demi-demons attacked, and then the third... I paced back and forth, feeling useless as I watched my friends fight while I did nothing.

"Dad! Let me help them!"

He shook his head and blocked me from leaving his and Chay's dad's protection. "They were aiming right at you tonight, Milayna. You aren't going out there. In fact, I should take you home."

"No! That'd put Mom and Benjamin in danger if one of them went to the house after me. Not to mention, I'd have no protection there. This is my fight. This is where I belong." I flung my arm toward the vicious fight between my friends and the wicked-assed demi-demons.

My dad turned toward the fight just as the demi-demons broke through our line of defense. The demi-demon tackled my dad. I ran to help when someone grabbed my arm and pulled me to a stop.

Turning, I looked at the guy that held me. I didn't know him, had never seen him before that night. I was distracted when he backhanded me across the face the first time. The second time he raised his hand, I was ready. I blocked his blow, jabbing the hand on my other arm into his side. He roared in pain and swung at me.

Holy freaky angel powers, Batman!

His swing came at me in slow motion, like time had slowed. I took advantage of the warning and kicked his arm away, getting in a palm-heel strike to his face, slicing open his lower lip. Blood dripped down his chin; his lips stretched into a slow smile when he wiped it away with the back of his hand. His teeth were stained pink, and he spat out a wad of blood and saliva. I watched it leave his mouth, and move, little by little, through the air and land next to my foot.

I was stupefied. Everyone around me was on slow motion, but I was on real time. I had absolutely no idea how I managed to tap into the power, but it was definitely one of the better powers I had, especially during a meeting with the demi-demons.

I was deep in concentration, fighting off the attacks of the demi-demon in front of me. He was relentless, coming in with jabs and punches one after another. All in the same slow motion as the others. I deflected his hits easily.

The sound of the others fighting was deafening. The groans of pain as flesh hit flesh, the smack of fists as they made contact, the howling of frustration when a blow didn't connect.

Between the sounds, the demi-demon I was fighting, and my fascination with my newly discovered power, I didn't sense the person behind me until it was too late. They wrapped their arms around me in a bear hug, pinning my arms to my body. I stomped on his ankle, and his grip released long enough for me to wriggle free, only to be hit hard across the jaw, sending

239   *Michelle K. Pickett*

me backward into the second demi-demon's grasp. My concentration on my power slipped and time jumped back to normal speed, jolting me like I'd been in a speeding car and someone slammed on the brakes.

The demi-demon lifted me off the ground and carried me to the center of the yard. The earth started shaking, a mound grew until the dirt gave way, and the pit opened up.

Oh, shit. Again? Really?

But instead of throwing me down into the abyss, which they could have easily done, they held me beside the hole, pressing down on my shoulders and forcing me to my knees.

I felt nauseous. I knew what was at the bottom of that pit. And I knew my time was running short. I wasn't a cat. I didn't have nine lives, and I was kind of fond of the one I had. I tried to work up enough spit to swallow and ease the burning in the back of my throat, and I screamed for someone to help me, but they were all involved in their own fights. I saw Chay glancing at me before he took a hard blow to the side of his head.

I knew no one was going to come to my rescue. I was on my own. I took a deep breath and remembered what one of my many self-defense teachers once told me.

"Being scared is a powerful emotion. It is only crippling if you let it be. Channel it. Rewire your brain to read being scared as being pissed the hell off. It's okay to be scared, Milayna. It's normal. It doesn't make you weak. You can use it to make yourself stronger," he said, and then he worked me over on the mats, teaching me move after move until they came naturally to me. And he taught me something else—there was no such thing as fighting dirty when your life was at stake. Use what you could, do what you could to survive.

I closed my eyes for a minute and pictured myself in that gym with my teacher, hearing him tell me to do whatever it took to survive, and the butterflies in my stomach and the hollowness in my chest abated just a little.

The first thing I saw was the glowing, yellowish-orange light coming from the bottom of the hole. Then I saw them. Gray arms dusted in a fine sheen of ash. They reached out and planted themselves on the ground, hefting the demon halfway out of the hole. He had two horns, curled like ram's horns. They looked like wood that had its bark scraped off.

Its black fingernails dug into the ground as it pulled itself up and halfway out of the hole. It pinned me with its black-eyed stare.

"You can't trust humans to do a demon's job, even if they are half demon," it hissed through needle-like teeth that gleamed white.

It pulled itself further out of the hole, and I knew if I was going to survive the night, I'd better do something. Fast.

Do whatever it takes to survive. There's no such thing as fighting dirty when your life is at stake.

I turned my head and bit the arm of the demi-demon holding my arms against my body. I clamped down and didn't let go until I tasted his sickening thick, warm blood. He screamed in pain and let go of my arms.

I landed a palm-heel strike in the middle of the demon's face. Its head bounced backward, its black eyes registering surprise. Swinging my legs around, I scrambled up from the ground. I gave the demon a roundhouse kick to the side of the head. It grabbed my ankle, and I fell on my side with a cry.

"Tsk, tsk. We know all about your little fighting games. We're prepared." The demon shook his head at me like he was disappointed. "I thought you'd be more of a challenge."

I pulled back my free leg and jammed my foot into the demon's arm. It bent downward at an odd angle, and he lost his grip on me. I scrambled out of his reach. I feigned a right, but jabbed a left. The demon pulled himself out of the hole further to hit me behind the knees and I went down again, but not before I gave him an okay kick to the head. He slid down the hole until just his head and shoulders were above ground, his arms still reaching out. I rolled to my back and gave him a quick kick to the forehead. His head snapped back. He lost his grip and slid down the side of the pit with a shriek of profanities.

Thank God I didn't take piano lessons.

Turning, I helped my dad with the demi-demon cornering him between the house and the porch. I jabbed him in the side, grabbed the back of his hair, and yanked his head back. Raising my knee between his legs, I nudged him.

"Apologize to my dad."

He didn't acknowledge me. I rammed my bent leg upward. He shrieked in pain. I let go and he fell to the ground, curled around himself.

"You should respect your elders," I said and walked away, looking for a place I could help.

Someone touched me lightly on the arm. I turned quickly, ready to defend myself. Chay grabbed my wrist as my fist flew toward him.

"Milayna, it's over," he said quietly and kissed my fist.

I looked around. The demi-demons and Evils were running in all directions. The dirt was shifting and filling the pit. The only evidence that anything had happened was a mound where the pit had been.

I could hear the wail of a siren in the distance

We sat around the kitchen table. My mom and Mrs. Roberts made the six of us a snack. They hovered like two mother hens, making sure we ate, that our cuts were cleaned and our bruises iced. It must've been hard on them watching us fight and not being able to help. Demi-angels had superior strength to humans, even if a human was schooled in martial arts and self-defense like my mother and Mrs. Roberts. There was really nothing they

Michelle K. Pickett

could do but watch from the sidelines. As strong, independent women, it was a position they both hated but had learned to live with, if not accept.

"Milayna, what are you doing? Do you have a headache?" my mom asked when she walked by.

I dropped my hands from where they pressed on my temples. "Um, no... I was just trying to make that spoon move." Everyone in the room looked at me like I'd lost my mind—I probably had. Chay pursed his lips to hide a grin. "Dad said we can sometimes sense what other people are thinking. Not read minds, but feel what they are thinking or feeling. Well, that's happened to me twice now." That got everyone's attention.

"What are you talking about?" Drew scooted his chair closer to me.

"I was fighting this demi-demon idiot tonight, and everything was normal. He hit me, I hit him, blah frickin' blah. Then it was like someone slowed time down. I could see his movements in slow motion, giving me time to prepare myself for the block. It was wicked cool, like I could sense what he was thinking before he threw his punches or kicks."

I took a drink of my Coke and sat up straighter. "And the night we found out Steven changed? Well, I felt what everyone in the room was feeling. All I had to do was look them in the eyes and it was like we connected somehow. It felt like static cling sparking between us." I moved my fingers to imitate little sparks in the air, moving my hand between Chay and me.

"Somehow, the person's feelings were communicated to me through that connection. Like, when I looked at Chay, I could feel the electrical current connect to him, and I felt a sense of calm, strength, a sense of bonding to the team, and I felt... I felt... well, that's all. When I looked at Steven, he only held eye contact a second or two and the emotion I felt the strongest was uneasiness. There was no tie to the group. Otherwise, I felt nothing." I let my hands fall. "That's when I was fairly certain he'd already changed. And it turned out I was right—well, the electrical current was right. Whatever. Anyway, I thought since that power was showing up, maybe I could get a handle on this telekinesis thing we're supposed to have. I can't seem to get it to work when I want it to, but it shows up anytime Chay and I... well, whatever." I shrugged a shoulder, wishing I could suck those last words back in.

"Anytime Chay and you what?" My dad lifted an eyebrow.

I gave him a quick smile, the tips of my cheekbones burning. Chay wouldn't make eye contact.

"Yeah, good luck. I've been trying forever and nothing," Drew grumbled. He spun his plate around on the table and scowled.

"Well, we need to work on developing our powers. I know I have them, but I don't know how I made them work. I mean, I tried to get the emotional electrical current thing. Sometimes it's there and other times, nada. And we all have telekinesis that we need to learn how to work. Because this can't go on." I pushed my plate away. "The fights are making us weaker. There's no way we can keep fighting and be able to fight off Azazel and his demons too."

The group murmured their agreement.

"Dad, there has to be a way of killing them." I looked at my father, who had one hip leaned against the countertop and his arm around my mother's waist.

"Milayna, we can't kill the demi-demons. They're half human!" he said in horror. His eyes wide.

"Not them, Dad. Geez. I meant the demons. How do we kill them? How do we protect ourselves from their strength?"

"We fight like you did tonight. You use what you learned in your training. It's no different. That's why your mother and I have tried to train you in personal defense and fighting skills almost since you were able to walk. And you rely on your teammates."

Except the thing I'm defending myself against is a demon with flaming hot skin who'd like nothing better than to throw me into the pit of Hell, and one of my team wants to help it do that.

"Well, there is one other thing," Chay's dad said from the corner of the room. He looked down at his hand and rubbed it with the fingers of the other.

"We'd never get one. I don't know anyone, angel or demi-angel, who's seen one." My dad shook his head.

"What?" I asked, hope stirring for the first time. I leaned toward Chay's dad. "Whatever it is, we need to try!" I said, talking so fast in my excitement that I wasn't sure anyone could understand me.

"There's a legend among angels that demons can be killed using a dagger," my dad said quietly.

"Good! Let's get one." I started to stand. "Chay? You want to drive?"

"Wait." My dad held up a hand. "There's more to it than just going to the local Gander Mountain and buying a knife, Milayna. If it were that easy, we would have done it years ago." My dad let out a breath of frustration and pushed off the counter. "No, these daggers are special. Legend says they are made from the very coals of Hell. One prick from its blade and a demon dies. We don't know who makes them, how, what they look like, nothing. In fact, we don't know if the legend is even true."

"So how do we get one?" Drew asked.

Chay's dad shrugged. "Don't know. I've never seen one. The Demons are too afraid to use them. The Demons higher in the hierarchy use them to keep the lower, servant demons and hobgoblins in line. I guess they have an immunity to them that makes them unafraid to use them. It's also said that demons give daggers to demi-demons. But as ferocious as they are, I've never seen a demi-demon use any kind of weapon to kill a demi-angel or a human."

"We need one of those daggers." Chay rolled his shoulders. "What about Azazel? Does he carry one?"

Michelle K. Pickett

Chay's dad shook his head. "I don't know, son. I've never seen Azazel, only his demons."

"Me either." This from my dad.

"I have," I whispered. The air in the room stilled, and everyone looked at me. "Not in the flesh, but in a dream. In a vision."

"What'd you see?" My dad's voice was hard.

"He looks like a man, but his skin is red, like he has a wicked bad sunburn. He has shoulder-length black hair slicked back on his head. It looks like he uses too much hair gel. In my vision, he wore a black robe. Tucked into the sash was a gold-jeweled handle. I didn't think about what it was until now, but I'm sure it's a knife of some sort."

"The only way to get our hands on that dagger is to take it from Azazel... who none of us have seen in the flesh." Chay flopped back in his chair, letting out a frustrated sigh.

"Or find someone he's given it to." I rolled my pop can between my hands.

"I don't think that'll get you the dagger. The legend says that a demi-demon who possesses it absorbs its strength, but also its evil. The person would be stronger than any of us and fueled by evil. Not someone you want to mess around with." My dad pulled Mom closer to him.

Chay's dad nodded, drumming his fingers against his thigh and tightening his other arm around Mrs. Roberts.

"And if a demi-angel gets the dagger? Does it still emanate evil?" I braced my forearms on the table and leaned forward.

Mr. Roberts made a sound in his throat and shook his head. He swallowed his mouthful of Coke and said, "The legend is that it gives evil to evil and enhanced power to destroy evil to anyone good who possesses it."

"We need that dagger, even if we do have to fight a much stronger demi-demon to get it." Chay threaded our fingers together. "We'll just have to keep Evils out of the picture while we do it, so we can focus all our energy on the demi-demons. So one prick and a Demon is toast. What happens if we get cut by the dagger?"

Mr. Roberts looked at Chay, and his face softened. The love and worry for his son was clear. "I don't know, son." He shook his head and looked at the floor. "We just don't know enough about it."

Evils. Hmm. Could they... what if? Jake.

"The Evils. Is there anything that says the dagger has to be used by a demi-demon? Could an Evil have it?" I looked between my dad and Mr. Roberts.

Mr. Roberts looked at my dad and lifted a shoulder. My dad looked at me and mimicked his shrug. "We don't know enough about it to even guess. Why?"

"There's one person I know who's turned so evil that he's not even himself any longer. He's cruel, sadistic, and I can see him and Azazel laughing over cigars and coffee," I said.

"Who?" everyone in the room asked, their words overlapping and echoing each other's. All except Chay. He knew the answer. A frown pulled at his lips, and he nodded.

"Jake," I whispered. "And I've seen a leather sheath on his belt. The kind that would hold a knife."

I stood on the back deck with Chay after everyone had gone home. He cupped one side of my face in his palm, gently rubbing his thumb across my skin.

"You're so beautiful," he murmured.

"Yeah, right," I said with a laugh. "I look like I lost a boxing match after ten rounds."

Chay leaned down and kissed my jaw lightly, just a whisper of a caress over the skin that was already swelling and turning a dusky red.

"I could kill them for what they've done to you," he ground out between clenched teeth.

"What they've done to everyone," I said, wrapping my arms around his neck. "But you wouldn't—couldn't—kill anyone. You're better than that. You have too much goodness in you. Right here." I put my hand over his heart.

Sliding my hand around the back of his neck, I nudged him to me. His eyes darkened and the blue-green depths swirled. He skimmed his lips over mine before pulling back. His mouth hovered over mine, just a sigh separating us. I could feel his breaths mixing with mine, and I said his name on a sigh. He sucked my lower lip into his mouth. Letting my lip slip from his mouth, he kissed along my jaw to my ear.

"You were made to fit in my arms." He kissed the hollow behind my ear, and my fingers fisted in his hair.

I pulled his mouth back to mine and his tongue delved between my lips, exploring every part of my mouth. Running along the length of my tongue, across my teeth, over the roof of my mouth—he touched everywhere. I leaned into him, wanting more. Always wanting more. His feel. His strength. His taste. Him.

The light clicked on, and Chay stepped back. I grinned. "I guess the fun's over."

"Yeah, but it was damn good while it lasted."

I gave him a quick kiss. "'Bye. Text me."

"I will," he promised. "I'll talk with you tomorrow, Milayna. I have a feeling we're gonna get a free pass from school."

Judging by the bruises covering his face, and the way mine throbbed,

Michelle K. Pickett

I figured he was right.

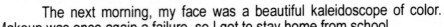

The next morning, my face was a beautiful kaleidoscope of color. Makeup was once again a failure, so I got to stay home from school.

Unfortunately, Chay had to go to school, so there was no one to make fun of soap operas with. Uncle Rory was my babysitter for the day, and he didn't see the appeal. So we watched the sports channel. It was torture. I'd rather have been at school.

27

Swim Practice

FIVE DAYS UNTIL MY BIRTHDAY.

Thursday, my mother booted me off to school even though I looked like I was on the wrong end of a catfight.

"I can't go to school looking like this, Mom! Give me one more day." Although another day with Uncle Rory and the sports channel and I was likely to pull my hair out strand by strand. Watching the sports channel all day was like Chinese water torture. It actually made me want to study chemistry.

"No, you can't miss any more school. If anyone asks, tell them you fell down the stairs."

I stomped up the stairs to my room, tripping on the top step, and landing on my hands and knees on the hallway floor.

"See, honey, falling down the stairs won't be a big stretch for you. You can even fall up them." She walked away, giggling.

"Ha freakin' ha," I muttered.

I called Chay for a ride, but his mother said he'd already left. He had a quiz to make up. I didn't even want to think about the amount of work I had to make up. The thought made my head pound. I had demons to deal with. I couldn't be worrying about chemistry labs and calculus. Who the hell cared what x equaled?

"So what's the official story?" Muriel asked, interrupting my thoughts. She had given me a ride to school. We walked from the student parking lot to our lockers.

Michelle K. Pickett

"Hmm?"

"Your face." She tilted her head to the side. "People are bound to notice."

I rolled my eyes. "Yeah. Um, I fell down the stairs."

She walked with me to chemistry, said she'd see me the next hour in calculus, and walked away. I looked through the door into the classroom. Chay sat at our lab area, his arms folded on the table, his head lying on them. I walked quietly to the desk and hefted my book bag up. It landed with a loud thwack next to him. He jumped up straight in his chair.

"Now you know how it feels," I said with a smile. "You look like hell, Chay."

"That was going to be my line." He stood, pulling out my chair for me, and I sat down. As he moved away, he let the tips of his fingers glide over the skin at the base of my neck. I shivered. "So, what's the story? Stairs?"

"Yep. Just tumbled down the darn things," I said loud enough for everyone to hear.

It wasn't like someone wasn't going to figure out our lie. Chay was bruised, I was bruised; Drew, Jeff, and Jen were all bruised. Not to mention the other side. I was sure they had their fair share of cuts and bruises, as well. It wouldn't take a rocket scientist to figure out there'd been a fight. The only real issue was to make sure no one knew what the fight was about.

"I missed you yesterday." He pushed a stray lock of hair behind my ear. His finger trailed down the side of my face.

"I missed you, too. Uncle Rory insisted on coming over. We ended up watching the sports channel all day. It was torture. I actually wanted to do homework."

"Well, I'm glad I'm better company than Uncle Rory."

"Slightly."

He laughed. I loved that sound, a slow rumbling deep in his chest. He flashed me a wide smile that crinkled the skin around his eyes like only a real smile can. And for a moment, time stood still and we weren't in chemistry class. We weren't fighting demi-demons or demons. We were just two people together. Normal. In love.

The teacher started class. We had a lab to work on. Since I didn't do the homework assignment because I was home—falling down stairs, apparently—I relied on Chay's notes. He bent his head close to mine, showing me the lab in the textbook... I breathed him in. He pointed out something in his notes... I stole glances as his profile. He explained the assignment... I watched his lips move and remembered how they felt against mine. When class was over, I had no idea what we did or even if I helped.

School lasted forever. When the last bell rang, I just wanted to get into the car with Chay and go home. My head pounded and my face throbbed. I wanted to crawl into a nice, warm bath and soak my aches and pains away.

"See ya in the gym." Muriel walked past me in the hallway with a wave.

Ugh, swim practice. I'd forgotten it was Thursday. I wanted to duck out, but I'd missed so many practices that I was going to get kicked off the team if I missed any more.

"I get to see you in that sexy swim hat." Chay waggled his eyebrows.

I groaned. Not only did I have to go to swim practice, the horrendous swimming cap would pull all my hair from my face and every ugly mark and bruise would show. At least with my hair down, it hid some of it. And I had a pimple on the side of my nose. It was like the cherry on top of everything else.

Can this day get any worse? I probably shouldn't ask that. The answer is most definitely 'yes.'

I dragged myself into the locker room and changed into my swimsuit. Picking up my swim cap, I sighed and bounced it in my hand a few times. Scrunching my nose at the ugly thing, I jammed it under the edge of the leg opening of my suit so it hung down my thigh, and left the locker room.

On my way to the pool, my coach walked by me. "Where's your cap, Jackson?" Her voice echoed off the sickly green, ceramic-tiled walls, making my head pound even more.

"It's so tight. It hurts to wear it. I was hoping I'd get some brownie points for looking like Frankenstein's kid, but no go, huh?"

"If you're swimming, you're wearing the cap."

"Fine," I muttered. I looked around. Chay sat on the bleachers overlooking the pool.

Maybe I won't look so bad from way up there.

I bent over, my hair hanging over my head. I grabbed it, twisted it into a knot, and shoved it all in the white swim cap before diving into the pool.

The water was cool and felt good against my bruised face. It muffled the sounds of the voices echoing in the pool area, making my head feel just the teensiest bit better. I stayed under water as long as I could, letting the air bubbles swirl around me. It wasn't until I felt a poke in the ribs and saw Muriel jerk her thumb upwards that I surfaced.

She sighed. "We're doing laps."

Hefting my body out of the water, I walked to my lane. I waited for the buzzer and dove into the water, pushing myself to swim as hard and fast as I could. The physical exertion felt good. By the time swim practice was over, the endorphins had kicked in and I was in a much better mood.

I was right behind Muriel. We were walking out of the girls' locker room after we'd showered and changed, and she was gossiping about something someone said during practice. I wasn't really listening. I stopped for just a second to adjust my things when he stepped out in front of me, separating

Michelle K. Pickett

me from Muriel, who walked into the hall, still talking.

I sucked in a breath. "Move, Edward," I said as forcefully as I could, trying to keep my voice firm. He wasn't a demi-angel who'd switched sides. No, he had an evil aura around him that only a demi-demon could. I really wanted to scream out to Muriel, but something held me back. I still wasn't completely convinced I could trust her.

Didn't she see him when she walked by? She would've had to... right?

"I know this isn't how you want to live, Milayna. I know you don't like your powers, that you don't like being a demi-angel." He stepped closer to me.

"You don't know anything about me." I moved to the side and tried to brush past him. He pushed me back.

"Oh, I think I do. Things can be different. You just have to renounce what you are. Go to Azazel and join his legion. Things would be so different for you. You wouldn't be plagued by those awful visions anymore." A smile spread across Edward's face. "Azazel will treat you like a princess. Fame, wealth, jewels. You'll have anything you want and more."

"Thanks, but no."

"You're just making it harder on yourself and those you love."

I stilled. Harder on those I love? Mom and Dad. Oh! Benjamin. He's so young. It's not fair for them to touch him. Not one damn hair on his head. Wait...

"Ah, I see you're thinking of the benefits of a life with us," he murmured.

I steeled myself. Things were already hard for those I loved. Azazel wouldn't make it any easier once he controlled my powers.

"No, I'm just thinking how stupid you are for asking. What kind of crap are you spouting? Things are already hard on the people I love. But mark my words, if Azazel so much as touches a hair on the head of anyone I love, I'll end him."

He let out a banshee-like scream and ran for me. I sidestepped him, and he ran into the wall behind me before he could stop. The force knocked him backward, and he fell on his ass.

"See? Stupid." I walked to the door. I wanted to run like hell, but I didn't want to show any weakness in front of him, so I forced myself to walk calmly and slowly.

"Bitch, you have no idea the shit storm you're bringing down on yourself. Personally, I can't wait to see it," he called, standing and brushing his khakis off.

"No doubt."

Just as I walked out of the locker room, Chay rounded the corner at a full run. He took the corner too fast and slipped, catching himself with his hand on the floor before he fell. His sneakers squeaked loudly against the tiled floor.

Milayna   250

He grabbed me. "Are you okay?"

"Yeah."

He folded me in his arms, kissing the top of my head. "What happened?" He put his finger under my chin and tipped my head back, grazing his lips over mine in a whisper-soft kiss.

"Where's Muriel?"

"I don't know. When she came down the hall alone, I asked where you were and she said she didn't know," he said. "That's when I knew something was wrong."

"I was right behind her. She was talking to me. How could she not realize something was wrong?" I chewed the corner of my bottom lip. I didn't understand why Muriel left without me, and I knew there was no way she didn't see the demi-demon go into the locker room when she exited. My mind did the math and circled around the answer, but I didn't like what I saw. I refused to even consider that she might be the traitor. No. She wouldn't turn.

Chay put his hands on my shoulders. "What happened?"

"I was walking behind Muriel out of the locker room." I waved at the door behind me. "Some of my things slipped, and I stopped for just a second to adjust them when Edward walked in front of me."

"Edward," Chay spat. "He's a demi-"

"Demi-demon, yeah, I know. What I don't know is how he slipped by Muriel without her seeing him. The entrance to the locker room is rounded. We walk in from the hallway and then follow the U-shaped curve around and into the locker room. There are no doorways or nooks where he could have been hiding. It's all one smooth, tiled wall."

"What did Edward do?" Chay threaded his fingers through mine.

"Just ran his mouth," I said, still distracted by Muriel and how she missed seeing Edward. Even if he had walked into the hallway after she left, she would have seen him. And besides, he didn't have time. He showed up too quickly after she walked by. He'd been in that hallway. I was sure of it.

"What'd he say?" Chay gave my hand a small squeeze when I didn't elaborate.

"Oh, you know, the same old stuff. Switch sides, Azazel is great, he won't kill you, your family will be safe, you'll have wealth, popularity, standard stuff like that."

Chay pushed me behind him. I looked up and saw Edward saunter past, a smile pulled across his crooked teeth.

"Chay," he said.

Chay nodded his head once in acknowledgement.

"Think you can keep her safe forever? I just proved we can get to her whenever we want," Edward taunted.

Chay didn't answer. He watched Edward walk by before pulling me around to face him. He kissed me softly on the forehead. "C'mon. Let's get

Michelle K. Pickett

outta here."

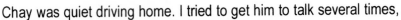

Chay was quiet driving home. I tried to get him to talk several times, but he only grunted in response. Finally, I gave up.

He pulled into my driveway and got out of the car, walking around to open my door for me. I slid out of the car and grabbed my bag. Chay lifted my bag from my shoulder and shut the car door. We walked up the front steps and onto the front porch. It was a cheery porch. Flowering plants hung from the rafters, and two wicker rockers sat side-by-side. My parents sat there on summer evenings, holding hands and talking about their day. I had only good memories of the house I'd grown up in, and it made me angry that those memories were being overshadowed by demons, fighting, and the constant threat of Azazel.

"You want to have something cold to drink and sit on the back deck? Or do you want to come over to my place? I just stocked my refrigerator with all your favorites." He grinned.

"Our parents aren't home. They aren't going to like—"

"I don't care." At the argument he saw forming on my lips, he said, "I don't care. I'm not leaving you alone. Besides, once your dad finds out what happened, he won't be mad."

"You can't tell my dad." I grabbed Chay's arm, my eyes wide. If it got out that we thought Muriel was a traitor, true or not, it would put a wedge the size of China between our families. I couldn't let that happen.

"We have to tell him."

"No," I shook my head.

"Why the hell not?" Chay's voice rose, and I flinched.

"Because if he thinks Muriel is involved, he'll go to Uncle Rory. If Muriel isn't involved, it will cause a lot of anger in my family. Maybe something that can't be repaired. If Muriel is involved, we don't want her to know that we know. So you can't tell my dad."

Chay licked his lips and looked at the sky before he nodded once. "Fine. We'll tell him you had a vision, but I'm not leaving you alone, Milayna."

I smiled. "I don't want you to."

"I'll meet you out back." He walked down the drive. I heard the gate to the backyard creak open before he closed and latched it.

I dropped my things on the foyer floor on my way to the kitchen to grab some cold Cokes and a bag of chips. I jumped when I saw Chay watching me through the patio door.

I opened the door. "What's wrong?"

"Let's go to my house." He filled the doorway, blocking my view outside. But I smelled the sulfur.

Milayna   252

"Why?" He didn't answer me. "Chay? Why?" When he didn't answer, I grabbed the pops and chips. I elbowed him in the ribs so he'd move from the door and I walked outside, laying the snacks on the patio table.

"This is so messed up! Like, mondo bizzarro." I watched as the six hobgoblins ran through my yard, cackling and spraying each other with the water hose. I dropped down in a deck chair and leaned back into the cushions. "This is so not how I imagined my senior year."

Chay laughed and sat down next to me. "They'll get tired sooner or later and leave."

"Yeah, I know. Wanna make out while we're waiting?" I asked with a smile.

"Stupid question." He moved closer to me and lowered his head to mine.

"Chay! Kissing Milayna? Naughty, naughty," the friendly goblin squealed. The other five stopped and looked at us. Scarface scowled.

"Get your kisses in now, boy. The day is almost here. Her birthday. No need to get her anything. She won't be around long enough to enjoy it," Scarface growled.

Michelle K. Pickett

28
My Mom

THREE DAYS UNTIL MY BIRTHDAY.

Jake loved the gym. He confronted me the first time in the gym. I supposed it was a logical choice. It was Saturday, so the gym was empty.

We'd finished another swim practice to get ready for a meet we had the next week. Muriel and I were on our way to the locker room, but we made a detour to the vending machines. The back way to the locker room was closest, but we had to cut through the gym. Big mistake.

We were talking about practice. Who did well, who sucked. Who was dating whom, who was cheating… all the good juice. We were halfway across the room when Jake and his friends appeared.

"Nice job at practice today." Jake smiled. The face I used to find so beautiful now disgusted me.

Neither Muriel nor I answered. We were sizing up the group, calculating our chances of getting out of the gym—through the doors. I wasn't in favor of taking a detour through Hell.

"Not speaking to me?" Jake raised an eyebrow at me and folded his arms across his chest. My stomach dropped when his biceps flexed, and not in the gooey-swoony way they would have a couple of months before. No, more like the how-the-hell-are-we-gonna-get-outta-this way.

I tried to swallow, but my mouth was too dry. My tongue stuck to the roof of my mouth and tasted sour.

Fear, Milayna, that's what it tastes like. Oh, shut up! I should be giving myself a pep talk, not telling myself I'm scared shitless.

I looked from side to side and bounced slightly on the balls of my feet. Closing my eyes for the count of three, I visualized somewhere calming to steady my racing heart. I didn't trust Jake, so I didn't dare keep my eyes closed long.

There were four of them. If Chay sensed trouble and came, we'd be fine. We could take them. If not, well, Muriel and I would be visiting a warmer climate, and it wouldn't be the Caribbean.

When I dropped my bag from my shoulder, it hit the floor with a loud thud. I kept the strap wrapped around my hand, tensing my fingers. Inhaling a deep breath through my nose, I blew it out slowly before inhaling another.

I stared at Jake, trying really hard not to look away, even though I wanted to watch the others. I had to trust Muriel for that and trusting her was something I was having trouble doing, especially since it was her idea to take the back way to the locker room.

"Maybe we can outrun them," Muriel whispered so low that I had to strain to hear her over the blood galloping behind my ears.

As if on cue, one of the Evils walked around and stood behind us. We'd have to plow through him to get out of the door. That would give Jake and his Azazel-loving homies time to catch us, and I'd rather fight Jake head on than have him gain the upper hand by grabbing me from behind.

"Doubtful." I shook my head slightly.

Jake stood directly in front of us, blocking our way to the locker room. His flunkies had circled us, one on the left and one on the right. The guy in the back blocked our way into the hall. There was nowhere to run.

Chay, come on. Please.

Jake rushed Muriel. The guy behind us ran to me. So did the guy on my left. I tightened my grip on the strap of my book bag. When they were close enough, I swung it around. It hit the first guy hard on the side of the head, knocking him backward. But it lost momentum and the second guy knocked it away.

He wasn't very large, no more than a couple inches taller than I was. But he was strong, and his skills were nearly equal to mine. The only good thing on my side was that the other guy was still holding the side of his head. He stumbled backward, hit the bleachers, and fell and hit his head a second time on the side of the seat. Guy number one was so sufficiently dazed that I didn't have to worry about him—yet.

The second guy jabbed me in the gut. The air whooshed from my lungs. While I was trying to recover from the hit, he hit me hard across the injured side of my face. Stars lit up in front of my eyes. I stumbled backward. My legs wobbled. My entire body hurt from the constant fighting and for a second, a tiny part of my mind wanted to give up. Just let what would happen... happen.

255   Michelle K. Pickett

Get it together. Stop being a freakin' baby. Fight!

And I did. I jabbed him in the side and gave a quick uppercut to the chin. Grabbing his arms, I tried to knee him in the crotch, but he recovered in time and threw me off him, punching me in the rib cage. I was sure I heard a crunch. The pain was blinding, and I couldn't stifle the scream that ripped from my mouth.

I heard one of the gym doors bang against the wall. Chay ran into the gym. I heard him tackle one of Azazel's homies. I didn't have time to look and see which one. My new bestie was advancing on me.

I watched him move around me. Protecting my side with one arm, I held the other ready for the block.

Expecting a blow to the face, his hands were raised to protect it. I punched his crotch several times in quick succession as hard as I could. He bent over, howling in pain. I locked my foot around the back of his leg and pushed him hard against the chest. He fell to the ground, his head bouncing off the gym floor once, like a deflated basketball.

I looked across the room at Jake. He pulled a small dagger from the waistband of his jeans. He watched Muriel while he turned the knife over and over in his hand. He tilted his head to the side, his expression thoughtful. The sunlight streaming through the windows glinted off the metallic blade.

"Muriel!" I screamed, but she was busy fighting a short, fat guy. He looked innocent enough, with his mop of curly, blond hair and deep dimples, but he was strong and faster than he looked. Muriel was struggling to keep up with his constant attacks.

Jake's gaze flicked to mine when I screamed Muriel's name. He bounced the dagger in his palm a few times and smirked at me before returning his gaze to Muriel. This time, his expression had purpose. He was focused.

I was too far away to get to Jake before he rushed Muriel. If I didn't do something, I knew he was going to hurt her. Jake had lost all his morals. He was the personification of evil. It was hard to believe he was the same person who fought alongside us just days before.

He moved toward Muriel. A sneer marred his face. His denim-blue eyes that I'd always loved were clouded with hate. Evil. He was going to stab Muriel. I had no doubt, and I was too far away to do anything to help her. Bile rose in the back of my throat, and I swallowed it down. It burned a trail to my stomach. Panic bubbled inside me and glued me in place. For several precious seconds I stood watching, doing nothing, my head void of any thought as I watched the events unfold in front of me. My heart banged against my chest so hard and fast that I couldn't breathe. Muriel was going to die, and I had a front-row seat. My hands started to shake. Sweat slithered down my spine and pooled at the base of my back.

I can't breathe... I can't breathe... Oh my... Muriel...

A strong wind blew through the gym and hit me. I stumbled. It knocked the panic out of me and forced me to move. My eyes darted around the gym, and my head bounced ideas around like someone was dribbling a basketball inside my skull. I searched for a way to help Muriel. Turning in a circle, I looked for anything I could use as a weapon.

Telekinesis.

"How?" I said through clenched teeth. "I've never made it happen on my own."

I have the power. Telekinesis. I can do it. I've done it, but I don't know how I did it! Information that would come in handy right about now. I need to kiss Chay to make it work!

I focused on the dagger, envisioning it flying from Jake's hand to mine. I tried to empty my mind—no small feat, considering that we were being attacked. Concentrating as hard as I could, I visualized the knife flying out of Jake's hand. I watched him run toward Muriel.

A strong jolt ran through my body, the kind you got when you stuck your tongue on the end of a nine-volt battery times ten. I shuddered, my hands started to tremble, and adrenaline-filled blood pulsed through my veins at an incredible rate. I could feel it run against the sides of my veins, throbbing as it pushed its way through my body.

I focused all my energy on the dagger. He raised it above Muriel, and my gaze locked on it. I watched as he lowered it toward Muriel's back. Reaching out my hand, I focused harder. The knife vibrated in his hand. I concentrated even harder. The vibration got stronger. Just as the tip pricked Muriel's back, it flew backward. I caught it as it whizzed by my head. Obviously, judging by the close proximity of the knife to my face, my aim needed some work.

Jake roared in anger. Realizing their defeat when they lost the dagger and giving me a way to protect myself from Hell's demons, the Evils ran out of the gym. Jake glared at me, his face contorted in an ugly sneer. "This isn't over, Milayna," he said through clenched teeth.

"I'm counting on it." My eyes locked on his. We stared at each other for what seemed like minutes, but was more likely a few seconds. He looked away first, the first sign of weakness he'd shown since the battles began. I was getting stronger. And we both knew it.

"You did it?" my dad asked with a huge smile when Chay brought me home.

"Yeah." I was still amazed it'd worked.

"How?" Drew asked.

The news of the attack spread quickly throughout the group, and ev-

257 *Michelle K. Pickett*

eryone had congregated in my small kitchen.

"I don't know. I just imagined the knife flying from his hand to mine. I concentrated on the image... and it just did."

"You know what this is, right? I mean, everybody realizes what she's done." Chay looked at me, his eyes soft. He reached out and trailed a finger down the side of my face.

"I just got us a kickass, demon-killing dagger is what I've done." I laughed when Chay chuckled.

"Keep it with you at all times, Milayna. Keep it on you. Not in your book bag, not in your purse. Keep it on you. We'll get you a sheath to carry it in. Maybe one that fits around your ankle where it won't be noticeable. I want you to have it whenever and wherever you are," my dad said. He turned the knife over and over in his hand.

"It sure is pretty for a dagger made from the coals of Hell." Muriel watched my dad roll it in his hand.

The dagger had a medium-length blade. A person would have to be close to their attacker to use it. The blade was engraved with a beautifully intricate design. But as pretty as the blade was, the handle was extraordinary. It was gold and embedded with small gemstones. Sapphires, rubies, emeralds, and diamonds glistened in the light and created rainbows on the ceiling and walls.

I didn't think something so beautiful could come from the bowels of a place as wretched as Hell.

Two days until my birthday.

Chay came over Sunday for a study date. It turned out to be more date than studying, which was fine with both of us. We sat on the back deck with our books covering the patio table. Charts and lab notes were everywhere. Pens and pencils lay unused next to them while we talked about everything except Azazel.

"What are you going to do after graduation?" I asked him. The thought that after high school our paths might lead us in different directions stole my breath, like someone was physically sucking it out of my lungs and I couldn't fill them again.

It was then, I knew. I wasn't ready to admit it to myself, or anyone else, but I knew. Chay was the air I breathed. The reason my world turned. Why I got out of bed early on the weekends, even after I repeatedly told him weekends were for sleeping in. The reason the stars twinkled in the night sky and the sun woke up every morning. The reason I wanted to beat Azazel. Because Chay was my reason—I could tackle anything.

"College."

Milayna   258

I wasn't sure I liked that answer. Of course I wanted him to go to college; I just didn't want him to leave.

"Where?" I held my breath, waiting for his answer.

He looked at the sky, and I watched the colors in his eyes change from blue to green. "Here for starters. I'll do my first two years of standard courses here, and then I'll decide where to transfer, if I transfer at all. And you?" He looked down at our hands, our fingers threaded together. He gently rubbed his thumb over the top of my hand.

I let out the breath I was holding. That was my plan too, and I smiled. We'd go to the same college, at least for two years. "The same."

"I was hoping that was your answer." He leaned over the table and kissed the tip of my nose.

"Hey, you wanna get out of here? We aren't getting any studying done anyway. Let's go do something." I shoved my junk in my book bag.

"A movie?"

"Sounds good. Let me tell my parents." I ran in the house and asked my parents if I could go. Naturally, they said yes. According to them, Chay was the next best thing since the invention of the wheel. I agreed with them wholeheartedly.

We got into Chay's car. He put the key into the ignition, and the motor roared to life. I looked around.

"Hey, you cleaned," I said with a laugh. The fast food cups were gone from the front seat, and the burger wrappers had been picked up. The floor had been vacuumed and the dash wiped off. Then I looked in the backseat. The fast food cups were thrown haphazardly on the floor covered by the wadded-up burger wrappers. The floor hadn't been vacuumed, and nothing had been wiped off.

"Yeah." He winked. "It's as clean as a hospital operating room."

"I can see. Very neat and tidy." I nodded, trying to hide my smile.

We picked a movie and got comfy in the theater's reclining seats. While we waited for it to start, we guessed the trivia questions flashing on the screen by unscrambling the letters to find the answer. Every time I answered before Chay, he'd pelt me with popcorn.

"I can't help it that you're slow!" I laughed so hard I snorted.

"Okay, Ms. Piggy."

I looked at him. "Did you just refer to me as a pig?" I raised my eyebrows at him.

"Um... it's because you snorted... I was jok—"

I started laughing again. "You're so gullible. But seriously, watch the pig jokes." I laughed so much that my sides hurt. And Chay threw so much popcorn at me that it piled up in my lap. I stood up, and it rained popcorn all over the theater floor.

The lights dimmed and the previews started. That was when I saw

259   *Michelle K. Pickett*

little red arms in the empty seat in front of me. The seat rocked back and forth, reclining and then straightening, then reclining again, followed by a high-pitched squeal of delight. Damn hobgoblins.

"What are you doing here?" I pulled the seat down and looked in the eyes of the pudgy imp who was making my life a living hell.

"We're on a date."

"You weren't invited," I said through clenched teeth.

"We thought you'd want to know about your mother."

The blood slowed in my veins and a ringing filled my ears. "What about her? You'd better not have touched my mother. She has nothing to do with this. I will see red splatters on the road with my tire tracks on them from where I've run you down if you've touched one hair on her head."

"You'll see." It smiled at me.

My stomach tightened so hard that I jerked back and my elbow knocked my pop out of its holder.

"I told you. The vision is already starting. See you at home, Milayna." He giggled and disappeared with a small puff of smoke.

My head started to pound. I shot out of the seat, the reclining back hitting me when it flew forward. "I need to go home."

"Milayna, they're just trying to scare you. Will it make you feel better if you call?"

"No, no, I'm having a vision. I need to get out of here." My hands started shaking, and the cold fingers of fear ran down my spine. I tripped trying to get out of the dark theater, stumbling on the stairs leading up to the exit.

"Are you okay, miss?" an attendant asked.

"She's just not feeling well." Chay helped me up the stairs and into the hallway.

My head pounded. My vision faded in and out. The ugly burgundy-and-gray carpeting on the theater's floor turned fuzzy, and a flash of my mother entered my vision. As soon as I saw her, the vision left and I saw the matted, dirty carpeting again.

"Take me home." I leaned on Chay for support. My hand fisted in his shirt. "Please."

'You might as well switch now before it's too late. Or too late for the ones you love. The ones you love. The ones you love.' Shayla's words rolled over and over in my head. I couldn't focus on anything else. What if I was too late? What if Azazel hurt my mom? I sucked in a breath to keep from crying and held it until my lungs burned. How could I forgive myself if my mom was hurt because of me? I couldn't. Azazel knew the guilt would eat me alive, little by little, like worms feasting on a corpse. 'Too late for the ones you love.'

Chay sped all the way to my house, talking on his cell phone. First, he called my dad, made sure everything was all right, and told him about my vision. Then he called his father and finally, he called the group. They met us when we arrived.

It wasn't long before the Evils and their demi-demon home fries showed up. I was still in the middle of a vision. My mother was all I saw. I couldn't tell what was going to happen or where. I just knew she was in danger. I could feel it in my bones. They were too cold. I could feel them under my skin like an ice-sculpture skeleton. The rest of me was overly hot, and sweat covered my skin and pooled under my hair.

The hobgoblins ran around me, skipping and singing in their shrill voices, in a language I didn't understand and really didn't care to. The friendly goblin grabbed my leg and tried to crawl up it. I kicked him off. Scarface growled, and his eyes turned black.

I held my pounding head in my hands, made my way to the swing on the deck, and fell onto it. The red midget climbed up and sat next to me, his stumpy legs kicking back and forth, trying to make the swing move.

My mother. Standing at the window.

The goblin next to me was getting annoyed that the swing wasn't moving. He stood up, his temper flaring. I reached out and pushed him off so hard he went flying across the deck. That didn't help his mood.

She's looking outside. There's screaming. Hobgoblins are running through the house.

My vision came and went as the images played through my head.

"Fight it, Milayna. Your mother's fine," Chay's dad said. "I'm going to stay with her."

A demon. He reaches out and touches her shoulder.

"Milayna, you need to fight the vision."

"I can't, Mr. Roberts!" I fisted my fingers in my hair and pulled until it hurt. "The images keep coming. I can't get them to stop." My voice shook with barely controlled tears. Fear, panic, and rage swirled through me as the vision bombarded my senses. I didn't know which emotion I felt the most, which would take over, but something bubbled under my skin, ready to burst free.

"It's not real. The goblins are forcing a vision on you so you're unable to protect yourself. You have to fight it." My dad squatted in front of me. "You're stronger than the vision. Fight it."

A demon... No! It's not real... it's not real.

"A demon is in the house!" I cried. "Dad, a demon—"

"Milayna," he said in calm, soothing tones, "the house is protected. Even if there is a demon inside, its power is drained."

Yes! There's a demon... no, it's not real. It's not real.

"Fight it, Milayna. The house is protected." I could hear the fight. I knew Chay and the others were taking on the group of Evils by themselves.

Fight it! Okay, okay, I can do this. It isn't real.

My head pounded, and my stomach clenched. I couldn't erase the images that flashed in my head. "Where's Mr. Roberts?"

Michelle K. Pickett

"In the house." My dad's voice.

"Chay?" I whispered.

"He's in the yard." My dad cleared his throat.

My mother. A demon. Hobgoblins running through the house... on the counter tops... on the table...

"No! It's not real!" I lifted my head and shook off the effects of the vision. My head pounded and the images still played out in my mind, but I had to help my group. I couldn't sit there and do nothing. Chay's dad was with my mom. She was fine.

Can I trust him?

I trusted Chay. I had to trust his dad.

I stood up and fought the vision.

It's not real.

I ran down the steps of the deck and into the fight. Jen was trying to fight off two demi-demons. I picked one and slammed into him. The more the vision attacked me, the harder I fought.

He turned and threw a punch. I saw it coming at me in the freaky slo-mo thing I had. Blocking it, I kicked him in the side. He tried to jab me, and I stepped to the side. He swung and missed, stumbling forward from the momentum. I used his moment of weakness to kick him on the side of his head. He went down. No major damage done, but he wouldn't get up anytime soon.

Demon. Looking at my mother.

My gaze swung to the house. My mother was standing at the window, watching the fight.

Demon. Looking out of the window. I can see the fight through its eyes.

I watched the window. There was nothing there. No demon. Just my mother.

It's not real. It's not real.

I turned and a fist hit me in the jaw. Stunned, it took me a second to recuperate, and I barely had time to block his next swing.

Jake.

I blocked the next two jabs he threw. Why didn't his swings come in slow motion like everyone else's? My freaky-magic-mojo didn't work on him.

Demon. Reaching out to grab my mother. No! It's not real.

Jake kicked me in the side and brought my thoughts back to the issue at hand. Getting my ass kicked, literally. The next kick I was ready for and grabbed his leg. I twisted it, and he fell with a grunt facedown on the ground. I stepped between his shoulder blades and pushed him down into the moist dirt.

"Don't screw with me," I bit out just before I kicked him in the side.

Demon. Demon. Demon.

I turned, my gaze searched frantically around the yard. Everyone was fighting. Chay was fighting a demi-demon. He had a cut above his eye; blood dripped down his face. Or maybe it was the same cut from the last fight. Who knew anymore?

Demon. Demon. Demon.

Something was wrong. My vision had changed. It wasn't my mother I saw through the demon's eyes. It was me.

It's not real.

But I had a sick feeling deep in my gut. Something was wrong. I could smell sulfur. The glowing coming from the backyard told me the demons were coming.

Jake used my distraction to sweep me feet out from under me. I hit the ground hard. He fisted his hand, pulling his arm back. I readied myself for the block. Chay ran into him and hit him with a palm-heel strike to the side of the head.

I smiled. "I think I love you."

"I know I love you." He winked.

Our first declaration of love and it comes during a fight with demi-demons. Totally screwed up, but completely perfect.

Sulfur. The ground shuddered. I scooted away and stood. The dirt moved, shifting to form a pit. A yellow light shown from it, and heat radiated from it. I shuddered when I saw gray arms reach out. I reached down, taking out the dagger from the sheath on my ankle. My hands shook so badly that it took three tries for me to get the knife out of the sheath. My stomach felt full, like I'd swallowed a hand full of rocks. It weighed me down, and I couldn't seem to move. I just stood in place and watched.

Demon. Demon. Demon.

Jake shoved me hard toward the pit. The smell of burning flesh and rotting meat filled the air. The demon reached for me. I held my breath, partly because I didn't want to retch—although yakking on the demon did have its appeal—and partly because I was too scared to take a breath.

Here it goes. Please let us be right.

I used both hands and speared the demon's gray arm with the dagger as it reached out of the pit. A scream pierced my ears, followed by a plume of black ash.

Wicked cool! Now we're gettin' somewhere.

A smile spread across my face. I wanted to jump up and down I was so excited, but I felt a hard push and stumbled toward the hole. I spread my legs wide, planting them on each side of the opening. Jake advanced on me. I pushed off on the balls of my feet, clearing the hole.

"Milayna, Milayna." Jake walked around the hole and stood in front of me, keeping me from moving away from the pit. I readied myself for a blow. "You can end this. It doesn't have to be this way. One word from you, and this all goes away." His waved his hand around the yard, his voice silky smooth,

Michelle K. Pickett

like he hadn't tried to beat me to a pulp minutes before. Or feed me to a demon. "Why are you fighting? Look around you. You're all tired of the fight. There are more of us. We'll win; it's inevitable."

"Listen, asswipe, did you not just see me kill that demon mo fo? I wouldn't get too cocky about who the winner is going to be," I yelled over the noise around us.

I wasn't able to watch the pit behind me. Jake had meant to block my view and distract me. Unfortunately, I let him.

I smelled it, and I knew I was in trouble. The demon grabbed my hand from behind. I tried to wrench it free. Its skin was unnaturally hot against my flesh. My first instinct was to drop the dagger and fight it off me, but I forced myself to tighten my grip on the handle.

I took a swing at it. But trying to hit something standing behind you is difficult at best, and it easily deflected my blow, grabbing my other wrist and jerking my arm behind me. I screamed in pain. It forced the hand holding the dagger toward my throat. I tried to pull away, but the way the demon held me, I couldn't get any leverage. I watched the blade inch closer and closer to my skin.

I'm dead. This is how it ends. Oh, God. I didn't think I'd be this scared. Is it gonna hurt? Where's my mom? Dad? Oh God, please don't let Ben see.

Tears clouded my vision, and my muscles burned and trembled as I fought to push the knife away from my neck. I felt a prick on my throat; a trickle of warmth ran down my chest. The demon laughed, and Jake smirked.

DO something! Now!

I closed my eyes. "I control my pain."

"What?" the demon hissed.

I moved my head to the side as far from the blade of the dagger as I could. Bending forward, I swung my head back. My head cracked against the side of the demon's and the dagger sliced the other side of my neck. I couldn't help the cry that escaped me.

The hit wasn't very hard, but it surprised him enough that I was able to twist my hand and break his hold. I swung around and stabbed it in the side of the neck—my eyes locked on its cold, black orbs.

It howled in pain. I watched it turn to black ash and dissolve in the air. I could feel warm, sticky blood oozing down my neck and soaking into my collar.

The demi-demons and Evils scattered in the darkness. The earth shifted under my feet. I stood, drained of every molecule of energy, and watched the pit crumble in on itself until it was just an ugly, brown scab in a sea of lush, green grass.

We filed into the house to clean up. My mother darted from place to place, complaining about the police response time. "I called them when the whole thing started," my mother complained, wiping the blood from Drew's face.

"Some fighting teenagers aren't high on their list when there are robberies and murders going on, Mom."

"How bad is that cut?" Chay stood in front of me and cupped my chin, turning my head to the side so he could see the cut on my neck. "Deep?"

"Not very. It's fine." I tried to brush his hand away.

He grabbed some gauze and sterile water and cleaned the blood away. "I don't think you need stitches. We'll have to see if the bleeding stops." He put a bandage over it and taped it in place. Chay cupped my chin in his hand and peered into my eyes. "Are you hurt anywhere else?" He placed a kiss on my forehead.

"I hurt everywhere." I gave a small laugh. "But, no. Let me clean your cut."

He had rubbed the blood with the back of his sleeve, smearing it over his face. Sitting down, he lifted his face to me. I rubbed it gently with a warm, wet cloth.

"It's not too bad. Just a lot of blood and dirt mostly." I put butterfly tape across it.

Chay wrapped his hands around my waist, his fingers tight against my skin. "I meant what I said."

My hands stilled, and I looked into his blue-green eyes. I knew exactly what he meant. My mind centered on the five words he'd said, and warmth built in my chest. A slow, languid contentedness flowed through me. It was different from the jolts of sizzling current I felt when we kissed. But it felt right. It fit, like my body had been missing that piece of the puzzle. The hot stuff still bubbled just under the surface, but this new emotion was stronger, permanent. It took our relationship somewhere new. A better place. Love.

I twirled a lock of his hair around my finger and looked into his eyes. "It was kind of a weird time and place."

"I know." He nodded, and one side of his mouth twitched in a half grin. "But our relationship is built on weird. Even so, I meant it."

I felt the sizzle run up my arm, through my chest, and reach out. The current connected to Chay and his emotions washed over me. I saw anger directed at Azazel. I saw rage directed at Jake—this time, I saw a memory to go with the emotion. It was me. The demon held me with the dagger at my throat; a trail of blood ran down my chest.

I saw protectiveness, caring, trust, longing, love—and there was another vision to go with his feelings. Me. The day he first met me. The day we had milkshakes at his uncle's shop. Him watching me sleep in his lap at the zoo. Me laughing at something he said, him wiping my tears away after the woman died at the waterway. Memory after memory of me and the emotions he felt with each one.

Tears filled my eyes. It was almost too much. It filled my heart. I knew

Michelle K. Pickett

I loved Chay. I knew it before that night. I couldn't remember my life without him in it; he'd filled a void I hadn't known existed. Without him, I was incomplete. But until that moment, seeing me through his eyes, I didn't know how strongly he felt. And the realization gave me the most exquisite joy. But it scared me at the same time. How could I live with myself if he was ever hurt because of his feelings for me? I looked down and broke our connection.

I licked my lips and swiped at my eyes. "Me too. With everything in me," I whispered.

He gripped the collar of my shirt and pulled me down to him. His kiss was whisper soft. So gentle. I opened my mouth to him and pressed myself closer, taking the kiss deeper. He groaned in my mouth. The people in the room faded. The memory of the fight and the circumstances that brought us to that point dissolved. We were just two people realizing how deep their feelings for each other ran.

"Get a room," Drew drawled, walking by to grab a Coke.

"No. No, no. There'll be no room getting," my dad said, and I laughed against Chay's lips.

Chay pulled back and grinned at me.

He's mine. How did I get so lucky?

"Did you notice Muriel tonight?" Chay asked after everyone had left. We swayed on the swing on the back deck.

I picked at a piece of peeling nail polish. "When?" I knew what he was going to say. I didn't want to hear it.

"During and after the fight."

I dropped my hand and sighed. "I didn't see her during," I said. "I was a little busy."

"I caught a glimpse of her. She was just watching. She didn't fight. And when we came in, everyone had injuries except her."

I looked at him. "What are you gettin' at?" As soon as our gazes touched, the electrical cord sparked to life. I sucked in a breath. He was worried and scared for me. Fear was associated with Muriel, but in a different way. He was scared of her. Or of what she could do.

"I don't know. I just think it's odd, that's all," he said. He gave me a quick kiss—too quick—and our connection was broken. "I'll see you tomorrow."

"Yeah." I touched my lips with my fingertips, my thoughts a million miles away.

"I'll pick you up."

Muriel didn't fight? Is she going to turn? Has she turned? I didn't get the same vibe off her that I did from Steven. But I don't really know how to use this electrical vibe thingy yet, so who knows if I even did it right.

It'd have been a huge victory for Azazel if he got Muriel, my best friend and cousin, to work against me. Someone I'd never suspect, close to me. Someone I loved and trusted.

Chay's warning rang in my ears. "You don't know who you can trust."

I had less than twenty-four hours. The next day was my birthday. One minute after one in the morning.

My mom offered to let me stay home from school, but I decided to go. I needed to be with Chay. And I wasn't showing any fear. I was going to act like it was any other day. Besides, safety in numbers. Staying home alone wasn't really an option.

Classes dragged on. Instructors babbled about inane subjects. Things I'd never use, even if I did live beyond my birthday. Who cared what x equaled? Or what ROI meant? I didn't care about the gross national product or microeconomics. What I needed was someone to teach me how to get through the next twenty-four hours so I lived to see swim practice the next day.

I sat at the kitchen table after school. My parents were there. Chay sat next to me, holding my hand. His dad was there, and so was Uncle Rory. The entire group was there.

"We need a plan for tonight. It'll be bad. There's no doubt," Mr. Roberts said.

"The church at the end of the street," Jeff suggested. "It should offer some type of protection, more than she's getting here. The demons have weakened it too much here."

"I don't know if a church will stop him." Chay jammed his fingers through his hair. It was mussed and falling over his forehead from him running his fingers through it all day. I reached up and smoothed it back into place. His gaze found mine, and I let myself get pulled into the blue-green depths, hardly hearing what the others were planning around us.

"It's as good a place as any," my dad said. "You hide her there. We'll stay here and try to keep them distracted long enough that her birth time passes before they realize where she is." He shook his head and rubbed his forehead. "I don't know. There are so many variables. Not all churches are protected. And some are more protected than others. I... I just don't know."

"There aren't many options left. It's a place away from here, but not too far that we can't get to her if we need to. It's a church. Chances are better that it'll give Milayna more protection than she'll have here. Surely, he and his demons can't do too much damage there." Mr. Roberts shrugged a shoulder. "At the very least, it's a place he might not think to look. He'll automatically expect her to be at one of our houses. He's not omnipresent. He doesn't

Michelle K. Pickett

know what we're doing, planning, saying." He ran a hand through his hair. He looked so much like Chay when he did that. "I don't know, my friend. I wish I had all the answers for you."

My dad frowned and nodded. He pinched the bridge of his nose. "Okay. That's the plan, then." He looked at my mom, and she gave him a quick nod.

"Then it's settled. When it starts, Jeff and I will take Milayna to the church." Muriel pulled her hair back and tied it in a messy bun.

I swung my head to look at the others. My dad was looking at the floor, his hand on his hip. He nodded his head.

Wait! Muriel?

"Okay." My dad looked up.

No, no. I don't trust her.

I turned to Chay. His expression told me he was thinking the same thing. He ran a finger down the side of my face and smiled. "Jeff will be with you."

I nodded and tried to smile back. I couldn't breathe. It felt like fear was wrapping around my throat like a scarf, squeezing tighter and tighter. I didn't want to leave. I wanted to lock myself in a closet with Chay and my family and just wait until it was over.

I want you to go. I trust you.

All there was left to do was wait.

29

Azazel

Less than twenty-four hours until my birthday.

Waiting was the hard part. I wanted to be alone with Chay. I wanted to be with my parents and brother. I wasn't sure who I wanted to be alone with the most. I did not want to be in a house full of people milling around, waiting for the fighting to start. But that was where I was.

Chay never left my side, not even to get something to drink. I was sure he would've sooner died of dehydration than leave me.

The clock became a ticking bomb. Every second counted down to the most important event in my life. Maybe the last event of my life. The sound of the constant tick, tick, tick reverberated through my skull until I thought I'd go crazy.

My hands were slick with sweat, and I had to let go of Chay's hand several times to wipe them on the legs of my jeans. My heart was in my throat, and butterflies the size of trucks were spinning around in my stomach like a tornado of brightly colored wings. I was sure if I opened my mouth to speak, they'd fly out. So I kept quiet and waited.

It was getting dark, and the autumn chill rolled in. I went upstairs to change into warmer clothing. Chay, of course, followed. He waited silently outside my door until I finished.

"You're still here?" I asked when I stepped into the hall.

He tilted his head, and his eyes roamed over my face before stopping on my eyes. "Where else would I be?"

Michelle K. Pickett

"I thought you'd have run away screaming by now." At his look of confusion, I tried to smile. "Haven't you heard? Being my friend is bad for your health."

"I thought I was more than a friend." He gently pushed me backward into my bedroom.

"You are. So much more. Chay, I... I'm not sure how to say this, but when I told you I loved you, it wasn't exactly the truth." I grabbed his hand that rested on my shoulder and kissed his palm. "What I feel for you has to be more than love. No one has ever made me feel like you." Rolling my bottom lip between my teeth, I looked at the floor. I thought he'd say something, but he remained silent. I took a shuddering breath. "I just wanted to tell you how happy you've made me the last few weeks, you know... just in case." My gaze swept up to meet his.

"Don't." His fist hit the doorjamb, and I flinched. "Just don't." He looked to the side, his jaw working. "You're talking like you're giving up. Don't you dare give up, Milayna. Don't. You. Dare."

I shook my head. "I'm not. I'm not giving up!"

"Then don't tell me any type of goodbye." I wanted to tell him I wasn't, but that was exactly what I'd been doing. So I nodded and squeezed his hand. "Good. Now that we have that settled, I want you to do something for me," he murmured.

"Okay."

He skimmed his hands up and down my arms before moving them up to cup my face. "I want you to hold on to something for me until this is over."

"Chay, I'm probably not the best—" He let me go when I pulled away.

"I'll want it back, so don't get too attached. Take your sweatshirt off."

"What?"

"Take your sweat—"

"I heard you, but there are people downstairs. Our parents are down there. I don't think me and you playing striptease is gonna be their idea of appropriate behavior."

He chuckled. "Just do it."

I pulled off my sweatshirt and stood in just my bra, with my arms across my middle, shivering. My breath hitched in my throat when he reached behind his neck and pulled his sweatshirt over his head. My stomach did a weird sort of cartwheel and my heart, well, it wasn't sure what to do.

Oh dear Lord, is he gonna take his clothes off, too? That'd be the best damn birthday present. Ever.

Disappointment flooded me. He wore a T-shirt underneath, but when he slipped out of his sweatshirt, it rose up and... wow... I was sure I forgot to breathe.

Damn, look at those abs. Can he be any more ripped? Breathe, I must remember to breathe. But, oh, is he screaming hawt. And if those jeans

Milayna

270

were any lower, I wouldn't give a damn that my parents are downstairs.

"Lift up your arms," he said. I just stared at him. "I've seen you in a swimsuit. Seeing you in a bra isn't that much different. Although seeing you in a bra next to your bed is kinda killing me right now, so please lift up your arms."

I did as he asked. He very gently lifted his sweatshirt, pulled it over my head, and held it while I slid my arms in the sleeves. He lifted my hair out of the collar before he placed his hand behind my neck and pulled me to him.

His mouth moved over mine; his velvet tongue dipped between my parted lips. He tasted slightly of apple cider and smelled of cinnamon and something all him. I sighed at the feel of him. He pulled me closer, kissing me deeper.

My fingers itched to run over his hard, muscled stomach. I moved my hands from his waist and slipped them under his shirt. My fingers grazed over his rippled abs and followed them to the tapered oblique muscles that dipped into the waistband of his jeans. He groaned and dropped his hands to my waist. He pulled me even closer to him, kissing me deeper still. When he lifted his head, we were both breathing hard and I was more than a little dizzy. It was pure bliss, a toe-curling kiss. The only kind he seemed to give—not that I was complaining or anything. The guy was a kissing god.

"Wow," I breathed.

"Yeah." He leaned his forehead against mine. "Now listen, Milayna, this is very important."

"Okay."

"That's my favorite sweatshirt." He grabbed a handful of the front of the shirt and yanked me toward him. "I want it back in the morning. It's only on loan for tonight."

I let out a breath and a small laugh. "Okay. On loan. Got it."

"I'm serious. I want it back two minutes after one tomorrow morning." He pulled me into a tight hug and kissed my forehead.

I closed my eyes and squeezed back my tears.

For the next hour, I sat on the couch next to Chay, his arm protectively around my waist, his thumb rubbing my skin just above my jeans. I wrapped myself in his sweatshirt. I loved how it felt. So soft and warm. It was so big on me that it draped over me like a blanket. And it smelled like him. I'd bend my face forward and inhale his scent, fresh and outdoorsy. It calmed me.

At eleven thirty, I smelled sulfur.

"It's beginning," I whispered. No one answered me. Chay pulled me closer to him.

With the smell of sulfur came the goblins. They ran around my yard,

Michelle K. Pickett

playing like they always did. We tried to ignore them, but their singing grated on my already fraying nerves.

At eleven forty-two, the demi-demons and Evils showed. They stood silently in a line in my front yard.

At eleven fifty-five, the ground shook and the dirt parted. A hole emerged, like someone was drilling their way out of the earth.

We walked outside. The first gray arms appeared, hefting themselves out of the hole. I'd never seen more than two demons at a time. That night, there were a dozen, maybe more, fighting to get out of the hole at the same time.

My parents kissed me. My mother was crying, and my dad was determined. "It'll be fine, honey." They pushed me toward Jeff's car.

Chay pulled me around to look at him. He framed my face in his hands and kissed me hard. "I want my sweatshirt back." He gave me a crooked grin. "And the person inside it."

I nodded and pulled his face to mine for another kiss.

"Go with Jeff, Milayna. You can't be here," he whispered, his lips skimming over mine when he spoke.

"You take me!"

"I can't." And he was right. Next to me, Chay was the strongest demi-angel in the group. If something were to happen to me, he was next in line to lead. He had to stay and fight. Both of us gone would weaken the group too much.

"Go! I'll be right behind you."

The smell of sulfur and charred flesh stirred in the air. I knew they were coming for me. I threw the dagger to Chay and let Muriel and Jeff push me through the open car door. This was it. Dozens of pointless fights brought us to this point. A culmination of the stupidity of flying fists and staining the earth red with blood.

The endgame.

Midnight, my birthday.

Jeff raced down the road to the church. He and Muriel hurried me inside, closing and bolting the door behind us. It wasn't until I turned and looked up at Jeff that I knew something was very wrong. When I looked at Muriel, I saw the same wide-eyed expression I was sure was on my face.

Jeff sneered. I always thought he was nice looking in an understated way. Dark hair but light eyes. Lean, but muscled. He was quiet and soft-spoken, but always friendly. But just then his normally friendly smile was cold and his light eyes glinted like shards of glass. "You knew there was a traitor in the group, yet you came with me like an idiot."

'Jeff and Shayla used to date,' Chay had told me. Why didn't that sink in? Then I saw him in the hall helping her pick up the books Lily dropped.

As I scrolled through my memory, I could pick out things that alone wouldn't cause alarm, but stringing them together, they all pointed straight to Jeff. Him stopping to talk to Shayla and Lily at the restaurant, Jeff not doing anything to help when Drew and Chay were hurt until he was told to call 911, holding the door open for Shayla and following her out of the school.

My heart sank. It wasn't Muriel I should've been afraid of. It was Jeff. Bile rose in my throat, and my body shook so badly that my teeth chattered. I had to grab onto Muriel to keep from falling.

"All this time, I thought it was you. I'm so sorry, Muriel," I said close to her ear. "I'm so sorry for doubting you."

"Me? Why me?" she whispered. Her hand squeezed mine tighter.

"You've been standoffish, we didn't talk or text anymore, you didn't help me when Jake was pulling me toward the pit, you—"

"Yeah, you don't have to keep listing things. I admit I've been weird. It's no excuse, but I've been scared. Everything was way more intense than anything we'd seen before, and I panicked. I let you down, and I'm so sorry. Maybe if I hadn't been such a coward, we wouldn't be here now."

"Don't. Don't you dare blame yourself. This was hard for all of us. So you were scared. That's normal. No matter what happens tonight, It. Is. Not. Your. Fault. I love you, Muriel."

Big tears rolled down Muriel's face when she hugged me. I could feel them pooling in the curve of my neck. "I love you, too. We'll beat this." She gave me one last squeeze, letting go when she felt me stiffen. "What?" When I didn't answer, she followed my gaze.

I saw him. I swallowed back my fear and tried to stand straight, show no weakness. But my body trembled and my arms wrapped around my middle almost without my consent.

He looked just like he did in my dream. He had the appearance of a man, unlike his demons.

"Hello, Milayna. I've waited a long time to meet you face-to-face." He leaned against a pillar leading into the church's sanctuary, his hands clasped in front of him.

"Azazel," I whispered. "But—"

"What? We're in a church?" He laughed. "You thought you'd be safe here? Stupid girl. Churches are open to any who wish to enter. There are no protective powers here to keep you safe. Come in, come in." He motioned us further into the church.

When I didn't move, Jeff shoved me hard and I stumbled forward. He grabbed Muriel by the arm and jerked her to stand next to me. "When he tells you to do something, you do it!" Jeff screamed. Spittle flew from his mouth, and the sound of his voice echoed through the old church. I wanted to cover

273   *Michelle K. Pickett*

my ears, but I forced my hands to stay at my sides.

"Now, now, boy, there's no need for screaming," Azazel said.

I felt two hands clamp down on my arms. I looked, but I already knew what I'd see. Their unnaturally hot skin burned through my sweatshirt. When I saw the sickly gray flesh of the demons holding me, I gagged.

The demons held me in place as Azazel circled me. Jake appeared out of the shadows and grabbed Muriel, restraining her. Steven, Lily, and Shayla stood next to him and watched. The hobgoblins waddled back and forth in front of them. Azazel's angels flew overhead. Their black wings flapped, and the fabric of their black robes billowed around them. Their banshee-like screams pierced my ears.

My betrayer watched, standing next to Azazel. He smirked at me. A self-satisfied sneer that said he was pleased with himself. He was too busy staring at me to see what was coming. With a flick of Azazel's bony finger, his minions descended, scratching and clawing at Jeff. His screams of pain filled the room, and I flinched. My stomach dropped, and my mouth went dry.

The demons held him motionless, his arms pinned to his sides and legs held together.

"Have you ever heard the fable of the scorpion and the frog?" Azazel asked Jeff. Walking to him, he scraped his fingernail under his chin, drawing blood.

"N... no." Jeff's voice was shrill. Beads of sweat covered his forehead, and he breathed in fast gasps.

"Please, don't do it. I'll do what you want, just let him and Muriel go," I pleaded. I knew what was coming. But my words fell on deaf—or evil—ears. He wouldn't let them go any more than he'd let me go.

"A scorpion needed a ride to the other side of a river, or was it a lake? Oh, I don't know. I never can remember."

"Please, show some mercy." It made me nauseous to plead with him.

"He betrayed you, and yet, you still beg for his life?" Azazel tsked. He waved off my pleas and continued his story. "Anyway, unable to swim, he asks a frog for a ride. The frog, of course, is leery of his would-be passenger. 'You'll sting me,' he whines. But the scorpion laughs at the frog. 'Why would I sting you? You'd sink, and I'd drown.' The frog thought for a moment and decided the scorpion's reasoning sounded logical, so he agreed to give him a ride to the other side. And this, well, is the part that concerns you, dear boy. About halfway to the other side, the scorpion stings the frog. As the frog is dying, he asks the scorpion why he would do such a thing. And do you know what he said?"

Jeff shook his head, his eyes wide with fear.

"He said, 'Because I'm a scorpion. It's my nature.' See, the scorpion couldn't change, or maybe he didn't want to. Either way, he doomed the frog and himself to an early death. Well, as most everyone in the room will agree,

I'm evil. It's my nature. So in this little scenario, I'd be the scorpion and you'd be... " He stopped and plucked a piece of lint off Jeff's shirt before he looked up at him and smiled. "Well, unfortunately, you're the frog."

Realizing what was about to happen, Jeff screamed, "But I helped you. You promised if I brought her to you, you'd let me cross over!"

"Oh, you're crossing over. Just not the way you thought. See, there's a problem with you. You came to me for what I could give you. That's what you care about—what I'll do for you. Well, I want people to worship me. Adore me." Azazel lifted his arms toward the ceiling and threw back his head as he talked. "Fall on their knees in front of me and declare their undying love and devotion. Fight to the death for me." He dropped his arms and looked at Jeff. "Not follow me because I can give them a seventy-inch plasma television and unlimited time with his girlfriend." He turned his back, dismissing Jeff.

With a nod of his head, one of the flying demon-angels swooped down and grabbed Jeff's head. With one swift twist, it broke his neck. The sound of bone crunching and cracking filled the room.

The demons holding him let go. His body crumpled and fell to the floor with a sickening thud, his face slack and open eyes staring straight ahead.

"No!" I screamed. My heartbeat throbbed in my ears. I could feel heat surge through my body and pictured my hands breaking Azazel's neck.

Jeff was a good person. Deep down, he was a good person. He didn't deserve that.

Jake and his friends stood silently watching. Muriel bent and vomited, the spray hitting Jake's leg.

"Hey, Jake!" I yelled. "Maybe your new bestie Azazel will tell you the same bedtime story just before one of his angels breaks your neck. Because it'll happen. As soon as he doesn't need you anymore, it'll happen."

"Whatever, Milayna. Right now, I think you have bigger problems to worry about," Jake mocked.

"Tsk, tsk, Milayna. Are you saying I'm not a man of my word?"

My body shook so hard I had to concentrate to keep my voice from wavering. I didn't want to show fear. I wouldn't give him the satisfaction. "You're not a man."

Azazel laughed. "You got me there. I'm not a man. I'm stronger."

"Doubtful."

"My, my, you have a lot of attitude for someone in your position. I'd consider treating me with a little more respect."

"Earn it. Let Muriel go."

"Mmm." He tapped one long fingernail against his thin lips. "Nope. Not gonna happen. I will do this, though. I'll kill her last. That'll give her the best chance of being rescued."

We're not getting rescued. It's two against... shit, two against all of Hell. Eh, those odds aren't too bad.

275   *Michelle K. Pickett*

"Okay, I think I've had enough chatter for one day. I'm growing bored with this whole ordeal, Milayna. It's time for us to end this." He waved his hand in the air like he was swishing a bug away. "Let go of her. She's not going anywhere."

With one final, painful squeeze, the demons let go of my arms. I stumbled forward, falling on my knees.

"Now see, if only you'd fallen on your knees in front of me sooner, this could have been avoided." Azazel chuckled and shook his head. "Such a pity."

I stood and brushed myself off. Squaring my shoulders and schooling my expression, I looked into Azazel's cold, dead eyes. "I'll never bow to you."

"And that is why you will die."

The floor began to shake, and I held out my arms to keep my balance. The tile broke, the pieces flying through the room like knives as they sailed past me. I felt blood ooze from a cut on my cheek. It ran down my face and neck.

As pieces flew at me, I waved them away with my hands, amazed that I could finally tap into my telekinetic power without thinking.

The floor broke open. Fissures spread across the concrete floor like fingers. The earth parted—sliced open like melted butter. The sound of the cracking concrete and churning earth was deafening. It drowned out even Muriel and the demons' screams, who lined the wall behind Azazel. Two held Muriel as she struggled to break free. The only sound was the groaning of the building as it gave way around us.

Pieces of the ceiling crashed to the floor as supports broke. As pieces fell above me, I raised my hand and flung them to the side. The chunks of ceiling followed the direction of my hands, landing just inches from Azazel.

"Wow! You're getting good at that. It's such a shame all your power will be wasted. Last chance, Milayna. Come with me. Think of all the fun we could have using your powers!"

I flung a piece of ceiling tile at him, knocking him in the shoulder hard enough that he stumbled backward. Jake and the line of demons shuffled toward the door of the church, dragging Muriel with them. They moved as far away from the falling ceiling and the pieces of concrete I was throwing toward Azazel as possible.

"I'll take that as a 'no.'" He steadied himself and brushed off his robe.

I turned in a circle, watching Azazel break away the floor little by little until I stood on a small surface, the hole in the floor like a moat encircling me.

I smelled it first. The stench of sulfur filled the air just moments before the smoke coiled up from the fissure. I saw the faint yellow glow coming from below. The earth gave way a little more, and I saw them. My stomach churned at the sight. So many people, such destruction. That would be my fate.

"Bow!"

"No!" I screamed. He flung his hand toward me, and a portion of the floor I stood on gave way.

"Do it or die," Azazel yelled.

"No." Fear clogged my throat, choking me.

He shrugged. "Okay." He gave a small wave. Barely a movement of his hand, like he was so bored he couldn't summon enough energy to do more. The small area of floor I stood on cracked a little more. I took a step back. My heels hung off the back, rocks and broken pieces of tile fell into the pit leading straight to Hell.

The clock chimed. One o'clock. I had one minute until the exact time of my birth. He'd do it any second now. He couldn't wait any longer. If he didn't kill me before the clock read one minute past one, I'd be immune to him and his demons. I'd be stronger. I closed my eyes and waited for the visions to tell me what to do. How the hell was I going to get out of this? When they finally came, the visions scrolled through my mind like credits after a movie. Faster and faster they came. I could hardly keep up. Scenario after scenario. Around and around they swirled, blending into each other.

They stopped, and I jerked forward with the abruptness. I opened my eyes and locked on Azazel's glare. I knew what had to be done.

"Oh dear. Sounds like your time has run out, Milayna."

"We'll see," I said with a shrug of one shoulder.

Oh, geez, I'm smart mouthing a demon. Maybe I should rethink this plan. I don't even know if it's possible… but the vision showed me.

The floor crumbled little by little, and the smell of sulfur and rotting flesh filled my nostrils, burning the back of my throat. The screams and groans of the people below roared in the room as the demonic angels cackled and flew in circles around my head.

I forced myself to relax. I pictured my parents and brother, Saturday morning breakfasts and family movie nights. I saw Muriel, whispering during sleepovers and joking around at the mall. Chay. His blue-green eyes, the feel of his hand in mine, the taste of his kiss.

When I listened very closely, when I really focused, I could hear them on the other side of the doors, trying to find a way inside. My mother was crying, and my dad was screaming. Chay called my name.

"It's okay," I whispered. "I love you all. So much."

Just as I felt the piece of support give way beneath me, I reached my hand down toward the small slab of floor I stood on, making a fist as though I was grabbing hold of it. In one motion, I dropped low, held on with one hand, and swung my other hand forward in the air. The floor followed the movement and sailed across the room, with me on it, right into Azazel.

We both fell hard. My head bounced against the floor. Stars, like Christmas twinkle lights, flickered in front of my eyes. The gold-and-bronze mosaic floor blurred. I tried to move, but my body was heavy, weighted.

Oh, shit, I didn't think that would work.

Michelle K. Pickett

Fat, red legs scurried toward me. Damn goblins. I was so over them! I reached my hand toward them and made a scooping motion. Their fat, red bodies suspended in air, stumpy legs kicking and violent curses spilling from their mouths. I moved my hand to the pit and dropped them in, back to their homeland down under.

Just like an invisible dump truck.

I tried to sit up, but I couldn't move. Lifting my head off the ground, I could see I was covered in debris. One swipe of my arm and the cement and pieces of ceiling tile flew off me. I jumped up and searched for Azazel.

He rushed me. I did a side sweep. He fell forward, trying to catch his balance with his hand on the ground. But his feet tangled in the hem of his robe and he face-planted in front of me.

"Sucks wearing a dress, huh?" I circled him. He planted his palms on the floor and tried to push himself up. I put my foot in the middle of his back, pressing him down. At the same time, I motioned for the barricade to lift from the door. People burst through, yelling and shouting as they stormed into the room. Out of my peripheral vision, I saw my group head straight for Jake and the rest of his little club.

Azazel used the small window when my attention was diverted, flipping and rolling out of reach. He stood with his back to me.

A chunk of plaster ceiling fell a few feet from me. I reached my hand toward it and flung it at Azazel. His back was still turned. He was close enough to the pit. If I could get one good hit in, he'd fall in and the nightmare would end.

I guided the piece of ceiling toward him, closer and closer, it was almost there. I picked up speed, moving my arm faster, putting as much power behind the throw as I could. It sailed closer and closer. It was almost to him. Just inches. Something clutched my stomach, excitement, anticipation, I wasn't sure. But my body had a current run through it, from my toes to the tips of my hair.

It's closer. So close. Almost. It's going to hit him...

His arm shot out, his hand flat, palm facing the piece of ceiling. "Did you really think it'd be that easy?" He turned to face me. The piece of ceiling moved slightly as he did. "Are you really that daft, to think your powers are stronger than mine?"

I pressed against the ceiling. He pressed back. It hung between us, moving a little one way and then the other. My arm started to shake against the force.

It must be almost time. Just hold on...

A tingling began in the middle of my chest and radiated down my arm. I felt it move through each finger. A wind blew through the church. My long, red waves whipped wildly around my head like Medusa's snakes.

The piece of ceiling started to move toward Azazel. He grunted with his effort to push it back. I pushed as hard as I could. My body vibrated from the force.

"Enough!" he screamed. He pulled back his arm and thrust it to the side, sending the piece of ceiling sailing to the left. I squeezed my hand together, and the chunk of ceiling exploded in the air. The dust carried away on the wind circling the room.

For a brief moment, Azazel looked shocked. He masked it quickly when I picked up a piece of concrete pillar and aimed it at him. I advanced. He raised his hand and pushed back. I pushed harder. Azazel took a step backward before he swiped his hand to the side, sending the chunk of concrete with it.

I immediately sent another large piece of building at Azazel. I shoved it at him, and he grunted with the effort of pushing it away. "What's the matter? Are you getting tired of our game?" I taunted.

Azazel narrowed his yellow eyes at me. "You'll be sorry you screwed with me, Milayna."

I smirked and guided the piece of cement above his head. I let it hover over him. He tried to swipe it away. I held it there. It was difficult at first, but it became easier and easier to resist his attempts to push me away. "It's raining." I gave him a slow smile.

"What?" He glared at me.

I squeezed, and the piece of concrete hovering over his head crumbled into dust. It rained over him, sticking in the goo that slicked back his jet-black hair.

I felt a current of electricity run over my skin, under my skin, through my veins, my bones. It wasn't painful, but it didn't exactly feel warm and fuzzy either.

A hot, dry breeze began swirling. It grew stronger and stronger around me, like I was the source, my energy created it. My hair whipped around my face, and I had to shield my eyes.

"Dad, what's happening?" I yelled over the roaring wind. "Your powers are greater than his. You're closing his portal."

"It's not time! I still have ten seconds," Azazel shrieked.

"There's one problem with that. Birth certificates aren't timed to the second. She was born at exactly thirty-seven seconds after one o'clock. The hospital rounded up, listing her birth time as one minute after one. If you weren't so blinded by your own arrogance and greed for power, you wouldn't have waited until the last possible second to squeeze the most power out of her if she'd turn. It's over, Azazel," my dad yelled.

"No!" Azazel fisted his hands and put them on either side of his head. A scream tore from deep within him.

The earth began to close, the screams of the damned growing quieter as the ground shifted. The demons flying around our heads swooped down

279 *Michelle K. Pickett*

into the craters. The last of the hobgoblins disappeared.

Chay wrapped me against him and kissed my forehead. "You are a badass, Milayna Jackson. Remind me to never piss you off."

With one last howl of anger, Azazel pushed Jake and the others into the pit, before following them himself.

The room grew silent. The quiet buzzed around us as we watched the earth move back into place.

"It's over," Muriel said, her voice small and trembling.

"Until next time," I whispered, running the back of my hand across my forehead to wipe away the sweat and grime. There was a sour taste in the back of my throat, covering a dull ache. I licked my lips and blew out a breath. Something rolled in my stomach and coiled around my insides. It felt heavy. Not painful. But I knew it was there... waiting. "I should have killed him."

I'd regret that decision.

30
The Day After

THE DOORBELL RANG AT FIVE O'CLOCK. BEN'S FEET THUD-ded down the hallway. I heard him open the door. He squealed, and I rushed down the stairs.

Ben!

I stepped off the bottom step and saw Ben standing at the door, smil-ing. "You scared the crap outta me! Who is it, Frog Freckle?" I ruffled his hair.

"Don't call me that." He turned with a frown and shuffled away.

I peeked around the door and my heart fluttered. "Chay," I breathed.

"Hey." He reached for my hand and I weaved my fingers with his seamlessly, almost without thought. Like they knew where they belonged and were drawn there.

"I didn't know you were coming over."

"No? You should have. I mean, we do have a date." He grinned.

"Huh?" My gaze snapped to his.

We do? I don't remember making any plans for after my birthday. I didn't figure I'd be here to keep them.

"Yeah, you told me if the Hounds of Hell thing didn't work out, you'd go out to dinner with me."

I laughed. "Oh, yeah. I do remember that."

"So? Are you ready?"

"Uh, no." I looked down at my sweatpants with holes in the knees and Chay's sweatshirt.

281   Michelle K. Pickett

"Hurry up!" he said when I stood there. "We have reservations."

"Where?" I looked closely at him then. He was dressed in a shirt and tie. I'd never seen him in anything but jeans and a T-shirt or sweats.

Where are we going? He's dressed... wow. I didn't think anything could look better on him than his jeans, but man, does he clean up good.

"The Grey Goose."

"But... but they're booked for weeks in advance—" I touched my fingers to my lips and squeezed my eyes shut. My skin tingled from the top of my head to my toes. My breath hitched when I opened my eyes and my gaze found his—the blue-green swirling together making a deep turquoise.

He cupped my face and skimmed his thumb over my cheek. I leaned into his hand. "I know. I made the reservation the day I asked you. I told you everything was going to work out, Milayna. When will you start listening to me?"

I pulled him in the door and kissed him. "Thank you," I whispered against his lips.

"Anything for you."

Knife. Bloody hands. Blue-green eyes.

I squeezed my eyes shut and shook my head to erase the images.

Chay put his thumb under my chin and tilted my face to his. "Everything okay?"

I smiled. "Yeah, it's great. I'll go change."

I hurried upstairs, fighting the vision I could feel pushing its way into my consciousness. My head throbbed, my stomach felt as though it was in a vice. I made my way to my bed and sat on the edge, my arms wrapped around my knees. I squeezed my eyes closed and waited for the vision to show me what it needed me to see.

Blood. Knife. Blue-green eyes.

And then I heard it:

"I'm coming to finish what Azazel started, Milayna..."

Milayna's Playlist

Angel: Natasha Bedingfield
Unwritten: Natasha Bedingfield
On the way Down: Ryan Cabrera
Higher: Creed
One last breath: Creed
Collide: Howie Day
Notorious:Duran Duran
Sweet Sacrifice: Evanescence
Whisper: Evanescence
Be Still: The Fray
Like You'll Never See Me Again: Alicia Keys
I'd Come for You: Nickelback
If Everyone Cared: Nickelback
Why Don't You and I: Santana and Alex Band
Fall for You: Secondhand Serenade
Everything Has Changed: Taylor Swift & Ed Sheeran

Acknowledgements

WHILE THE IDEA FOR A STORY MAY COME FROM ONE MIND, the resulting book comes from many hands. Several people deserve my thanks and appreciation for the development of Milayna, and I know I will surely forget someone. So if that someone happens to be you, trust me, you have a special place not only in this book, but in my heart.

First to my husband, your never-ending support and encouragement are priceless to me. There are many days I question, *"Why, just why?"* You are always there to answer, *"Because you are meant to."* I have it in writing, Larry. And you know words are eternal, as is my love.

To my family, I know there are times you get sick to death of only seeing the top of my head peeking over my laptop lid. But I also know that even in your frustration, you support me. I see it in the monster drawings and story ideas Evan gives me. I hear it every time one of my twins, Aleigha or Alana, tell someone their mom is an author. I know it because only a family that loves me would listen to my never-ending *'what-if-I-wrote-it-this-way'* questions. I love you all.

To the staff at Clean Teen Publishing… what's there to say? You are amazeballs. Thank you for making me part of your family. There's nowhere else I'd rather be. You are all "Rockstars," and I thank God for you every day.

Anna Masrud, thank you for all your tireless work, under ridiculous deadlines, always with the most positive, encouraging attitude. I'd work with you again in a second.

Bloggers, reviewers, and the online writing community as a whole—authors would be nowhere without you. Technology opened a door to a new way of marketing our books, but you pushed us through. Your work spreading the word about the books you love is priceless, and appreciated by me, and all authors. A simple *thank you* doesn't seem near enough for what you do.

Finally, to the people who have spent their time reading my story. I never can seem to find the right words to express the amount of thankfulness and appreciation I have for you. Thank you for spending time with me and my crazy mind and the people who live there. There are so many books to choose from, and I am very honored and humbled that you chose to spend your time with mine.

I hope to see you for the second book in the trilogy, "Milayna's Angel." Azazel won't join us, but someone meaner and sneakier will enter Milayna's life, and will stop at nothing, and use anyone, in attempt to finish what Azazel started!

If I possess one molecule of talent it is from Him and it is to Him I give glory, Michelle

Author's Note: Nothing in this book is religiously or biblically based and should not be taken as such. This is a work of fiction, meant for entertainment purposes only. If you have religious questions, I encourage you to speak with your clergy member, or visit www.crossview.net.

About the Author

IF ASKED, MICHELLE WILL TELL YOU SHE IS A WIFE, MOTHER, AUTHOR, reader, and M&M connoisseur, especially peanut butter, which she eats way too many of while she writes. Red Bull or Monster Khaos are her coffee of choice, she has an abnormal obsession with hoodies and can't write without one, and hates to cook, but loves to watch cooking shows. Michelle is a hopeful romantic who loves a swoon-worthy ending that gives her butterflies for days, and books that keep her thinking of them long after she's turned the last page.

Born and raised in Flint, Michigan, she now lives in a sleepy suburb of Houston, Texas with her extremely supportive husband, four amazing children, a 125-pound rescued "lap dog," and two crazy rescued cats.

Michelle writes across genres in the young adult and new adult age groups and loves to hear from readers, bloggers and other authors!

Website:www.Michelle-Pickett.com
Email:Michelle@Michelle-Pickett.com
Blog:www.Michelle-Pickett.com/blog
Facebook: www.Facebook.com/michellepickettauthor
Twitter:http://www.twitter.com/michelle_kp

CPSIA information can be obtained at www.ICGtesting.com
Printed in the USA
LVOW12s2123030215

425586LV00001B/1/P